BOOKS BY BLANCHE D'ALPUGET

Mediator: A Biography of Sir Richard Kirby
Monkeys in the Dark (fiction)
Turtle Beach (fiction)
Robert J. Hawke: A Biography
Winter in Jerusalem

WINTER IN JERUSALEM

BLANCHE D'ALPUGET

SIMON AND SCHUSTER
NEW YORK

Winter in Jerusalem is fiction; similarity between its characters and persons living or dead is coincidental. As to the scenes set in hotels, restaurants, and hospitals in Israel: the buildings are real, but the staff and events are imaginary.

PUBLISHED BY SIMON & SCHUSTER
A DIVISION OF SIMON & SCHUSTER, INC.
SIMON & SCHUSTER BUILDING
ROCKEFELLER CENTER
1230 AVENUE OF THE AMERICAS
NEW YORK, NEW YORK 10020
SIMON AND SCHUSTER AND COLOPHON ARE
REGISTERED TRADEMARKS OF SIMON & SCHUSTER, INC.
DESIGNED BY BONNI LEON
MANUFACTURED IN THE UNITED STATES OF AMERICA
2   4   6   8   10   9   7   5   3   1
LIBRARY OF CONGRESS CATALOGING-IN-PUBLICATION
DATA
D'ALPUGET, BLANCHE, DATE–
WINTER IN JERUSALEM.
I. TITLE.
PR9619.3.D24W56   1986   823   86-1758
ISBN: 0-671-49808-8

ACKNOWLEDGMENTS

I wish to thank the Literature Board
of the Australia Council and I.L. of Melbourne for material assistance in research-
ing this book.

—B. d'A.

FOR MY MOTHER,
JOSIE,
WITH LOVE AND RESPECT

ONE

She said, "To Jerusalem." Then, to herself, "Yer-ush-al-ay-im," and felt her lips burn on the name, as if from a seraph's kiss.

Danielle Green was looking for something. She had just clambered out of a taxi into the chaos of Yo'el Moshe Salomon Street and if she could find a way to cross the road with two suitcases and a shoulder bag without being run over, then locate the ticket office in the Tel Aviv Central Bus Station—the cab driver was shouting, "There! You go!" and pointing at a scabrous green building that looked like a large public lavatory—and if in the ticket office she could discover which, from the scores of red-and-white buses arriving and departing every few minutes, was the one for Jerusalem—if I can accomplish all that, she was thinking, without losing my traveler's checks or my address book or my nerve, I will, for the moment, be happy.

Fifteen minutes earlier, a clerk in the beachside hotel where she had spent the night had said, "You want to catch a bus?" and had waggled his upturned hand back and forth from the wrist in a gesture indicating helplessness in the face of unreason. His expression had been relaxed, as if to say he knew that this was the way of the world: remote from good sense, self-damaging, yet mysteriously pleased.

Last night when she had arrived from the airport and had made inquiries about traveling the following morning, the clerk had become heated, telling Danielle she must take a taxi all the way from Tel Aviv to Jerusalem. He had crossed his arms and stared at her when she rejected his advice. In the moment of silence between them, she had realized that this man detected foolishness in everything about her—in every tourist—from voice to shoes. But then he seemed to catch the thrill of an impractical adventure. "So catch a bus," he'd replied, and smiled.

He rather enjoyed the look of her, her contradictory appearance. She had remarkable tobacco-colored hair, shiny, and as thick as a mountain sheep's fleece, and a fine-boned face that was almost pretty in repose. However, when she smiled or grinned, there was such a gap between her front teeth that she seemed to have played a trick, cracking herself in halves, and that, inside, there was a witch. She was dressed in a navy pullover, jeans, and elaborate boots of the same bright tan color as her hair, with a snakeskin curling around each ankle and up the calf. The boots came from a shop on Rodeo Drive. Danielle had bought them three days earlier when Bennie Kidron, sauntering beside her with his hands in his pockets, had whistled at them. "They'd look great on you," he'd said. She'd heard the message: you need clothes as equipment because you're not attractive enough to dress badly, and she'd dashed in and bought them— five hundred dollars' worth of consoling discomfort.

She winced as she heaved her suitcases from the cab to the pavement of Salomon Street: the blister on her right heel had burst. The taxi driver said, "All right. Sixty dollars," but she shook her head. She had decided not to explain either to the clerk or now, to the cabbie (who at first had offered to drive her to Jerusalem for a mere ninety dollars—in dollars, not shekels), why she wanted to go by bus. She'd had two lessons already in things going wrong. Both had occurred at the airport, last night.

At the immigration desk she'd felt sick when the clerk suddenly asked: "Any relatives in Israel?"

"A father."

"His name and address?"

"Professor D. Garin." She didn't know his address; she thought he lived in Jerusalem. No—she didn't know if he had moved recently. She didn't know his former address in the city, but yes, yes, she was *sure* he lived in . . .

The clerk was about to tell her to step aside to be questioned, but she'd pleaded: "I'm trying to find him. I've not seen him since I was a child." Abruptly, he had let her pass. But within minutes she'd got involved in a debate about the rights and wrongs of what she was doing to earn her keep.

TWO

She was a screenwriter, about to earn $300,000 (plus five profit points) which, after years of snatching at a living—writing television soap operas by the episode; commercials—would give her financial security for the first time in her life. She was under contract to Kidron Productions. For Bennie Kidron's special reasons the company was registered in Hong Kong and could be discovered there in a filing cabinet on the eighth floor of the Seiko Building, in the office of Peter Liu, chartered accountant. Otherwise Kidron Productions was a third-floor suite of rooms on El Camino Drive, Los Angeles, where Bennie Kidron, chairman and managing director, was to be found drunk, sober, and in between, several days each week. Danielle was to write the script for a film based on the Zealots' Revolt, that colonial upheaval which had seen the destruction of the Temple and the sacking of Jerusalem in 70 A.D., and finally, three years later, the mass suicide of the Zealots in their desert fortress, Masada. Its title was to be *Eleazar*, after the leader of the Zealots, who had given his followers the signal to die.

Although it had all happened so long ago, last night at the airport, when talking to some of the people who had been on her flight, Danielle had mentioned the research she was to do in

Israel and had sparked a political argument. She was chatting with a middle-aged man with kindly blue eyes and the sort of paunch that, until recent years, had meant its owner had made a success of his life. There was no warning: this mild, avuncular character abruptly wanted to fight.

"Masada. Masada. It's an allegory for what the Likud government is doing to Israel," he said. He shook his finger at Danielle. "That was a civil war, and it brought ruin. Now we have another one." He turned to his daughter who apparently held different views. "You see! The fatalism of Islam is infecting Israel and even people from *Hollywood* perceive things which you . . ." He continued in Hebrew, attracting a small crowd of homecomers, all of whom seemed to agree with him. But from a few feet away a couple of young Middle East Jews muttered to each other and one yelled something at the man with blue eyes.

She hadn't known what to do. She'd begun the conversation in a voice of modest triumph, expecting to be admired, but now she expected that at any moment the man would turn and denounce her as another foreigner who sought to flagellate Israel— from God-knows-what base motives, malice or profit. She'd stood on the sidelines listening to the argument, until inattention had come to save her from further embarrassment and she began imagining all the things she could have told him instead, things that would have made the man with blue eyes embrace her. For example, that she was born in Jerusalem; that her parent's other child, Geoffrey, had been shot by a sniper during the War of Independence, and before that they'd all fled their house in the eastern sector of the city . . . She imagined herself announcing, "I'm like a bird answering a homing call. I've flown from the other side of the world . . ." Her thoughts moved to the house she'd first known, in East Jerusalem: it was built by a Turk for his wives, with stone walls that at the height of summer gave out a faint, cooling smell of minerals. And it had an internal sky, she recalled: in the biggest room the ceiling was painted shiny black and spangled with gold thorns to represent the light of stars. There was a crescent moon beneath which her nurse would lie her on cushions each afternoon, saying, "Contemplate Allah, then sleep." Danielle imagined herself telling the man, "I spoke Arabic, until I was four. My parents got on well with the Arabs, until—" Until someone killed my brother. We'd moved to West Jerusalem when the War of Independence began. Geoffrey was shot in the

Jaffa Road. My father's mind snapped—not immediately, but a few nights later when an Arab doctor, a junior colleague of his before the war, sneaked into West Jerusalem to offer us his condolences. My father drove him away. That same night he turned on my mother, and me. He called us "daughters of Babylon." As soon as we could, she and I fled, all the way to Sydney. A carnival town, my mother said; we'll be safe here. "So you see," she heard herself telling the man and his daughter, "this is a pilgrimage for me. I haven't seen my father for more than thirty years. He's old now, and living alone, I believe." She was thinking, I want to go up to Jerusalem full of love for him. Oh, Jerusalem—it makes me tremble to say your name.

She had begun to smile.

Danielle had moved away from the arguing group and gone to wait by herself at the luggage carousel. While there she had the sensation that one of the black-browed young men was standing just behind her and she clung to the strap of her shoulder bag. But when she had glanced around, he was a good distance away, watching the paunchy father with blue eyes; his expression was as calm as a lion's.

THREE

The cab driver, who also drove a tank, he said, put his hands on his hips and looked at the suitcases, looked at Danielle—or rather, at her snake boots and her hair—looked back at the suitcases. He had the grave expression of an insurance broker assessing damages for which his company would have to pay. "Forty-five dollars," he said. Danielle shook her head.

She would not tell him that she was catching a bus to Jerusalem because from its windows she could have a wider view of the countryside through which, in due course, she would march a Roman army of horses, plumed helmets, and legionnaires. Audiences would see the majesty of a column of ten thousand men winding through the hills; reality would be six hundred extras, hired for three days, being rushed from one point to another in buses, shouting and cursing and complaining about the order against smoking. Inevitably one of them would be wearing a wristwatch . . .

She explained to the taxi driver, "I have a sentimental reason for going by bus. My last view of Jerusalem was from a bus, in 1949."

The cabbie had pioneer manners, blunt and pregnant with aggression. But he was warm-natured, too.

"You weren't born," he said.

"I was. I was four years old."

He shook his head slowly, as if to remark, All women are liars. "Peace," he said, and went.

She stood, gazing around. She had landed in the middle of a market and shopping area teeming with activity that seemed as random as an ant-heap. Civilians and soldiers in battle dress, carrying automatic rifles, were hurrying past. There was an atmosphere of rush, as if the clock would stop suddenly and lives would be petrified as at Pompeii, in the act of unfinished business. Traders shouted for custom, Arabic-sounding music blared from a record shop, the pavements were cluttered with innumerable gee-gaws for sale, and the dank February air smelled of diesel exhaust, roasting meat, coffee, and cigarette smoke. A man came at a fast trot along the gutter, carrying a large brass tray, put it in the trunk of his car, slammed the door and turned defiantly to another man who had chased him from the brass shop. They shouted and waved their arms at each other until a policewoman strolled toward them, when they stopped arguing, offered each other cigarettes and settled to a friendly chat. A child would have realized that this was a habitat of thieves.

Danielle felt paralyzed, caught in one of those moments when it seemed inevitable that her life had brought her to this street, this market, this bus station in the Middle East. All the solid rock of reason turned for a moment to vapor beneath her feet, dispersed, and for an instant revealed a different scene. She was standing on a savannah, surrounded by tall grass; a red earth path led forward for a few yards, then was hidden by the grass; ahead of her was a mountain. She had to climb it.

The moment of sorcery left her feeling unsteady on her feet.

And one of them had begun to throb. She realized she must find a pharmacy and had just picked up her suitcases again when a smiling young man walked toward her with his hands outstretched.

"I almost didn't recognize you," he said. "Wonderful that you've come to Tel Aviv." He had a cupid's mouth and long eyelashes. His brown eyes looked deeply into hers with an expression that was at once serious, insolent, and caressing. Danielle had never seen him before.

FOUR

She waited for him to play out his pantomime of astonishment at his mistake—he was sure she was Ingrid and that they had met in Copenhagen last summer—then told him she needed to buy Band-Aids and Mercurochrome. Menachem, the name he used to introduce himself, offered to kiss her foot.

"I worship you, from the feet up," he said.

She said she would prefer medication. Menachem shrugged.

"I'm not going to schlepp all this luggage," he added and went into the schwarma stall on the pavement behind them where he fell into an argument with the owner, who repeatedly shook his head and appealed for support from a group of soldiers lounging at a chipped Formica table. They agreed that he, the stall holder, should not allow Danielle's suitcases to stay in the place unless she or Menachem stayed with them. She did not need to understand Hebrew to know what they were saying: Who knows what's inside? Maybe she's a terrorist. Any unaccompanied parcel or bag in a public place . . .

Menachem returned to Danielle, his mouth in a pout for the benefit of the men inside, but for her, crafty eyes.

"I've told them you are my cousin from Argentina," he whispered and said aloud, "Will you agree to open them?"

No, she thought, I will not go through that again, the gynecological examination that every traveler to Israel undergoes.— Passengers had stood morose and chastened while security officers plunged up to the wrists into their intimate possessions. A young woman was asked to step into a private room; half an hour later she returned to the public area with her cheeks flushed and, behind her glance, the desire to run. A security officer led her by the elbow. "We're sorry—but we have to be careful," he was saying. As fingers had probed through Danielle's belongings her sense of violation had made her swing her head suddenly, feeling that from behind, too, she was being observed. The search had continued, calmly, automatically, jangling memories in every mind: We can't take risks; we can't take risks. "Yes," she said.

A middle-aged soldier drinking beer sauntered over to read the address tags on her suitcases. He too was from Sydney, he said. Then, in argot: "Is china here" (he meant Menachem) "giving you the tom-tits?"

"She'll be apples," Danielle replied. The code phrase worked.

He made some announcement in Hebrew that settled the question: there seemed no need to open the second bag. He, the former Australian, was gone when she returned half an hour later.

Danielle had three times refused Menachem's invitation to go with him to a place close by. Just for one hour. "You will not be disappointed," he murmured breathing softly against her ear. He asked her no questions about herself but devoted the time as they pushed and were jostled along Salomon Street to praising his business acumen. He was a toy importer, specializing in helium balloons. "I am the balloon king of Israel," he said. He was planning to take over Western Europe.

When he began to nuzzle her neck, Danielle told him in a firm voice that she was in business herself, that she was easily ten years older than he—she had, in fact, an eighteen-year-old daughter—and that she did not go to bed with boys who introduced themselves in the street. Menachem listened with indifference. On her third refusal he stopped walking to look at her again and a brazen smile spread over his lips and eyes.

"I know women," he announced. "I know when women are in love. You are in love."

"Don't be ridiculous," she replied. But Menachem had started to laugh.

"You're blushing about it!"

All the way back along Salomon Street he murmured: "Your lover is not here, is he? So spend the time with me. I will teach you wonderful things . . ." She held her chin up and her lips pressed together in a small haughty smile, seeing herself through his eyes—just a foreign woman standing in the street, as irresistibly vulnerable as a rabbit to a man with a gun.

There were guns everywhere, hanging on shoulder straps, snuggled into armpits, grasped between knees. In the hotel last night an elderly American had accosted her for the pleasure of sharing a revelation: "Look at these wonderful kids," he said, "with their Uzis and Galils. Can you imagine New York if every kid of eighteen had a *rifle?*"

When they had reached the schwarma stall again and Danielle had gathered her bags she turned to Menachem and said, "I'd just love to. You're very handsome. But I don't want to catch herpes," and left him.

FIVE

A Russian grandfather gave information about bus schedules from a booth at the rear of the terminal building that some unkind person—like me, Danielle thought—might have said not only housed public lavatories but also stank of them and was generally such an eyesore that one regretted the Egyptians had failed to knock it down with shelling in 1948 and had only made a hole in the pavement outside. Such a poisonous smell came from the area marked "mesdames" that its pollutants could have contained, she felt, radioactivity. She was suffering a vague, general irritation, mostly with herself for her resort to offensiveness to get rid of Menachem: a woman should be able to say no in such a way that the man takes her seriously, she thought. But if one were dealing with a man incapable of hearing the woman, a sort of wise monkey with his paws on his ears . . .

She cheered up at the idea that in their scene was a neat little allegory for the mechanics of the Arab-Israeli conflict: the Arabs had refused to *hear* what the Jews had said about staying in Israel . . .

Or maybe, she thought, it's the other way around, now: maybe we have an attack of selective inattention to protect us from the truth, and maybe the Ayatollah's Islamic Revolution is serious about its goal of exterminating . . .

Her eyes moved away from the information booth to a news-stand close by where there were dailies and weeklies in various languages and Hebrew novels with bright pornographic jacket illustrations. A few feet beyond it a religious with a white beard was urging young men who passed by to stop and pray. He had on hand prayer books and phylacteries but—as the Russian explained to Danielle—no water for the ritual wash. Therefore the young men were washing by rubbing their hands on the peeling green paint of the walls. The Russian had a low opinion of religion and considered the old party with the white beard a nuisance. "Go back to New York!" he called several times but was ignored by the Pious One, who was by now absorbed in mumbling. On the cement floor alongside the information stand two disabled beggars had a pitch. They kept up a spirited discussion with the news vendor between shouting demands for money. Their voices sometimes drowned the cries of a man selling tokens for the nearby telephones and another offering cheese pies, cans of Coke, and quoit-shaped rolls from a tray.

"And that, darling," the Russian said, pointing to a notice board, "is photographs of missing persons. And beside them . . ." An army couple were kissing each other in a trance of tenderness, the boy clasping a rifle to his girl's back. "After the battlefield, the bedroom. *Nu*, it's the rule of Nature." The Russian beamed, all sunshine, wrinkles, and a gold front tooth.

Another rule here, Danielle thought, is: the greatest possible variety in the smallest possible space.

The interior of the building was the size of a living room in a suburban house, badly ventilated and poorly lit. The seventy-seven—or whatever—countries from which Jews had come to Israel each seemed to have a representative inside it—along with characters like me, she thought, and that black American dressed up as King Solomon, selling incense and patchouli oil in the doorway, who just told me he is a *real* Hebrew and that he has three wives.

"Ah aim th' Lawd," he said, plucking with long fine fingers at the folds of his yellow robe. He was born in Dallas, he said.

She was about to make for the exit to the bus bays when a flash of white light startled her. A photographer was crouched on one knee, apparently focusing on the newsstand's parade of naked women, some of them masturbating, some trussed with black leather thongs. She turned back to the grandfather.

"He's taking a funny sort of picture," she said. "Nude women in the foreground and boys praying in the background."

The Russian leaned over his counter to see what she meant, grasped it, and shrugged. "Darling—this is a free country. What can I do?" His open hands rose in the air as if controlled by a will so much greater than his own that objections were futile.

She shrugged back.

She had spoken out of an impulse to amuse the sweet old man, not really knowing if what she claimed were true or not. But she continued to watch the photographer as he darted about on bent legs and saw that he did have a stubby, wide-angle lens on his camera. He was as quick as a spider. He had just caught an expression of animal stupidity on the face of a soldier who had stopped to pray, a boy whose face in the next moment looked human again. The camera seized frame after frame of the same scene.

Then his roll of film was finished. He straightened up and strolled outside, taking the exit opposite the one that led past the plutonium lavatories.

Danielle saw him again a few minutes later. As she took her place with her luggage in the bus line, there, a couple of yards away, was the photographer, snapping a group of nuns gathered around a food vendor. Something about him puzzled her, something tormenting, like a word on the tip of the tongue. He was swarthy, with a huge curved nose like a fin, too big for a big man, and he was short and slight. That nose was troubling him, for he kept sniffing, ruching up the skin on its slopes into ridges. He was warmly dressed, with a natty dark cap, a tartan scarf, and a black leather jacket. It was only ten o'clock but the day, after a promising start, was growing cold again. His face quivered with sudden agony: a sneeze exploded.

—It's Wili Djugash!

She wondered how long he had been out of jail, and what had become of London's Most Brilliant Photographer. Also, of the silver Jaguar, and the van emblazoned "Wili's Doggie Carriage" that had carted around the five Afghan hounds to his outdoor assignments.

She continued to watch him, remembering her own taste of the exuberance of the 1960s in London—of being twenty years old, having a husband who knew the real story about everything, having a job as a copywriter in Hamish & Bruce. She'd met Wili through Hamish & Bruce; he'd walked into her office one day, said, "You're the new popsie? I'm Djugash—it's Huguenot French —come to lunch." He spoke English like an elocution mistress. That evening Patrick had roared, "Huguenot French? Wili's father was a seaman from Odessa who fell overboard on top of his mother one night. Huguenot French! He's an East End bastard." Then, a few months later, she remembered, Patrick had announced, "There's a rumor your friend Wili has got his prick in the Cusack till. Old man Cusack and his son are gunning for him." She had not learned the full details, for she had to return to Sydney and Australian press reporting of the Photographer– Teenage Heiress Scandal was scant. It ended with Wili sentenced to seven years in jail. A picture of him beside a Black Maria carried a caption saying, "Wili Djugash, the society photographer who eloped with 15-year-old Hon. Tamsin Cusack, has been convicted of burglary and assault. He says he will go on a hunger strike in prison."

He was certainly slimmer.

There was a double coincidence in seeing him again, here, for the one person Danielle knew in Israel, her beloved Alice Sadler, had been Wili's teacher too, but in England, at a progressive school founded soon after the war. She wondered if he had seen Alice already.

Danielle watched him patting at his jacket pockets for a fresh handkerchief: he was always the first in London to catch the new strains of influenza. Around Hamish & Bruce any unidentified illness was known as "The Wilies."

The nuns were eating cheese pies made with flaky pastry. They had strained, yearning eyes that reached out as if they wanted something specific, but were not sure how to recognize it. Even as they ate, they kept watching for it. One noticed the camera and began brushing her mouth and chin with flustered movements, while Wili turned his machine vertically and snapped once more, a smile on his small, rather feminine lips. The traffic noise drowned out other sounds, but Danielle could hear in memory a snigger, a little *eh-eh-eh* in the back of the throat Wili made when he was pleased with a shot.

Just then the bus that was already full of passengers pulled out and, like clockwork, another pulled up at the front of the bay and everyone corralled between the iron railings of the line began pushing and shoving. A trio of the Pious, two older men and a beardless youth, were immediately in front of Danielle. Behind her were two tired-looking soldiers with kitbags. The soldiers had only enough energy to keep themselves upright, but the Hasidim had spent the past ten minutes in constant minor activity, the men talking animatedly to each other and consulting a religious text, the boy nervously curling his earlocks around his index finger, fluttering his hands to the brim of his handsome black hat, and then, as the new bus pulled up, using his pointing finger again to help him count, over and over, the number of passengers in front of him. As they approached the head of the line the boy peered backward, anxiety impressed into a face too young for it. He was as pale and tall as a sprout germinated in darkness. His clear, worried eyes looked not past Danielle but through her, by some process of mental discipline that allowed him not to see that which was forbidden. The hair stood on her scalp: this time she felt certain there *was* somebody watching her from back there, some shadow, original and dark. She swung around wildly, ready to say "Father!" but there was only a line of men and women paying her no attention and the two soldiers, who grinned.

"You speak English?" one asked. She nodded. "You won't get on this bus," he said. "Sweetie-pie has it all figured out: if you board, he'll have to sit next to you."

He jerked his thumb at the adolescent Hasid. "God doesn't let them sit next to women."

His companion muttered. "Bloody shirkers. I say, fuck the religious."

When they reached the head of the line the Hasidim had an excited exchange with the bus driver, who appeared to be cursing them, but nevertheless he beckoned to a man standing alone behind Danielle and the two soldiers and ordered him to enter the bus as its final passenger.

"See?" the soldier said. "And what do they do for this country?"

Danielle felt hostile and uneasy: she had been the victim of an injustice, but it was such an ironic one. Those religious men, supposedly concerned with the immaterial and the spiritual, had just revealed that their true obsession was with the body and its physical purity. So she knew she should not be upset: they were frightened of women, in general; that was their problem, in general.

Her hostility passed and its place filled with a niggling anxiety. She had thought of herself as cast from a single piece, but in recent months she had begun to doubt—and worse, different parts no longer seemed to fit together. Which was bewildering. Wasn't she thirty-eight years old, the winner of an award at Cannes, and with the screenplay of *Eleazar*, getting the chance to win an Oscar? For some reason she could not diagnose, she knew that even if she had more luck, more success, the comfort it would bring would leave her feeling incomplete. And so she was going back to Jerusalem, to heal something.

The Hasidim were now on the bus.

"What should they be doing for the country?" she asked.

The soldier patted his rifle; his companion nodded in agreement.

The bus moved off, giving Danielle a clear view of Wili, but she avoided looking at him directly; within seconds she would be able to board and escape him altogether. However, something seemed to have happened to him in the few minutes he had been out of sight and she found herself glancing in his direction. He had hung his camera around his neck and was hitting himself on the thighs, the chest, the rump, and talking aloud. Then she realized: He's been robbed!

Danielle hesitated, stepped over her suitcases and ran up to him. He did not recognize her. She had to repeat, "Danielle Green—oh, Reilly—I was married to Patrick Reilly of the *Sunday Times*. From the Bruce agency. Remember?"

He jerked as if she had slapped him. Then he threw his arms around her saying, "Princess!" (And how well she remembered that salutation of his, and how it irritated her. She suspected that within it was a sneer—"Jewish Australian Princess.")

Danielle riffled through the currency she had in her shoulder bag and pulled out a wad of hundred-shekel notes.

"Here's fifty dollars' worth," she said. "I'll be in the American Colony Hotel in Jerusalem."

People were shouting at her to get on the bus or to move her suitcases or to do *something*—to stop wasting their *time*—but Wili, sudden tears in his eyes, had caught her by the elbows and was refusing to let go.

"Hey, Wili," she said, "Alice Sadler is living in Jerusalem." His attention caught, she managed to twist free. "Have you seen her?"

"That old fart." He seemed to be grasping only parts of what she said.

She called "American Colony" over her shoulder as she mounted the steps to the bus and knew he had heard this time because he nodded vigorously.

SIX

February was only a few days old but already the people of Jerusalem were forcasting that this would be the coldest winter in forty years.

When she got out of bed that morning Alice Sadler discovered that the solar-heating tank on the roof of her apartment building had again proved itself ineffectual and she had no hot water at all. It would take two hours for the electrically heated boiler to produce some, but Alice could not afford to switch it on. Inflation was already running at 120 percent and everything cost a fortune. She looked out at the sky, of which she had a good view from her top-floor apartment. It was the color of metal, right across to Jordan.

"Israel needs all the rain she can get," Alice said to cheer herself up. Then she added, "Jerusalem the Golden with milk and honey blest, *my foot!*"

In her kitchen, which had the same stone-tiled floors as the rest of her shabby rooms and smelled of gas, she was too cold to boil the kettle for a cup of tea. Boiling the kettle took a good five minutes because the water had the hard nature of the city and despite scrubbing out every couple of weeks and soaking with half a lemon, it left on the inside of the kettle an unbudgeable deposit of limestone, a lining of that same rock the local Arabs called "Jew's head" because it was so tough. She went back to

bed and there, guiltily, let her hand slide to the switch of her
electric blanket. Alice allowed herself few weaknesses; the electric blanket was a gift from her friend David, and normally she
used it for only half an hour at night, the time before sleeping
that she devoted to a memory exercise with cards. Although her
passport said she was born in 1898 Alice suspected that in a few
weeks she would turn eighty-six, not eighty-five. The records had
been lost in a synagogue fire and her mother, beautiful and frivo-
lous, was vague about dates. Alice excused her as a creature
trapped by the mannerisms of her era. To exercise her own wits
Alice translated some Virgil each morning while she ate her
granola.

She listened to the BBC foreign news broadcast, but without
taking much in because she had slept poorly after the excitement
of speaking to Danielle in Tel Aviv. Finally she read a few pages
of a new feminist book called *All Women Are Goddesses*. She'd
liked the title, although it was glib. The authors argued (and she
agreed with them) that Eve, far from being the cause of the Fall
of Man, had led Adam from his bucolic stupor into a subtler
realm of thought. They were just getting themselves muddled in
their argument when Alice glanced at her bedside clock, saw it was
past nine, and realized that she had to get out of bed and hurry.

Outside the city was already rowdy. There were the sparrows
to feed—only four fluffed into gray dandelions had had the patience to wait on her balcony—and downstairs Arik, who lived in
the communal garbage container left parked in the street, was
stiff-legged with temper because his breakfast was late.

He drank the milk while she was still pouring it, throat and
chest vibrating with a noise like a propeller.

Alice hid the saucer in her mailbox in the foyer and the milk
container beneath her morning's copy of the *Jerusalem Post*. She
said to Arik, "Off you go, before *she* comes," and climbed back
up the stairs. He washed himself, then strolled outside to the
pavement and sprayed a new Alfa Sud that had been parked
there overnight. When Alice's landlady came downstairs soon
afterward, she noticed that the door of her new car stank. She
turned back into the foyer and shouted in English up the stairwell, "You bloody old woman with cats," and repeated it, more
vividly, in Hungarian.

The landlady was given to emotional upheaval and overeat-
ing, and had a permanently sore back from getting about in very
high-heeled shoes. On the days she saw Alice striding out in a

woolen suit and walking boots, beret at a jaunty angle over her white hair, Ruth muttered to the window panes, "Old skeleton. English lesbian."

"Get out of my building!" she'd say. "This isn't the British Empire anymore. This is the Israeli Empire. And you'll never give it away, Peacenownik!"

She daydreamed about evicting Alice, moving herself into the top-floor apartment, and on its balcony having summer evening parties with handsome men. When she heard David slowly climbing the stairs or Gideon pounding up them three at a time to Alice's apartment, she would open her front door and croon, "Sha-lom. Going up for some fun?"

For Gideon, Alice's spare bedroom was permanently available for a night or an afternoon with his Yemenite girl, Tikva. They were both twenty, both in the army.

The day Gideon, blushing as deeply as the marvel he held by the wrist, had pushed her through Alice's front door the old woman had cried, "A celebration for the eyes!" The girl's beauty restored confidence in a generous God. Along her upper lip a faint gray mustache was the essential flaw, the perfecting inconsistency, in her appearance. After army service Tikva hoped to get a job as a typist.

When Alice announced, "I'm going to switch off my hearing aid now and have a rest," the pair of them would stare at the rug, then tiptoe from the curtained-off parlor.

Alice worried that the bed was too small for them. Tikva was of average height, but Gideon's body had grown in one of those leaps one saw often in kibbutz-born children, as if nature wanted to erase all at once the constriction of the centuries. He was almost six feet three with a smile as open as daybreak, a son so different from his father that it was hard to believe, as it is with the males and females of certain birds, that they were of one species. There was sweet nature, health—and the faintest hint of swinishness—about Gideon, not all excused by his age or the army, but due to being one of the new breed of men in Israel. Each month he washed her windows, leaving gray trickles around the edges. At the beginning of summer he appeared with a mouth full of nails and a hammer to re-rig the canvas awning on her balcony. They would sit under it drinking mint tea, surrounded by geraniums and the hot, antiseptic smell of the pine trees. Alice said, "If something happens to me—if I have a fall— you won't let them take me to hospital will you, love?"

Gideon nodded and looked away.

She had ready a cocktail in a drawer of her bedside table and
had explained to Gideon what each pill was. He had listened as
if it were just an army routine, another task to perform. Sometimes she regretted the absence in him of Jewish ecstasy—and despair. Gideon had grown up knowing that thirty-two years in the
army lay ahead, three of them full time, then reserve duty until he
was fifty. "It's not a birthright Jacob would have envied," Alice
told him. He and his friends had a hybrid quality: grafted to the
warrior needed by the state there was a branch of Esau's peasant
temperament. Gideon's father, Amos, said when his eyes rested
on his giant son, "The New Jew," and his lips buckled with a
smile like paper being burnt.

At a pinch Gideon would help Tikva take off her parka; Alice
remembered David, at almost the same age, kissing the insteps
of her feet as he removed her shoes, calling her *Elfe*—she, already a woman of forty. He'd been as sentimental as any German boy.

David came to lunch bringing a bunch of white and pale purple irises, pretending gaiety, but with sad eyes. He had turned
seventy a few months earlier and had given up the room he had
been allowed to keep after retirement at the Givat Ram campus
of the university. "No head for figures anymore," he'd said, tapping above his ear. He had fine hands. Sometimes he held them
out and remarked sardonically, "Worker's paws," while Alice
had thought, sardonically, "Yes—and what destruction they have
wrought." They'd met on the day in 1939 when he had arrived as
a refugee in London and had been lovers ever since—through all
his other love affairs, his marriages, through World War II, when
he had worked on the Manhattan Project, and since then, in Israel, on God-knows-what. When Hiroshima was vaporized she'd
shouted at him, "What an intellectual debauch you have enjoyed—and what a hangover!"

David—he still called himself Heinrik in those days—had replied mildly, "That's why I need you."

"You're pale, darling," she said.

"I have been loitering in the city." He was already acquiring
that shrunken look, as if life were leaking from him somewhere.
They tried to chat about politics and university gossip. When he
stood to leave, the world capsized; he saw black space and pulses
of yellow lightning.

"Elfe! Elfe!"

She could not rise quickly enough to help him. David lurched and fell back again on the settee.

They allowed silence. Then:

"So. I'm collapsing now. Like our country. Poor Israel. Poor me." His charming, weary smile returned, but Alice did not see it. She sat looking into her palm, cupped inside the other in her lap, a serene old woman watching the end. It was not just a bad government and a vile, unjust war, matters that could be fixed up by installing a different group of politicians; the spiritual values of Zionism were dying. She saw the decline everywhere, in people like Amos . . .

"When I was young . . ."

—When I was young I believed that after the Great War there could be no more wars, and that the Revolution in Russia would save the world. My heart broke when I realized what Stalin was doing. There's been nothing since to compare with that agony, not even Hitler.

". . . I was a mad optimist," Alice said aloud. "Now I'm just an optimist. Buck up, love. Life's too long to be gloomy."

After lunch Alice felt worn out. Her nap turned into a deep sleep from which she woke with a little yell when the doorbell rang. It was already darkening outside. From her parlor window she could see the sky over the Mountains of Moab thick with snowclouds.

"That will be Danielle," she told herself and wondered how often the poor girl had tried to ring her: the telephone system was a scandal.

"I'm doing it as fast as I can," she called through the door, kept double-locked against burglars, who were brazen enough for even top-floor apartments. There was no reply from the other side, where there were four steep steps immediately in front of the door so that whoever was standing there was first seen from above.

"What color is your hair these days?" Alice called. She did not catch Danielle's reply and realized her hearing aid was turned off.

The end of the barrel of an automatic rifle reared at her and the humiliation of never knowing one's moment of death lifted. Alice held herself erect, knowing she must stay conscious, must watch it all.

SEVEN

Her lithe stride up the steps of the bus and her hand waving from the sleeve of a tatty fox jacket created another image for Wili: that jacket when it was glossy and thick; Danielle caressing its sleeve, saying, "Patrick gave it to me." Pause; her trying to look brazen: "I suspect it fell off a truck." Fragments of the past rushed together and Wili reexperienced his dislike of Danielle's spouse. He'd not been surprised when he read that Reilly had been killed in a car accident and that the popsie traveling with him was suing for the ruin of her face. That was Reilly: cocksure and knockabout. Danielle had been pregnant, Wili remembered, and had flown back to Australia. The thought occurred to him: she'll barely know what happened to me.

"Princess," he whispered in a tone that was reverent and smug, valuing her, suddenly, as someone to talk to, someone new who would learn the whole story, firsthand, from him.

Then he remembered he had just been robbed of five hundred dollars in cash. There was a beetle-eyed policewoman not twenty yards away; Wili decided he had better do the normal thing and report the theft. He wasted twenty minutes at the police station. They offered to drive him home. "Thanks awfully, chaps, but

Wili will make it alone." He had to show them Danielle's shekels before they would let him go off by himself.

He walked to Jaffa. There he changed into laborer's clothes, waited, and at four o'clock took a shared taxi to Gaza. It was dark by the time he arrived and trudged off through the mud alleyways between concrete-block houses.

"An opportunity arose today," he told his friends that night. They were always on the lookout for opportunities because they were free, taking no orders—not from Moscow, not from Damascus, not from Tehran, not from Fatah. They floated and waited. Waited: to win the honor of real men—in a big bang! or in the "factories for men" the Israelis prepared for them, the jails. While they waited they kept busy with their usual work, "our high jinks," as they called it. They burgled, they traded in false passports, they robbed tourists, and sometimes sold hashish.

They despised Wili and were polite to him; among themselves they called him "our useful parasite." Over the years Wili had been obliged to be especially useful to one of them, Issa, who'd lived in London and called himself Jazzy. It was Jazzy who'd told Wili to think up a photographic assignment for himself in Israel.

"We need some photographs ourselves," he'd explained. "You'll be doing nothing illegal, Wili, I promise you." Wili was not in a position to refuse. "I'd be delighted. Delighted," he'd said. He made Jazzy sick.

Inside the bus two women soldiers checked the passengers against the luggage. There was a brief commotion when nobody claimed a red nylon haversack. The soldiers blew their whistles; the bus stopped; people started making for the exits. Then a sleepy ginger-haired youth remembered it was his, the soldiers shouted at him, and the others, grumbling, returned to their seats. Reassured that there would be no explosions on this ride, they set off again.

Danielle had chosen to sit next to a lump of a woman in an army uniform who allowed her the window seat. She spoke French. "We have problems in Israel," she said and her thick-lidded eyes strayed suspiciously over Danielle's hair, as if it might be one of them. "Terrorists."

"I was born in Jerusalem," Danielle replied.

"And now?"

"Sydney."

"Nice for you." She turned away and began searching inside a large black handbag while Danielle watched in astonishment. She was so used to assuming sisterhood among women that hostility from a female stranger was an experience to think about.

The soldier drew out a letter handwritten in Hebrew and read through its three paragraphs twice. A large tear rolled down her cheek. It was followed by others. After a few seconds she leaned forward with her head and arms on the handbag and sobbed loudly. Danielle looked around at the other passengers. All were either young and in uniform or, if older, in nondescript civilian dress. She caught an eye here and there and each told her the same thing: Don't interfere. The passengers did not talk to each other; there was a subdued inward-focused air, a discontent. It did not go along with the "general bond of love in Israel" she had been led to expect.

Timidly, she patted the heaving back, wondering if offering the soldier a peppermint candy would be taken as an insult. After a while, when there was no response to her comfort, Danielle decided to ignore the noise alongside her.

Once clear of the chaotic traffic around the bus terminal they moved fast into the outskirts of the city, an area even shabbier than the center, with rows of decaying concrete apartment blocks, each one's functional ugliness increased by the dozens of solar-heating panels and tanks on its roof. The suburbs looked as if they had been flung up in a housing emergency without time to plant gardens then, or since. Vacant lots were strewn with building rubble and rubbish in such an easy way it seemed not illegal but a municipal policy in favor of littering. "Tel Aviv is beautiful," people had told her; she realized they meant it was emotionally beautiful, its existence a triumph of the spirit. But there was something unnerving about the ugliness, because it suggested people were willing to turn their lives into corridors, to narrow their sympathies and be stifled now in the service of the future. Ten thousand times in Jewish history Jews had said, Our present pain will bring joyous rebirth. But this was the rebirth. And this bit of it, at least, looked like another ghetto.

The housing, she thought, seemed inside out: bedding and rugs hung over balconies, revealing to the eyes of the street the activities within. Women were leaning from their apartment windows, pinning laundry onto clotheslines stretched across the outside walls of the buildings. Time cracked.

—I remember handing clothespins to my mother, who was leaning out the window, hanging sheets on the line. It rained. We laughed and cheered and ran out with every bowl and saucer. We had baths, then washed the clothes in the bathwater. Geoffrey was still alive then. He and I washed the kitten, for which Papa gave him a beating.

Two days later Geoffrey was dead.

Danielle straightened her back and cautiously surveyed the passengers again. None of the older men was vaguely familiar. *He* was not on the bus, as he had not been on the airplane, nor at the airport, nor in the hotel, nor in the streets of Tel Aviv passed by her taxi. Nor was he in the bus terminal, nor in Salomon Street, shopping.

The bus had reached a highway that passed vast dark green groves of citrus trees. These were followed by a featureless plain. The soldier stopped weeping and accepted a peppermint. Danielle had taken out her map of Israel and was checking the road signs against it.

"What are you looking for?" the soldier asked. Her eyes wandered again to Danielle's hair.

"I'm trying to find out where I am."

"We are coming to the Valley of Ayalon. That is where Joshua made the moon stand still."

On the other side of the valley the foothills of the Judean mountains were now in view and a different sort of excitement, not the watchful anxiety of the past day, but a pleasurable thrill, began to spread through Danielle. She and Bennie would tour the whole area by car, but in the meantime she could roughly assess the landscape for "impossibles": electricity and telephone lines, telecommunications stations on the tops of hills, the technology that made a nightmare of location work for historical sequences. The Sea of Galilee, people said, was useless now for Jesus movies; what audiences saw these days was a Canadian lake.

Bennie had said, "This is going to be a *big* movie. We'll shoot in seventy millimeter. Big views. Giant people. Real heroes." His feet were on his desk, he was making a mess of the end of his Monte Cristo, his shirt was open halfway down his woolly chest. The California sky behind him made a halo for his hair, which was like thick dark whorls on a centaur's head. He looked down at the tip of his cigar and Danielle saw a luster on his eyelids that reminded her of the skin of pearls. "We'll win an Oscar.

Hey, let's win an Oscar, girl." When Bennie smiled, it was as if a beautiful woman were stroking him.

After a while she'd asked: "Have you anyone in mind for Eleazar?"

"I'll cast an unknown. For this, we use unknowns. And I promise you—they'll be stars overnight."

And that too, she reflected, came from deep inside Bennie: his belief in nobodies making history.

He said he had left Israel fifteen years earlier for a vacation in Cyprus, just weeks before the Six-Day War. At first she had believed he had taken part in it. "It was a miracle," he said. "Everyone, my parents, all our friends, thought we would be slaughtered by the Arabs. A joke went around: last person, turn off the lights. But after six days of fighting, Israel owned all Jerusalem, the West Bank of the Jordan, the Golan Heights—"

"Where were you?"

"Me! I was fighting every inch of the way." Listening to reports on the radio. "Six days. And on the seventh—He rested. That's how it was."

He had not returned even for a holiday; now he was going to make a film in which the central incident was one of Yahweh's earlier, nasty miracles: spurning His people, He had sent a mighty wind-change to sweep the Zealots' fire away from the Roman siege engines and back upon their own ranks. When He did that, Eleazar ordered suicide for every man, woman, and child. The Zealots died free, but with an act—according to Bennie—of rebuke to God.

"It's the story of a hero struggling with Yahweh," he said. "It's about being trapped inside something, an idea, not knowing if it's real or an illusion. I want your script to convey . . ." She had waited for him to finish the sentence. At last she asked:

"What? The tragedy of a false premise?"

He'd squinted through the fragrant blue smoke. "Danielle! Twenty-five million dollars above the line and you want to write it as a *tragedy*? The box, girl. Let's not forget the box office." He'd begun to laugh, throwing his head back. There was something insolent and intoxicated about him; he tossed some peanuts into his mouth. "You want the bankers to put me in jail?" He mumbled as he chewed the nuts, "You gotta think of an upbeat ending for me."

She had nodded, remembering the mortgage on her house.

❊   ❊   ❊

"Chinese scientists have proved that the Bible is accurate," the soldier said. "There was an eclipse when Joshua commanded the moon to stand still. It's been in the newspapers."

"Do you believe in miracles?"

The soldier fiddled with the clasp of her handbag. "Maybe." Her tone was offended. She hesitated, then asked the question that had been flickering between them for some time. "Are you Jewish?"

"Yes. My father is."

"And your mother?"

"No."

"You aren't, then."

"I'm not Christian, either," Danielle replied but the soldier was not interested in her anymore. She shrugged and took out some knitting.

In a week Bennie would arrive. He'd said, "So spend a few days with your father, smell the air in Jerusalem, look at the colors, then you and I will start work. I'll hire a car and a chauffeur. Later we'll do it by helicopter and small plane. I'll even hire a stills photographer for you." For *you*, she'd thought.

He had come around to her side of the desk and pressed his fist against her chin, making clicking noises with his tongue. "You'll win an Oscar," he'd said. Later that afternoon when she reminded him that she had already worked four months on the project and made two trips from Australia to see him he'd said, "Do I owe you some money?" and while he was reading something on his desk had scribbled a check for fifteen thousand dollars which, Danielle noticed afterward, he had predated to the day that it had been due.

The diesel engine churned throatily, someone snored, and the bus began climbing into the foothills. Abruptly the air became chillier and some passengers stood up to take parkas from the luggage racks. They passed Bab el-Wad and signs that directed to Castel, Abu Ghosh, Mevasseret Zion. The names whispered the languages of waves of conquerors. At last they had come to the beauty Bennie had promised her, not ravishing, as he had described it, but as she remembered: austere and gentle. The hills had a female roundness, as if here a woman had lain stretched to receive into herself a sky god and waited an eon, for her skin was cracked in long horizontal seams of stone, like ribs. Her nakedness had been covered in part with young forests of pine;

elsewhere black-green cypresses as pointed as spears spurted upward. She thought, This is the real Helen, still breathing.

Lying by the side of the road were burnt-out armored vehicles: trucks, what looked like a homemade tank, a destroyed bus.
They were painted with a reddish antirust substance to preserve
them as memorials of the war of 1948. Glitter from a hilltop drew
her eye: up there was a sculpture of giant silver-colored spears
clustered as if grasped in a mighty fist. She felt dizzy. These memorials were for a war that had torn her life as if it were a boot
rag. And in a few more hours—a day, maybe, for she felt a cow-
ardly tiredness overcoming her—she would have to confront the
torn-off part: Professor Dan Garin, as Dr. Daniel Green was now
known. The spears seemed to threaten from above with a message as ancient as the stories of Creation; looking up at them—
they could have been held in Yahweh's fist, or Jupiter's, or Aga-
memnon's—she recalled some lines of Virgil she had translated
for Alice. But the Latin words and the exact music of the poetry
had escaped and she remembered only the meaning now: When
Aeneas fled Troy, he carried his father on his back into exile.
That bastard, Danielle thought. He did not send one penny for
my education.

On another hilltop there was a Jerusalem dormitory suburb, a
great round structure of lion-colored masonry that seemed at
first to be a medieval castle, but on closer examination turned
out to be a stone honeycomb for individual families. Ahead a
tower soared.

"What's that?" she asked the soldier, who had finished a sleeve.

"The Hilton. From whichever road you approach Jerusalem
you always see the Hilton."

"What bliss."

She was staying there?

"I can't afford to. But I like the idea of Hiltons—they're so uniform. So *orthodox.*"

"Of course it is kosher," the soldier agreed, somewhat surprised.

They passed the civic welcome, which she translated. Clipped
shrubs planted on the right-hand side of the road said in Hebrew, "Blessed Are They Who Ascend to Jerusalem."

"May I kiss you?"

The soldier understood immediately; she rubbed her cold nose
and cheeks against Danielle's face, crooning something in Hebrew.

EIGHT

Danielle glimpsed him a dozen times, first at the Jerusalem bus terminal, then from the windows of her taxi, but each time he turned away and was transformed into some other old man. After a while a voice in her head said, "Stop looking *for*. Just look." The city rolled out before her like a magical path that revealed the past and concealed the future, and did this all at once so that for an instant she felt time sliding backward and forward, like water in a tipped bowl, and was as giddy and exhilarated as if she had been dancing in a circle.

"Slow down!" she cried. The Old City walls were ahead, those marvelous tawny blocks of stone rising, rising, with crenellations on the topmost layer and slits for shooting arrows. She was drunk with bizarre impulses, trying to reach her arm seventy feet and let her fingers brush the Damascus Gate as they whizzed past. They accelerated through traffic lights she did not remember and she gazed back at the walls, convinced that if she looked harder she would see something on them she needed to see. The cab driver kept muttering, "I'm from West Jerusalem." He was anxious to return there. He was anxious. Slowly, as if her mind were a simple structure like a starfish limb that needed time to make the connection between sensation and grasping, slowly she perceived that something had happened, some incident was affecting everything and everyone. The idea crept all over her—from the air, from eyes in the streets, from the cab driver's voice. People were boarding up their shops. He turned on the radio for a news broadcast, but she could not understand a word, except for the driver's exclamation of *"Mamzer!"*

In the lobby of the American Colony Hotel the Arab staff gathered in groups of three or four, glancing uneasily as they whispered to each other. The manager scolded them from the desk and they scattered for a few minutes to attend to the guests, then regrouped in a corridor or a corner where he could not see them.

Danielle stared fixedly at the youngest bellboy: Ahmed, according to the white plastic nametag pinned to his jacket. The jacket was green, too tight and too short. as if he were filling in for somebody else, an unfortunate; he, Ahmed, favorite son of a sheik, was above worrying about his appearance. He exuded an amiable laziness.

When at length he allowed his attention to be trapped, he split his face with a smile. "Welcome. Double welcome." He wanted her to stop pestering him.

"Please come here."

He complied with the air of a benevolent merchant dealing with a customer who has set her heart on a caprice.

"What is going on, Ahmed?"

He had no idea what she meant.

"I saw people, just now, boarding up their shops."

That was because it was cold. Or perhaps there was a holiday. In Jerusalem there were many holidays: this was the Holy City—she could see, tomorrow, beautiful shrines, Christian . . .

She nodded.

"They are killing each other," Ahmed said.

"Who?"

"The Jews." His sweet smile followed her as she returned along the corridor, boots clattering on the broad flags of creamy-pink stone as slippery as satin. She ran past the carpets hanging on the walls, up the stairs, to the garden room with its luxuriant trees in pots, past the balcony where Lawrence had strolled, to the white-painted double door, and over the threshold. Alice's number was still busy.

NINE

The head, hidden by a soft-brimmed khaki hat, turned up to Alice: Gideon's cheeks were streaming with tears. He rushed past her and into the spare bedroom.

When she entered it with a cup of tea he had stopped sobbing and looked as if he might be asleep, lying face down with his boots on, so that she was torn between anxiety to know what had happened and concern that he should recover undisturbed. However, he was awake, and swung his legs over the side of the bed to sit contemplating his boots.

"I ran here," he said. He had come from the parliament building.

"Take your time, love." But it exploded from him—the shouting: Peace Now! Peace Now! Down with Sharon! Down with Begin! and the other chant: "Begin, King of Israel! Father! Father!" and then

A world had ended. A young man—his name was Emil Grunsweig—had been blown to pieces in front of the Knesset. For the first time since the founding of the state, Jew had murdered Jew for political reasons.

Gideon said, "I'm not going back to Lebanon. I'm going to refuse duty."

This war has closed the gates of Eden; now Cain has murdered Abel, Alice thought. "You'll be court-martialed," she said, and let him be, while she returned to the kitchen.

Their kibbutz had been in the Galilee, in spring as green as Ireland, with brown sheep up to their bellies in pasture and whole hillsides and valleys suddenly, briefly, in glory with wildflowers. The earth would sigh in her sleep one night and next morning her breath on the fields was visible in an acre of red poppies or a streaming mile of purple lupins, or buttercups. Alice had taught English during the day and at night sat in the bomb shelter with the children. There was a mountain behind their settlement, honeycombed at its peak. Nightly fire spat from the cells of the comb. In summer the mountainside itself caught fire—maybe the Syrians threw a lighted cigarette from their bunker, or maybe it was a fragment of glass concentrating the heat among the dry summer grasses; in summer the flowers died and the grass turned to ashen bristles revealing a black skin beneath. Gideon had been terrified of the mountain. His father had tried to reason him out of his fear, explaining it was people—not the mountain itself—who made fires by day and deadly fire by night, but Amos's arguments had only seemed to increase the child's sense of horror.

Alice felt weary as she moved around the kitchen, preparing a supper for Gideon—grating carrots, slicing capsicums and cucumbers. He was still vegetarian. It had been an irreligious kibbutz, but they maintained the meat and dairy laws in the kitchen for the sake of the income from foreign tourists staying in the guesthouse. However they behaved at home, diaspora Jews liked to keep kosher in Israel. She remembered the day Gideon had decided he would not eat flesh; he was about four years old. I was leading him into the children's dining area when he said, "I'm not having meat." I said, "But supper will be dairy." When I looked down into his solemn face I realized he meant something else. "Meat is killed animals. It's terrified animals." He was pleading with me to understand for him something he *knew* but could not express. A month later the June war began. Gideon was calm throughout. "Daddy will come back," he insisted, and, "Daddy's been nearly killed, but he won't die."

His psychic power had vanished as inexplicably as it had alighted, with only his vegetarianism as a reminder—to Alice—of its existence. Amos was too intellectually vigorous for such ideas, which he grouped under the general heading of "Swiss mysticism." He thought all mountain scenery conflicted with a reasoning life—and after his marriage collapsed, he left the kibbutz. For the past six years he had taught law at the Hebrew University full time, "Like a *proper* Yid."

Alice sighed as she assembled the vegetables in a glass salad bowl. Something—that war fever, the grandeur of an army on the move, of a hundred thousand men all urged in one direction, will-less but seized with a mad delight in the energy of their numbers—something had swept Gideon over the border to Lebanon nine months ago. One night the telephone rang and it was he, shouting, "Alice! I'm in Beirut!" He sounded as if he had discovered the secret of immortality. Even Amos, who for weeks before had said, "We *cannot* attack—there is no justification for an offensive," even he had gone, cursing the government as fascist and knowing from the outset that they would not stop at the Awali River but would go all the way to Beirut—and even to Amman and Damascus, if Fortune smiled. "Giantism—Israel has an attack of giantism," he'd said. But he'd gone; he'd wanted that delicious bite which promises: kill thine enemy that you may live. What bitter fruit it had been.

Gideon had brought back bottles of Arpege and Veuve Cliquot, which now needed dusting; his father had returned empty-handed and silent. He was not fit enough for active service. "I've been an ambassador," Amos said. "Honest man sent abroad to lie for his country." He had handled the foreign press.

This would be the end for Gideon: court-martial, jail, dishonorable discharge. No job for him. No room for him in Israel. And Amos would die from a broken heart: two sons in voluntary exile, *yordim*. It was a word with doom inside it, "those who have descended."

Alice could hear Gideon continuously dialing the telephone, probably trying to get through to Amos. Then she heard "Father?" and switched off her hearing aid.

TEN

Later that evening Amos telephoned her, his voice sounding as if he had smoked sixty cigarettes in the past few hours. She knew how he would be sitting, leaning his forehead against the heel of his hand; his hair was rigid, his face was hollowed in the cheeks, and his skin kippered from compulsive smoking. For an ugly man Amos was one of the most attractive Alice had known, never without a girlfriend since Miki had left him and taken their elder boy off to New York. He had fought to keep Gideon and bring him up single-handed, rebuffing women eager to move in. His only surviving relation, an older sister, did his washing every week—"So why have a woman live with me?" Alice had answered, "For your soul." She had also tried nagging him about cigarettes: "Alice, lung cancer is a Western luxury. It takes *time*. It's for the *goyim*."

Over the telephone he said, "I'm going to kill Gideon." He was going to break his arms. Gideon was behaving like a self-indulgent child: of course the war was rotten, and the government was rotten, and there was a civil war in Israel, the nation sinking into primordial tribal hatreds—blacks against whites, religious against secular, Likud against Alignment, new towns against kibbutzim. "But this is not the time to give up!"

"Please don't shout."

The sound of his indrawn breath could have been a sob but he was only lighting another cigarette. "Alice, if Giddy throws it in—" What would he have done it all for?

He sat for a long time remembering what it had been like to be starving, to be so buckled with hunger that gnawing wood was a comfort. Then returning from Russia in 1946, to a void: house, street, shops, synagogue—the whole had vanished. Two little Polish girls were playing with a hoop; one pinched her nose and exclaimed, "Yech! A Yid!"

He locked his apartment and went down to the street where his car was parked on the pavement. The car population of the city had bred wantonly in the past couple of years: the country was on a spending and gambling spree, wages fully indexed, everybody chasing goods before inflation snatched them further away. His landlord wanted Amos to buy the apartment, for one hundred thousand dollars. He'd been saving for six months, going without this and that. The car, a 1978 Cortina, needed servicing and had only one windshield wiper.

It was raining lightly as he drove into town and the wiper, without its mate, looked absurd thrashing away alone. Against the other window the lobster joint of its lost companion twitched in sympathy. He found a parking spot on Hillel Street and entered the humous restaurant where military people ate and where he, sometimes, met friends. The place was so popular there was often a line. The owner thought of himself as a character and had signs on the walls saying CHEW DON'T TALK and SWALLOW DON'T CHEW. If allowed a year he would not be able to exhaust the subject of how his wife ran off with another man. The story—installments, additional details, important points—came with the humous: you ate, he smoked a cigar and told you about his wife. The only people he left alone were the rough boys from Intelligence whose aura of disciplined violence, that special relaxed-after-the-kill air of theirs, announced their identity.

A university acquaintance in uniform left some younger men and came to join Amos. He had been on reserve duty in Sidon, he said, and began talking in the compulsive monotone of fatigue, as much to himself as to Amos.

". . . arresting people suspected of terrorism. Any whom we thought might be PLO, we handed over to Shin Beth for ques-

tioning. One of the men we'd picked up drove a Mercedes. I had
two Yemenites helping me. They said they *knew* this man was
PLO. I asked how. They said the Mercedes: it was a mark of pre-
ferment. Then they said, 'Questioning him is a waste of time.'
Amos, I didn't know what they meant at first. They were kids—
one was nineteen. He said, 'We've been ambushed five times in
the past month. Why waste time questioning him?' And then the
other put in, 'We could use a nice car.' I forbade it. I quoted
military regulations. I quoted Talmud. Nothing touched them.
Legally, politically, ethically . . . They kept on saying, 'We've
been in this town for eight months. We've got a week's leave.' "

He ordered another Turkish coffee.

"And then?" Amos asked.

"Next morning they came to me and said that during the night
the suspect had tried to escape. His Mercedes is out there. Somewhere."

They smoked in silence for a while. There were only half a
dozen tables in the restaurant, the owner was in the back making
coffee, and it was unusually quiet. Weapons were stacked against
chair legs and walls, the diners focused on their dishes of humous
and salad, tearing spongy round loaves to use as scoops, chewing
not talking, fathoms deep for a while in an animal calm.

Amos said, "My son is going with a Yemenite girl. Beautiful
creature. She doesn't speak. Blushes if you look at her. Tikva—
her name is Tikva." His eyes brimmed with horrified amusement.
Then all at once they were both roaring with laughter, intoxicated. Amos had a rich baritone and after the first words the
young soldiers, grinning, bemused, turned around to listen, then
join in singing. A couple clapped their hands over their hearts as
they bellowed with him the national anthem, *Hatikva*.

Later, walking back to his car, Amos had another attack of *fou
rire*. He was forty-seven years old, he'd topped first-year law at
Harvard, and what did he have to show for it? This absurd vehicle with one windshield wiper.

"C'mon," he urged as he pumped the accelerator. "Pretend
you're a Merc."

He did not feel like calling in on Mira: she would expect him,
at this time of night, to have come to make love.

ELEVEN

Danielle woke up in a room brightly lit with lamps beneath a domed ceiling painted the color of a spring sky. The stone walls were whitewashed and three feet thick; she imagined lounging in the window recesses to watch laden donkeys and Ethiopian monks in black beehive hats and all sorts of people jostling on the street outside. The walls gave out a faint, cold smell of minerals.

She sighed, forcing herself to see this space as a hotel room, and in Israel, not Palestine. It was snowing outside, at some stage of night: her watch was on Los Angeles time and she did not know if it were evening or early morning, what day of the week or what date. She had traveled from Sydney to Los Angeles, stayed overnight; Los Angeles to Tel Aviv, overnight; Tel Aviv to Jerusalem . . .

After she had checked in at the hotel she had gone for a walk. But the streets had retreated from her, ducking away like actors into the wings behind a screen of fatigue within her. Their house had been only five minutes on foot from the American Colony, but although everything looked familiar, nothing was exact and for a few minutes she had stood paralyzed, totally lost, although she could see the white tower of the Sheik Jarrah Mosque, right

beside the hotel, and had only to walk toward it. She came across
Mandlebaum's house, walls patched up where they had been
bombed. It was a museum now, in a quiet street which had been
in Jordan from 1948 to 1967. Again, there was the strange tip
back and forth: time *and* space could slide like water in a bowl.

She got off the bed, stiff in her joints and with her feet throbbing. She had gone to sleep in her fox jacket, for the room
was unspeakably cold. Ahmed had said her central heating was
"cracked"; he'd looked sorry about it.

Danielle walked gingerly across the marble tiles to the big
brass table where some benevolent hand had placed a piece of
chocolate cake, a cup of cold cocoa, and a tepid hot-water bottle
wrapped in a white napkin.

But the bathwater was hot. The bathroom was up a flight of
stairs, with a view over the area of Nahlat Shimon, now veiled
by night and snow. Public lighting from the street cast an orange
haze and transformed the falling snow into flakes of gold.

I remembered a permanent summertime, she thought. All four
of us would walk to the American Colony in the evenings to sit
by the bougainvillea, palms, and lemon trees in its courtyard,
feeling cooled by the fountain. The sky was a rectangle of washing blue above the stone walls and sometimes a silver balloon
would slide into it, the twinkling fist of Polaris holding tight to
its string. I said, "Toys in the air." Father bought me an extra
slice of cake.

A loud buzzing noise started up just outside the bathroom
window and then a voice began crying out, high, rigid, panic-
stricken. It quaked up to a pitch of longing, turned to vapor,
vanished, shimmered back into existence—then yearned upward
again. The muezzin sounded so close he could have been standing at the other end of the bathtub. She hollered *"Allahu Akbar!"*
back at him, and giggled. A muezzin had visited Dr. Green once
for medical advice—I asked him why he had only three teeth and
he said Allah had taken the others to stop him eating too much.

She realized she was very hungry herself and that because of
the prayer times it must be either around midnight or four in the
morning.

After a long wait Ahmed arrived with an omelette and another
hot-water bottle, which he served from a tray. He didn't know
what time it was, either. "Late," he said, smiling and shrugging.

In the kitchen they had been discussing the testimony of the

Israeli chief of staff, who last week had said, "All the Arabs are the same whether in Arabe, Ramallah, or Gaza. All of them should be finished off." And then, today, the newspaper had reported him saying: "To punish the parents for the deeds of the children—this works well with Arabs." Ahmed liked this woman with the djinn smile. He wondered why she wanted to contact the old man who gave speeches calling for the expulsion of all Arabs from Israel and the rebuilding of the Temple; when she'd asked him to look for the professor's name in the Hebrew telephone book he had said he could not find it. But she had tipped him all the same.

TWELVE

Alice tottered a bit when she stepped back from her front door, laughing and clapping her hands.

"Thy hair is as a flock of goats that cometh down from Gilead! Oh, let me look at you. The screenwriter!"

For Danielle it was always amazing to connect Alice with her age, to see her shaky on her legs as a woman of eighty-five had a right to be, for she was such a girlish creature, her eyes so bright with communication, her voice so gay—and with all that she had a quality of knowing, of knowledge of the goals of life. She looked a schoolgirl nine hundred years old.

Danielle thought: She brings out in me the urge, almost uterine, to exaggerate; to make everything brighter and more dramatic.

"My God, Alice! This place smells like a coal mine," she said, and they went off into peals of laughter.

"The wicked landlady will not fix the gas for me. I'll go up in a fireball one day. And the prime minister will blame the PLO."

"There'll be summary vengeance."

"Yes. A couple of planes will whiz up to Lebanon and bomb some camp."

They deflated.

"You've come at a sorry time," Alice said. "I didn't think I'd live to see . . ."

Chastened, she looked at the floor. —We've lost it all so quickly. All the fun of the 1930s and of the fifties and sixties has gone. Israel was "God and us" in those days.

"You're limping," she said. "You mustn't fall sick here."

She led Danielle into the kitchen where the reek of gas hammered their noses until the kettle was boiled for tea, and the stove could be turned off. Alice had herbal ointment for foot blisters and made Danielle remove her soft red leather walking boots, red leg warmers, and the socks with toe pockets.

"Toed socks!" she said. "I invented them, I believe, for my trip to Moscow in 1925. I knew I was going to freeze and wouldn't be able to wash."

Danielle looked around at the leaky stove, the refrigerator that made digestive noises, the cold-water sink. Alice saved pieces of string and plastic bags; they were heaped on a peg behind the door; she had breadcrusts stored in a plastic container and bean sprouts growing feebly in a jar by the window. Danielle wondered if she were getting enough to eat.

"It's not Darling Point, with harbor views," Alice said. She had sold everything when she turned sixty-five and run off to Israel again. After a while snapshots had arrived: Alice outside the children's house of the kibbutz; milking a cow. A note said, "When I came here in 1930 it was half-swamp and we slept in tents. The achievement!" Looking at the frugality of her existence in Jerusalem Danielle wondered at the ends of life, the loose fringes to its garment: Miss Sadler—suffragette, pacifist, Communist fellow-traveler, Zionist, abortion-law reformer, feminist radical, member of Amnesty International, and the Voluntary Euthanasia Society. She had wanted to save the world. Now she saved plastic bags. And she seemed happier than ever.

"Since you're getting on a bit . . ." she said tentatively. Alice was tottering about the kitchen, refusing help with the tea things. She gave a snort.

"You think I should return to Australia? Yes. It would be more comfortable." There was gaiety in her eyes. "But, my dear, the spirit. At my age, it's the *spirit*."

"Won't it travel?"

"It does not need to. It's contented everywhere. Especially here."

They went to the parlor where there was an electric heater

and a blue woolen curtain enclosing the room's warmth. Danielle
was unwilling to yield up her cheerfulness, but as she settled herself on the settee beside a pile of *Listener* magazines she experienced a sudden thud, as if her armor had crashed to the ground.
Without intending to she began relating her problems: *Eleazar*
was her big chance, but she would not be paid much until the
script was complete (and accepted), so she had gone into debt to
keep herself going: "I've had to put up my house in Avalon as
collateral." There were difficulties with the producer, who wanted
her to move to Los Angeles, but she could not leave Katherine
alone in Sydney during her first year at university. Then there
was the dog. "The dreadful woman from whom I bought the
house, Mrs. Wellsmore, is staying in it while I'm away, minding
Emma. She has a diet of gin, cigarettes, and aspirin, and I expect
she smokes in bed."

Alice listened to the undercurrent, to Danielle's voice saying,
"I've reached a crossroads—and I'm lost." A few months ago her
letters had sounded so confident; she had announced: I'm through
with men! Radical celibacy equals peace of mind.

A deep breath turned into a sigh. "The worst problem is I
think I've fallen in love with the producer-director. He's a crook."

Alice folded her hands and closed her eyes. There was some
weakness in Danielle's nature that drew her to tainted men—
including Patrick, for whom she'd grieved for years, although he
was a drunk and unfaithful. As a child there had been an incident with one of Bonny's admirers. Of course, living alone with
her mother, who was more or less a geisha . . . Rich men paid
the rent and the school fees for Bonny, who was a real beauty
and as high-handed as a duchess, her haughtiness that of a
woman made bitter when still young. The mother had been kept
in furs and the daughter in trifles like Swiss watches. But it was
always on the edge, and the girl had been scarred: she looked
for God in men, someone to save her.

"You told me you were never going to fall in love again, after—
what was his name?—the last one?"

"James." Danielle's voice was glum. She'd helped James get a
lead role in a production of *Arturo Ui*, whereupon he'd turned
layabout, and wouldn't help with the shopping.

Sipping the hot clear tea, Alice contemplated that aspect of
women that whispers, "You're not really good enough; you'll
never achieve what you could if you were a man." The serpent

says, "But if you *love* a man, if you become his soul for him, you can guide him to happiness—and that will be an achievement." She had listened to its seductive murmur for more than sixty years.

Danielle, also sipping tea, pictured Bennie—he with the Filipino servant, he who ate all his meals in restaurants, who drove a white Corniche (discounted at $40,000 a year, thanks to the tax laws of California), Bennie Kidron: supermarket shopping?

"Is he a real crook?"

"He has a certain reputation in Los Angeles. He had money troubles after his partner died in a helicopter accident. The partner, Raphael Schultz, was the"—she grimaced—"genius *auter*, as they say. He was famous in the seventies for low-budget, cult movies." Kidron was the salesman of the team; he raised the money, he did deals. "Now he wants to be a director. I doubt if he could direct traffic—and he's hired me because he needs a writer who will feed him every line. But he's full of charm, when it suits him. And always full of cheek." Bennie had said, "I'm gonna make fifteen, twenty million out of this. I *need* fifteen." What he needed it for was not clear. Danielle was now sitting in silence, realizing she was already deeply in conspiracy with Bennie, that her discretion about his greed sealed it like a vow.

There was a delicate query in Alice's raised eyebrows.

"We're not lovers!" she replied quickly. "Nor does he give the slightest sign of finding me interesting."

So much the worse, Alice thought.

Alice had a habit of punctuating conversations with periods of quiet during which she sat with her eyes closed. When she opened them it was the signal to begin a fresh topic. Danielle enjoyed the orderliness this gave, but she dreaded what had to come next: her father.

"I tried to find his telephone number . . ."

"You *shall* find it, my dear. You have to. You knew you had to return to Jerusalem, and now that you're here you know you must find him. Your mind will never have peace until you do. You told me that yourself, once."

"But it's not in the Hebrew phone book."

Alice thought that a poor excuse. Danielle should know how small Jerusalem was, that "everybody knows everybody." There were invisible structures, like the crystalline lattice in a saturated solution. All the pre-Independence people knew each other; all the German-speakers; all the Anglophones; the Second Aliya; the Herut people. The country was a laminate of clans.

"He's religiously—how that word is misused—active," Alice added. "My born-again Christian girls know of him." And David had told her: Professor Garin, retired, was still as troublesome as he ever had been since 1948 when his crusading against the Arabs had not been recognized for what it was: a form of madness. It was restricted, however, to a single area of his mind so that Garin had been able to continue his research, begun under the British who had sent him to Palestine, and had attained the status of professor in the medical school where his work on viruses had been outstanding. For thirty years he had been writing pamphlets calling for the rebuilding of the Temple (prophecy said that on its third building the Temple could not be destroyed). Alice had seen them occasionally. They usually began with the motto "He who rules Jerusalem rules Israel, and he who rules the Temple Mount rules Jerusalem." Since 1967 Garin's pamphlets had been taken more seriously. She gazed at Danielle, whose face had become small and anxious with questions beneath its rug of copper hair.

"He's considered a prophet, by some. He's part of the shadow spreading over this country—it's a fearful thing." The Christian girls spoke of Satan's wing darkening the Jerusalem sky, but they meant something different: they prayed for Israel to bomb Damascus, "for Damascus shall be in heaps," the Bible said. When they mentioned Islam they said "Satan."

"I wasn't prepared for something I saw at the airport," Danielle said. "What I can only describe as racial tension between some European Israelis and some Middle Eastern ones."

"The blacks! My dear, that's what the Sephardim are called. They're the dogsbodies—Arabs aside—and they're blamed for everything. And, you know, I think it *suits*—" The doorbell rang. "That will be Suzie from the home-help agency. She'll know how to find Garin."

The young woman who followed Alice back into the parlor was so thin Danielle guessed she suffered from anorexia nervosa. She had pretty dark hair and eyes, but there was something feral in her expression; she looked uncertain, almost suspicious, as she stood close to the blue woolen curtain, her glance directed down over her long Indian cotton dress, thick maroon stockings, and clumpy sandals.

"This is Marilyn, who's going to clean for me today because Suzie, who normally comes, has a cold."

In Danielle's warm hand Marilyn's fingers were icy and all bones.

"You're freezing!"

Both recoiled.

There was a hint of perverse pleasure in the girl's expression: "I lost my gloves yesterday," she said. "But Jesus will send me another pair," and Danielle realized there was a challenge thrown at her from Marilyn's eyes. She thought: scavenger's eyes.

Alice had gone to make more tea. When she returned she found them watching each other as warily as strange cats. She could see what Danielle was thinking: that Marilyn needed a bath. She had folded the skirts of her dowdy cotton dress over her knees in a manner suggesting that invisible men, across the room, were leering at them; her hair, in particular, did smell unwashed, especially alongside Danielle, who would as soon go out without wearing scent as Alice would without wearing her beret.

Marilyn was saying she had a brother in the movie business. The rest of the story shimmered, waiting, while she attended to the modesty of her knees once more. "He died very young." She turned a brilliant smile on Alice. "He's with the Lord now."

It's not often, Danielle was thinking, that I meet someone I loathe on sight. But there was something fascinating alloyed to Marilyn's repulsiveness, she found, and was curious to know more about her: *why* born-again Christian? (Why not est?) Why Israel? Why a cleaner's job?—She'd said she had a degree in sociology from UCLA; her manner was that of a girl who'd grown up with servants; maybe she even came from Bel Air.

Alice had gone off to show her the broom closet and was away a long time. She returned holding a photograph of Jesus and sat down with a thump.

"Those girls have the Lord right under their thumbs, you know. When Suzie misses a bus it's Jesus who sends her another one. She's told me! The Egged bus company has nothing to do with it . . . How d'you think you're going to get on with Marilyn?"

Danielle thought not at all.

Again Alice sat in contemplation of the troubles of the young. When she had turned eighty something extraordinary had happened—her earnestness fell away like an old skin, sloughed off. She stood naked in front of her bedroom mirror one morning and looked at her straight, thin body as if it were brand-new, its wrinkles a puppy-looseness. She was platinum and white, like an old moonbeam. And she began to laugh at herself, knowing that the body didn't matter any longer—she could throw it out the window, go parachuting, leap on a tiger's back—she no longer cared if she had a body or not. All the terrible heat of emotion it had generated, the turmoil and anxiety, the passions for mankind and men, all those ideas and plans that made her life fizz and spit . . . What a game they had been. What a struggle—like Israel's: he who struggled with God. The mirror showed her a column of white marble that rose on its toes. Soon she'd been able to throw it away to join the other stones in Jerusalem—because now inside, now outside, now surrounding it, there was something else, immortal and unalterable. But one cannot explain these things to the young, she thought. One can only encourage them, try to give them the nerve to walk into fire, and pass through it: Danielle's a plucky girl. But immature.

Time and again she had remarked on the emotional greenness of these bright young women whose careers reached heights her own generation had not dreamed of. In Danielle she saw an authentic example of the late-twentieth-century Western woman, reared in prosperity at a forced pace. The process left them glossy as their tomatoes, which were colored scarlet from gassing, but undeveloped within. It was a sort of vulgarity, and a sign of the times.

"You've got your work cut out, dearest. Marilyn is Professor Garin's daily help." She handed over a slip of paper with a telephone number and an address. "His wife, it must have been his third, died recently and Marilyn, from the way she spoke, is his keeper. He's told her he has no children. It's as well for you to know what you're up against."

She saw self-righteousness in Danielle's expression and thought: Fear. But if you succumb to it you'll spend another twenty years in assuring yourself you did not.

"Do you know why you want to see him?" she asked.

"Sentimentality."

But Alice, even through the distortion caused by her hearing aid, heard the facile note in Danielle's voice, and thought, I'll not indulge her.

"In my experience," she replied, "Sentimentality is a cloak for lies we tell ourselves. You can do better than that."

Silence. And noises from another room of Marilyn moving furniture. Danielle was thinking: Something happened to me after I won the award at Cannes for *The Lovers* . . .

—Not one thing, but many. The most banal was that I wondered, "Is this all there is? Do I now just go on writing bigger and better—or worse—movies till I drop?"

"I had a mild attack of existential *angst*," she said, "Nothing, however, to distress for long your average bear . . ." She listened to herself trying to be amusing. But some slight gesture from Alice conveyed that the old woman was *really* attending to her, that nothing she said would be dismissed as trivial and that her nervous defenses were unnecessary.

"You know, Alice, I thought of that film—*The Lovers*—as a clever, feminist look at sadism. And masochism, of course."

Alice had seen it; the story was simple, an old favorite in fact: supposedly set in the nineteenth century it was about a poor farmgirl who becomes the mistress of a rich, tyrannical landowner, trapped into it by love for her starving parents, brothers, and sisters. At length, having befriended a terrible bull owned by the lover, she rebels and escapes, riding off on the animal's back.

"But the idea for it came from television news pictures of a matador being gored. I kept wondering, 'Why do they fight bulls?' Suddenly I started seeing pictures of bulls everywhere— every time I opened a magazine or a newspaper."

—Like the girl, who had an obsession about the farm bull. She saw it everywhere, watching her, tracking her when she went to the fields, waiting to trample her down.

"Then, at Cannes, an elderly judge came up to me and asked, 'Why does she escape on the bull? Why not on a bicycle?' I wasn't sure. He went on about mythology and the interpretations the other judges had made when assessing the film. Then he said, 'Mademoiselle, pour moi.' For him, the bull was the energy of life. The Life Force. And the girl was Soul. I told him, 'Listen—*The Lovers* is about victimization, and overcoming it.' And he replied, 'Ma petite, you are lucky because you have written *something good* in your sleep.'"

They heard Jerusalem surging outside, Marilyn scraping chair legs across the floor, the momentary hiss of the thermostat on Alice's electric heater.

". . . absurd," Danielle was saying. "It sounds absurd. I began to think I was the girl."

"And who or what is the bull, my dear?"

—Some part of me, also. Or him. My father. Men. Patrick. Even James. "I don't know. But I imagined it, so it's mine, somehow." Alice was nodding, but Danielle had shocked herself, feeling as if, all of a sudden, she had molted.

"Zeus appeared as a bull. Or a swan—or anything else that took his fancy. Yahweh, too, for that matter . . ." Alice's reedy voice was far away. "I was translating some Virgil this morning . . ."

Danielle waited, straining to seem attentive. At length she asked, "Did you tell Marilyn that Professor Green-Garin does, in fact, have a daughter?"

Alice sighed. She had, she said, and Marilyn had remarked: "Your friend has made a mistake. He has only me, Miss Sadler." Then she had given Alice the picture of Jesus and asked her to join in prayer with her, after she'd mopped the kitchen floor.

A needle twirled in Danielle's chest. "So *she's* his daughter! That unwashed hippie! He even has a granddaughter. What about all the photographs of Katherine I sent him?"

Without warning her, Danielle's body began to sob. Alice came to sit beside her and rubbed her back. She spoke quietly, saying things Danielle could not hear at first for they reached her like signals in a fog. At length she was able to listen. Alice was saying: "Remember you're not powerless. Remember you're a widow who brought up a child single-handed, got her launched into university to study engineering, and made a career for yourself at the same time. And here you are, not yet forty, setting out on a great adventure. A discovery."

Danielle inhaled as if air were liquid, to be gulped.

"What discovery?" Her voice bridled.

Alice chirruped, "To know yourself. What else is there, my dear?"

Marilyn had the rugs rolled up, had piled the small chairs on top of the dining table in the salon, as Jerusalem called its living rooms, and was already mopping the stone-tiled floor. She turned to smile, looking up over the mop handle. Danielle thought, You and your broomstick. They made the singsong "Sha-lom" at each other. Ironic, Danielle thought, how in this battleground of a country people never tire of saying "Peace." You say it in greeting and parting, even answering the telephone. Peace. Peace. As if in Jerusalem there could ever be peace. Even Alice had the habit: "Shalom, love," she said at the door.

A man about seventy was on the stairway, resting to catch his breath. He carried a bunch of violets and although he was sagging from exhaustion his face brightened as Danielle galloped down the steps toward him. He made a gesture with his free hand, trying to tip his astrakhan hat. Half-dead, he retained that charm of a man who loves women. They were in each other's presence for only a second but it was so agreeable that when Danielle reached the foyer and opened her umbrella against the snow she felt as if something had been restored to her.

"For the American Colony?" the cab driver asked.

"No. I want to go to the Old City. Jaffa Gate."

THIRTEEN

##

Her taxi moved fitfully through the narrow hilly streets of this central European West Jerusalem. It was a town of apartment buildings faced with cream-colored stone, with pine trees and dark-leafed winter jasmine in the front gardens. There were laundromats, banks, bakery windows luscious with chocolate tortes and poppyseed cakes, and cars parked on asphalt pavements richly manured by dogs. Danielle muttered to herself: I am a Hottentot. I've never heard of David, Solomon, Jezebel, Herod, Salome, Rabbi Jesus of Nazareth, Caiaphas, Titus, Bar Kochbah, Mohammed, Goddefroi de Bouillon, Saladin, Richard Coeur de Lion. The Lion's Gate, the Golden Gate, el-Burak, the Hill of Evil Counsel, the Mount of Anointing, the Mount of Olives, the Temple Mount. The Via Dolorosa, Suleiman the Magnificent, the el-Aqsa, the Dome of the Rock, the Valley of the Cheesemakers. The Tenth Legion. The Wall. These are unknown to me . . . I am just *looking*.

What stately names! Uttered under the breath they expand to blossoming centuries.

It stopped snowing. They passed a street still half-destroyed from the war of '67; ahead the purple-gray sky rested a few yards above the Old City walls like a dark wing—but to her, all at once, it was the great protecting wing of the Shekinah. She walked through the Jaffa Gate, past the sandbags and men with submachine guns, and was instantly lost and at home.

Once she found herself drinking a thimble of coffee perfumed with cardamom while in the background a bunch of young men played Space Invaders and older ones smoked hookahs, but mainly she wandered without direction, passing window shutters and doorways painted blue to ward off the Evil Eye. The very air jittered with a violence of mind and sensual distraction that made every yard she walked and every minute that ticked away seem like provinces and months spent in some normal place. The past leaned upon the present. Invisible boundaries, as commanding as barbed wire, appeared at street corners: here ends the Greek Orthodox quarter; here begins the Moslem quarter; Danger—Jews unwelcome past this point. Foreign women take care to be modestly dressed . . . Something had stung her neck: a group of ragamuffins was surrounding her at a prudent distance, their leader, about ten years old, with his hands on his hips.

Behind her a merchant was offering for sale a statue of the Madonna, its face inlaid with mother-of-pearl. "See the beauty," he called to Danielle.

Men dressed in the style favored by Christ went by; the Yasser Arafat three-day beard was popular—on both Arabs and Jews— and an old party got up as an amateur-dramatics Turk stomped along banging the stones with a stout pole, followed by some Assyrian kings with square beards and diamond crosses hung around their necks. "That's the Pope," someone said. But it was only the Greek Pope.

The environment recalled too much of the past and confused it with the present, making her feel slightly mad. She looked into the face of every older man she passed: he was not in them. When she turned to rebuke the person behind who had shoved her, Danielle met with a donkey's muzzle. The donkey tapped his delicate forefoot peevishly; his back was laden with kerosene tins and behind him eight men inside a Mercedes Benz waved fists out the window. The donkey said, "What do they expect me to do? Fly?" Since no one could move, the owner began beating him on the rump, and yelling. A sign said Via Dolorosa.

It had taken her about a minute to realize—or remember—that

the merest glance sideways at the wares of the souk would bring out like wasps from a disturbed hive men saying, "Yes, please? What is it you want?" in voices at once obsequious, threatening, and suggestive, as if anything at all could be made available and they could recognize a corrupt soul.

Pretending to help her try on a sheepskin jerkin a boy had fluttered his hands over her breasts and as she pulled back he had grabbed a handful of her hair as if by accident. "Welcome," he said. An older man watched from a rush-bottomed stool in the corner of the shop. Outside someone had followed her ten yards muttering "fuck-fuck-fuck-suck-my-cock" until she'd had the nerve to swing around and hiss, "Suck it yourself!" He had scrambled back, eyes rolling white, like a dog unjustly kicked. Extremes touched each other: in the streets, misogyny; in antique shop windows, clay figurines of the Mother Goddess, who became the Abomination.

She stopped to look at an Abominable Female (price, $200, guaranteed a genuine Caananite artifact), wondering if her father now recited the daily prayer: Thank you, Lord, for not creating me a woman. What monsters that insult has spawned, she thought.

She was aware of other dissonances. Although the Old City belonged so intimately to the people, there was an insistent suggestion of conflict between their vitality and the funereal stillness of its stone. The walled town was time-defying, like a pyramid. Enclosed by masonry of such mighty age flesh seemed tender, weak, and poignantly impermanent, at the farthest remove from eternal life. It was as if the builders had constructed a daily reminder for themselves that bodies are only meat and bones. She shivered all over at the idea that underneath lay collected a lake of the human blood shed century after century in these lanes: a sharp blow to the paving could make it gush again.

Suddenly she found she had escaped the crowds of the souk and was alone in a Crusader church. It was free of decoration inside and out, except for a cross on the wall of the apse. The altar table had a white cloth and two lighted candles, their pale, straight forms like the translucent bodies of saints. There were rows of pews and nothing more—thousands of tons of masonry leapt upward as if weightless. She was shaken by contact with genius, its fire drawn down, somehow, into the hands of stone-cutters who believed the earth was flat. Her footsteps on the flagging made a soft thunder.

It was bitterly cold inside the church, which was filled with a dim gray light except where, entering at a round window, a silvery ramp of sunshine maybe sixty feet long ran down to the altar. There was a saying, she recalled: Jerusalem's sunshine is the outermost garment of God.

She was about to leave when a group of pilgrims came in following a guide. From forty feet away she could hear his whispers about the acoustics of St. Anne's; he suggested they sing. Danielle was half-way to the door. "Please stay, Miss," the guide called and his mouth could have been cupped against her ear. The pilgrims' voices rose—and then, something happened. Angels came to sing. Her body was permeated by their vibrations and she felt she had expanded so far the boundaries of her skin disappeared, and she'd turned into waves and dots and riffles of light.

She went outside when they began the second hymn. She was weeping, but not distressed. She felt, rather, a mixture of joy and compassion for all beings. It was a calming sensation and she leaned against the wall of the church, smiling. The world on its permanent errand went here and there in front of her.

After a while she became aware that a pair of eyes were fixed on her.

"Wili."

"*Prin*-cess!" His approach was an exercise in stagecraft: arms flung wide; two steps forward; say "Princess"; halt; smile; another two steps. Hug.

His skin shone from cold cream and he seemed to have spilt on himself the contents of a bottle of *Kouros*. It was a scent she loathed.

He was sucking a throat lozenge.

He's been watching me, she realized, he can see I've been crying, but he's such an egomaniac that all he'll be interested in will be my praise for his cleverness in finding me.

"Well, how did you do it?" she asked.

"Someone told me." Lips pursed smugly. He had an aluminum suitcase on the ground beside him, open. The insides were a nest of foam-rubber hollows for extra lenses and film spools. He shut it with a snap. "I don't let them x-ray *this*." He wrinkled his nose and made the *eh-eh-eh* snigger. Danielle felt too peaceful to be irritated. She allowed him to take her arm and lead her off.

"*How* did I find you? Well, you had a coffee in the Moses Cafe. You talked to a friend of mine in the antique shop just over there . . ." Wili looked meaningfully into her face. "You see, darling, I know lots of people here."

Her vague response displeased him and he changed the subject: he was taking snaps for what would be The Book on the holy places and the religious in Israel. And he was working with "a very talented, a very beautiful lady. Who lives in Germany."

"We may marry," he said.

Danielle made a polite face.

"Helga and I share a great many views," he added. His sharp eyes were full of questions and secrets. Danielle thought, If I were not in such a soft mood . . .

As they walked Wili greeted several passersby, in Arabic. From their courteous responses it was impossible for her to guess whether they knew him or not. The Arabs in Jerusalem wore masks of calm behind which flitted restlessness, agitation, or despair.

"Aren't they wonderful? Aren't they great human beings?" he said every time a man returned his attention. He took Danielle's silence for agreement and squeezed her arm. Then he made an irrelevant remark, as seemingly trite as his others, but with an energy that jarred; afterward it echoed to Danielle and disturbed her. He said, "What's lost on the battlefield is made up for in the bedroom."

She said, "Wili—that's the PLO line. The Arabs used to say that in 1948. It hasn't worked yet."

"Not yet"—with a spike through "*yet.*" "Whose side are you on, politically?"

"Neither. They're both right. I think history is a series of experiments, most of them ending in catastrophe. How can one take it personally?" She was still feeling vague.

Wili stopped abruptly, jerking her to a halt. "Princess, that is a very, very perceptive statement." He added, "From your point of view."

Danielle wanted to leave the Old City through the Lion's Gate and walk around the outside of the walls, but Wili said it was getting too late, that more snow might fall, and that he knew a quick way to reach Herod's Gate which would take them straight on to Sultan Suleiman Street.

"And I want to show you something. For your political education."

They were in the Moslem Quarter, a quiet residential area where children with eyes as bright as licorice balls laughed and ran around in the laneways and delicious aromas drifted from windows cut in the stone walls. There was also the smell of drains. Wili said, "Look!"

Above their heads a long pole projected from a second-story window. From it hung a white rectangle of cloth with a horizontal blue stripe near the top, another near the bottom and in the center a blue Star of David.

—The Israeli flag! In a Moslem area!

"Nice people, your Gush Emunim," Wili said and set off jauntily again. They stopped inside the Old City once more only, at a pharmacy near Herod's Gate where he inquired about nettle tonic for his scalp. Apparently his Arabic was rudimentary, for the pharmacist replied in English. Wili gesticulated, trying to make his hands a dictionary. Then he took off his peaked cap and the problem was revealed: all his luxuriant black hair, which Danielle remembered him wearing to his shoulders, like the Beatles, had vanished. Now there was only a dark gauze through which his yellowish scalp shone. The pharmacist nodded solemnly, reached under the counter and withdrew a small dark-brown bottle, which he blew on to remove the dust.

"Can I smell it?" Wili asked; he had already re-covered his scalp.

The pharmacist's sigh said that if smelling would make Wili happy, he should smell; if he wanted to set a match to it, he could do so. He, the pharmacist, was familiar with humanity and would not object: folly defeated him.

Wili passed the bottle to Danielle who jerked back from the punch of Friar's Balsam.

"That's the stuff," Wili said.

She realized he had, with that great nose of his, almost no sense of smell. This struck her as doubly unfair, for Wili's nose made him not merely ugly but also ridiculous, as if he had been fitted out by a joke shop, born a clown and fated to the circus— that thrilling glimpse of the netherworld where everything is upside down, in rebellion, on the verge of death, the human fly, men transformed to birds without wings leaping between trapeze swings, animals hurtling through hoops of fire, the clowns themselves with faces as white, sad, astonished, and mute as Lazarus. All afternoon ideas for *Eleazar* had been jumping in and out of her mind. Suddenly she was sure that Eleazar too had suffered a tragicomic disfigurement of mind or body, that his extremes had some painful source as intimate, so to speak, as the nose on his face: if she were patient she knew that she could hit upon a film metaphor to convey what it was that had made him the Zealot. It would not be an insight to appeal to the audience of eighteen- to twenty-five-year-olds whom Bennie aimed to please.

It was already dark by the time they reached the hotel, a five-minute walk from the Old City. They agreed to meet for dinner at seven.

Back in her room Danielle took a few deep breaths before dialing the number Alice had given her. Marilyn answered the phone, in Hebrew.

—How dare she speak Hebrew? It's my language, not hers, she thought, and heard her voice mimicking her mother's haughty, languid tone. If Professor Garin were out, when was he expected to return? Oh, not this evening? At six-thirty in the morning? "I'll be asleep."

Marilyn made a noise that was cheerful and disapproving; it said "early to bed, early to rise . . ." and that people who were self-controlled found it easy to make telephone calls at that time of morning.

"Professor Garin is always up at five and at his desk writing by five-fifteen," Marilyn said. She asked what message Danielle would like to leave and whether Green had an "e" on the end.

Danielle said he could spell it. "It was his name for almost forty years."

Marilyn said "amazing!" in the shocked, tolerant voice of a maiden aunt listening to a tall story.

Danielle blew on one sweating palm, then the other, when she had put down the telephone.

There was a knock on the door: Ahmed carried a silver tray on which lay her hair dryer and a message from reception.

"Fixed," he said. The hair dryer was not fixed. She had asked him to remove the plug and replace it with one that would fit a socket in her room. Some took around two-pronged plugs, some rectangular-pronged; others three-pronged, rectangular, and round. Ahmed had explained their diversity with this remark:

"Here is the Middle East."

"All you've done is take the plug off," she said.

Ahmed agreed that was so; before she could stop him, he had poked the exposed wires into his mouth, rolled them around on his tongue and, wetted, shoved them into a socket. Danielle stood back aghast as he pressed the On button—there were no switches to the sockets—and held the whirring machine up to his hair. The voltage was two hundred and ten.

"You'll be electrocuted!"

Ahmed was enjoying the hot currents of air on his face. "Don't afraid," he said. His smile had all the tenderness and contempt of the Oriental male for the female. After an argument he went off to get a plug.

The message was a telegram from Bennie. It said GO FOR IT GIRL ARRIVING SOON LOVE B K.

Arriving soon? He was due to arrive in another four days, precisely. Danielle took from her suitcase the international-time indicator that told her it was about nine-thirty in the morning in Los Angeles, a good time to call. Instead she stood in the center of the room as if in a vacuum, her will sucked away.

Wili Djugash had chosen the restaurant on Sultan Suleiman Street because he had eaten there before and felt confident about the hygiene of the place. He put his traveling utensils—a folding knife, fork, and spoon—into his pocket before he set out for the American Colony at a quarter to seven, feeling that lightness of heart that comes from trivial successes. He thought he had evaded telling Danielle where he was staying; in fact, she had not asked.

He took the hill at a trot, picturing himself setting forth, over kebabs and grilled chicken, "My Prison Experience" and "My Liberation." Of course, she would have read something in the newspapers; the whole world knew they had jailed him. He imagined a candle on the table and its glow in her eyes. Maybe she would weep.

The streets were inky; some had sidewalks, some did not, it was necessary to press against the walls of houses as cars went by. Halted for a moment Wili realized he had stepped in donkey dung.

He felt sick!

Should he run back and change his shoes? Should he dash down to the Damascus Gate and look for a shoe-shine man? At this hour they would have gone home.

Fortunately he was wearing gloves. With a gloved hand he could remove the shoe and find a faucet somewhere—maybe at the American Colony.

Danielle said, "Give it to me, for God's sake. I'm not squeam-

ish." After a few minutes she returned to the foyer with a clean,
wet shoe.

"What a great lady you are." He had been impressed by her
friendly relations with the staff: a young man called Ahmed had
gone off with her and the shoe. Wili had heard them joking together, something about this being the Middle East. He took it
as a good omen that she was staying in the American Colony
rather than in one of the multistory West Jerusalem hotels. As
Jazzy was always reminding him, one could never believe what
people said about their political sympathies; however, a Zionist
would not choose the American Colony.

"Good hotel?" he asked casually.

"Heaven."

"So you like the Palestinians?"

"What a peculiar idea." She meant: one likes some and not
others, but Wili translated it as "How could you doubt that I
would?" and gave her arm a squeeze.

He was going to enjoy showing her his photographs of Helga,
"the lady I told you about. So like you, Princess. *So* like you."

Afterward Danielle often remembered the dumb hilarity grip-
ping her from groin to neck as she looked at Helga-so-like-her:
nineteen years old, hair plaited into eight hundred dreadlocks,
clenched fist for the camera, ancestors from the Ivory Coast.

"She's very pretty."

—Wonder if she dresses well? You can't tell with nudes.

"Afro-German," Wili agreed. If he had not looked so solemn
as he added, "You and Helga are the same sort of woman," Danielle might not have released that shriek of laughter.

Then, because she had insulted him; because she had to defend herself for having made a despicable, racist remark—her
noise had become "a remark"—she thought it was funny to be
compared to a black lady, did she? she thought black people
were funny? he supposed—if only all this had not taken place
within moments of sitting down to table she might not have gone
too far in her desire to mollify him, and ended by inviting him
to take the site stills when she and Bennie began their location
tour.

Her original intention had been to have dinner with him, get
back her fifty dollars, and never see him again.

For his part Wili could barely believe his luck. *Their* luck.
"Fine by me," he'd said.

FOURTEEN

L istening to Wili's story she thought, The quality that makes people interesting is different in each one, but bores are all the same.

She was ashamed of her lack of compassion. However wildly he exaggerated, Wili had been victimized. He had been beaten up (by persons unknown, one in the uniform of a Guards offi-cer—the Hon. Tamsin's brother was in the Guards); he'd been sued for libeling the family; he'd been bankrupted by litigation. In Parliament an MP had demanded he be "sent back to Bombay along with all the other wogs." But compassion, she realized, is a willful emotion that wells up and slinks away according to a tide of its own. Her attention to Wili would spurt, then subside as her mind wandered to her own collection of family myths. She tried to see them afresh, clearly: the tear made by Geoffrey's death, the grief . . . Did my father, she was wondering, beat up Bonny from frustration—because the real villains were out of reach? Bonny had told her, again and again, "He made *me* the scapegoat!" But Danielle knew her mother had been a flirt, even in those days, that she'd hypnotized the Arab doctor who came to visit them in West Jerusalem . . . Then there was cousin Rachela, the illegal immigrant they were hiding. She remembered: I went into Bonny's room one day and found her brushing her hair into sparks. She said, "Your cousin finds my appearance frightening. Frightening! That's what she told your father." The golden filaments crackled. "What's the use? He's in love with her!" Bright fragments exploded; Bonny's image disappeared and in its place: the wooden backing of a looking glass. "A whore for the SS—that's how our dear Rachela survived the Holocaust. And how are we to survive?"

He married Rachela later, but she died from tuberculosis, already too far gone with the disease when they carried her ashore and smuggled her into the house. Bonny used to say, "When I married your father in 1935 he didn't know Yom Kippur from Pancake Day. The war . . . the war . . ."

Wili was saying, "I knew you would understand." She blinked away tears, and he reached out to grasp her hand.

Then he straightened up, cleared his throat, said, "Well, well . . ." and, in the tone of a man who has put the past behind him, told the waiter to bring more wine.

They were seated on the mezzanine floor of the restaurant alongside one other group, a party of Americans in high spirits. They pointed out to each other the "ethnic" gravy stains on the tablecloths and laughed loudly at a wall papered floor to ceiling to resemble a Swiss Alp. Downstairs there was a concrete floor and a glass counter displaying cooked dishes. There the tables were occupied by silent men playing a game that looked like backgammon. From time to time they darted angry glances at the noise upstairs.

From the Americans' conversation it was impossible to tell if they were nominal Christians or nominal Jews: they shouted *"l'chayim"* as they clinked glasses and said *"be'te'avon"* as they fell to their food, but they could have learned these expressions from a guidebook. A young man began telling his experiences as a volunteer kibbutz worker:

"I'll never look at a sheep again. For those animals I slaved like a black."

Wili turned his head away from them and muttered the best-known curse in Arabic.

"And they were exported to Saudi Arabia!" said the kibbutz volunteer.

The conversation moved on to the exigencies of economics. A woman said, "Keep your voice down, George." Someone else said, "They can't understand English." George swung his head defiantly and said, "So Israel's major export is weaponry. I'll tell you something, Bob. The survival of this country depends, ultimately, upon the Bomb."

There were cries of protest from the women; the men munched gloomily. George said, "Israel's survival is a microcosm of the problems of world survival in the face of the nuclear terror. What saves this country from being overrun is they know in Damascus that Israel has nuclear weapons."

The waiter said, "Kebabs."

"And *will use them* if necessary."

The waiter said, "Parsley salad."

The kibbutz volunteer roared, "But when the Syrians get their own bomb they can wipe out most of the population with one strike on Tel Aviv." He added in triumphant gloom, "And Israel can never have a second-strike capacity."

The waiter said, "Fools."

Heads turned, as a shoal, in his direction. He was referring to an extra plate of beans.

When he had gone George hissed, "Morty, technological progress will . . ." but Danielle and Wili could not hear what it would do.

Wili pinched the bridge of his nose, and frowned. "Business, Princess," he said. "Of course I'll do the location shots for you. I'll be very honest: Wili needs the money, these days. But tell me—this film." He was still holding his nose on. "Is it, like their nonsense about having nuclear weapons, going to be another Jewish propaganda exercise?"

She thought of replying, "Your political views bore me. And so does this cacophony of moral claims and counterclaims." Instead she said, "That's a snide question."

"Oh. I didn't realize you were so sensitive."

She glared at him, willing him to drop his gaze, but his eyes held steady and after a few seconds it was she who looked at her wristwatch.

Wili polished his traveling cutlery with his table napkin and put it back in his pocket. Downstairs at the door he announced, "I've got to piss." His mood had changed abruptly and he was debonair again.

"Try going through that door with a top hat over it," Danielle said.

He tutted. "Never in public lavatories."

Off Nablus Road he found a convenient laneway from which he returned smiling. Danielle asked how, if never in public lavatories, he managed on airplanes.

"I order a tall glass of water. I take it into the lavatory, throw out the water, and pee in the glass."

"Oh, terrific."

"Just a matter of personal hygiene." He sounded flattered.

She walked back to the hotel thinking, I have made a terrible mistake; his obsession with cleanliness is a projection of some filthiness in himself.

In her room she felt so jittery she telephoned Australia, first Katherine, then Mrs. Wellsmore. For no good reason she burst into tears after speaking to Emma, who whined quizzically, then barked into the telephone. Mrs. Wellsmore said Emma had been naughty: she had killed a possum two nights ago and the neighbors had threatened to report her to the department.

"What department?"

"How should I know, dear? I never owned a dog. Never could afford one."

Danielle told her it was snowing: Mrs. Wellsmore hated cold weather.

"Snowing? I've never had the opportunity to see snow myself, dear. Never had your sort of money." She ended by promising she would ring Danielle's Sydney lawyer if anything should come of the neighbors' threat.

Ahmed brought a pot of cocoa. Outside her room the indoor garden area behind him was brightly lit, yellow light bouncing off its big brass table and white walls, and Ahmed, framed against it, had an aura of gold. He lowered his eyes when he saw her smudged mascara and poured the cocoa with his head bent so far his chin hit his chest.

"What is it?"

"Very problems. Very tense, Jerusalem."

The gingerly way he opened and closed the double doors, wringing silence from the ancient fittings, the way he turned his dirty black shoes into the pads of a cat—these things told her that he had something he wanted to say. She scribbled herself a note: Ask Ahmed.

At some stage that night she had a nightmare: a brown monochrome painting she had seen, a Daumier of Don Quixote on his horse, came to life. In the painting the mad knight was trotting along a leafy country lane but in dream he was moving through the covered souks of Jerusalem. Now and then he flicked his visor open and each time he did he revealed a different person: a man she had seen in the souk; Wili; someone who might have been her father; a man who resembled Bennie Kidron but was maybe an actor. The rider carried a crusader's shield. Suddenly he was no longer in the Old City but galloping along the Gaza Road. His horse went so fast its caparison streamed and changed to the red-and-white sides of an Egged bus. Then the horse itself changed into a bus, hurtling like a firebird. The crusader was running beside it. He threw his shield on the ground and it exploded in a ball of fire. Bodies flew in the air. A voice shouted, *"Allahu Akbar!"* and she woke.

Ahmed also woke for the prayer, which he made in his room. During contemplation his mind wandered, however, and he remembered the man who had come into the hotel that evening and asked questions about the lady in room one. "I talked to her today in the Old City," he said, "and I am conquered." He gave Ahmed ten dollars and asked him to give to the lady his card. Ahmed had been busy with the pilgrims from Tennessee and now he could not remember where he'd put the card.

A recorded male voice speaking Hebrew answered Professor Garin's telephone. There was a beep. Danielle left her name and number and asked for her call to be returned. Her heart had been flying ever since her alarm clock had rung. She lay back in bed, trying to be calm, but her mind seemed to bump against the walls of her skull like a trapped insect. After a while she got up and distracted herself with bathing and dressing. One of her heels seemed worse this morning: a blush of inflammation had crept around her ankle.

She left the door to the bathroom open, ready to leap out, but by seven-thirty there had been no ring.

She rushed downstairs, in case he should call at that moment, running to the reception desk to tell the staff that she would take any calls that came through. The desk was surrounded by English pilgrims, older women in sensible shoes and a few surviving husbands, who stood together being jovial about the girls' plans for today. Danielle heard one say, "If Gwen insists we visit the Holy Sepulcher again . . ." Their pastor wore a turtleneck sweater and a Harris tweed jacket. He was saying, "Ladies,

ladies, if I may suggest," but their attention was on the desk manager. His brown eyes drowned in sweet, patient melancholy, his hotelier's unintrusive gaze seeing all, forgiving all. At last Danielle got through to him. One of the women said, "*Everyone* pushes in this country. Manners are something which don't exist." Danielle tried to apologize to her but she was not to be mollified. "It's no good doing it, then being sorry afterward," the woman replied.

Danielle snapped, "Vot do you expect? I'm a Chew."

Oh! She was so sorry. She hadn't meant . . .

Meant *what?* Danielle thought. I'm sorry I was rude, but you're an anti-Semite, and I hate you.

There was no message for her during breakfast; the corpulent headwaiter, whose mustache was like a whale's tail, watched over her regretfully, tutting about her poor appetite. His impassive, professional manner was disturbed this morning because in his pocket was the card of the man who had pestered Ahmed the night before. A disagreeable type. His companion had hung around outside the gate. The headwaiter had no intention of upsetting the Australian lady by telling her she had been followed from the Old City but he wanted to warn her to stay away from the souk.

Danielle listened to his rigmarole about a nephew who would take her shopping there, only to the honest merchants, and would bargain for her. "Better you wait for my nephew," he said. "Today comes Shabbat. Better you not shopping. People going to Temple Mount. Sometimes . . . not nice." What was not nice? Trouble. But what was the trouble?

He wagged his head from side to side. "Temple Mount trouble. Sometimes other people wanting to pray there also."

She realized he was, with that Oriental delicacy of reference that is at once enchanting and maddening, referring to Jewish extremists wishing to pray on the Islamic enclave of the Mount. Since somewhere beneath its contemporary buildings was the site of the Holy of Holies no pious Jew would go up there in case he sullied sacred ground; those who did, if not merely sightseers, had political motives.

"It will be there next week, like this week, like last four thousand years," the headwaiter said. "You see Abraham, Isaac, the Prophet Jesus, the Prophet Mohammed next week, just the same."

After breakfast she went quickly back to her room. She could hear the telephone ringing as she wrestled with the antique brass lock; the line went dead just as she lifted the receiver. There was no message at the desk for her but, yes, the clerk remembered that someone had called. A lady. Old? No, he thought—young, like her. Danielle calculated: he will spend the morning writing, then have lunch and a nap. If I've not had a call by two o'clock, I'll go there uninvited.

It was snowing, blowing, raining, and sleeting by turns. There had been a flood in a low-lying area of East Jerusalem during the night and an old Turkish drain had collapsed, leaving a crater in the street. Telephones had been affected; an exchange was partly under water and it was estimated that thirty thousand lines were out of order. When Wili woke that morning he looked at the slate sky and decided to spend the morning working indoors. He took a taxi to the Damascus Gate, then struggled against the wind, holding close to the wall until he reached the Jaffa Gate where he took another taxi to the Hilton and began photographing. A few people stared at him and looked around to see who his subject was. By midday he had a pictorial record of the public areas of the hotel, and nobody had challenged him. The weather had improved a little and he was able to walk from the Hilton to the bus station. By that evening he was again in Gaza—Egypt, as he called it. His darkroom was ready. One of the boys asked if he could be a witness. In the black-red glowing room with its sharp smell of nitrates he shivered with voluptuous excitement watching Wili tip the trays of liquid. Images swam onto the pieces of paper like ghosts taking on flesh as Wili talked to them—"Come on, that's it. Yes. Yes!" They started to laugh. "Adios, Hilton. Adios."

Wili worked all night, printing and collating. This was the work he had come to Israel to do: make detailed maps of the public areas of West Jerusalem's international hotels—because what his friends wanted to do, if an opportunity arose to help them, was to stuff a room with plastic explosives. The tactics were the same as for burglary: they needed familiarity with the hotels in advance but dared not snoop around themselves. "We'll make history," Jazzy said. "*Any* big tourist hotel . . . We will be known as the Sons of Saladin!"

In case the Australian woman moved from the American Colony to a West Jerusalem hotel, where her old friend, Wili, might get access to her room, Jazzy had told him to photograph her also, so that all the boys would be able to recognize her. Jazzy had seen her for himself that morning in the Old City and had engaged her in conversation for a few moments: pleasantries, a word of welcome.

He passed around the prints of Danielle: full-face, profile left; profile right; back-of-head; smiling to herself. "Make another set and give them to her. She'll be impressed." He himself was impressed with the progress Wili had made during his dinner with the woman, that he had managed to get a job as her site photographer. It meant that when the producer arrived Wili could go into his hotel room also. And where Wili could enter, Jazzy and Saeed could enter, too. Perhaps he had underestimated Wili's ability to get on with women; or perhaps it was that losers attracted each other. "Doesn't she look vulnerable?" he added, and as he tossed his hair off his forehead he caught Saeed's eye.

Danielle wondered as she dragged on the Rodeo Drive boots and felt them scald her heels why she believed, to her core, that she could not meet her father in comfortable clothes. "I'm dressing up as a mark of respect," she answered herself, in too much of a hurry to think what *that* might mean. She had already arranged to have her hair done. It had taken eight telephone calls to find a salon with an opening since this was Friday and every woman in the city, it seemed, was titivating for the Sabbath.

The man who shampooed her was a creamy-skinned black. From Iran, he said. He had recently come back from Lebanon and thanked God he was only on reserve duty these days. "When I made my first parachute jump I was nineteen. I tell you, I was so excited. But now . . ." and he reached for the cigarette left burning on the edge of the basin. Israel chain-smoked, she'd noticed: bank tellers took a drag in between thumbing out notes, post office clerks lit up while selling public telephone tokens or sheets of the small, dun-colored postage stamps printed without a cover price because of inflation. She wondered if she could ask him to move the cigarette; the smoke was stinging her eyes.

He was saying he enjoyed hairdressing better than soldiering, but he didn't like hairdressing—"It's a job." Then he led her to the dressing table where he first checked in the glass the symmetry of his short black beard; she watched him snip off a tiny bunch of unruly hairs. The service was certainly different from that at Avalon, where the customers' hair was done before the staff's. But one has to bear in mind, Danielle told herself, that Charles of Coiffeur Charles—strawberry blond one week and lilac the next—will never jump out of anything higher than a double bed. She was in a forgiving mood. The Iranian was saying he couldn't see his girlfriend as often as he would like because she was still in the army full time.

"It makes her nervous."

Nervous?

Again, that look of helplessness, the unvoiced question: What can I do?

"She doesn't like some of her duties. She gets upset . . ."

So, what did he think of the war? He didn't know.

"But I hate the Peacenowniks. We have to fight. Otherwise . . . Listen, my family was in business in Tehran. We'd been there for centuries. Now the Khomeinis call Jews 'spiders.' They want to take over everything, the whole Middle East. You can see them walking around in East Jerusalem already—women with white veils over their heads and long coats. *Khomeinis.* Already in our capital. My elder brother was going to study to be a doctor. What job does he have? He's a chauffeur." Immigrants usually romanticize the riches they have left behind, she thought, but this boy is telling the truth—the fluency of his English, the elegance of his bearing, his whole demeanor marks him as upper middle class. He inhaled smoke, his free hand still massaging her scalp—as if, she thought, the right and left are disconnected, with an abyss between.

Seated in front of other mirrors there were women in states of dampness, semiattentive to the work of the hairdressers, some having their fingernails painted by pretty, hard-looking girls who argued with them about which colors to apply, as the hairdressers were arguing with their clients about styles, their voices gritty with assertiveness. There seemed to be no calm place, no space, no time to halt the struggle.

A terrific *bang!* shook the front window. A manicurist jumped, upsetting a bottle of polish. Some of the hairdressers switched off their blowers; someone hurried to the door to look out and returned shrugging. Someone else turned on the radio. Danielle's attendant took no notice except to concentrate more determinedly on the curling tongs. After a while he said, "Maybe the Messiah just came," and he grinned, astonished at his own wit.

Most offices closed at midday and by half past one the streets were emptying. Grilles were pulled down on shopfronts and cafes; Danielle had not had time for lunch. In Zion Square a hawker was selling off cheap daffodils and irises; late shoppers were hurrying home with the last plaited loaves of *challa* from bakeries. The sky was cold iron, but at least it had stopped sleeting and the wind had abated to gusts. She had to juggle with all her paraphernalia: the shoulder bag, umbrella, book wrapped in red cellophane, album of photographs, bunch of white roses. She laid them out on the backseat of the Mercedes taxi, anxious that nothing should be crushed.

The ride was too short. Then the steps to the apartment building, just another stone-faced block, the same four stories, the same shape as its neighbors in Jabotinsky Street, with the same few steps to climb to the tiny front garden.

His apartment was on the second floor, one of two on the landing, its varnished front door identical to the one opposite, with a peephole and a ceramic name-tile giving the name in Hebrew and Roman script. She pressed the buzzer and as she waited heard a telephone inside begin to ring, then stop. No one came to the door. Danielle buzzed again. A flicker made her aware that she was being examined through the peephole. Well, take a look, she thought. Stepping close to the door she saw, miles away, Marilyn's distrustful dark eye.

"I tried to ring you at the hotel," Marilyn said. Her face was pale and she seemed angry, or frightened, or both. "Professor Garin had a mild heart attack at seven o'clock this morning, while he was in the bathroom."

Danielle had a queer sense of holding an intelligent conversation in her sleep. Marilyn made no gesture to invite her inside, rather she seemed to be blocking the doorway. When the telephone began ringing again, she said, "Excuse me" and Danielle stepped into the hall, narrow and ill lit, with overcoats hanging from pegs. There was an old-widower atmosphere: she saw spindly wooden furniture in the room ahead, laden bookshelves, knickknacks on small tables, but everything was lifeless and the colors were unpleasant—burnt-orange cushions and dark red chairs—and carelessly chosen. An open newspaper sprawled on a settee; a philodendron in an earthenware pot was turning yellow and dropping its leaves. There were some frightful oil paintings—a dancing Hasid; someone's attempt to copy van Gogh's sunflowers; a Galilee scene.

"Oh, Daddy," she sighed. Where were the Oriental rugs, and the carved chairs from Damascus? Surely Arab *furniture* was not forbidden, too?

Marilyn was speaking in English to the caller. Danielle heard, "Yeah. He's asleep now and his condition is stable. Praise the Lord."

Leather-bound volumes of the Talmud stood to attention in tall black ranks on the shelves of his study, which was otherwise as spartan and insensitive as the rest of the apartment. The only thing worth a second glance was a large painting that was not exactly good but had something to it, something that twanged at the mind and set it vibrating. It showed the Temple Mount, viewed from the west. In the lower foreground dark figures as small as ants prayed at the Wall; above the Wall were the Mount itself, the el-Aqsa Mosque, and the Dome of the Rock shrine, its cupola shining dully. But the lion! Lying on the mount, with tail twitched around the el-Aqsa, paw resting on the Dome, was a huge lion. The top-heavy head had turned to stare out of the painting, past your shoulder, back into history. The lion was resting, but its eyes remembered that it was a king and at any moment it would splatter the cupola like egg yolk. Its tail could flick the el-Aqsa to rubble. Behind the lion the sky was twilit— which had a different meaning here: not the end, but the approach of a new day.

Marilyn said, "Professor Garin says that in other countries people study the past to understand the past. In Israel, we study the past to build the future. Isn't it an inspiring picture?"

Danielle said, "Hmm," but Marilyn required only slight encouragement: would Danielle like coffee and cookies? or lunch?— it was dairy, she always made dairy for Professor Garin's lunch, but he wouldn't be eating it today, so they could share it. She spoke in short bursts, leading the way out of the study, swinging her thin arms—"Why don't you sit there?"—as if she owned the place. The man she had been speaking to on the telephone, Matti, was so interesting—he lived near Hebron.

"On the West Bank?"

"In Judea. Some people are narrow-minded about the Christian contribution to Zion, but Matti grew up in Nebraska and understands the Christian mission in the Holy Land. He has supported our oil well from the beginning." . . . Danielle had heard about the oil well, hadn't she? Gracious!

There was a history of miraculous events, leading to an ex-

ploration for oil in Israel on the coast north of Netanya. Already
five million dollars had been spent; drilling was down to eighteen
thousand feet. "You know what it says in Deuteronomy 33?"

"Not offhand."

Marilyn was tolerant. "Well, the Lord was speaking about
Asher, whose tribe was allotted the land where we are drilling.
And the Lord said, Let him dip his foot in oil. Danielle, when
we find it, the shekel will be worth *gold.*"

But what if the Lord meant olive oil? Danielle wondered.
"Amazing," she murmured.

Marilyn pumped her head, with a strange, inwardly-fixed expression. Danielle had seen that look often in the past few days—
the Hasidim had it, their eyes did not rest upon the outer world
either.

"Marilyn . . . my father?"

She surfaced. "Do you want to leave a message for Professor
Garin?"

"No. I want to see him."

There was a spark of amusement, quickly smothered.

"Professor Garin's only child, a boy, was killed during the War
of Independence." Marilyn's tone was sugary but crisp, as if
she'd almost exhausted her capacity to indulge her visitor.

Never argue with the servants, Danielle thought.

"Well, all the same, I have brought him some presents from
relations in Australia. And I must deliver them in person. Which
hospital is he in?"

She could feel Marilyn's eye watching through the peephole
after the front door was closed.

Danielle finally found a taxi on the Gaza Road, having walked
blindly in that direction, stamping up the hill of Jabotinsky
Street, across Albert Einstein Square, down the slope of Molcho,
then along Radak Street, with its pretty Turkish villas, one of
which had a brass sign announcing in English that the occupant
specialized in "Women's Diseases." People were waiting in a
bus shelter, cringing back from the rain, looking at their watches,
then up the road. A man dashed out and managed to nab the
taxi she thought was stopping for her. When a second one came
by five minutes later she ran onto the roadway in front of it,
waving her umbrella. The red cellophane around the book she
had brought for him had a thin coat of mud on it when she
picked it up from where it had fallen.

"No. It's too far. I have to be at the depot in half an hour."
He wanted to shut the door again.

"Please. My father has had a heart attack."

He drove at high speed. "You make me illegal. I lose my
license if I'm on the road after Shabbat."

"But for taking someone to hospital?"

He made a disgusted noise in his throat. "How do I know
what you want in the hospital? Maybe you're a nurse going late
to work." They skidded at the lights. "You make me lose my
license." He said, "Shabbat Shalom" and was gone, without looking at his tip.

The ground floor of the hospital was deserted except for a
couple of people who shook their heads when she spoke to them
in English. It was a tall, modern building with glass partitions
and corridors leading off in all directions; the signs were in
Hebrew and English but they pointed to destinations she did
not want: x-rays, pathology, eye clinic. There was nobody at the
information desk and its typewriters had covers on them as if
they were caged birds put to sleep for the night. After wandering about she came across a European-looking man standing in
front of a bank of elevators. He spoke English. "Try the seventh
floor," he said. They waited together. "It doesn't want to come,"
he said. "What time is it?"

He thought that maybe the hospital had already switched over
to the automatic Sabbath elevators, although it seemed too early.
Then a lift opened for them, but although he pressed Up it went
down. "It doesn't like me," he said and got out in the basement.
Danielle stayed in the carriage, which rocked gently and bumped
its door open and shut when she pressed its buttons. It was sighing but stubborn. Without warning it decided to ascend. She
was back on the ground floor. A woman in a white uniform
called, "Use the Sabbath elevator" and pointed off to the left.
A long walk later she found herself at the end of a narrow corridor in front of a door which, when she opened it, revealed fire-
fighting equipment. She passed more people on the way back,
but they did not speak English. Then she saw a steel door, and,
opening that, found a stairway.

The rose petals flopped on the open blooms and buds lurched
like ashamed white faces; the red cellophane was torn. But she
had, at last, found his ward and someone willing to spend a few
seconds speaking to her, a woman from Sydney, oddly enough.

"The form says clearly, look here—oh, you can't read it, give it back to me—here, 'No children.' He has no relations. It says here. Mrs. Green, I trained at Royal North Shore, and if we had people barging in to see patients, we told them to go and they went. Now—look at that Mrs. Rubenstein, she's still crying over there. I had to get a male nurse to *drag* her out this morning. Her husband is very ill, but he's not going to die . . . *Gveret Rubenstein!* Oh, if she doesn't shut up in a minute . . . Look at that! It's temper. She's not hysterical. *Gveret Rubenstein!* She'll break that chair. No. I'm sorry. You can't see Professor Garin."

"When is his doctor doing the ward rounds?"

She didn't know; they don't tell the nurses. That was the son-in-law! My God, she was going to call a male nurse.

The son-in-law was tall, slim, elegant, and wearing a gray homburg. "Come, Mother," he said in English and taking Mrs. Rubenstein by the elbow he escorted her through the double doors. Danielle hesitated, then followed in his regal wake.

On the other side there was a wide corridor, full of people—nurses, physicians in green cotton jackets, visitors in civilian, religious, and battle dress. There was a quiet but cheerful atmosphere. The wards opened on either side of the passage; whole families were gathered around beds in some; a man wearing a white satin skullcap stood reading from a prayer book. He reached over the plastic swing table suspended above the foot of one bed and broke the *challa*, then poured wine into a liqueur-sized glass of lapis lazuli blue. Danielle tiptoed along, looking in doorways. A physician stood back for her to pass.

"Professor Garin?"

He pointed down the corridor. Other families were softly chanting prayers.

"Excuse me." The doctor had followed her. "Are you a relation of Professor Garin?"

"Yes."

"He doesn't want visits from his relations."

The physician, a round little man, perhaps a Russian, looked down at the cream linoleum and chuckled. "*Nu*—he hasn't got any. Especially he has not got a daughter from Australia."

She gave a huge sigh, so tired now she felt no fight left in her. "What's *wrong* with him?"

"He has angina. He overexcites himself. He can go home on Sunday."

"*Why* won't he see me?"

He had small, perfect hands so pink and clean they looked brand-new. There it was—the gesture of open palms. "I'm a heart specialist. Not a psychiatrist." He seemed worn-out, as if he had been on his feet all day in an operating theater. "Maybe I'm in the wrong job. In my next life . . ." His eyes twinkled and persuaded her with professional charm. He had taken her arm and was gently shepherding her back toward the double doors.

"I've come all this way . . ." She could hear herself whining.

They had reached the doors. "You travel but you don't necessarily arrive," he said. He took the dead flowers and the album and the book in its torn wrapping. On the other side again, her eye pressed against the door's black rubber baffle, she could see his stocky torso returning down the corridor.

The Royal North Shore nurse said, "You're a nice one, sneaking in like that," but she gave Danielle a cup of tea and a biscuit all the same.

Downstairs, outside, she felt as if she had plunged her head into an icebucket. It was spitting with snow and thrillingly cold. Perhaps, she thought, a taxi will go past—one headed for East Jerusalem or Bethlehem. She started to walk, juggling the umbrella. The snow was playful, dancing in circles with the wind; when the umbrella jerked back as her foot slipped in a pothole an eddy of it swirled against the side of her face in a swarm of stinging needles. My body must still be warm, she thought, from the tea. It's twelve hours since I've eaten.

This was not a built-up area and the streetlights were separated by great stretches of blackness. At her shoulder, behind her back, some sort of open space—maybe a field or wasteland—gaped like a cold, open oven. She came to another light and in its chemical orange glare saw for a moment that the old fox fur on her jacket had turned golden. But her hands—

—Where are my gloves?

She could not remember putting them down. Her hands were a jaundiced color under the light. They had stopped burning and throbbing; now they only ached with cold. Her watch said 8:05; she had been walking for twenty-five minutes. It seemed longer. "You wretched things," she said aloud to her boots. No car went past. The next streetlight appeared to be hundreds of yards away, and was set high. She began to climb the hill. Hands, face, and feet were aching now and somewhere in the jacket there was a split between two pelts, because a shaft of ice had entered and was slicing at her ribs. A taxi flew by, then a couple of cars full of people. She thought of trying to hitch. Just to Alice's place. It could only be a mile or so. But this hill. And in these boots: four-inch heels.

When she reached the next streetlight, she stopped to check her road map; halted, the rhythmn of movement turned off, she became aware of another horrifying sort of music: every fiber in her legs was jumping and fluttering as if an orchestra were playing soundlessly inside limbs with a life of their own, beyond her will. She could feel her armpits streaming and knew it was fright as much as effort.

The map was incomprehensible: she was sure she had passed that park, or field, or whatever it was, but the darkness was still there at her left shoulder, and across the road there was a void. Her legs said, Keep walking! and her mind answered, But we're lost. The snow had turned back into sleet. A truck went past, and another car. She could not do it. It looked so simple when you saw other people do it, jerk a thumb—but a voice was saying, Only an Arab will stop. Even here, in West Jerusalem, it will be an Arab. There will be two or three of them in the car and you won't have a chance. You'll be found over in the field, or maybe they'll go to the trouble of burying you and you won't be found at all.

Another car went past. The voice said, See the color of the license plates? They're from the West Bank. I warned you.

Her nose was running and swollen water stood at the lower rims of her eyes; vision became a dark blur. Then utter stillness. Something—a man—had moved out of the night at her back. She could not see his face nor make out anything of this form, but she knew he was large, the color of coffee, and angry with her: enraged. He had some weapon in his hand, a cosh. She stood still for him to hit her, which he did—half a dozen stunning blows on the head. He talked quietly as his arm flailed: I am here every minute, he said. If you don't accept me, you will die forever, like an acorn thrown to the pigs. The final blow shuddering on her skull satisfied him.

He was gone, returned to the dark.

The car, a mustard-colored Alfa Sud, began slowing fifty yards before it pulled up level with her on the opposite side of the road. The woman tried Hebrew, then switched to English. "Are

you crazy? Shabbat Shalom. You're crazy to be hitchhiking."
She gave Danielle a good looking-over, with the interior light
switched on, shaking her head, allowing her hands to fly from
the steering wheel to emphasize the admonishment. All right,
she was a tourist, but didn't she read the newspapers? A Danish
girl had been murdered, hitchhiking down in the Negev. And
her own niece, still in the army, just a few weeks ago was threatened by a man who gave her a lift—he had his Uzi on the backseat. A few years ago girls could hitchhike, but now . . . This
was the Middle East.

They looked at each other's hair, that special index among
women that measures age, social status, indicates—even in its
deceitfulness—happiness and discontent. The woman's was sil-
very-brown; her French roll was loosening. No paint on her
fingernails, none on her face. A lawyer's briefcase and a scuffed
lizard handbag tossed to the backseat to make room for her passenger. Dutch, she said; been living in Jerusalem since just after
the war. Things had changed: Begin, King of Israel! Who could
have believe it? A rabble taking over. This had been *the most*
democratic state in the world—and it still was in a lot of ways,
anybody could say anything—but *Elohim!* a king! They could
be back in the days of the Judges, petitioning God for a king so
they could be like all the other nations—whom, incidentally, they
had wanted to be different from—and then anointing Saul. Who,
by the way, was crazy. Begin was also crazy—you've heard his
motto? We Fight, Therefore We Are. The Sephardim kiss his photograph. And as for Peres: who'd vote for a man who lost his
nerve when he was heckled, and screamed at the crowd? Begin
might be crazy, but he has dignity. As for that Sharon—Arik the
Unstoppable . . . Her sister was leaving the country, going back
to Amsterdam. Already her son had a plastic left hand—twenty-
three years old and a plastic hand. Who'd have children? Why
have children if you have to feed them to a war machine? You
know who persecutes Israel now? Israelis! Why live here if you
get called an Ashken-Nazi? My neighbor—she runs a small pub-
lishing company—had a swastika painted on her car. She lived
through the war. The blacks should have been in Europe in 1942.
Do you know Amsterdam?

Her shrug at Danielle's "no" was a resignation from further
interest in her. Her frankness tipped upside down and became
the opposite: inward brooding, resentment.

They had reached Rahavia, and Alice's street.

"Yes, yes. Shabbat Shalom." Impatient to be gone, a woman living in a gale, eyes red with grit.

The note still thumbtacked to Alice's front door said "Please ring LOUDLY." Danielle rang a second time, then began knocking. Nothing happened. She sat on the steps to rest for a few seconds.

When she opened her eyes again it was totally dark—the stairwell light had a timer that kept it on for only a couple of minutes—and she experienced pain that was almost audible, as if her body had become a sheet of freezing tin that shuddered and clanged as fists beat on it.

She could not stand up, at first. Then, very slowly, antennae crept out; a foot slid into the dark, trembling to sense a step; a hand found a patch of wall that burnt it with cold. An inch at a time she moved herself toward the glowing circle on the wall of the stairwell that could save her from pitching down, neck broken, nose and teeth smashed. Suddenly she had it. Pushed. The lights turned on.

An exquisite whiff of food seeped out from a doorway lower down.

Its glass eye observed her for a long time, then there was the sound of bolts being drawn. A mouth breathing wine fumes spoke to her through a narrow shaft. I'm going to keel over, Danielle thought.

"Please. Please," she said.

There was the sound of a door chain being unhitched. Three of them looked at her: a chubby nondescript young man in a crocheted skullcap, a wan young woman about seven months pregnant, and a harridan with a brass perm who had drunk too much Sabbath wine. She wore one high-heeled shoe and held the other in her hand.

"Alice has gone away." She made a movement as if to close the door. The gesture came of itself, shockingly naked. Danielle did what Patrick had done when he was a police roundsman: she put her foot in the door.

"Give me something to eat."

Who had spoken? Who stared at their startled faces with eyes as blank and indifferent to their lives as a demiurge? It said, Assuage my hunger or I shall eat *you*. Who was it?

—I. Barbarous with the fear of disintegrating.

Her face twitched into apology, a smile.

There were candles on the Sabbath table, flakes of crust from the broken bread, an asterisk where wine had spilt. They fed her, the offerings coming in wrong order—first the pudding, then slices of roasted meat, some bread. She didn't try to talk. They whispered among themselves in Hebrew, then grew braver and discussed her aloud. When she looked up at them, their glances flinched away and they began whispering again, darting smiles at her. The harridan, both feet crushing down on high heels now, said in English, "You were hungry." Her angry, cruel eyes, a layer of iridescent blue shadow painted on the wrinkles of the lids, blinked rapidly. "I know what it is to be hungry."

The woman—"I'm Ruth"—offered to drive Danielle home, causing her son-in-law to look away, abstract himself, as men do when confronted by the intimacies that only females should deal with—birth, menstruation, diapers. He stared at the curtains, a male knowing how to remain master of life by distancing himself from its mess, which at this moment was the emotional and religious mess these women were creating with their talk of driving on Shabbat. But maybe it would save a life! How could a woman walk through East Jerusalem at midnight? It was madness! Rahavia, West Jerusalem—you could walk there at three in the morning. But the Nablus Road? Those alleyways? The mother-in-law appealed to him; he studied the curtains.

"No. I really don't want you to," Danielle repeated but her wishes were irrevelant to this struggle between them that was as old as the laws of Judaism, as ancient as the yearnings of women to be beloved in the eyes of God. She watched Ruth thrashing in a net and thought, Men gave us God as they give us babies; our hearts open with love, our breasts with milk—but as we gaze down we meet eyes narrowed and lips mouthing, "temptress, slut, whore"—yet the milk still flows.

"The Law is the Law," he said. The wife's attention slipped from mother to husband, her palms resting on the barrel beneath the folds of her dress. "Sit down," he ordered her. She appeared grateful as she sank behind the weight of her majestic belly.

Danielle thought suddenly, I can't bear this.

"Thank-you-all-very-much. I'm going now," she said, and left.

FIFTEEN

Tikva and Gideon had leave that weekend. Tikva was driven down from Sidon in an armored vehicle, leaving before dawn on Friday morning; a few hours later Gideon hitched with an American couple, the man a diplomat, who drove him all the way from Be'er Sheva to Jerusalem in their Mercedes with a stereophonic sound system. Diplomatic staff were forbidden to offer soldiers lifts and soldiers were forbidden to accept, for security reasons. Gideon pretended he could not speak English—understood just a bit—so there was no harm done; they didn't ask him questions. It was to guard against loose talk to well-informed and curious foreigners that the law against diplomatic rides was made. They gave him the backseat; the wife asked her husband to turn down the Beethoven, but he knew what was what.

"It's not necessary, dear. These kids can sleep on their feet. It's the first thing the army teaches them—learn to sleep any time you get the chance. And the second thing . . ." he took a quick look over his shoulder.

"Yes?" She was young, maybe his second wife, attending to what he said with an expression of reverence in her round, translucent blue eyes. Gideon's were closed.

"The second is: how to finagle the system. To survive Israeli Army training! . . ." He laughed to himself. Gideon decided he liked the American, whose accent was similar to his father's. He listened for a while longer, then indeed went to sleep. He dreamed of Tikva. She kept changing, appearing one moment in azure robes, then in white; then wearing something he could not make out because they were in darkness and she had taken his hand to lead him through a subterranean corridor, some sort of labyrinth, over an underground river. There was a fire in the distance. "Look—our children," she said, and children came running toward them with outstretched arms, wanting Gideon to pick them up, but they were out of reach.

When he awoke, the music had stopped, the man and woman were silent; they had passed Sodom and were on the flat road beside the Salt Sea, that area of utter stillness. The car purred and they three breathed. Nothing else lived, not a tree, not a blade of grass; it was nonbeing in an exquisite, sculptured landscape. Dun-colored towers rose beside a stretch of turquoise water, hardly water at all, more like a beautifully-colored embalming fluid. The English name for it was better: Dead Sea.

"You've had a good sleep," the woman said.

"I dreamed."

"Oh, really?" She turned around to stare at him, as if dreaming were a curiosity reserved to special people. "What about?"

"My soul." He remembered he barely spoke English. "I dreamed my soul."

She sighed. "Did you hear that, Stanley? This young man has been dreaming about his soul." Her glance rested on the Uzi lying beside Gideon; he had slept with his right hand resting over the trigger mechanism.

Stanley flicked a look in the rear-vision mirror, amused, quizzical. "That must have been an edifying experience." He said it fast, too fast for anyone who was not fluent. Gideon gave an idiot smile. Stanley tried again. "Been up in Lebanon, have you?" Same smile, same uncomprehending shake of the head. "*Habla inglés,*" Stanley said to his wife. She clattered the cassette boxes, chose a Vivaldi; Stanley patted her knee. "Good. Something lively."

The great Masada mountain loomed at their left shoulder as the car was pursued by its shadow through this valley where nothing lived.

Gideon was looking forward to meeting Alice's friend, the woman who would write a movie about Masada. He would try to tell her what he had experienced, wearing his new fatigues, that first time he had climbed the Serpent Path up to its summit, how his heart felt the size of a cabbage, bursting—my ancestors! A race of giants!—with pride, incredulity, awe. Maybe what one of the Americans in his unit said was true: that memory is not something stored inside people's brains but is, rather, a field outside the dimension of time—and the brain is just like a television set that can be tuned to receive it. The American said scientists were now working to prove this, and that he was, too—he had returned to Israel "to tune myself to our past." They had all experienced shivers of it, on Masada.

Their sergeant had undone his pants and sent a thread unraveling hundreds of meters down to the skeleton of a Roman camp. "Look here, you young fuckers—this is what we're going to do to the Arabs." He'd ordered Gideon to drink water; next day he'd ordered him to climb ten times up and down the mountain beneath the Monastery of Temptation. "Next time I say piss, you'll piss," he'd said. Gideon was not going to tell the Australian that. He'd told Tikva.

The Australian woman did not turn up. They telephoned her hotel, but she had not returned all day and the message Alice had left in the morning, inviting Danielle to dine that night at Amos's apartment, was still pigeonholed beside her room key, the desk clerk said. Alice fretted: "I should have pinned a note on my front door for her," and "She probably doesn't know there's no transport on the Sabbath—she could be stuck *anywhere*." Amos was in a bad mood: he had cooked for six people—himself, Gideon, Tikva, Alice, Alice's friend, and Mira—and only four had turned up. At the last moment Mira had telephoned to say she had to visit her sister-in-law, but would try to come over for coffee. By nine-fifteen she had not arrived.

"You bloody women!" he said to Alice. Her faded hazel eyes through the lenses of her spectacles were supernaturally large; their very size gave the impression that they saw too much. Amos winced away from them and from her quiet remark, "You're tired, love," which said: Such ·disgust, Amos? Such disillusion with politics, such a feeling of impotence with the course of events that now you are cursing Mira, whom you were in love with a year ago? How long since you've made love with her?

He could tell her how long: Rosh Hashanah. Five months. He and Mira had gone to the protest demonstration outside Begin's house that Saturday morning when they had heard of the slaughter up at Sabra and Shatila; they'd both been tear-gassed.

But he'd got it full in the face, he was staggering, helpless; Mira had to lead him home. I was a blind man, he remembered, boiling water pouring from my eyes and nose and mouth. It wasn't the physical pain; it was the rage. Gas! On an Israeli crowd! What have we come to? I couldn't stop asking it.

Afterward, the window shutters closed against the pounding heat outside, he'd lain on his bed staring at the ceiling. "We're turning to savages," he'd said. "It's just tawdry." Mira wanted to comfort him, but something had gone wrong with her: she'd been infected, somehow, by the mood of the day, the heat, the screaming. "Let me encourage him," she'd said. Amos wondered, Why does she try to please me like this—and why do I have to pretend? It was so seedy, so textbook. But the warmth of her mouth was luxurious and he let her continue, alone.

He'd grinned at her when she looked up: the black stuff she'd put on her eyes again after they had showered off the poison had resmudged. "Go wash your face," he said. He still felt detached from her and was thinking about the temperature up there, outside Beirut. The bodies would be high by now, iridescent flies sizzling in their nostrils. Mira was sniveling in the bathroom; she came out and said, "You don't love me."

"I do. I do." He did. He took her to concerts; he fed her cat when she was away; he advised her on university politics, knowing the quicksands better than she.

When the door closed on her he was seized without warning by a fit of irritation. "Love me! You don't love me. You must love me," he moaned to himself, thinking Mira's thoughts. He felt trapped, violently frustrated, and began to grind his teeth. When the fit had passed he sat quietly, still naked, and drank vodka from the bottle.

That had happened five months ago. The Black New Year, as it was called. And seven months from now, when the year changed to 5744, the letters would spell TASHMAD. Destruction. Seven months until the beginning of the Year of Destruction. Already the religious were saying that 5744 should be changed to 5745 so that Israel could fiddle the arithmetic, skip the thirteenth floor as hoteliers do, installing elevators whose boards flash 1, 2, 3, up to 12, then 14.

Amos turned to Gideon. "Have you had any news?"

They had all been avoiding the subject, all been thinking of little else during the evening, held to silence by the strong pain that exists inside a family.

Gideon shook his head.

"What are the rumors?"

"We'll be going back up there next week."

"Have you thought over what I said?"

Gideon nodded; Amos lit another cigarette. "Can I have one?" Gideon asked.

His father said, "Oh, shit. You little shit. You're going to refuse duty." He turned to Alice. "No. Stay. You, too, Tikva. We're all going to hear what Giddy has to say."

Gideon had nothing to say: he was simply going to refuse duty in Lebanon. And be court-martialed. Two of his friends had made the same decision.

Amos held his head in one palm, blowing smoke at the tablecloth. After a while he said, "You want to know what a court-martial is like? You think it's a fancy show, some TV drama with you playing the hero? I'll tell you something: I court-martialed men during the October War—little bastards who dropped their weapons and ran away from the Syrians. And you know what? It takes three minutes. Giddy, you'll go into a room, the charge will be read, you'll plead guilty, and that's it. On the next convenient transport you'll be taken to the slammer—for twenty-eight or thirty-five days, depending upon the rank of the officer who sentences you. And in jail you'll be with a mob of hooligans—malingerers, insubordinate thugs, the alienated riff-raff of the settlement towns, kids who have no interest in politics or ethnics or any of the nice things you think about. In New York they'd be muggers; in Israel, because they go through the army, they're in jail. Listen, you're in a good unit, you've all looked after each other . . ."

"You bet," Gideon replied. "Every one of us can dismantle a bus by now. Do you know how much stuff we've smuggled? What you can fit inside the chassis of a bus when you remove the cladding . . . ? Dad: guys are getting ready to go into business with the things they bring back. One bus broke down and started giving out a wonderful smell; when the driver opened it up to look for what was wrong he found the whole thing full of bottles of French perfume . . ."

Amos whacked at the smoke. "That's irrelevant." But it's not, he thought; it's a symptom of the rot. He said, "Gideon, this government is scared. The army is scared."

He was thinking, Ever since the war of '73 rebuilding national morale in the army has been critical. We're on a seesaw—the mad confidence after '67 was shattered in '73, but you're too young to remember how terrifying it was during that October when we thought we'd lost the country, when we were going to be slaughtered to the last . . . child. So national confidence has been built up, built up—to the point where our idiot leaders have picked a fight we can't win. *We're* demoralized, the Arabs are equally demoralized. It's too absurd!"

He said, "The army is scared because refusal of duty is unknown in Israel. How many of you are there in Yesh Ge'vul? A couple of hundred? Unless there are thousands of you, unless there is a general mutiny against the war—you know what the reaction will be? Punish the ringleaders. Grind their faces. When you get out of jail you'll be ordered to Lebanon again. That is my fear. Oh, yes—you didn't think of that, did you? And what will you do? Serve another sentence? And another? This war is not going to end quickly. For the moment forget your ethics, forget politics and Begin and Shamir and Sharon; forget The Little Thing, then The Big Thing—oh, it's all right in front of Alice, she knows about those dreams, that Israel could reorganize Lebanon and then do the Big Thing in Syria and Jordan. We had an attack of imagination, we thought Israel was invincible, we'd recouped the dignity we lost in '73 and we could rule the Middle East. Forget all that and remember this: we survive on bluff. We *cannot* run away from Lebanon. We've got to see it through, whatever the cost, because once Israel starts running to sand . . . Do you know why you exist? Because your grandmother read *Mein Kampf* and believed every word of it was seriously meant, but she could not convince my father until September 1939. She was a realist. I'm a realist."

"It didn't save her," Gideon said.

—No, but it saved me and my sister and father. We made it to the Russian border. All our other relations stayed behind in Lodz, telling each other, This is just a war between the Germans and the Poles; when Germany has got the provinces it wants . . .

Amos waved away the gauze of smoke. "That was an accident." His mother had been shot for stealing food. The Ukrainian who did it had been almost apologetic, his square face smiling at them, asking them not to take it personally. He had a peasant's sense of hierarchy: first the mistress, then the maid—Christiana, our nanny who'd chosen to flee with us because she loved me and my sister. She and Mama had been stealing to keep us alive—me in particular, because I had a weak chest. My father said to me afterward, "Because of you I lost the light of my life."

That was the first injury a woman did me.

Gideon said, "But *you* demonstrated. Before I did. You said . . ."

"I said. I said . . ."

"And you still do. You go around saying, 'Our leaders are crazy.' But you want me to cooperate with them?"

"I don't want you to be thrown out of the army."

"Then you're a hypocrite."

Amos's lips buckled; the whoop of laughter escaped. "Giddy! What it is to be twenty years old!" His hand ruffling the hair of his son's big head was a little simian paw and in his eyes was the yearning that is sometimes in the faces of intelligent animals as they look at humans and try to communicate across the gulf of human reasoning. Gideon jerked his head away.

The doorbell rang. Five people surged in: two women with chocolate cakes, husbands, and a political scientist from UCLA on contract to the *Washington Post* to write a series of articles on the New Right in Israel. Alice knew them all except the American, Phil Abrahams, who bear-hugged Amos. "Phil's luggage is lost," they cried, and "We had the most dreadful experience driving here—Saul took a wrong turn and we almost ended up in the religious area. My God, we could have been stoned!" Saul said, "Jerusalem on Shabbat is more dangerous than anywhere over the Green Line. Or the Red Line." The apartment exploded with hilarity, like applause. Look at the size of Gideon! What a son. And this was Tikva . . . Amos is always boasting, but of course we hadn't believed . . . Such a wonder! I'm a young man again. His wife said, "Gershon, speak English, for Phil. Tikva might not want so much cake." Of course she does— and Gideon was in Yesh Ge'vul? Bravo! The youth of Israel— they had sense. We're too old, the Desert Generation. Old men, old wounds. Look at me, born in Berlin . . . now if I'd been born in the Galilee. "You stick to your principles, Gideon. We're the Desert Generation, we'll all die out. Then you young people will be able to take over. You'll make peace. Peace outside, peace inside—see, here is a boy whose grandparents were Polish and Russian, and a girl who comes from the Yemen . . . This is how it will happen. Through love. See, Alice agrees with me."

"She turns off her hearing aid when you arrive," Amos said.

Where's the Australian woman? Lost? Good God, and on a night like this. Should we look for her? Garin's daughter! We will not look for her. Phil, you must interview our Professor Garin. He's one of their mystics. A Yahwehist. A thug, like Rabbi Kahane, whom he admires, by the way—but he has English polish. The American fundamentalist Christians love him: he's the most polite Israeli they've ever met. He is Khomeini with a medical degree and a BBC accent; he is our Reverend Ian Paisley. Why do Judaism, Christianity, and Islam produce such thugs? Buddhism doesn't. Buddhism's had not one war in two thousand five hundred years. Do you know why, Alice? Of course she does but she's not listening. Garin should be in jail—not our Gideon. But you stick to your principles. And Tikva, you must have another slice of Shoshana's cake. Do you know Goethe, my dear? Amos, how do you translate . . . ?

Amos cut him short, in German, "Gershon, Tikva's mother is illiterate. Just tell her she's pretty and leave Goethe out of it."

"Allow an old man to be romantic. You used to be."

"I could kick your guts for encouraging Gideon."

"Why? Why? Oh, Shoshana, I've upset Amos. Shoshana says I'm an intelligent idiot. Amos, dear boy . . ."

Phil had sat beside Alice saying, "Please don't let me disturb you. I'm terribly tired, myself."

"I catnap."

"Wish I could." His big frame slumped; he needed a shave.

Alice had switched on her hearing aid for him; he had a pleasant, deep voice. He said, "This country seems to be at breaking point. People have classical alienation—the sense they have no control over outside events and the fear they have none over their own lives."

"Quite right," Alice chirruped. "Maybe it's the beginning of Wisdom."

He liked that; a smile like a drop of dye spreading across paper moved from the center to the boundaries of his large, good-natured face.

"But why does it take so long?"

"Ooooh. Our love affair with God is a great obstacle, you know. The story of Yahweh and His Chosen is the stormiest romance in history. And look what we've named the State! I remember the debates in the forties over what this country should be called after it became independent. There were any number of names. But we chose Israel. D'you know your Hebrew? D'you know it means 'He who struggles with God'?"

Phil picked up her hand and pressed it to his bristly cheek. Then he began to laugh, head thrown back on the brown vinyl of the settee. "In America . . . oh, it's so funny—my university colleagues believe that what holds Israel together is the Arabs. What will they say when I tell them . . ." The room had turned to look at him.

". . . it's really a fight with God!"

Departing after midnight the guests remarked to each other what a jolly evening it had been. When Amos was in good form . . . "I adore his maliciousness," Gershon said. "But he is *wrong* about Wittgenstein. And Hegel." Shoshana said, "Darling, shut up."

SIXTEEN

The reading room in the American Colony Hotel had a gorgeous paneled and painted Turkish ceiling and was furnished as a good English common room with settees, easy chairs, and a writing desk. One entered it from the indoor garden area on the other side of which was room one. Ahmed discovered the room had been burgled when he took a tray of drinks to the reading room and noticed that number one's door was ajar.

They had everything tidied up by eleven P.M., had reironed the clothes thrown on the floor, put the underwear back in drawers, stacked the papers left scattered on the desk, wiped up the powder the police used to collect fingerprints. When Danielle arrived and the night manager bounded from his office with a smile and an armful of yellow and white chrysanthemums for her, there was no sign of an intruder. Look, she now had a new lock, stainless steel, with a bolt mechanism. Of course there would be no charge for her stay these past few days; the management insisted: complimentary. But, please, there were certain formalities. With the police.

She had walked from the Sha'arei Zedek hospital in West Jerusalem! Allah be praised for giving fortitude. Maybe she had her passport and money with her, in the shoulder bag? God is Great!

The night manager had in his pocket the international tele-
grammed message that said DELAYED. ENJOY. LOVE BENNIE, but
now was not the appropriate time for a disappointment. He
would take her himself to the police station. Yes, tomorrow. Now
she must sleep.

He could not believe his ears at first. "You speak Arabic?"

"No," she said. The words had jumped into her mouth.

He closed her doors gingerly, listening for the dead lock to
thump into place. "Contemplate Allah, then sleep"—she'd said it
so sweetly, standing up, eyes shut, rocking with weariness.

Jazzy had taken her jewelry, for the look of the thing, and as
an added encouragement to her to move to a West Jerusalem
hotel. It was worthless, gold-plated rubbish, except for a small
pair of diamond stud earrings, the sort of present a man gave
to a woman for reassurance. Then he did a second room, the
one directly above the stairs to the right; he did not want her to
think she had been singled out. The next job yielded two English
passports, three thousand dollars in traveler's checks, a couple
of hundred in cash, and a cashmere pullover, so it was time well
spent. He returned to the dinner dance downstairs.

The English girl was half-drunk. Jazzy, who was calling himself Yoram to the English girl and her mother he had met in the
souk that morning, picked up her limp hand from the tablecloth
and, holding it in his two, raised it to his lips.

"You make me struggle with myself," he said. "I have been
praying, just now, for the strength to resist you. I asked
God . . ." Her breath stank of whiskey and cigarettes, even
her fingernails smelt of them.

"Is that why you were so long?"

"Yes. When you are my wife . . ." His gaze fondled her.

"Yoram!" She didn't know if she could live on a kibbutz; she
meant—she wasn't even Jewish—and he was a fighter pilot! She'd
worry about him.

Jazzy bowed his head. "My country must come first, darling."

He had noticed the fat headwaiter staring at him when he
returned to the dining room. The last time they had seen each
other Jazzy was wearing a mustache and looked older. He saw
the headwaiter's hand move distractedly to the thick growth on
his own lip.

"I feel bad in this place," he said. "I want to be alone with you. No—no. I promise! I won't even try to kiss you if you hate me so much."

He swung his leather shoulder bag on to his shoulder, shook his arm so that the gold bracelet slopped down to the back of his hand, plucked at the creases of his mohair trousers, and glanced at the tassles on the imitation Gucci shoes. The bag was imitation Gucci, too. If the whore weren't so tipsy she might have noticed that it had more contents than when they had arrived.

"Where will I take you?" Jazzy asked.

She looked at him with eyes like a dog's. "To the YWCA, please. I promised Mummy."

He drew his head back, holding his chest into his chin. "Very well, Angie. If that is what you want. If you reject me . . ."

For a moment he thought she would change her mind, and invite him to try to seduce her, in which case he had his British-imperialists-who-sold-us-out-to-the-Arabs speech ready. He was due to meet his fence in half an hour.

The policeman said, "You were lucky. He was a professional—he was wearing surgeon's gloves. That type is dangerous if caught in the act. Fortunately, he found what he wanted in the other room."

Danielle was invited to see the forensic laboratory and the mass spectrometer that in its first week had solved two murders. The crime rate? Well, it wasn't as bad as in Europe, or *America,* but there was—how could he put it?—an alienated class: people and the children of people who had come to Israel without an idealized cause, who came because they had to, then found life difficult. There was a mafia: drugs, prostitution, the food markets. Tourists came to the Holy Land expecting angels. And then, in East Jerusalem, there were the Arabs.

When the manager left them alone for a few moments he said, "Move to a hotel in West Jerusalem. You'll be safer."

She was still exhausted. The East Jerusalem doctor had prescribed an antibiotic cream for her infected heels and told her she must walk as little as possible for two days.

She tried to take a siesta when they returned from the police station but as soon as she closed her eyes they flew open again, ready for the intruder with surgeon's gloves. She saw his face smeared mongoloid under the stocking mask.

When she decided she could not sleep, there was nothing to do but work. Ahmed brought two more hot-water bottles and she settled herself to *Eleazar*. She wrote:

> • *Opening shot of Mediterranean beach, gentle swell of sea.*
> • *Contrast to the desert setting of Masada; symbolic suggestion (by seascape) of renewal of life, of variety and metamorphosis.*
> • *To convey agony of Eleazar's decision about suicide— check New Testament and Gnostic gospels for descriptions of Jesus' behavior before crucifixion.*
> • *Is Eleazar a Rabbi, like Jesus of Nazareth?*
> • *Problems of martyrdom: joyously embraced by Christians as form of liberation. Zealots similarly?*

"Bugger Bennie," she said aloud. He didn't want anything too complicated. His idea was a 1980s version of *Quo Vadis*, with the same wicked Romans, and with benighted Jews replacing benighted Christians. "And bugger you, skulking in hospital with angina."

She must have slept, for suddenly she was wide awake in the dark, struggling for the threads of a conversation she had been holding in dream. Her partner had been that shadow met on the roadway last night. But in the dream he had revealed himself fully. He was wearing barbaric princely dress: a lion's skin over his back, its fanged red-bucket mouth gaping around his head, and perched on one hand a dove with a ruby eye. They were in Africa, or some tropical country; the haze was a cold mist, not heat. He had bare feet and toes like the bowls of wooden spoons yet his hands were long and delicate with velvety black skin. He had turned a wrist for her to see the pink lining of his palm.

What had he said?

"I change. I cause change."

She asked, "Into what?"

"Into whatever comes next."

Then he had done something odd: he dropped to his hands and knees, showing her the back of a wild animal. "Piggy-back," he'd squealed. It was so frightening she had woken up.

Her watch said it was five-thirty; the evening star had risen, Queen Shabbat departed, and a new day begun all at once. She could now ring her father without breaking the Law. But as she stretched toward it the telephone started to ring.

It was an hour before Danielle had finished talking to Alice, then a man called Phil Abrahams who was trying to contact her father. Next, Wili, who wanted to know when they were to begin work. The desk clerk interrupted them to say he had a call from Australia.

Katherine said, "Mummy—there've been terrible bushfires— hundreds of houses." The line was poor and their voices tangled in panic. From the knotted umbilical of sound words here and there throbbed: "Ours is . . . safe . . . I drove up . . . millions destroyed."

"What? In Avalon?"

"No . . . Victoria. Wasn't it on television? They said it was on TV in Moscow. Don't you . . . ?"

"It's all different here."

The tinge of rebuke: "I thought you'd be worried."

"I would have been. Thank you, darling. Are you"—I fall back into the role—"wearing sunscreen? And a hat, on the beach?"

Katherine had a holiday waitressing job at Bondi, where she shared a flat with four other students. Imagining her shouldering a surfboard across the esplanade, as graceful as a palm tree, Danielle filled with longing and anxiety.

Exasperation: "Mother!"

Danielle thought, But I yearn to see you and touch you. "Okay. Don't get in a huff," she said.

What about Grandfather?

"You were right," Danielle shouted. "He's an old bastard."

—But I have not given up. On the contrary.

A woman, not Marilyn, answered his telephone. There were voices in the background as if there were a party in his room. The woman spoke English irritatingly, that is, fluently, but with a mishmash of accents—a leetle French, ze Hongare-ian maybe, a touch of Yank—that made her sound, Danielle thought, as if she owns no language at all, has no respect for any. And she was insufferably ladylike: "Really, I am not sure that Professor Garin is well enough to talk with you on the telephone." She called Danielle "Madame." As requested, Madame waited, hearing his room muffled by a hand held over the receiver. Then: "He will speak to you now."

In the pause she began to tremble. What would she say? She needed time, but the voice was in her ear suddenly, intimately: "Hello? Dan Garin speaking." Such a civilized, British voice. All her vulnerability to authority rushed into her throat and choked her.

"Um. How are you?" Much better, thank you. The heart specialist said . . . something. She was in too great a panic to take in the interminable, grave details. Already they had been talking how long—two hours?—her face felt hot with embarrassment for the banality of her responses: "Oh, that's interesting" and "Oh, dear." And then—it was like one of those agonizing conversations when you're in love and *he* hasn't called for a week; finally you can't bear it: you telephone and say, "Hi, did you get my postcard?"

There is a room in hell, she thought, where paralyzed women sit beside telephones waiting for their lovers to ring. "Did you get my flowers?"

"Flowers?" Oh yes. A kind thought.

—A *thought*. Yes. They were dead, he took one look and ordered them thrown away.

Was she enjoying Jerusalem? It's changed a great deal. Some inspiring restorations in the Old City. And more to come. Ha-ha. The room around him was going ha-ha, she found herself ha-haing. Then it came out:

"Are you going to see me or not?"

Silence.

"Allow me to take your number once more—Judith, would you pass me a pen, please?—and I shall ring you back. At the moment I am—ah—holding court, as my young friend Matti describes it. So, perhaps it would be more convenient for both of us, and I would be more considerate to my visitors who have come all this way, if later . . ."

For a few seconds after she replaced the receiver she felt elated, but it was only the tail-end effects of adrenaline. They burnt out, reeking from her armpits.

Did he notice they were roses, for love? she wondered. And white, for peace?

Garin was saying: "I don't know why, but she came here on Friday afternoon and pressed upon Dr. Wilensky a bunch of dead flowers and this picture book illustrated with photographs of scantily-clad Australians, who seem to spend their lives swimming. The country appears to be a sort of well-appointed health farm. Would you like the book, Judith?" He added, "Thank you, my dear," as Judith passed him a dish on which she had arranged segments of peeled orange.

The room service menu was limited, but Danielle decided to have dinner in her room all the same, in case he rang her back while she was between floors. By nine o'clock the telephone had not rung.

There was one Mogadon left, one she was saving for the twenty-hour flight from Rome to Sydney. She took it and had the first serene sleep in weeks, waking to the chime of Sunday church bells vibrating from the Old City.

The hotel was deserted. Its pilgrim tour groups, who occupied the cheaper modern wing, had breakfasted and left for divine services by the time she entered the dining room. The English couple who had been robbed on the same night as she had moved out; the Swiss businessman who had exchanged nods with her had gone to Jericho; and the Brazilian family had decided they could not bear the cold and had left that morning for Eilat. She booked a call for five P.M. local time to Bennie's house in Los Angeles and spent the day in the reading room, working on her notes, grateful to be housebound.

The letter and pamphlets arrived, courier delivered, at three that afternoon.

Garin had rehearsed its opening words—*My dearest Danielle, I write to you now*—many times in the past thirty-odd years but personal emotional expression did not come easily to him, and he had a demanding life: students, lectures to prepare, laboratory work, faculty meetings, annual military service, the newsletter. He was not one of those from whose eyes scales had recently fallen, after the miracle of '67 and the warning of '73, dates when the divine plan had revealed itself to many good young people. It had come to him back in 1949 that his life had been a series of revelatory events: marrying a gentile woman; applying for a post in Palestine because she wanted to travel; the homecoming of his dear Rachela; the destruction of Geoffrey. God wove a seamless garment in which each thread had its pur-

pose and moment. It had been meant that their few thousands
would win the War of Independence (so-called) against the
Arab millions—who were, incidentally, a fiction commonly agreed
upon, a twentieth-century circus invented by British imperial
policies.

There *were* no Arabs, in fact—or very few; but there were a
great number of people in this part of the world who believed
they were Arabs because they spoke a certain language, which
he also spoke. Did that make him an Arab? This absurd—and
absurdly believed—political sleight-of-hand was one of the problems he had confronted in the past thirty-odd years. In Israel itself there were few capable of understanding that "The Arabs"
were a figment invented by T. E. Lawrence, styled "of Arabia."
Real Arabs, as distinct from the Arab Circus, lived in a medieval
desert kingdom that floated on oil and the extortion of money
from pilgrims who traveled to it annually to walk round and
round in a circle, at the center of which was a large black stone.
With them there was no argument. Holding the cities of Mecca
and Medina, their concern with Jerusalem, which ranked only
third among Islamic sacred sites, was footling. However, since
the founding of the Jewish state this nonsensical enemy propaganda had been believed and its pernicious influence was now
worldwide. Israel cowered before a shadow Goliath. The imaginary giant waved a toy pistol, the so-called oil weapon, and
with this hypnotic instrument had robbed the banks of many
unfortunate Third World countries, and more egregiously, those
of the *soi-disant* civilized world: Japan, Western Europe, and
America. That is to say, of the nations in decay. He referred to
them as the Lands of the Living Dead when he addressed the
good young people who were fleeing their birthplaces to Israel.
They were states in which drugs, boredom, and lack of meaning
had attained such a hold that the females considered themselves
lacking in sophistication if they had not been sodomized by the
age of sixteen. Regrettably there was, as ever with the Jews,
backsliding: in Tel Aviv, a city of Hebrew-speaking Philistines,
one could find similar attitudes.

He had composed his address to his daughter so many times—
then waited: no letter had come from her telling him that she
was ready to ascend. Instead her mother wrote demanding money
for the fees at her Anglican school. He could read between the
lines: the child was turning into a savage. She had given up her

piano lessons; she refused ballet classes. He had written, "If you want Danielle to enjoy 'the outdoor life,' send her home and I shall arrange for her to live on a kibbutz."

The kibbutzim were, in those days, decent places where people built the Land. Nowadays they had Olympic-sized swimming pools and were the luxurious domain of milquetoasts and traitors, who proclaimed the joys of "Peace Now," a slogan none of them was able to define but which seemed to mean abandoning the country and their lives to the merciful disciples of one Yasser Arafat, a murderer who spent his spare time holding press conferences and was too busy to shave.

After a while Bonny had found some source of funds for those famous school fees, although as he had pointed out to her the problem would be easily overcome were Danielle to have her schooling in Israel, where it was virtually free. Then he had stopped writing. The girl did not write either, except for an impertinent note announcing that her final examinations had won her a place in medical school but, lacking funds, she intended instead to write ad copy for a living. A few years later she sent some photographs of a baby with the message: Your granddaughter, Katherine Reilly—her father died in an accident four months before she was born.

That was the moment, of all others, for her to come home; she could have found an Israeli husband in no time if she had one tenth of her mother's looks. He disliked the term "shiksa" as descriptive of gentile women, who were not *all,* as it suggested, damaged goods. Bonny, for example, had been made, fashioned, to lead him to Palestine in 1936—*Das Ewig-Weibliche zeiht uns hinan,* as it were.

So here, in Jerusalem, was Danielle.

He had been composing his thoughts for her when he had suffered what he believed was a cardiac infarction but which that competent little fellow Wilensky insisted was slight angina.

The letter said:

> *My dearest Danielle,*
> *I write to you now with joy and misgivings: joy that*
> *you have recognized your insoluble connection with*

Eretz Israel, with Judea and Shomron, and misgivings as to your future course.

I have lived for more than three decades as a father without a child and much as I appreciate your filial feelings, I must tell you that I am not given to the vice of curiosity. I do not pant to see you from the spur of inquisitiveness. I wish to meet a daughter whose heart is sound, whose mind is unclouded by the folly of the age, one who, in short, understands the great undertaking of the Jewish people in their obedience to the guidance of God, Who, having scourged them with His great weeding-out, the so-called Holocaust in Europe, has re-established His beloved and precious remnant in Eretz Israel.

Before we meet, therefore, I ask you to consider deeply: Have you Returned? Is your presence in Jerusalem the first step toward a permanent settlement in the Land? Do you know the truth of the saying that your ancestor, Abraham (of course, I am ready to recognize you as a Jew, despite your mother), was the first Zionist? We but follow his mighty footprints which mark out, forever, Our Land.

I ask myself also: does Danielle know that, as with those who found their way here from Egypt after cleansing in the desert, we too must purify the Land of its Philistine inhabitants? We must make It a temple. In fact we must rebuild His Temple. We must cleanse the Mount of its blasphemies. It is a Divine canon and, indeed, the deepest wish of every Jew. Those who have remained in exile, in America, in Europe, all over the globe, annually pray "Next year in Jerusalem!" Here we say, "Next Year in Jerusalem Rebuilt!" And it is, my dear, The Temple that shall be rebuilt. My question is: do you join in this great undertaking? If so, I welcome you with open arms and rejoicing. If not, my answer to your question is: No. You and I shall not see each other again. The dry bones, the dead, come to life in Eretz Israel; outside this land is the domain of the living dead.

Please do not be hasty. As a child you were eager and filled with curiosity. Do not now allow those qualities to rule you and, from curiosity about me, profess sentiments you do not hold firm.

In conclusion I quote to you the lines of our great national poet, Bialik:

We are the brave!
Last of the enslaved!
First to be free!

He signed it "Dan Garin."

"No 'Love, Father,' or any of that nonsense," she muttered.

She read it through again. Oh, yes—the life of glory for him and all of them. "Every Jew." How glibly he asserted. How easy to insinuate that after the Holocaust "every Jew" felt an inner rage for heroism—and of one type only: Violence. What did he fancy would happen when the Temple Mount was "cleansed"?

There are twelve million Jews in the world, she calculated, and four hundred, maybe seven hundred, million Moslems. The destruction of their third most holy shrine would pass without a shiver among them, no doubt? A couple of speeches in the United Nations, some tooth-gnashing from the Ayatollah Khomeini, the rulers of Pakistan in pique ordering a few hands cut off, but then they would all settle down. That's how you picture it, don't you, Father dear? So simple and reasonable. After all, the Temple was there before the el-Aqsa or the Dome of the Rock, and Jews and Arabs are members of the same family, united in their devotion to the Cosmic Father. They would all shrug and say "It is Allah's will" and return to what they like doing best: raping their grand-daughters and trading. One could observe how spontaneously Christians, Jews, and Moslems shared their hearts with each other by looking at the television set and seeing them do it in Lebanon. "For bloody example," she said aloud, and realized she had fled from her father—off into the safety of theorizing.

The two pamphlets he had enclosed contained many biblical quotations: one proved that the Menorah, stolen by the Romans when they sacked Jerusalem in 70 A.D., was now in the cellars of the Vatican, and the Pope should be told to give it back; the other was about Marilyn's oil well, that miraculous hole in the ground into which five million dollars had been poured and which, soon after reaching 20,000 feet, would pour it all back to the surface transmuted into gold.

Why not? Why not!

She realized she should not shout in the reading room of the American Colony Hotel.

Even I know you don't strike oil at that depth, she was thinking. Why not just strike gold? Spare oneself the technicalities of putting it into barrels and refining it into gasoline and kerosene and leftovers that have to be made into plastic bags . . . *This* was the solution! This had vision, and verve.

"The Israeli shekel will be worth gold." Deuteronomy 33, verse 24, which one was directed to read, did not actually say that. It read in full: "Let Asher be blessed with children; let him be acceptable to his brethren, and let him dip his foot in oil." The pamphlet had printed only the final phrase about oily feet—but the Lord's intention was clear from those few words. Yes, indeedy.

Danielle put the Bible down and tried to think about what one meant when one said that someone was mad. A few days ago, in a bank, an Israeli had told her he was not worried about the country's economic situation. "There'll be a miracle," he said and shrugged. "Israel has had economic problems in the past." What form did he think the miracle would take? she asked. He found this obtuse; "America will pay." But what if it won't? He was getting sick of her. "You don't understand love," he said. "You don't understand what Israel *means*, not just to American Jews, but to American gentiles. If Israel fails . . ." Maybe *I* am crazy, she thought. I'm in a temper—and distracted. But why can't I think about *him?*

She was so agitated she left the reading room without noticing where she was going and in her socks walked out on to the balcony. The afternoon was cold and fine. After so much rain it was luminously blue overhead, only the eastern horizon showing a grainy haze of mauve that would gradually deepen to the violet that on clear winter evenings was the glory of a Jerusalem sky. The mauve haze was already Jordanian territory. In the center of town outside the YMCA building she'd seen a signpost saying "Beirut, 150 Km." If you left out the Negev, the country was only the size of Sydney, she mused, and it had the population of Sydney plus one of the big country towns. It was claustrophobically small, a kernel, a spark.

What, in their heads, does the globe look like? she wondered. A huge ink stain of forbidden territory, here and there a dim glow of welcome, but the only real beacon America? Thoughts rushed in disorder. She tried to make sense of how things were here, in Israel, by thinking of some parallel in ordinary life . . . The friend who telephones at three in the morning to say her husband has beaten her up again: she holds you to ransom because she is helpless to control her life. But secretly, secretly, her weakness makes you feel good.

—So perhaps the Americans will save Israel.

—Perhaps they will make it a condition that people like my father are put in the loony bin.

It was almost five o'clock and sunset was changing the city stone to rose. She remembered the phone call she'd booked. In Los Angeles Bennie's Filipino servant would have cleaned the ashtray in the Corniche and would be making breakfast. For one? Had there been a starlet for the night? Would their limbs be tangled when the international operator began to dial and would his gasped "Hello, yes?" come from the shock of broken sleep, or from a different disconnection?

"Daaaanielle! Wake me, of course not. I've been awake for hours. At least three minutes. Dog, get off. You know I've been given a wolf? Yesterday. No—last week sometime. Hey, dog!"

There was a crashing sound, a yelp.

Bennie said, "I didn't like that lamp anyway."

Everything in his life was expendable.

"Daaaanielle! How are you? Enjoying? Written the movie yet?" She'd forgotten that talking to him was like the passenger ride in a sportscar driven too fast. "Last night I got this great idea, did I tell you? Well—oh, yes, coffee. Thank you, Ferdy. Isn't that something? He has the same name as the president of the Philippines. Best cook in the world. Danielle, can you hold a minute? I've got to drink coffee. I'm dying. Last night—oh, I haven't been to bed for two days. I think my nose is falling off. It just did! It's on the floor. Oh, Danielle—last night I had so much coke. You having a great time? I've had a brilliant idea. At the party last night I talked to a man who told me there are hermits living in caves just a few miles from Masada. Near the Monastery of Somethingorother."

"Temptation," she said.

"Yeah? Great name for a monastery. What do they all do in there? Think about dames?"

"No. It's where Jesus was tempted to avoid crucifixion."

"Terrific. Well, about these hermits. I want real hermits in

Eleazar. Imagine the blurb stories: 'Blah-blah-blah-blah, AND REAL HERMITS.' You like it?"

"No."

"Danielle? Why yer being nasty to me? I'm a noseless wreck. I'll have to book in for plastic surgery."

"Hermits refuse to play in movies, Bennie."

"Yeah?"

"I checked with Hermits Equity."

"Listen—I'm so disappointed I'll have to drink some coffee. You've ruined my day." She waited while he made slurping noises; from other grating sounds it seemed as if Ferdy were sweeping up the shattered lamp. "Hey!" He startled her. "Did I tell you I got the money? Stitched it all up last night, in New York."

—The hell you did.

"That's why I've been delayed—been running around town, stitching up the money-money-money. And you know that bitch Marguerita Schultz, the widow of poor Raphael? She put a rock through my window. Why? She's berserk. You know she's trying to blackmail me? She's trying to steal the company from me and she's hired a shyster lawyer who says I owe her five big ones. Five million smacks! Just hand it over, Bennie. I told her lawyer, 'You want to see my books? You wanna see my tax returns? The company's not worth a quarter of that. You can go to hell.' So she puts a rock through my window. And she's harassing my secretary. She made a big scene in the office, said she'd slam an injunction on the distribution of *Eleazar* and a couple of little movies I've got coming out. But I've fixed her. Called the police right away—Danielle: Can you imagine *me*, calling the police?"

Danielle had begun to sketch Marguerita Schultz throwing a rock. She pictured a big-boned, dark woman, maybe partly Mexican, certainly from the south—a southern belle gone to fat. She drew a whiskey bottle in Marguerita's rock-throwing hand.

"She looked so funny when the police carried her away," Bennie was saying. "You know she's a cripple? I shouldn't say that. She's not much of a cripple . . ."

That ruined the drawing.

"What do you mean?"

"Aw—" Bennie did not want to talk about it. "She was in the same accident as Raphael. She's all fixed up, really. You know she tried to kill me with that rock? If I'd been in the car when

she threw it . . . hold on. Orange juice has arrived. Thank you,
Ferdy. He makes the best orange juice. Not as good as in Israel,
though. You been drinking lots of the orange juice?"

He stopped talking and made noises as if eating toast.

Danielle said, "When *are* you coming? I've organized a whole
series of interviews with university people here who've studied
the Zealots and Masada. But when they're finished I'll be stuck
until you arrive."

"Never get stuck," Bennie said. "I tell you what: I'll finish
breakfast, get dressed, and jump on a plane. We'll go and find
hermits."

"Bennie. I have got to know when you're arriving. I can't plan
otherwise."

"Plan, plan, plan. You remind me of the army. Here, I've got
a flight schedule. Wrong one. Ferdy! He can't hear me. Danielle,
can you hold? I've got so many flight schedules and airline tickets here—I promise you, my secretary has had me booked on every plane to Israel for the past month. They're getting mad at
me. Look, I've got tickets. Danielle, what's it say? I can't read it.
I'm going blind."

"Hold it closer to the phone."

"Yeah. Can you read it now?"

She was sketching what she imagined was the scene in Bennie's bedroom. He would have hired an interior decorator and
everything would be in matching pairs: pairs of sidetables, pairs
of bedside lamps (until recently), pairs of chairs, on which he
would throw his clothes, a king-sized bed with a mechanism
that elevated the head section so he could sit comfortably while
talking on the telephone. She covered the bed with unused airline tickets and added, at its foot, a small airplane.

"It says you're leaving next Thursday," she said.

"How did you know? That's amazing! You got it right. I'm going to Rome first, to talk to a set dresser. He's a genius—he's
done sets for Coppola. I'm going to offer him anything he asks."

"Have you called him yet?"

"Yes. Not yet. Today. Right now I'm calling him. What time is
it in Rome?"

You'll arrive in Rome, she was thinking, and you'll meet the
movie crowd. They'll invite you to a party in a nobleman's villa
at which, it will be rumored, Sophia Loren will be in attendance.
Ten days later you'll remember you were en route to Israel.

"I think you should fly direct and talk to the set dresser on the way home."

"Danielle—why are you so anxious? You worry about everything. Never worry. I learned that in the army. Listen: I'll be there on Thursday. No—hold on. If I leave Los Angeles on a Thursday—what's the date today?"

"Just tell me the flight number. I'll find out this end."

"You got a pen?"

"Yairs." She added a final touch to the figure of Bennie she had drawn, flicking his satyr's curls down the back of his neck.

The operator rang back to say the call had cost seventy-eight dollars. And seventeen cents.

She asked to be connected to international telegrams and sent one saying CONFIRM I WILL MEET ALITALIA 43 AT LOD AIRPORT. He responded to that kind of gesture. Sometimes, sentimentality was the only thing that kept Bennie fit for human company. She felt filled to bursting with the distress of responsibility he stimulated, her anxious foibles blown up, out of proportion. I turn into the wretched, toiling little Ant, while he's the Grasshopper, she thought. All very well for him to be lying in the meadow, chewing tobacco and playing the fiddle. I've got a daughter to get through engineering, a house to pay off, a dog who frets for me, I owe the bank $80,000—

She had a vision of Bennie, in their hired airplane, insisting on taking the controls, sweet-talking the pilot. The ground came flying up to meet them.

"Settle down," she told herself.

SEVENTEEN

Bennie read the newspaper, drank more coffee and orange juice, then spent three hours on the telephones he had beside his bed. He made calls on both at the same time, saying, "Sam—can you hold a minute?" and, "Louis, I'll be with you in a sec." Bennie got a lot of work done this way, although on Saturday mornings there could be frustrations because people were sometimes doing things with their families. He got hold of his stockbroker and discussed the tactics for Monday morning, and located his lawyer, whose wife said at first that he couldn't be disturbed, he was in his studio, painting. "Sam's painting? Why? Debbie—don't I pay him enough to buy all the junk in the Guggenheim?"

Sam thought the Schultz situation was looking difficult: the fact that she had smashed the windshield of his Corniche would not affect any decision about the authenticity of Raphael's will. Bennie said, "Sam—it's a fake. It's got to be a fake. Raphael and I—listen, we *loved* each other. We drew up wills at the same time, each partner leaving everything to the other. It's impossible he would have written a later one, leaving his share to that witch. She's forged it."

Sam said, "Bennie, I have kept Marguerita off your back for three years. You've had full control of the company in that time, you've made twelve million bucks. If the handwriting experts—"

Bennie said, "Sam: I'm not going to do it. I'd prefer to go bankrupt. Hey! *Can* I go bankrupt?"

Sam sighed. "If you want to, it's possible, Bennie."

Bennie thought they should look into it—after the *Eleazar* money was tied up. Monday morning they would sign for certain? Sam was a genius. He should get a Nobel Prize. On the subject of painting: Bennie had bought a crayon drawing a few weeks ago. Sam had to have it. Ferdy would bring it around. Yeah, a Gauguin. Sam definitely would love it and he, Bennie, didn't want it anymore.

"Do me a favor, will you? Take it."

"He needs parents," Sam said to Debbie when he had put down the telephone. "Bachelors are always looking for parents."

"Did you invite him to lunch?" she asked.

Sam looked at his vase of brushes arranged as a fistful of stiff flowers. The painting with which he had awoken that morning had vanished, sucked like water through a plug into the telephone. Yet he could not tell Bennie to hire someone else to do his legal work; the kid's nature was seductive. Years ago Sam had stopped sending him bills, since he never paid them anyway. Now they had a cellar full of crates of Dom Perignon; Debbie had a chinchilla jacket. And the Gauguin drawing would be coming this afternoon.

"Darling," Sam said, "Bennie never comes to lunch on Saturdays. Do you know why? Come here and I'll show you."

Bennie did not take women to his house, where he and Ferdy had a perfect routine. He took them to the Beverly Wilshire. If he were to take a woman home she would create the full tragedy. Like that Danielle. What a nag!

While he was shaving he allowed himself to imagine the location work in Israel. Danielle is going to drive me crazy, with her worrying over every little detail. But he realized, at least she's interesting to talk to. Not like—Jesus, what's her name? The one I'm taking to lunch. Was she dumb! But what a body: Brigitte Bardot in 1963. Maybe they're plastic. Every second tit these days is plastic. If she's plastic I won't have dinner with her. Kiss-kiss-you're wonderful. Good-bye, *motek*—that's Hebrew; wonderful language, I'll teach you—gotta rush now, having dinner with my folks. My mother has a nervous breakdown if I'm late.

Bennie's mother lived in Tel Aviv. Twice a year he sent her the airfare to America. Day one was bad, devoted to telling Bennie about the fight she had had with his father over her visit to their eldest son; day two was better—he took her shopping on Rodeo Drive. Day three she raised the subject of matrimony and by lunchtime had produced the photographs of all the suitable wives she had collected for him in the past six months; day four she sacked Ferdy; day five she moved into a hotel, in tears. He remembered childhood, feeling overwhelmed by her needs, never being sure if what he gave was enough. Gradually he had learned to promise, then disappoint, and he'd felt strong.

Bennie rinsed off the last of the lather and trailed two fingers along his jawbone. It felt like satin. "Kiss me," he said. The face in the mirror leaned forward to press against his lips a long, cool kiss.

Gideon's and Tikva's leave was for three days. On Saturday evening, when the city came to life again, they went in to Ben Yehuda Street and ate pizzas and ice cream, walking around holding hands and looking in shop windows. On Sunday Gideon took her to the Old City. All of Christian Europe, South America, Japan, and Korea was taking photographs and buying junk. African men in striped robes and their women in cotton headdresses worn with the dignity of crowns went surging around them, the native born, the only two of that kind wandering hand in hand, not caring where they were going. On Sunday evening when they had to go to separate bus lines each felt a chill down the side where they had been joined.

"Driving past Masada I had a dream about you."

People called Tikva's eyes black, but they were the color of coffee grounds, with whites so clear they reminded Gideon of the white porcelain her mother brought out of a cabinet in her bedroom when she served him food. The mother talked a lot; Tikva, like him, was silent but more so than he. In their long, wordless spaces Gideon sensed sometimes the meaning of what the American said about brains being like television sets that tune to other lives. Her eyes were like tuning mechanisms. "What? What?" they asked.

"I dreamed you took me underground and at the end you showed me a fire."

A fire!

"It's all right. We had lots of children. I woke up with a hard-on. You'll miss your bus."

He waited until she had boarded, then loped off toward his own line. Amos was standing in it, his chest heaving as if he had been walking fast. Gideon had pleaded with his father to stop smoking: on his last medical check Amos's military profile, the measure of fitness, had been so low he had refused to tell Gideon what it was. Seeing him, people never guessed, because Amos had a big chest, there was no gray in his hair and he carried his head tipped back slightly so his chin jutted at the world. And he had not caught a cold or suffered a day's illness in the ten years Gideon could remember.

"I thought I'd missed you," Amos said. "I skipped a faculty meeting and I'm parked illegally. Giddy, I must talk to you. We've got twenty minutes. I can say it in three. Oh, all these fucking people. I'll buy you coffee. Okay? Fuck it. We'll talk here then, if you want to."

Gideon said, "Daddy, keep your voice down. We'll have coffee."

There was an unoccupied table next to the window of the cafe through which they could keep an eye on the bus lines—not that there was any need to, for from the chaos of the terminal Egged buses streamed out, on time, like intelligent action arising from primal confusion.

Amos said, "I'm not going over the military and political arguments again. I only want to say this: you are about to take the first step toward abandoning Israel. This is how it starts, in the army. You get disillusioned—one thing and another—then you think, 'a trip abroad, to America.' You speak English, your mother will send you the money—I'm not giving it to you!—your brother will get you a job, cars cost nothing, gas costs nothing, every second man is a fairy, so the women will be knocking you down in the rush . . . Listen: this is the only country in the world where *everybody* can leave and go live with family somewhere else. Somewhere out there, there's always an alternative, some cousin in Rio or Manchester or Minneapolis. The Diaspora is a magnet. And you start to feel it now, when everything is going to pieces in Israel. You know you'll be welcomed as a hero: fine boy, went to jail for his beliefs, the great Jewish tradition of dissent. The young, the beautiful, and the brave—oh, it'll be marvelous for you. You'll be invited to give speeches: The Purity of the Weapon—Israel's weapons are no longer pure. Every liberal

in Manhattan will be pleased for you to date his daughter.
You'll make them feel good—'Here's an ethical *sabra*.' Out there
the ones who think they think are ashamed of Israel now. All
through the fifties and sixties and even some of the seventies this
country was Glamorville. You're Israeli? Wow! We've read about
your miracles in agriculture and science and—well, you certainly
showed those Ay-rabs . . . They basked in the reflected glory.
Every fund-raising dinner to buy trees for Israel made them feel
as if they were building the Galilee with their own hands, sweating away in their minks and tuxedos. A tuxedo? It's a suit men
wear to fund-raising dinners. I don't own one. Nobody I know
owns one. Your brother probably does. Listen, Gideon, I've never
spilled my heart to you before. I'm asking you: Don't do it. It's
the first step. You refuse duty, you get thrown out of the army:
you will want to join the many. We are the few. Are you listening to me?" Do you hear what I have left unsaid, he wondered.
Israel is the Jews' last chance. The temptation to become gentiles
is irresistible in the Diaspora; it became irresistible with the
Paris Sanhedrin of 1807. Century after century we'd survived
thanks to legal oppression—theirs and our own, the way the
Christian sect survived thanks to the Roman policy of public tor-
ture. But we're not going to take over an empire. We'll fade into
impalpability. We've been fading since the beginning of the
nineteenth century, by losing our boundary lines. *I want* the
Jews to survive. I don't need to give a reason, any more than a
giraffe needs to give a reason for the length of its neck. It *is*. It
is a limb of God. You know why I don't bleed about the poor,
bloody benighted Palestinians?—because theirs is an argument
over property, not being. They can grow grapes on the other side
of the Jordan River. But if Israel disintegrates, in another two
hundred years the Jews will have vanished.

—So we're giraffes. But imagine the world without them—the
little Martian horns, rainbow neck bending for the mauve-colored
tongue to lick a foal: I saw that when I was fourteen years old,
in the Bronx Zoo, and I whispered the secret name of God.

"What's making you smile?" Gideon said. "You spill your heart,
then you grin at me when I'm thinking about what you've said.
You're always laughing at me. You talk German to Gershon so I
can't understand."

"And you talk Arabic with Tikva. Oh, shit. I wasn't laughing
at you. I'm as proud as hell of you."

EIGHTEEN

___

119

Alice whipped off her beret for Danielle to take a look and just as quickly put it back on again, pulling it well down for warmth. She had gone to sleep while having her hair cut; when she awoke she discovered she had left an inch of hair all over and her neck was being clippered. "What have you been thinking about?" she demanded of the hairdresser.

The girl did not seem to know. She said, "Maybe my brother. He's in the Golani brigade."

Danielle took Alice by the elbow and conducted her indoors.

Alice had insisted on making the trip to see Danielle, rather than letting Danielle visit her when the doctor had ordered rest. Danielle had begged her to take a taxi and allow her to pay for it, but Alice had caught a bus to King George Street and walked from there. The day was as clear and crisp as a sheet of ice. In the Street of the Prophets she could smell the tang from a stand of pine trees—she remembered the whole city scented with pine only five or ten years ago—and in one of her balcony boxes that morning she had seen the first green ear tip of a daffodil. In West Jerusalem everyone was in a good mood for the Purim holiday, children and teenagers off school for the day already out wearing funny costumes, masks, and painted faces. Young mothers had dressed up to amuse their children and strolled along with green glitter around their eyes; some of their little ones were turned out as Arabs—or maybe it was Biblical style. Purim was the only jolly festival in the calendar; it scored Jews 1, Goyim 0, for a change; in the form of triangular pastries people ate the ears of a Persian prince.

"Here," said Alice. "I've bought you some Haman's Ears. And you should see the Pious Ones, swaggering around in their shtreimls! They all got drunk last night. I've seen them *reeling* through Mea Sha'arim at Purim: that's the Law—drunk on Purim." There had been only one seat on the bus, next to a Hasid. "He slapped his hand on it to stop me sitting there. I said to him, 'Do you imagine I'm menstruating at the age of eighty-six?' and sat straight down. He pulled his hand away just in time. In a great paddy he was. Got up. Got off the bus. Polluted."

Alice thought Danielle could ignore Professor Garin's conditions for meeting and that she should visit him regardless.

"Beard him. He's a guilty man. He's ashamed of the way he has treated you and Bonny and Katherine, and now that his chicken has come home to roost, he's in a funk. You go and roost on him."

"But they won't let me see him at the hospital. And if he's at home he won't allow me through the front door."

Alice contemplated her food.

They were lunching in the poolside restaurant of the hotel, seated next to a glass wall that gave a view of a small swimming pool, palm trees, and the white tower of a mosque. Alice's Salade Orientale was described on the menu as "a delicate concoction of cold diced chicken in a light, curry-flavored mayonnaise."

She said, "I last ate this in a cricket club in Malaysia. You know, there was something about the British Raj: no country ever quite recovers from it."

The thought linked: "I remember when I was lobbying Ernest Bevin about Palestine. He was an awful fellow, such a bully and a liar. He refused to meet our delegation. So I sat in his waiting room for fourteen hours a day, for three days. He used to charge past me with his head down. Then he gave in. I was told the minister would see me for ten minutes. He and I argued for two hours, *and* he ended by inviting me to eat with him in the Members' dining room. That's a politician for you, dearest. They can't tolerate pressure, because underneath that invisible coating of oil they wear they are not real ducks at all, but clay pigeons. You go and roost on Garin. You must come to terms with the past and transcend it, or *it* will dominate *you*."

Wili arrived at the same time as their slices of chocolate cake. When he saw Alice he performed his greeting routine, with an added flourish. "The Queen!" he said. "How are you, Darling Teacher? You know, Princess, we always called her Queen Alice at school."

"I heard it as Old Cow," Alice said. She had never liked him, he had been one of those slippery children, sycophantic and vicious by turns, too small to defend himself adequately in the playground. But a few days after some boy had bloodied Wili's nose that child's satchel would be discovered slashed; Wili always had an alibi. In class he was eager to clean the blackboard or carry a teacher's books. They were exceptionally bright children at that place, the first of the opportunity schools in the East End. Some of them were top men in medicine and law by now.

He had left early, in 1950, telling a story that his mother needed him to go to work, but Alice had met Mrs. Djugash one day in the fish shop and she said Wili had run off; she assumed he had a messenger's job on a newspaper. "It's one mouth less, and I've still got five to feed." If there ever had been a Mr. Djugash he had not been around for years and the eponymous little ones arrived by some influence known only to their dam; the two smallest were the color of mahogany, with peppercorn hair. Wili had taken the devil of a teasing over this sister and brother. As she recalled, his nickname changed from Schnozzle to Sambo. Sometimes, when he was trotting along beside her with an armful of books, she could hear him screaming for the derision to stop. Alice had tried: she awarded him better marks for composition than he deserved, which gave him the idea he could run away and conquer Fleet Street. And oddly enough, he'd succeeded, but not as a writer. Danielle said he used to earn £ 1000 a week, in 1964. Then five years in jail. No wonder he's a nervous wreck, Alice thought. His entire body was a fidget. And his voice was unrecognizable. Wili had spoken such good Cockney once—rhyming slang, not an *aitch* in his alphabet, and glottal stops that would strangle a West Londoner.

No—Wili would not take "a coffee"; bad for the liver. But he took "a tea"; Alice noticed the gold ring on his little finger crooked above the handle of the cup, and its crest of a boar.

"Yairs—my mother's people came from Wales." The statement tripped off his tongue with the ease of many repetitions and was followed by a flick of defiance in his eyes.

"Well, when *is* this berk of a producer-director going to arrive, Princess?" He had brought an envelope of prints for Danielle, the pictures he had taken of her outside St. Anne's.

"I had no idea you'd taken photographs of me."

"Best eyes in the business, Princess. You can tell Whatsisface Kidron. Tell him Wili gets the snaps."

"You've got the job, Wili," Danielle said. "Relax." And then, to withdraw from the hostility that had jumped out of her mouth, before she'd had a thought: "He's delighted I've found you. He's an easygoing guy, very . . . fluid."

Wili wanted all the details: Which hotels would they be staying in at the Dead Sea? Would the aerial work be in a chopper or a plane? How many days would they travel by road? He laid a spiral-bound notebook on the table, took out a pen, polished it on the paper napkin (as he had polished his teaspoon and then not used it), and was poised to record her answers. Danielle kept shaking her head.

"Bennie does everything on the spur of the moment. I just don't know." She was feeling increasingly tense.

He made some irritable scratches on the paper. "Princess, I have to work out what film I need, which lenses, lighting, tripods—"

"Bring the lot."

"I can't carry everything. It's physically impossible."

"So hire an assistant. Bennie won't mind."

Alice said, "Oh, Lord!" In lunging forward in some gesture of surprise or pleasure Wili had knocked over his teacup, scalding her lap.

When he had left, Alice said, "You made his day, promising him an assistant. Did you notice he stopped that horrid sniffing?"

They sat in silence for a while, soothing themselves with the charm of their surroundings. Danielle was thinking, Perhaps I should move to a West Jerusalem hotel, as Wili also suggested. A voice in her head was droning: Something's wrong. I feel bad.

Perhaps it is this hotel, she thought—but it's so poetic and dotty . . . I like listening to the Christian pilgrims telling each other their "experiences of Jesus," and their dreams. At breakfast that morning she'd heard one talking about a dream of a spider with a sapphire crown. "That's your bad feeling toward Gerry, but you can convert it into a beautiful jewel," another explained. In a corner alone an officer from the United Nations headquarters breakfasted on muesli, grains of which he carefully removed from his handlebar mustache, while day after day he practiced drawings of camels in a notebook. The head waiter was the judge of his efforts; at the end of the meal both men adopted grave, mustache-stroking silence to contemplate the morning's artwork.

"I wonder if I've done the wrong thing," Danielle said. "I've just spent an extra thousand dollars of Bennie's money, by the time you add up transportation and hotel bills for a fourth person."

"A thousand," Alice piped. She lived on £36 a week, which got smaller every month, chewed up by the ever-strengthening American dollar. A lot of people on sterling pensions were feeling the bite. Danielle looked embarrassed. "Well, love, you told me yourself it was a world of illusion—not just the film at the end of it, but the whole environment."

Danielle hummed. "But there's a moment when the guillotine drops. The budget is settled and that's it: if a scene isn't right, too bad. There's no money for extra footage." She added, "And often the writer cops the blame."

"And then?"

Danielle shrugged. "I don't know. Legal hassles . . ."

She's way out of her depth with this film and so is her young crook of a producer-director from the sound of him, Alice realized.

It looked like rain so she gave in to Danielle about a taxi home. The driver was an Arab and got lost for a few minutes in the web of small streets behind the Gaza Road. He was a loquacious, jolly fellow—owned the taxi, he said, had just got married. (Alice understood: married a second wife.) When they passed a pair of Hasidim in flying-saucer fur hats he cried, "Look! Look! Fancy dress every week for them. I like them. You ask, 'When will the Messiah come?' They say, 'Next week!' They're happy. Every morning they get out of bed and say, 'Messiah will come today.' And next morning, they say it again. Happy people. Good women, always." He patted his belly. On a corner there was a group of young men in ordinary dress with knitted *kippot* flapping in the wind, anchored to their hair with bobby pins. They had to jump back to the footpath to avoid the cab. Alice tutted at her driver.

"You know what we say?" he asked. "Excuse, lady: they wear shit on their heads."

"They believe they are preparing for the Messiah, also."

He cleared his antrums emphatically. "In an atom bomb. In a gun. In a tank. The daddy sleeps with a gun under his bed: what does the son learn?" He fell to brooding and talking to himself in Arabic. "I want peace," he said.

"Everyone wants peace. No one is prepared to make it."

He thought that was a good one, and refused her tip.

The light was poor; the colors would be muddy. Even so Wili banged off a couple more rolls of film on the Purim festival crowds, got what he thought might be a good frame of a fat Dominican giving directions to a bunch of Israeli teenagers dressed as cowboys and cowgirls in front of the Moses Cafe. He then packed up, caught a sherut to Tel Aviv and a private taxi to Jaffa. The question was: Who? Who could they use as the assistant cameraman?

Jazzy said, "Saeed. He knows some Greek. We have a Greek passport."

Yusuf, who specialized in altering passports, said he would need three days to fix it properly.

"We have *time*," Jazzy said. "I know the Jewish mentality: this Kidron has not been back since 1967. I know what he'll want to do—go and look at the Wall. He'll want to enter the Old City, put on the cardboard skullcap, stick his little prayer between the stones: 'Thank you, God. All these years on Passover I've said Next Year in Yerushalayim, and now I'm here.' I know them. He'll want to spend a day feasting his eyes on el Quds. We can get everything ready." In imagination the details of their work were like individual notes gathering the energy of music; sensual pleasure spread through Jazzy as he pictured and saw each sequence, leading to the fountain of sound.

They had a party. Around midnight Jazzy put his hands on Wili's shoulders and, steadying himself, was able to lift one and tap at the side of his nose, but his finger missed and he only flicked himself on the tip. "Kidron will stay in the lovely, modern West Jerusalem Plaza. He is not the type for the King David. The Hilton is too far away from the Old City. The Plaza, Wili, is our bride. You and Saeed will be going into the Plaza." They rocked from side to side, their eyes radiating to each other the invisible, exquisite light that lovers exchange.

"Bang!" Jazzy said. "Bang! Bang!"

David had his own key to Alice's apartment. He kept a violin there that he had played well when he was younger, but had rarely touched in recent years. When she opened her front door she heard him playing a piece by Shostakovitch they both loved. His astrakhan hat was on its hall peg, his navy Aquascutum overcoat beneath it, both worn scruffy but of such quality they hung on to him. She sniffed a lapel and grimaced: he was turning into a dirty old man—he, with the shapely, soft hands that he still manicured as if they would survive forever. Not those hands, but their work, she thought. There could be bang upon bang upon bang until the planet was a brilliant firework, a display slowly fading from the cosmos. Maybe that was God's intention: to wreck a toy that could not assemble itself into friendly play.

She had discussed this possibility with her friend Father Gilot of the Dominicans, who came to tea on Wednesdays in a swirl of white skirts that smelled of Gauloises. Bernard Gilot, being one of those men who very young, only in their thirties, had grasped certain ideas, was inclined to agree with her that earth was a training ground for the game of hide-and-seek with God. David had listened to them with an ironic, baffled smile.

Alice stood in her hallway trying to catch the music: her hearing aid was an imperfect instrument, like memory. After a while two parts of her, memory and crumbling body, came together so that she heard the music in its perfection inside herself, as Shostakovitch had. "Poor wretch," she said.

David announced, "The biopsy is positive. I've got, they guess, maybe six months."

"I'll come with you!"

No, no—he would not hear of that; she must live on.

Why?

He didn't know.

"In that case," Alice said, "let's have a cup of tea."

NINETEEN

—

Danielle went directly from her father's place to the Old City, through the Dung Gate. The houses that had crowded up to the Wall had been demolished and now there was a broad plaza in front of it bounded by a wide flight of steps. One could sit on them and gaze at the Wall on the other side of the plaza and see the Islamic buildings on top of the Temple Mount.

In the precincts of the Wall they had searched her handbag briefly; people wanting to go on to the Mount were submitting themselves to more thorough searches—there were sandbags and men with walkie-talkies and sharpshooter rifles on their shoulders. She did not feel like being re-searched.

She wanted a peaceful spot, somewhere in which to think about what had happened in Professor Garin's apartment that morning. This was as good as any: a blank wall.

As walls go it was pleasant enough, about ninety feet tall, oblong cream stones more or less of the same size and undecorated.

It had an irregularity she noticed; a few feet from its base there was a band of bathtub grime at the height of the hands and foreheads that had rubbed against it. How many? How many, she wondered, since Eleazar's revolutionary friends had set fire to the buildings above and Roman legionnaires had finished the job, wrecked the city stone by stone, and sowed its earth with salt? They had left this wall. From laziness? As a reminder of what happened to colonials who misbehaved? Maybe because they were great engineers and had some technical reason. The stones were smooth with oil from the millions who had returned to them; from where she was sitting she could see around all the lower masonry the faint white outline made by prayer slips poked into crevices.

An accommodating sort of wall, she thought. It allowed people to hammer it with their fists, inject it with demands, tell it about family tragedies. Access to it was divided by a partition, the left side for males, the smaller one, on the right, for women. No part of it looks bored, angry, or mad, she thought. Nor does it hide from view.

Danielle flung her map of Jerusalem onto the steps below.

Christ's honey bun had opened the door to her. "This will be a surprise for him," Marilyn had said. Danielle was invited to "take a seat in the salon." Had she read today's *Jerusalem Post?*

By the time Marilyn returned she had almost finished its four pages, not that any of the stories had made sense. The words could have been lottery numbers churned in a barrel and popping out at random. But her ears had snatched and gobbled the tiniest sounds: Marilyn's cajoling whine, male harrumphing. They switched from English to Hebrew; Danielle could tell he was asking questions and Marilyn was stalling with her replies, turning shrill. There was a long silence. A drawer banged shut; a cupboard door squealed. There was a noise of pillows being thumped.

Marilyn entered the salon with her fingers interlaced, her palms facing the floor. Fetching pose, Danielle thought. Victorian handmaiden. You need a frilly white blouse and a corset. Why can't you wash your damned hair?

"I don't know how to say this, Danielle," Marilyn was saying. "But Professor Garin has a slight infection. We wouldn't like you to catch it."

"It's a risk I'll take." She felt reckless enough for anything: Have a glass of arsenic? Yes! Why not? I drink it for breakfast.

"Well, in that case."

❊   ❊   ❊

Professor Garin was sitting up in bed wearing a dressing gown, a red beanie, and a black eye-mask.

As she stood in the doorway Danielle thought, My legs won't move.

Rage like a geyser spurted from her gut to her hair roots and her legs did move, carried her straight to the end of the bed and kicked it. Three times.

His arms flew up. "Marilyn, what's happening? I can't see!"

Danielle said, "You bastard! How dare you? You don't want to see me? Don't then." She gave the bed another kick.

"Aaaah." The alarmed quaver had left his voice; the Prophet was recovering himself. "Is this Danielle? Shaking heaven and earth?"

She sat on the end of the bed and looked at him. What could you tell from a bit of nose, a mouth, and a chin that had not been shaved that morning and bore a winter stubble? She looked at his hands, then at her own: her fingers had a slight plumpness at the base and tapered to almond-shaped nails. She could see the resemblance to his very large ones, age-spotted on their backs.

"Are you present, Danielle?"

Again she refused to reply.

"Danielle, my dear girl, if you are sitting there on the end of the bed, as I feel that you are, I think you might do me the courtesy of speaking."

"I think you might do me the courtesy, after thirty-four years, of taking off that eye-mask and hat."

The thin lips smiled.

"You must try to be reasonable. Danielle. Are you there?"

I could hit him, she thought. I could pull off his bloody beanie and . . . "You are crazy, Father. And destructive. I think your plan for the Temple Mount is criminal."

"Ah-ah-ah," the mouth said. A pedagogic finger waved at her. "Criminal, you say. Stay, dear child. Hear what *I* have to say."

She stood up. The action jerked her aware: I'm about to leave; I'll never see him again—and rushing from somewhere came a bolt of love. She teetered, then moved to the head of the bed. His ear was the only part of him she could kiss without offending him more than she had already. But as she bent toward it he moved his head slightly, away from her, and suddenly the flood of affection boiled into rage again.

She bent down and uttered a piercing scream into the ear. Then she walked out. Marilyn, quite the little housewife in an apron now and a pair of yellow rubber gloves, came running from the kitchen. They collided.

"Get out of my way," Danielle said.

Over there, a hundred yards away, people were talking to the stones, chanting to them, kissing them, rocking to and fro, working themselves into the rhythm of prayer. On the men's side the base of the wall seethed with black figures; a boy was lifted onto shoulders; a whirling dance began. Women stood on tiptoe on their side of the barrier, watching the men.

That's the way of it, ladies, Danielle was thinking. It's a boys' religion. But you lucky women, you're allowed to watch. While they get drunk on God.

Her buttocks were numb with cold. She had a scarf in her handbag which she knotted under her chin before she reached the women's section of the Wall.

There was plenty of space, empty yards of it because most of the women had left to become spectators of the performance next door. But at the moment of plunging forward she couldn't do it—bridled, as one sometimes is at the edge of cold water, victim suddenly of an unreasoning fear. Voices cry "Jump!" and "Come on!" She closed her eyes and leapt.

Next moment she was reeling from a whack on the side of her face. She came to, gasping, pressed against something as slippery and hard as wax.

—*Now* I'm in Jerusalem!

Her face burned. Turning aside she saw an old Sephardi woman giving the stones what sounded like a scolding. Danielle waited until she felt her heart slowing then put her lips to a crack. "Hello," she said. It replied, "I'm here."

She said, "I want to thank you."

It was courteous.

What did I expect, she wondered—the ill-temper of the streets outside? the obsession with time?

It said, "I'm always here. Stay as long as you like. I shall listen."

After that she felt braver and began to talk without embarrassment. She told it about her father's intolerable behavior and Bennie's unreliability. "I'm chained to Bennie: I've got myself into a second bad marriage with his film contract," she said.

Patrick had been unreliable, too—when he was twenty-five he already lived on the edge of a sense of futility. "If he hadn't died, we would have divorced. But I can't divorce Bennie Kidron. He's offered me the chance to move into the big league . . . My wretched father didn't give me an opportunity to tell him what I've achieved."

"I know about it."

How?

It did not answer.

She opened her eyes a little: there were the minuscule white snail shells of hundreds of slips of rolled paper pushed length-wise into a crack. Beyond them she could see deep inside, into blackness. It was unbearably cold, her jaws trembled and her body shook, but she continued to hold her eye to the pinhead of dark where there was nothing, neither stone nor crumbs of paper. It spoke to her, saying: "God abides in all and governs all."

The cold became agony. She stepped back, stamping and rub-bing her hands together. Before she turned to go, she patted the wall boldly, affectionately, like a sailor patting the timbers of his boat. Dear old thing, she thought.

"There is only the necessary and the impossible," it told her. "There is only One Being." But she was not paying attention.

Crossing the plaza a young soldier began to walk alongside her. He was blond and snub-nosed, as mild as an egg. To Danielle he seemed a nice kid, unsure whether he wanted to practice his English, try to seduce her or just pass the time being helpful to a tourist. She decided for him:

"Where's the closest place we can buy coffee? I'll pay."

They ate baklavas oozing pale honey. He said he was from the north, from a kibbutz; he'd met a Swedish girl two years ago who had come as a volunteer worker. His parents would not allow them to marry, although her family had treated him like a son. He'd stayed in their house in Stockholm for six months. Now she didn't write to him.

He wanted to pay for his share of the cakes; Danielle insisted; in return he offered to escort her to the Temple Mount. "You don't go alone," he said. And, "Look." An Arab boy walked past with a kerosene can on his head. "They use their heads for *that*. You need your head all your life . . ."

Up on the Mount he became silent. It was a silencing place, a plateau miles above the world, acres of flagging, with here and there a delicate archway, a stand of pine trees, a font for washing before entering the holy buildings. They looked from a distance at the Dome of the Rock. Beneath the great gold moon of roof verses from the Koran swooped around the upper walls on skis, painted in a blue so bright it stung. But as they walked closer she saw the craftsmanship was mediocre, rivets and ugly seams marred the cupola: it didn't stand up to close scrutiny.

"She won't write to me because of what happened in Lebanon," he was saying. "In the camps. What can I do? I'm Israeli. I'm in the army."

Danielle took his hand. I know what it is, she thought, to feel that your life is lived inside a tunnel scattered with booby-traps.

They had to decide which exit; there were many, with charming names—the Wool Merchants' Gate; the Wheat Gate; the Cottonworkers' Gate; the Chain Gate.

"Here's one for you," she said. It was the Iron Gate. There was a metal threshold to the doorway. "There's a poem in English that says, 'And tear our Pleasures with rough strife, Through the Iron gates of Life.'"

He smiled at that. Shoulder to shoulder they could not fit through but they swiveled as a pair of fish can, and, bellies together, slid over the lintel, laughing and breathless. On the other side he kissed her on the forehead.

"Our gate," he said. He wanted to kiss her lips but she drew back, shaking her head.

TWENTY

At the airport Bennie said, "No way. Are you crazy? No way am I going to Jerusalem tonight."

But: what about his booking at the Plaza? And where would he stay in Tel Aviv?

"And what will I do now?"

He was looking around, grinning. Other passengers with luggage trolleys were trying to maneuver past them as they had halted to argue, blocking the exit.

People leaned over its iron railing, some watching for friends and relations, others, taxi drivers, shouting for passengers.

"What a mess," Bennie said. "I love it."

He was wearing blue jeans, white sneakers, and a pale pink jacket made of leather that felt like silk. "Rome," he said. "I went a day early. Hired the set dresser, bought this . . ." He had sticking plaster over his eyebrow and a bruised cheek. ". . . busted my head." How?

Bennie giggled: he couldn't remember. And no way was he going to Jerusalem tonight. "Danielle, I need sleep."

On the way in from Lod to Tel Aviv he stopped the taxi for her to buy a toothbrush. It was raining heavily; in the beam of the headlights raindrops jumped from the black roadway like a shoal of tiny fish. Bennie said, "It'll be fine tomorrow."

He got them rooms at the Hilton, farewelling her with "See you at breakfast, girl," and "Ooops—this elevator hates me. You see that? It tried to bite."

Maybe it was the sea air, maybe relief that he had actually arrived. Maybe it was something else—the lazy walk, the way he looked over women with the air of a man appraising a smorgasbord. Danielle had thought, You'll be fat by the time you're forty—and with all that hair on your chest you'll be losing it on top.

While she had waited for him behind the glass partition at the airport not knowing if he were on the flight or not, she had been so anxious that when he had come into view, unshaven, beaten up like a sailor, shoving along the luggage trolley with his foot, her heart had bumped about. But not in the way she had feared it would. She'd thought: Here comes my money.

"Hullo, Prodigal," she'd said.

"Get stuffed," Bennie had replied. "I'm a sick man—cancha see?"

In her Hilton room three floors above his she had her second sound sleep in months.

At ten, when breakfast finished, his phone number was still busy. He opened the door saying, "Danielle—take a seat." Trousers and shirts were spreadeagled on the floor; he seemed to have slept in both double beds—naked as a cub, she thought. Bennie was not the sort to own a pair of pajamas. He went back to the telephone retucking the white bathtowel he wore and continued his electric shaving as he talked to Los Angeles. "Yeah, Sam. We'll screw her—sorry it's noisy here—I said, 'We're gonna screw the witch.' How's the other thing moving? You know, in New York?"

Danielle wrote him a note: I'll see you in the lobby.

He came sauntering toward her, hands in pockets, smiling, at eleven o'clock. "See?" he said. "Beautiful weather. We'll go for a walk. We'll have lunch on the beachfront. We'll go to Diezengoff . . ."

Danielle thought, And we'll miss the last sherut to Jerusalem, because it's Friday. But you go ahead and screw things up—I'm not going to complain. She loathed the feeling of underwear worn for a second day; her hair was a mess because she had no brush, only a comb, and her face, without cleanser, toner, and moisturizer, felt greasy: small humiliations. Women are fated to them—by this sort of man, she thought. He commands the relationship but takes no responsibility for its details.

Bennie stared at her fox jacket. "Why are you wearing that thing? God, what is it? Monkey?"

She was too hot in the jacket, but only after she had handed it in at the desk did she realize: *This* is how he demoralizes me; he attacks my weak point.

"Now you look great," Bennie said and she heard the message, I'm not going to lunch with a woman who's ugly *and* wearing a tatty old fur. He was dressed in loose cream trousers and shirt, both of raw silk.

She bought a pair of sandshoes in a shop they passed and said to him, "Here. You carry my boots," but he tipped the salesman ten dollars to take them to the hotel.

It was too cold for swimming, except for a pair of husky men who were frolicking with a ball; other people played Ping-Pong on the beach or sat in deck chairs looking at the flat green sea that seemed to move only at its edge, the little waves running forward to bow, then withdraw. Danielle cursed: It would not do at all for the opening scene, which needed a lively, bright blue surf.

"So we'll do it in Hawaii," Bennie said. "What's another hundred grand for the title shots, to you?" He snorted.

There was an esplanade paved in swirls of red and black, set out with umbrellas, and behind that restaurants and soft drink and ice-cream stalls. The tall hotels clustered together, then there were hundreds of yards of derelict buildings, buckled asphalt, and peeling walls.

"I lost my virginity in one of those lanes. That was the big deal when you were fifteen: to go to a brothel in Tel Aviv. I was so innocent! And you know who was in the next cubicle? A guy with . . ." He twirled his finger alongside his chin. "I said to him, 'Hey, Curly, what are you doing here?' and he quoted Talmud at me—said, 'If you have a passion you cannot master, put on a black cloak, go to another town, and indulge it there.' Isn't that cute? I love 'em."

"Did you go back?"

"Sure. Hundreds of times. Told my folks I was going camping. Played hooky from school."

How did he afford it?

Bennie shrugged. "Sold stuff. I dunno." He strolled along,

kicking at the sand and smiling to himself. "You ever been to a brothel? You should. In Bangkok they've got special ones for women, with real nice Thai boys. You'd love it."

"Why would I?" He was spoiling for a fight, she knew.

"Aah, you want everything under control. You could say to the boy, 'Do this, Do that.' You love being the boss." His tone was mild, oiled, almost feminine. Danielle took his arm companionably.

"How is the terrible Mrs. Schultz treating you?" she asked.

"That bitch! I'm going to break her in half."

By the time they had taken another turn and Bennie had announced he was hungry for lunch his good temper had returned, but Danielle realized that, in humoring him, she had somehow dulled her own wits. She felt relaxed but wooden-headed, in no state to argue her ideas about the shape of the film. While he was ordering their fish she went to the women's room and looked at the scruffy hick in the mirror. "You're artistic," she said and took handfuls of her hair and threw it upward, creating a fluffy mess; an application of charcoal eyeliner improved the bohemian effect. She grinned at the memory of her assurances to Wili that Kidron was easygoing.

"Tell, tell, tell," Bennie said when she sat down. "I want to know *everything*."

He interrupted only to say, "Brilliant" and "I love it! A great scene." When he listened he did so with concentration; his beautiful long eyelids flashed intermittently as he glanced at his fish before pushing it away, uneaten. He picked at the salad, groping in the dish for olives, and he bit a pickled cucumber in two, dropped one part, then held up the other saying, "What's this? They give me half a cucumber?" She thought, If you can't use your imagination and eat lunch at the same time you must be slightly half-witted. But overriding this thought was her mood, luxurious now from the flattery of his attention. Later she remembered that lunch and laughed at her vanity.

It was, however, the best meal she'd had in Israel and she wanted to eat the lot in case this evening everything was shut for the Sabbath, with only hotel dining rooms open and serving kosher Friday-night food. There had been signs in the Hilton's foyer asking guests not to smoke in public areas during Shabbat. She had not mentioned to Bennie that the last shared taxis for Jerusalem left at about four o'clock and felt a thrill of devious-

ness when he said, "Let's go to Diezengoff. Gotta say hullo to the
best street in the world. We'll have coffee on the sidewalk." It
was fine by her if they strolled about and arrived back at the
Hilton at 4:30 to discover they were trapped. He had forgotten
so much of Israel: on the beach he had said, "It's all changed. I
don't remember those buildings." He said now: "Or I can pick
up the car and we'll drive there."

"The car?"

"I hired a car this morning. You don't think I was going to ride
in a sherut to Jerusalem, do you? What's funny?"

"Wouldn't you ever like to do what *ordinary* people do?" she
said. "Just for the experience? You're back here for the first time
since—"

Bennie cut in. "Ordinary people are losers." He turned smiling gray-green eyes to her. "I'm a winner."

At whose expense? she wondered.

But his improvidence was an intoxicant. Bennie was paying for
everything—her sandshoes, lunch, their hotel bills—with an offhand air of noblesse oblige that made her feel narrow, middle-
class, and mediocre. In the shoe shop she had objected, "But it
was *my* idea to buy sandshoes," while he had said, "Danielle,
Danielle," in a tone that pleaded with her not to make a scene,
not to embarrass him again as she had with her mangy fur jacket.
One of his gold credit cards had already landed with a clatter on
the counter.

She had expected Diezengoff to be closed, as Ben Yehuda
Street in Jerusalem would be by this time on Friday, but it was
still full of people and the cafes were open. Tall, ravishing girls
and boys walked hand in hand and kissed between tonguefuls of
ice cream; there were hardly any uniformed soldiers; the clothes
were a parade of winter fashions for the well-to-do.

"This is Israel," Bennie said. "I'd like to have an address in
Diezengoff—a video outlet. Or something." He was watching
their waitress; she had long fair hair and a weasel face (Danielle
thought she was a goy, maybe of Irish stock). She wore the latest
in baggy jeans, tied at the waist with a piece of cotton rope,
suggesting she might really be a sailor who had just jumped ship.
There was a corkscrew in her front pocket that she wielded with
a practiced jerk over bottles of wine demanded by a laughing
group at the back table.

"She's pretty," Bennie said.

"She looks corrupt."

"Nah. She's real pretty."

"She thinks you are, too."

He acknowledged the compliment from both women with a faint smile that turned to an expression of panic. "Danielle. Don't move an inch." He ducked his head under the table as if looking for something. "Quick. Get the bill." His hand groped up with a fistful of notes.

Their table was deserted when she came back from the cashier's desk; she found Bennie standing hard against a wall of the cafe, apparently examining the mural.

"That was my mother," he said. "We're getting out of here."

They had to walk in the wrong direction until they could cut down a side street and head back toward the Hilton.

"She's a very beautiful woman," he said.

Danielle thought, She could look like a prizefighter in a wig, but I know what you mean: you're terrified of her, and you call that love. "Where's your father?" she asked.

"Around. He owns a trucking company. They're still married, they still live together. He's a bastard."

"So's mine."

Bennie said: "Shake."

They were bright-eyed, astonished with the discovery of a glimpse of their own faces in each other's. Bennie said, "Hey, you want an ice cream?"

When they arrived at the hotel and the car was waiting, the navy blue Mercedes he'd ordered, Bennie said, "This is going to be a great trip. We're going to enjoy, eh? That's what life is for." He tossed her jacket onto the backseat with: "Danielle's monkey suit. Next time I'm in Rome I'll get you one of these," and plucked at the collar of his kid jacket. "Maybe in lilac. You should wear lilac."

She wondered, Why don't you say it straight? "You, Danielle, just haven't got it. You're just high-paid help. You're a loser."

Go on, break the speed limit, you hairy-chested pig, she thought.

When they passed Bab el-Wad and began the ascent to Jerusalem Bennie asked, "Why is it so cold?"

"Don't you know?"

He looked wary.

"It's a bad winter," she explained. "Up in Lebanon the Syrian soldiers have been freezing to death. More than a hundred of them died of exposure when the Red Cross wasn't allowed to rescue them."

"That explains it." There was the same tone of caution in his voice.

He was one of those terrifyingly effective drivers who drive fast and talk at the same time, looking away from the road. He glanced at her again. "I've got a confession to make."

She waited. Then:

"I was—ah—exaggerating when I said I knew Jerusalem well. I thought the climate was warm."

I must not sound sarcastic, she thought. "How badly do you know it?"

He laughed, throwing his head back in that insolent way. "Never been there. Never laid eyes on the joint."

"So, all those script conferences we had . . . ?"

"Listen. I had maps. I had photographs. I'd asked people questions."

"Have you been to Masada?"

"Nope."

"The Dead Sea?"

"No."

"Ter-rific."

"You're making fun of me—and I've got a busted head. That schmuck of an Italian." Bennie swore he'd done nothing to provoke the fellow. Danielle pulled him back with "It's a good thing I hired Wili Djugash for us. He's been traveling around Israel for years. He did a series for *Vogue* on top of Masada."

The self-righteousness worked in a way she'd not expected. Bennie said, "Danielle—I don't need a seeing-eye dog to find my way around."

In another ten minutes they would pass the fortress settlements on the outskirts of Jerusalem. Already the taste of tension was returning.

Only half a dozen other Sabbath-breaking vehicles were on the highway ahead of them. At least *he* will not be traveling in one of them, Danielle thought. Marilyn, or perhaps that woman with the phony voice, will be lighting his Shabbat candles. Bonny used to; I watched her face become a priestess's over the flames. Then I would be sent to bed and from there could hear them laughing—Jews, Arabs, Armenians, French, Italians, the English-man with the glass eye who did conjuring tricks with it to make me squeal.

Bennie noted her silence and wondered if he had gone too far: she was not only a nag and always fishing for compliments, she was also moody. "I'm real pleased you hired Wili. We want the best."

"He is, but he's a creep."

"Five years in jail, what do you expect? Poor bastard. Jesus I'd hate to go to jail."

His eyes were fixed on the lights of the city ahead. "Listen—I'm not feeling well. Maybe I've got a concussion. I'm going to pull into that gas station." It was closed. He stopped the car, got out and wandered off into the dark. Across the valley lights sig-naled from the fortresses. Danielle opened the windows to re-lease the cigar smoke and, sticking her head out into the night, she smelled the pine resin. The moon was speeding overhead. Bennie came back saying, "Can you drive this thing? I'm all dizzy. I think that schmuck—you know, I was unconscious for half an hour? had to be carried onto the plane—no, really, I was a stretcher case."

She had never driven on the right-hand side of the road. "Will you keep an eye on me at intersections?"

"Just put it in Go," Bennie said.

She found she could navigate without his help, even if he had been capable of giving it. He had become so quiet he really might have been ill; when she stopped at traffic lights and took a look at him he seemed stunned, lying still in the seat and breathing slowly in the top of his chest as if his heart, grown huge, was trying to escape from beneath his jacket.

"My best friend was killed," he said. "The guy who took me to the brothel. In '73 he was blown away."

She felt kinder toward him.

There's pain when your history is dug up, she was thinking. "Keep your eyes closed," she said. "I'll show you something soon."

It took only an extra few minutes to drive past the Old City and up to the Mount of Olives. She stopped in the car park out-side the Intercontinental Hotel. By day tourists went there for a view over the Old City and to have their photographs taken sitting on a camel. Danielle had walked up to the Mount of

Olives yesterday morning, before going to lunch at the university with Alice's friend, Amos, and the American political scientist who wanted to ask about her father. She had planned to take Bennie here straight from the airport, last night. But of course he had mucked that up.

The Temple Mount lay spread as a feast, stage-lit from below by the orange spotlights around the Old City walls. Bennie jumped out, saying, "Where are we?" He staggered and clasped his head. Suddenly he wasn't acting.

She continued sitting in the car, and could hear him blowing his nose. After a while she joined him, leaning against the stone wall of the viewing platform.

"There, below us to the left, is your valley."

He didn't understand.

"That's the Kidron Valley. And that's the Golden Gate."

"There is no gate." The things he knew and did not know were equally surprising; she began to explain, to his long sighs. Then something she said triggered it all, and Bennie remembered: "So the Messiah will start from this very spot, descend from here, go across the Kidron Valley, the Golden Gate will open . . . hey!" At length he added, "Israel *had* to take this bit of territory, didn't she?"

Danielle shrugged.

"Aw—you're not an Israeli," he said.

And what the hell are you? she thought.

He wanted her to leave him there. She traced on the map the route he could take to walk to the Plaza; as she drove off with his luggage she saw in the rear-view mirror that he was still leaning against the stone wall, smoking a cigar.

At the Plaza she left a message for him to telephone her if he got in before midnight "so I'll know you're safe." There was no real danger, but . . . He had wads of cash and would be walking through unlit walled lanes in occupied territory before he reached West Jerusalem. When she returned from supper, there was no message from Bennie.

But there were already eight from Wili. At the American Colony the desk manager had greeted her with discreet, soulful glances of rebuke as he handed her the folio of messages, plus a letter. His look said he hoped there would be no repetition of what he had had to put up with on her account during the past twenty-four hours. Ahmed, who had taken to sitting about in Danielle's room and drinking coffee which neither of them paid for, followed her up the stairs.

"I've only got half an hour to get dressed before I go out. You turn on the bath for me, and be quick."

He ran up the steps to the bathroom and played about with the bathwater while she read the letter, which said:

> *Dear Princess!*
>
> *What is going on? You and Mr. Kidron have disappeared. I have checked every hotel in Jerusalem looking for you two. At the Plaza they said Kidron telexed from Rome to say he would not be arriving on Thursday and now they don't know when to expect him.*
>
> *I have lined up an excellent assistant cameraman but his time is limited. I cannot fool him about with all this confusion. I will ring you first thing Saturday morning. Hopefully you will be there.*
>
> > *Ciao for now,*
> > *Wili.*

It was printed in capitals, except for his signature, which was a firework of something like copperplate almost filling the bottom of the page.

Ahmed returned. "He waited four hours last night. Today, eight hours. Very anger. I told him, Madame has gone to Eilat. Back in five days." He was surveying the clothes Danielle had laid out on the bed, shaking his head. "More beautiful if you wear a skirt," he said.

Danielle gave him a dollar to go away and slid into the bath knowing that if Amos and Phil arrived on time to collect her Ahmed would stall them, not as a favor to her but for the rapture of invention. He was capable of denying that she was staying in his hotel—or even that it was the American Colony. Some days he told Danielle he was thirty years old and married to two wives; on others he was eighteen, a bachelor, and working as a servant to earn enough to study motor mechanics. (He had already confided to one of the other boys that Danielle had asked him to marry her and he would soon be leaving for Austria—where she owned a hotel.) Life was full of surprises for Ahmed, and a constant pleasure.

Lying in the warm water she went over why she was meant to be in a rush, how she would explain Bennie's absence—he, too, had been invited—and how it had all come about in the first place.

At lunch, two days ago: a repentant meeting (for her) with Alice's friend Amos, whose Friday-night dinner of the week before she had had to cut, because of the hospital affair. Alice had arranged a get-together at the Mt. Scopus campus of the Hebrew University so Danielle could apologize to Amos, and meet Phil. She had liked him much better than Amos, who had accepted her explanation with the air of a man who had no time for the intricacies of the Green-Garin family, from whom he expected that sort of behavior, anyway. Phil was large and cuddlesome; Amos was trim, tough, and all nerves. He had a superbright line of patter, jokes, and political opinions that masked whatever it was he was really thinking about—which was not lunch. He'd wolfed his food as if eating were a time-wasting exercise, and it tasted all the same to him. She had watched his rebarbative profile dipping toward his plate, and his yellow eyes, and had thought of an eagle. He had no time for coffee, but had rushed Danielle from the dining room and insisted on driving her to the station to catch the bus to Lod, asking riddles like "What's the difference between Israel and a lunatic asylum?" with fierce amusement in his face. She had gathered Amos was an associate professor of something and that his recent book, about Marxism and the theory of law, was already considered a classic—"which means it'll sell three thousand copies." He asked, "You know what Marxism is?" She did, kind of—but he had another joke up his sleeve: "No-no-no. Marxism is the opiate of the intellectuals." As she was alighting from his car he had said, "Come to after-dinner supper on Friday. Bring your director," and slammed the door.

At nine o'clock she found the big amiable Phil waiting for her in the foyer with a grave expression, his head inclined to Ahmed, whose eyes were rolling with the drama of what he had to say.

"I'm glad to see you all in one piece!" he called in greeting. "From what he's been telling me . . ."

Ahmed had backed away as if Danielle, clean, dressed, smelling beautiful, appearing in the lobby of the American Colony Hotel at nine P.M. were a supernatural event.

She moved a lot of orange peel, chocolate wrappers, and books to make room for herself on the backseat and explained to Amos that her director would not be coming because he was feeling ill.

Amos said, "Tell him to be healthy." Everything he said was emphatic. He added, "The fucking doctors are threatening to go on strike."

From the front seat Phil looked around to raise eyebrows in apology for his friend. "Amos's son has been court-martialed for refusing duty in Lebanon. He only found out this morning."

She mouthed words of sympathy that Amos seemed to find as interesting as bird twitter and to which he did not bother to reply. Phil launched on a story of his adventures in pursuit of the radical right. He had arranged an appointment with Professor Garin on Sunday morning: maybe he could *persuade* . . . ?

"Thanks. I'll think about it," Danielle said.

Amos was driving too fast, hunched over the wheel. When she had ridden with him two days ago his Cortina had seemed okay, but after Bennie's Mercedes it felt like a sardine tin and she wanted to cry out, "Go easy!"

But he suddenly cried out, "What! Garin will see you, Phil, and he won't see her?" He had stiff hair, like a barrister's wig, but black. Turning around almost to face her it seemed to be standing on end. "What did you do to him, for Christ's sake?"

Assume it's *my* fault, she thought.

"I haunt him," she said dryly.

Amos didn't find that amusing, either.

They had arrived somewhere. Phil helped her out and the three of them set off toward an ill-lit series of lanes to terrace houses on a steep hill; not far away they could see the Zion Gate in the wall of the Old City. Amos started to swear. This used to be a slum, he explained. "But if you forget about the Wolfson apartments—reserved for arms manufacturers who are also connoisseurs of art—Yemen Moshe is . . ." He joined thumb and index finger to make a rough circle and kissed them apart. "Only left-wing people can afford to live here, only the ideologically sound . . . Shit, Phil—where are we? Which is Mira's place?"

They had walked along one cobbled lane, but that was not the right one, then entered another that looked identically, neatly antique. They were now in a third.

Phil said, "How should I know? I haven't been to her new house."

The eagle-head swung around. "Phil: is Israel at war? Have

we moved the house to confuse the enemy? God, why do women move? They actually enjoy doing it. You know, there is not an armchair in the world that some woman has not moved."

Phil thought they should try an alley to the left. Amos said, "The solution to everything is interior decoration. In my next life—"

"You said you were going to be a New Zealand botanist."

Amos grabbed Danielle's elbow to save her slipping. "There's a pogrom coming for *them*, kiddo," he said to Phil. His yellow eyes glared into her face, like lamps, for a moment. "Danielle, be smart: the smart reincarnation money is on interior decorators. In Fiji. Ah!"

They had found it. "Mira's bijou," Amos said.

As the door opened Danielle realized she was rather seriously underdressed. Her fox whimpered as she took it off and hung it beside a burgundy Persian lamb. The mink collar of a scarlet cape hanging below a Chagall lithograph squealed rudely.

Why have I worn this jumper knitted with a kangaroo across the front and a koala eating gumleaves on the back? she wondered, as she looked at Mira's black taffeta skirt and peacock-colored silk jacket over a blouse so exquisitely ruffled it might actually have been done with goffering tongs. A Siamese walked up, sniffed Danielle's boot and walked away with its tail in a flagpole. Mira, coiffeured and manicured, was saying, "*Everything* is in chaos"; she asked them to excuse the mess. Tim-tim (the cat, Danielle gathered) was being simply *foul* . . . Mira was dark, and in her forties. She lectured in nineteenth-century English literature, Amos had said. She asked sympathetically about Bennie: if there was anything she could do? If he needed a doctor . . . ?

Ten people were gathered in the salon. There were more taffeta ruffles; one of the men was wearing Bally shoes, Danielle noted, and the painting in an alcove did appear to be a genuine Matisse. They were talking about books: a man in a black velvet jacket with a pipe he used like a conductor's baton was saying, "Jonathan, anyone who has not read Flaubert is doomed. It is a serious illness, like . . ." he hesitated to think of what such ignorance might be like, ". . . never having seen Jerusalem. You will lose weight, you will grow pale, your hair will fall out."

Ah-ha! they shouted at the appearance of Amos, Phil, and Danielle. Two of the men tried to stand up to greet them but they had to struggle and kick their legs to rise at all from the low leather-covered settees. Jonathan managed to uncoil himself and stand upright; the others made do with thrashing about, and the women stayed seated, waving. Danielle realized she needed to pee.

She had plenty of time, in the bathroom, to examine the elegant tiling and smell the expensive soap. The door, once shut, would not open again. She tried knocking and calling "Yooo-hoooo," then sat on the edge of the bidet to wait, thinking that after all it was a good thing Bennie had not come: Flaubert was not his forte. After fifteen minutes Amos opened the door.

"Why are you hiding in the bathroom?" he demanded. Enlightened, he added, "You see? This is Israel. You spend a quarter of a million bucks on an apartment and the bathroom door—ah, fuck it. I *told* Mira . . ."

He seemed to have told the rest of them, too: when Danielle went back into the salon and sat beside Phil the room felt jagged. Conversation was skidding everywhere, darting around and away from an epicenter: politics; the war.

The man who loved Flaubert said, "Rabbi Kahane is a terrorist. He's no better than Arafat."

A woman Danielle matched with the scarlet cloak said, "Worse! Because he's a Jew."

" 'Because he's a Jew!' " Amos was back. "Don't talk horseshit, Shula. The famous Jewish concern with morality and legality and nonviolence is the product of—"

Apparently they all knew what he was going to say, that it was the product of Diaspora life, a eunuch's virtue, because as he did they shouted him down with remarks like "Judaism is above all a legal system. Yahweh is a *legal* God." Danielle sat quietly, trying to hear what they were really saying.

Phil whispered, "We have turned out to be the ghosts at this banquet." Amos had told them about Gideon's court-martial, and he had explained his study of the Right. "Then Mira added you were writing a movie about the Zealots." That piece of news, Phil said, had turned the conversation to the graffiti in the religious districts, the slogans saying "In Blood and Fire Israel Fell—In Blood and Fire Israel Shall Rise." And from them, to Rabbi Kahane.

Flaubert had lit his pipe in agitation. "The low-grade terrorism we need to control the West Bank will in time be the low-grade terrorism the Israeli government needs to control the rest of the country." He sucked and blew. "State terrorism and private-enterprise terrorism are in the same rut."

Phil whispered, "He's right."

Jonathan, who was fair and seemed a bundle of languid affectations—Winchester? Eton? Danielle wondered—said, "I didn't come to this country to . . ."

She thought, But why did you come to Israel? Why did you leave Sloane Square, you rich wimp?

Mira said, "Neither did I."

Danielle was thinking: Israel is the country in which Jews can't be gassed and roasted. They can live forever here, from generation to generation. It's a *duty* to stay in it.

The sense of things coming unstuck was like vapor off black water.

Amos said, "So Jacob desires Rachel, but lifts the wedding veil and finds he's been married to ugly Leah."

"Yes, but," they cried.

"But nothing. We wanted it to be beautiful. It isn't. Our dusky brethren have seen to that—and *we have too,* by treating the Sephardim as resident aliens for thirty years. But we're good 'n married to them. And meanwhile Israeli policy has made terror respectable. It's an administrative matter when *we* make reprisal raids."

How could he! Shula wanted to know. Amos was going too far. Israeli schoolchildren should be massacred at Maalot and we accept it like sheep? Our diplomats are murdered . . . What alternative?

When the noise had lessened, Amos said, "I didn't say there *was* an alternative. I said there are consequences."

Mira offered Danielle crackers and cheese.

Jonathan murmured he would prefer the Stilton. "And what are the consequences?" He made it sound idle.

"In our lifetime this country will become another nasty little Middle Eastern state." Amos tipped his chair backward and defied them all, arms crossed over his chest, grinning.

His cynicism! Shula was sorry—she realized Amos was upset about Gideon—but his cynicism was disgusting. And intolerable. "*Zionism,* Herzl's Zionism, was a moral appeal for a home for homeless people. Its authority was and is our ethical compassion. Look at what we've done for the Arabs in education, medical services, financially! Look at what we've done for the Sephardim—my God, we didn't even know the blacks existed—who arrived here in tens of thousands, illiterate, penniless."

Flaubert's admirer said, "My dear Shula, that is all true. But we have also reduced the West Bank Palestinians to the legal status they enjoyed under the Ottoman Empire. The happiest moment of our lives, as Amos has implied with admirable brevity, was imagining the delights that lay before us: Jews in our own land, on the brink of a great adventure."

Amos gave Flaubert a nod of thanks.

Someone said that Begin had taught Israel to hate: "He's presented the rest of the world as corrupt and dangerous, and now our kids believe every gentile carries a knife."

Danielle was thinking, I am listening to the spirit of the age. Which is fear. But it's out in the open, in Israel. There's no muffler.

Amos grinned at him. "Have you noticed, Hirsh, that nothing shapes reality like violence?" he asked.

The room missed a beat.

Danielle began thinking, Survival is the condition of everything else, but it is only a condition of what has value; it may have no value on its own account. Out of the silence Mira's voice lifted to say, "If only women were in charge . . ."

A woman exclaimed, "I refuse to be labeled a feminist, but what Mira suggests . . ."

Danielle thought of asking, "In refusing feminism, what do you think you are rejecting?" but didn't have the nerve. The war of the sexes was shaping up; she and Phil, wordlessly, agreed to remain noncombatant.

Phil said to her, "All this worry about morality . . . What about the economy! It's impossible to have one-hundred-percent wage and salary indexation and one-hundred-and-thirty-percent inflation without . . ."

She nodded.

He made a gesture as if tearing his hair. "This country has been sleeping in a featherbed, economically, and they refuse to wake up. They believe it will be feathers forever. But I tell you: it's going to turn into nails. And world Jewry—that is, America—won't pay for Israel forever. Especially in the state it has reached." His chest collapsed. "Maybe the export of adrenaline will save the shekel."

He shut his eyes, then blinked a couple of times. "Can you sleep here? I can't. Or I have nightmares."

Hirsh was saying that Golda Meir had proved to be *the* most stupid prime minister: she lost opportunities to make peace; she had to share the blame for the October war . . .

"She had a vocabulary of five hundred words," someone agreed.

What are women? Hearts! Governed by a great muscle that goes squeeze-squeeze-squeeze.

Golda didn't start any wars!

No, but—

Danielle said, "So do I—have nightmares, that is. I've even had . . . sort of . . . visions. That's never happened to me before. There's something about this city . . ."

Phil smiled wearily. "I saw my father in the street three days ago. My mother and I and my brothers escaped through Switzerland in January 1939, but he stayed on in Warsaw to look after the business. He died in a cattle truck in 1942. And I saw him in West Jerusalem."

She felt very curious. The dead alive, the living dead, he had written. "Did you speak to him?"

Phil shook his head. "You know," he said after a while, "it's something ontological, rather than psychological."

She could not think of any response. At length Phil added, "It's that which makes the mystic Right so interesting: they're on to something, some underground disturbance . . . You know your father wants to throw the Moslems off the Temple Mount?"

"Yes."

"Maybe it will take another fifty years. But it's an idea with a taproot that in this soil . . . I'm glad to say I'll be dead."

Amos, who had gone in to fight for the female side but had switched to the male, had heard the end of the sentence. "Phil! What's this defeatist talk? What do you mean you're going to die? That's your Keynesian fairy stuff again. He was the fairy who said, We'll all be dead in the long run."

The glint in his eye caught Danielle like a whip. She wanted to do something to ease his pain, to stroke him, as you would a wild creature distraught at being caged. She leaned over and patted his knee.

"What is it?" Amos demanded. She had startled him. "You want to go home?"

To Phil he said, "Listen, baby, in Israel we'll all be dead in the short run. Haven't you noticed that time moves more quickly in this country?"

Phil said, "Yes, and *I* want to go home."

At the American Colony Amos helped Danielle from the backseat. "Are these Ay-rabs looking after you?"

"Yes."

He double-clicked his tongue. "That's what they're here for, Madam: they collect the garbage, they pick up the dog shit, they bring you the meal you've ordered . . . Have you ever tried to order a meal from an Israeli waiter? I tell you, don't bother. He won't bring it. You order chicken, he'll give you fish; you order fish, you'll get a steak."

On impulse she kissed his cheek. If he moved it was only to flinch.

"I'll be in touch," Phil called.

In her room the force of the evening gathered in retrospect around a trifle, an exchange between Amos and the small, passionate woman called Shula. She was, Danielle guessed, in her mid-fifties; from various remarks she had realized that Shula was Palestinian-born and as a girl had worked "illegally"—that is, against the British. The males had reined back their powers of debate when arguing with Shula, in whose burning gray eyes and sun-battered skin one could see a lost, fair prettiness. All night she had clung to expressing self-pity she made national: everyone else was in the wrong and to blame for the state of Israel; she—Israel—was by nature perfect. Amos had objected aggressively until Shula had said: "I understand you perfectly, Amos. Underneath you're all tears. But you've turned them into acid—and being cynical is all you've got. What happens when you lose that?" Amos had squirmed in his seat, grinning. He said, "I'll toss in my chips." But he could not resist a comic flourish. "Hey, Phil," he called, "is that psychological—or *ontological?*"

She remembered she had had an insight into Amos at the time but was so tired now she had forgotten it. He had looked ferocious as he had argued with Shula.

TWENTY-ONE

From Bennie's room there was a view over the gardens of West Jerusalem and the Old City. When Wili and his assistant, who did not speak after the introductions, had been shown out Bennie led Danielle on to the balcony. For a while he leaned on the railing, drinking up the view and flicking his cigar ash into the cold, sweet daylight fourteen stories high. His eye had a purple bruise around it now but the sticking plaster was gone.

He had no particular explanation as to where he had been for the past two days, except: "I been working my butt off."

He had rented Danielle an apartment on King George V Street, just across the road from the Plaza.

"I don't want you staying in East Jerusalem. It's not safe. Listen, I got you a nice little place. You can have it until Passover. You've got a garden. You've got good pictures on the walls. I looked at three hundred apartments yesterday and every one was hideous. Israelis have the worst taste in the world. I got brain damage. Danielle—for you I got brain damage." He rocked his head from side to side and said, singsong, "'But *I* like the American Colony. It reminds me of Mom and Dad and my Arab nurse.' Danielle—don't be a pain in the ass. I've paid already. You want a maid? I'll hire one."

She had to admit that staying in the center of town just across the road from Bennie and the American Express office would be more convenient. But according to the terms of her contract with Kidron Productions, she had to pay her own accommodation expenses: how much had the apartment cost? what did she owe him?

"*Nothing.* The guy who owns it—he's a real good painter—is a friend. He gave it to me."

She knew from Alice what short-term rents were like in the chic areas of West Jerusalem.

"You can't work in the hotel room," Bennie said. "I want my writer very, very calm. I gotta be in New York to spend Passover with my grandmother. I wanna know you're safe. I don't want you spending Pesah with a bunch of goys." He blew some cigar smoke in her face. "You know what they do to us at Passover?"

She whacked the smoke away.

"Sure. It's because we killed God."

Bennie grimaced. "Nah. It's because we've murdered all those Christian babies to get their blood to soak our matzah. Listen, don't argue. Take the apartment."

It was a charming, raffish sort of place, perhaps once the servants' quarters of the Turkish house above. There was one large room furnished with rugs and divans, a kitchen in a corner, a tiny bedroom, and a bathroom. The owner's paints, brushes, and easel were lying about; a kitchen cupboard was full of cans and jars of food and an inch of clouding black coffee stood in the chimney-pot *finyan* on the stove. There was something about the way Bennie was standing in the middle of the room looking at the pictures, the shelves of books, the African mask with its slanting cowrie-shell eyes—something superstitious: he did not want to touch anything.

Danielle said, "Tell me the truth. What's happened to the owner?"

Bennie shrugged. "He got called up a couple of weeks ago. Now he's missing. His mother can't afford to go on paying the rent. I told her this terrific Australian lady, a widow . . . Listen, Danielle: people here are poor. I walked all round the Jewish Market area yesterday. They're so poor it's hideous."

She had jumped up. "I'm not going to stay—"

Bennie said, "I don't think the mother was telling me the truth. I think the son is in jail. Now do you feel okay?"

*   *   *

That afternoon, working over their maps and the schedule in Bennie's room, he said, "Hey! You want some hash? I bought some great stuff yesterday off an Armenian. He told me about the apartment I got you. The painter was dealing: he got busted—poor guy couldn't make a living as a painter."

"So you got the key from the Armenian?"

Bennie, as he had sometimes done before, reached over and pressed his bunched fist against her chin. "You're smart," he said. "Even if you do fit me up with a PLO photographer."

He was sure that Wili's assistant was not Greek. "But why?" Danielle insisted; Bennie's head swayed left to right.

"I'm a businessman. I have hunches. That Ari smelt bad. He and Wili Whatsit smelt like a pair of cats. I'm not having them in the car with us."

Bennie had handed back the blue Mercedes to the rental agency and hired another, a private taxi driven by an Arab, to take him and Danielle next morning to the Dead Sea. Wili and his assistant were to travel there by whatever means they liked: "That's your problem, fellas."

Wili, little finger crooked as he sipped the Plaza room-service coffee, had said, "I see. I see." His eyes had darted fierce accusation at Danielle. Bennie had also said, "You get paid when I see the pictures. I don't pay cameramen whose flashes don't work, or who forget to take off the lens cover."

When they'd left Danielle had said, "You didn't have to be so rude."

Bennie was tossing peanuts in the air and catching them like a seal.

"Why not?"

She thought, Because the temptation to prey, and to be preyed upon . . . He tossed her a nut, which she caught by hand. "You're the only woman I know who can catch nuts," Bennie said.

He had ruined the city for her. He would never admit it directly, but he hated Jerusalem. He complained of the cold, of the unshaven men, of the litter in the streets. He disliked the wallpaper in his suite; he disliked the food; he disliked the foyer decorations—which were no better at the Hilton, he said. The only decent-looking hotel was the King David, but he wasn't going to move there because it was full of octogenarian billionaires being danced around by official schnorrers: "We've paid for every goddamned olive tree in this country ten times over. What do they spend the money on?" She muttered, "Tanks," but he wasn't listening. His list of discontents was endless: "Look at that!" An old man in a black homburg and an ancient pinstripe three-piece suit was trudging, resting on his wife's arm, trudging again up the hill toward them.

"But look at the story in him," Danielle said. "He was upper class, he lost everything . . ."

"He should be in a home," Bennie said.

This city was a palace to me, she thought. You're transforming it into a slum. All my energy is wasting in a struggle to keep on course against the gale of your . . .

"Haven't they got plastic surgeons in this country?" Bennie was asking. "Everyone has eye warts and moles on their faces. And look at their lousy tee—" He stopped suddenly, with an "ooops!" grin, a quick glance at Danielle's teeth. "You know what I'm being charged to telephone L.A.?" he continued. "And it took me forty-five minutes to get through yesterday."

Danielle said steadily, "You give me a pain in the arse."

He shrugged. "And I think your idea for the end of the movie is lousy. What's the point of having the whole thing told in flashback by the woman who didn't commit suicide and who escaped with a grandmother and a couple of kids? Having her—who the hell is she, anyway?—recounting the full catastrophe to a Jewish traitor, who joined the Romans?"

"That is accepted as *historically accurate*." As if it were a piece of metal twisted back and forth by Bennie, she felt her temper snap. "I've spent hours talking to people from the archeology and history departments at Mount Scopus. If you want a boys' adventure story—" Her voice was rising and she started away from him at a run, rushing to escape the anger. There was a restaurant, the Savion, just ahead, on the opposite side of the road. Somehow she got through the traffic.

It was dark inside. She ordered coffee and a crescent-shaped cake; when the waitress moved away Danielle felt that the man sitting across the room from her, reading a newspaper, was observing her. The *Jerusalem Post* hid him, except his hands, but in the poor light she could not make out if they were those she had seen before, resting on the counterpane. Three discreetly dressed Rehavia matrons were the only other patrons. Danielle thought of getting up, marching over to him and saying, "Excuse me, aren't you . . . ?" She felt shocked, and pleased, to realize that since Bennie's arrival she had barely thought of her father. Bennie had forced the pace—even when he had vanished for two days the knowledge that he was at large in the city had shifted her attention to the short-term, the pragmatic, the acqusitive.

Her food and drink arrived and she was able to stop shivering with anger. At least Bennie makes me concentrate on what I am *now*, she thought: a go-getter, like him.

Memories of the past days returned: she had treated the academics who had given her their time and knowledge like computers, prodding them back to the point if they became discursive. "I see you are single-minded," one had rebuked her gently when she had let him know, with a little tap of her foot, that the excavations at Herodian were all very well—yes, Herod deserved to be counted among the great engineer-architect kings—but it was his design of Masada that interested her. And if he could shut up about Herodian . . . "Well, Miss Green, here is the model of Herod's palace on the north face of Masada." Reconstruction was difficult because the Zealots—*nu*, they were primitives in their own time, fundamentalists. They had no respect for palaces. What they wanted from Masada was its position, its apparent invulnerability. They didn't give a hoot for its Roman baths; they camped in the dining halls. You could say they were hippies: very pious, warrior hippies.

He said, "If you want to understand the Zealots talk to the hard-core of the Gush Emunim. Talk to Rabbi Levinger."

And Kahane? she'd asked.

"Don't say that name!" He had slapped his hands over his ears.

Could the Zealots have been influenced by the followers of Jesus? she'd wondered. "Could they have expected to be saved by a Second Coming? It was a fashionable idea then."

"*Nu*—fashionable then, fashionable now."

The man opposite, without lowering his newspaper, turned a page. Danielle drained her cup. One-two-three. She was able to walk steadily toward him.

"Excuse me."

The newspaper came down. It was just a face. Sixty-five years

old? Seventy? The mouth, the chin—she could not tell; you always look at the eyes: she'd looked at an eye-mask. The hands?
The ears? They were similar.

"Would you tell me the time, please?" Her voice was husky.

He held out his arm for her to read from his watch.

"Thank you."

He nodded.

Bennie was seated on the Savion's terrace, chewing a leaf and
spitting bits of it onto the marble paving. He stood up and put
his arm around her shoulder. The whiff of his kid jacket and his
own body smell, something like apples and sweat, made her
breathe deeply as if she were sighing. Bennie grinned. "Better?"

"Yes."

"I realized: Danielle is getting her period."

She thought: What's the use of arguing?

"Are you constipated?" he added, solicitously.

"Bennie!"

"No—listen: I wanna look after you."

He was charming with Alice, held her hands between his, kissed
her three times when taking leave. Alice's telephone had been
out of order, again, and they had called in for a few minutes only
so Danielle could let Alice know her new address and that she
would be out of town for a week.

"You mind that road," Alice said. "There have been a lot of
deaths on it."

Bennie did not seem to notice the gas stench, or Alice's furniture. When they got downstairs he said, "She's wonderful. I want
to buy her a present. What can I buy her?"

"Dinner?"

"Maybe she'd like a trip."

"Don't be silly."

"Jesus, you're a tight-fisted bitch. You've got a quarter million
bucks and you won't buy your grandmother—"

"She's *not* my grandmother. Nor have I got a quarter of a million dollars: I've got eighty thousand dollars' worth of debts."

Bennie was rambling on, half to himself: "She'd love New
York. She could stay with my *bubeh*. That's it. Alice should
spend Passover in Manhattan. Danielle, will you write that down
for me? Tickets for Alice. Just make a note."

They were walking back up the steepest part of Gaza Road. There was a cool gray sunset, the color, in music, of an oboe's voice. She stopped, took out her notebook and wrote the first line of a limerick:

A young man from Israel called Bennie

"You'd make a good secretary," he said.

She nodded: "penny" would end the second line; for the final rhyme, "one too many." Perhaps he'll have a heart attack, she thought, and gave him a smile. He was complaining, now, about Passover in Jerusalem.

"'This isn't kosher. That isn't kosher.' Have you noticed the way the women whine? 'You can't buy whiskey—it isn't kosher-for-Pesah.' There's none of that crap in Tel Aviv."

Danielle said quietly, "The Judas trees will be in bloom by the time we get back to Jerusalem. They have purple flowers. For blood."

"Blood makes me faint." He meant it to sound offensive—that women, being monthly bleeders . . .

She felt manic. "You'll enjoy directing the suicide scene," she replied. "You know, it happened at this time of year, in the spring. Passover. Easter. The blood of the lamb. The pagan spring festivals, with blood libations for the crops and the Mother Goddess. Yum-yum-yum."

"Danielle! Stop teasing me." Between the fingers clutching his head a dark tendril of hair escaped.

They stopped walking and looked at each other. Danielle thought, Why are we clawing at each other like children? What are we trying to rip away? "Isn't it a lovely evening?" she said.

A group of Rehavia shops had reopened for late trading; their neon and yellow electric lights seemed to suck up what was left of the day, hastening a duplicitous twilight. Danielle could not be sure whom she had seen—then: "Hello Marilyn."

So La Pucelle has dressed up today as a Russian peasant girl, Danielle thought. Marilyn was wearing a brightly printed skirt, thick maroon stockings, and a little wicker basket. Her hair was clean.

"Why, Danielle." Smiling, pleased, she was very pretty. She looked ready to drop a curtsey to Bennie. "Yes, I've heard about Bennie." Graceful switch of the peasant basket to left arm so she could shake Bennie's hand. "I'm Richard Trembole's sister."

When she was out of earshot Bennie exploded. "It isn't true! Sugar Tits turned religious."

"Sugar Tits?"

"You bet. Raphael told me." Bennie hmmned. "They say she found her brother's body. Dead a week. Poor kid."

Danielle realized the poor kid was Marilyn.

A few minutes later they were back at the Plaza. Bennie asked, "You want to eat with me?" saying, You don't want to, do you? Danielle did not. He said he could not bear one more meal in a hotel, but he had a great idea: he would call on Danielle's father—Marilyn let him in. "You know me, girl—I could sell the Brooklyn Bridge. By the time I'm through, your father will be pleading, 'Bennie, bring me my daughter.' What's the address again?"

"Have fun," she said as she was leaving. She had intended to sound careless but her throat strangled the words and they came out grim. She tried to recoup: "Don't forget: the car will be here at six-thirty. If you're still asleep . . ."

"Who—*me?*"

Marilyn won't go to bed with him, Danielle told herself as she groped the doorway for its light switch: Sugar Tits has changed. When I first saw her I sensed she'd been a hippie tart. A year from now she'll be rock-and-rolling with Baghwan in Oregon— but right now, Marilyn is a nun.

She flinched from the abrupt glare of a naked bulb. The African mask was smiling at her, its cowrie eyes puckered around their slits.

At half past eight that night she chewed a Mogadon Phil had given her, took her telephone off the hook, checked the front door lock, shut the bedroom door, set her alarm for 5:15, and lay down on the painter's hard bed waiting to fall into a sleep from which, she hoped, she would remember nothing.

TWENTY-
TWO

Her first thought, when the alarm rang, was of Marilyn and Bennie. She felt a doomed curiosity about them as if all night her thoughts had played on nothing else and that this question in her waking mind arose as a shadow from the underworld of sleep. It had a peculiar feeling of incompleteness, as if she had lost an aspect of herself.

But by six-twenty-five when she strode across King George Street to the hotel and saw in the dim light that Bennie was already waiting for her, hands in his pockets, lounging against the big white car, saying something that made the chauffeur bounce with laughter—when she saw that everything was in order, her spirits zipped.

"They were out," Bennie said; she returned his hug with gratitude.

"Now we've gotta wait. Wili's assistant let him down—didn't turn up this morning. Wili's up in my room having a piss and resorting his gear." Bennie had felt sorry for Wili; he had invited him to travel with them in the Mercedes. "Meet Akram."

As they shook hands a Morse code flashed between Danielle and Akram: the gap between his front teeth was even wider than hers. He was short and plump and his round brown face had tiny handles for ears, like a hippopotamus's.

"Best driver in Israel," Bennie said. Akram had another squeezing fit of laughter. A horseshoe was welded to the front grille of his car; at the back there was a brass eye with a blue iris, and a baby's white bootie dangled from the rear-view mirror.

"For lucky." The bootie was that of his youngest.

"Akram's been explaining to me how it is with the rich guys in Gaza," Bennie said. "Four wives, hundreds of girl friends—"

"Very gentleman," Akram said. "In Jericho also—"

Danielle thought, Trust Bennie to find a sex maniac as our driver. I'm going to have to listen to their bedroom adventures . . .

Bennie was saying, "You know Jericho was the town where merchants used to take their blonds in winter?" It seemed the playground atmosphere had been affected since '67, when the city moved from Jordan. "Where the hell is that photographer?"

Just then Wili came running toward them, balancing his tripod on one shoulder, his aluminum camera bag in his other hand. As his nose hit the cold morning air he stopped and sneezed.

"You had a call from Los Angeles—here."

Bennie read the slip of paper and swore in a language Danielle did not understand. "Give me two minutes," he said.

He strolled back to them, hands in pockets again, grinning. "Let's go."

In the interim Wili had fussed: loading his gear in the trunk— "Careful! And don't squash the lunch boxes,"—was Danielle feeling well? Princess, you're looking marvelous—isn't this exciting? Oh, he'd manage without that berk of an assistant.

"Bennie thought he was a Palestinian," Danielle said.

Wili looked grave. "I was relieved when he changed his mind about the job." He added that he was impressed with Kidron; *very.*

When Bennie said, "I'm shutting this," and closed the glass partition between Akram and Wili in the front seats and him and Danielle in the back, Wili said, "Of course. You two have important business," and he turned to help shut the glass. Bennie rolled his eyes. In their sealed compartment he said to Danielle, "What the hell did you tell him about me? He's been crawling up my ass since six o'clock this morning."

She made an impatient noise. "He's a parasite. Forget it. His work is excellent."

Bennie said, "It better be." Then, "Aw—c'mon, we're going to enjoy," and he rubbed an unpowered punch against her jaw.

He and Danielle had allowed six hours, by car, for finding locations for the Roman army's march from Jerusalem. The city in flames would be a studio job; men crucified outside its walls would also be filmed indoors. Danielle said, "You must get Research to check the shape of the crosses—I think they were like *X*s or capital *T*s. The Christian ones are inaccurate." Bennie said, "Yeah, yeah."

She had nothing much to do. The army's route was a production problem, one of finding several lengths of road with a bend at one end and long enough to fit the six hundred extras who would be filmed again and again on the different sections, marching first in one direction, then its opposite, to give the illusion of an iron-scaled serpent hunting the ragged Zealots. They had chosen an area called the Ephraim Hills, between Jerusalem and Lod, and drove back and forth, back and forth. Bennie tapped on the glass for Akram to stop; he and Wili would jump out; Bennie said, "Take this—take that."

Danielle moved to the front seat and she and Akram drove off to measure the distance, which she marked on the site sheets and collated with their road maps. Akram had a cache of oranges and chocolate bars and a thermos flask of coffee and pressed her to eat and drink at every stop. Bennie was not allowing time for any of them to have a proper lunch. At three o'clock he slapped one palm against the other and announced, "That's it. We've got it." He pulled Danielle from the car, pointed to Wili to take the front seat again, slammed his door and instantly appeared to sleep. The two others looked around at Danielle, asking, "What now?"

"Go to the Dead Sea, I guess."

Bennie, with his eyes closed, said: "Stop in Jerusalem first. I gotta check something at the hotel."

Wili thought he would faint.

What if Saeed and Jazzy were still in Kidron's suite, removing the bathroom paneling with the tools in the second camera bag?

Jazzy had been furious when Wili and Saeed had reported how badly their first meeting with Kidron had taken shape. Saeed was in tears; Jazzy had roared, "*Why* was he suspicious of you?" and Saeed had rocked, helpless, whispering, "He's more clever than we thought." Jazzy, drawing close to Saeed, had smelled the sweet rottenness of his breath—bad teeth, maybe, but also the stink of fear. It aroused in him an avid sensuality. "Leave us," he said to Wili.

When Jazzy came through he curtain he said, "Saeed and I will work inside the hotel. You are certain we have three days?" Wili had replied, "He told me: Bring gear for three days; maybe we'll be away five." Jazzy said, "That had better be true, for Kidron's sake."

The back of the car was warm and scented by Bennie's kid jacket. After a while Danielle dozed off, too. She awoke to a squeaking noise: Wili was scratching his fingernail on the glass partition. He put a finger to his lips and pointed at Bennie. She slid the glass open as silently as possible. A whisper:

"Princess, do you know why we are stopping in Jerusalem?"

She shook her head.

"I'm feeling queasy. I get carsick. I'd like to ask Akram to drop me first, at Damascus Gate, so I can go to a pharmacy." She nodded.

Wili added, "I'll come on down tomorrow morning. Meet you at the base of Masada at nine-thirty."

When they drew up at the Plaza Bennie opened his eyes, swung his head from side to side and asked, "Where's Jugnose? You eat him for afternoon tea, Danielle?"

"Very sick. Liking vomit," Akram said.

Wili had jumped from the car at some traffic lights; all his photographic equipment was still in the trunk.

Bennie said, "Jesus Christ! He starts screwing us around already?" Danielle objected that Wili was not interfering with their plans; their itinerary scheduled work on day two to begin at nine-thirty at Masada. Bennie said, "Oh, stuff it. I'm just going to check they changed my room so that Schultz bitch can't find me again."

He returned in a good mood. "They moved my stuff at seven this morning. Marguerita is going to spend a lot of money ringing room 1423 and getting no answer." He offered Danielle a handful of sunflower seeds.

"But she'll find you through the switchboard again."

Bennie went on munching the seeds: his front teeth cracked the shell, his tongue extracted the kernel, his breath blew the husk from his lips—all this in one deft flow of movement. Danielle tried to do it and got an enamel-shattering bite of broken shell and pulp. Bennie spat a husk on the ground.

"Uh-uh. I've wised the manager. The only people who need to know where I am, now know. I sent cables. Anyone who wants to speak to Bennie has gotta know his room number. The others get told he's not staying there." He had ordered Wili's box of extra camera equipment stored in the porter's lodge: "In case I get sick of the schmuck."

She asked what was amusing.

Bennie replied that she really didn't understand business, did she? She did not understand that the site work today had saved three days of work by a preproduction team—saved like fifteen thousand smacks, girl. And who had the day's photographs, in the trunk of the car? And who was going to get them out, right now, and drop them into a Kodak shop—Akram would know the closest one—to be developed? "I don't *need* Jugnose anymore," Bennie added. "Site photographs on Masada aren't essential." This evening he would calculate for her the number of minutes she had for the army scene. "And you can go away and play with them: SOLDIER ONE says; SOLDIER TWO says; SOLDIER THREE scratches his balls. Listen—" Business was taking opportunities; business was about winning.

Akram's eyes rolled in wonder as he helped Bennie break the lock on the camera bag with a screwdriver from the car's tool kit. Danielle watched passively.

She was thinking, This is how he became a millionaire: through theft, through snatching people's work for himself.

—He'll do the same to me, if he can.

When he returned from the Kodak shop Bennie said, "I might have a tantrum in the morning. If Juggy is late, or if he complains about me getting the films developed quick-smart . . . Danielle: you ever seen me have a tantrum?"

"Not a big one, Bennie."

"You'll enjoy it. Now, let's go to Jericho."

The sky was on fire as they swept along the southern perimeter of the Old City walls, past the Basilica of Agony's gaudy facade, and turned into the Jericho Road. Bennie lit a cigar. He had left the dividing window open and called, "Akram—you know this song?" He began to sing in Hebrew, a good baritone. Akram joined in, countertenor. Danielle caught the odd word—Jerusalem; Jericho; wall. They sang on and on, four verses marked off by a refrain. She glanced at Bennie's profile in silhouette; at the back of his head his centaur curls disappeared in the dark.

"I'll translate a bit for you," he said. "The chorus goes—um, 'Jerusalem of gold, of copper, and of light, Am I not a harp for all your songs?' and then it says, 'No one frequents the Temple Mount . . . and we can't go down to the Dead Sea by way of Jericho.' Then the last verse: 'We've come back . . . the shofar calls from the Temple Mount, dum, dum, dum, And we'll go again to the Dead Sea, By way of Jericho.' Terrific, huh? It was written just before the '67 war."

"It's nice."

"Nice! For Christ's sake—it should be the national anthem. Not that *Hatikva.* That sounds like the Polish national anthem: 'Poland is not dead yet.' But it soon will be. The hope. What's the good of hope? I tell you, Danielle: hope is the Jewish vice."

"Is that so?" Her jaw was so tense she could barely move it.

"What's wrong with you now?" Bennie demanded.

She muttered, "I'll tell you later."

"We're going to have dinner in Jericho," Bennie announced. "Akram knows a top place. We'll be there in twenty minutes. Terrific, hey?"

They had passed shabby Arab villages, Bethlehem, West Bank settlement towns, and were now winding slowly down through the Judean Hills. It was very dark, with not much traffic, but Akram was taking the descent cautiously; around a bend distant lights flashed and up close the red eyes of taillights. Bennie said, "Got your passport?" Vehicles going in both directions were being checked. Three had been ordered to the side of the road; a family stood rigid while soldiers with flashlights knelt on the backseat palpating the interior; a white bassinet with a pink bunny rug was being examined by hand and flashlight. A soldier, maybe nineteen years old, put his head in the window; they held out their passports but he did not bother to look, replied with one word to Bennie's question and jerked his head for Akram to drive on.

"What did he say?"

"Routine. They always say that."

—As if you'd know: when you skipped the country the PLO barely existed; the West Bank and Gaza had not been captured.

Bennie added, "If my father were driving on this road, he'd have a gun in the car."

She had opened her window to release the cigar smoke. Night

air still heated by the day blew in and she caught intermittently the almost imperceptible breath of the desert. They had already passed a sign saying they were now at sea level; the car continued downward, they were a submarine on wheels diving into warm, dense stillness. The lights of Jericho glittered, disappeared, flitted once more from the depths below. Then the groves of the city, sweet Jericho, rose up and flooded the car.

"Cop that," Bennie said. He opened his window and flicked his cigar into the dark.

Orange blossom and balsam; a swooning fragrance. You knew why Cleopatra had asked for Jericho from Anthony as a love-gift, Danielle thought. It smelt lazy and voluptuous. The other sinful cities of the plains, Sodom and Gomorrah to the south, had been swallowed, but Jericho . . .

It was seedy. There were fruit peelings in the streets, frightful plastic junk for sale in grime-fronted shops, goat droppings, 1958 Chevrolets with leopard-patterned seatcovers and raccoon tails on their antennae.

Only one palace, of the Umayyads, remained—a ruin now, Akram said. The ancient city was a mound of earth—there, on the right, that hump; perhaps they couldn't see it in the dark. Soldiers lounged against an armored car in the square. If the Gush Emumin are around, she was thinking, their presence is discreet—even though, being committed to making Biblical arguments for possession, they ought surely be staking a claim here?

Bennie trod softly through the perfumed night; so did she. Akram, however, was at home. He had relations here—well, not many left, now. He gestured vaguely to the east. Their family orchards and fields were close by; tomorrow, or when Mr. Bennie liked, they would go and pick fruit. But now they would have the best food, prepared by his friend: everything for their pleasure.

We are standing fathoms below the sea, not wet; we are surrounded by desert—and a magical fecundity. She was feeling dreamy from the decision she had taken—or rather, which had taken her, while in the parking lot of the Plaza she had watched Bennie break open and steal from Wili's camera bag. The question was, When?

It was an excellent meal Akram ordered for them. The dishes were like those of East Jerusalem but each was prepared with a delicacy of touch with the spices on the chicken and lamb and in the combination of herbs in the salads that lifted it—the table with rose-patterned oilcloth cover, the aluminum cutlery, the thick unstemmed glasses from which they drank wine—lifted it all to a different plane.

Although it was chilly outside, Bennie liked her idea that they should move to the terrace for coffee. The owner joined them for a while, bringing a bottle of aniseed liqueur. On the house—would they not honor him? Madame would perhaps like water with hers? Ladies sometimes did. He spoke to them as if they were royalty and he was used to the whims of princes. A cigar . . . ? If Mr. Kidron insisted, but . . . He made a gesture to one of the boy waiters who had served them using only their right hands, their left arms held immobile across their chests. The boy returned with a basket of oranges, grapefruit, and pomelos. Please: for their journey tomorrow.

He and Akram withdrew, leaving the bottle of arak on the table. Danielle waited until the coffee waiter had gone, too. They were alone on the terrace beneath a pergola heavy with bougainvillea; small insects swarmed to the light above and somewhere outside a goat bleated.

She said, "I'm not going to argue with you about what you did today. I just want to make something clear."

The legs of their chairs grated backward at almost the same moment. Bennie stood still; erect, but not tense. "Don't close your fist," he said. "You'll hurt yourself." The blow knocked his head ninety degrees.

She sat down again carefully; under the table she shook her hand to dissipate the sting.

Bennie thought, She's not angry because I took Wili's films. That's her excuse, the self-righteous bitch. She's mad because I had Marilyn last night. What Danielle still wants is to get laid.

She saw pleasure in his eyes.

—I've made a fool of myself.

"More arak?"

"Thanks. Just a bit."

He winced as he took a mouthful, excused himself, and went out to the pavement to spit.

"I didn't mean to cut you."

"That's okay." He grinned. "*Yesh Ge'vul,* huh? Like the son of that friend of yours."

"*Yesh Ge'vul.*"

"You know, Danielle, your Hebrew is getting better. The accent is good . . . Now, listen: I've got us top-floor rooms at the Moriah Hotel. I'm getting up at dawn to see the sunrise over the Dead Sea. I'll work on the march scenes for you as soon as we book in."

He's let me off the hook, she realized.

When Akram rejoined them at the table she was explaining her idea for juxtaposing the opening scene—maybe behind the credits—of the Mediterranean waves with an image of the Dead Sea's stillness. "To me they make together metaphors about life and death, and how the soul is balanced between them. But I've no hope of getting that across unless . . ."

Bennie, lounging in his chair, was staring at her with eyebrows raised. She sat with her head bowed, fiddling with spoons and crumbs on the oilcloth, talking as if to herself.

". . . because it's ungraspable," she was saying. "Water is—"

"You bet," Bennie said. "C'mon. I'll pay the check and we'll go."

TWENTY-
THREE

━━

While they waited, he asked, "Am
I going to make it? Will I get there?"

There was the thirty big ones he needed, in his hand, all his
own, to invest as he wished, diversify: energy resources—they
were nonrenewable, so the price could only go up; new tech—if
you got onto the right buzz on that. Look at Wang, a Chinaman,
one of the richest guys in the world, now. The trouble with
movies: you could put your heart and soul in them, for zero return. Movies were *fashion*. Flavor-of-the-month. He was telling
her: he could lose not just his pants but his balls as well, on
this one.

He was haunted by the fear of having arrived too late in the
field, "Like Israel," he said. "If Jews had come here a century
earlier they could have done what they liked to the local inhabitants—killed 'em all, like you did in Australia, and nobody
would have sneezed." What's Israel now? "A pariah, for doing
the same thing everyone else did, but a bit too late." After a
while he added, "The movies need a new golden age. But the
home-video industry might save me. What's going to happen to
me, girl?"

"You'll make it," she said, and wondered, Why do women
nurse men?

It was still dark on his balcony; directly opposite them a denser blackness gaining in volume marked the Mountains of Moab. Had Moses stood there, gazing across at the land on which he, of the Desert Generation, would never be allowed to set foot? Bennie wanted to know. "Or maybe they murdered him, like Freud said, because his Law was too harsh?"

"Maybe. Moses was a murderer himself. Maybe he had to pay for it, in the end." Danielle sighed: dawn was taking its time in coming. But now, at last, there was a sucking-down of night, the sky became paler, paler, and then—just there along the mountain ridge, its color-of-nothing changed to a line of pink. There were no clouds, not a wisp of something more substantial for the light to play upon. Pinkness seeped upward into air; a momentary breeze lifted the stench of sulphur from mineral baths further along the shore; there was not one bird song, all around was silence, except for the low metallic churning of a generator below the hotel's grounds. A bit of greenery, some grass, and a few dispirited-looking date palms grew in the garden below but apart from that there was nothing to see other than desert encircling a jewel. The Dead Sea.

They were both disappointed. They had expected some brassy blare of noise or light—but what was it? Placid, soundless. "Just a throb from out there in the universe, brushing against the earth," she said.

He peeled another orange and spat the seeds over the balcony. "You know what? We should have stayed in our rooms with the blackout curtains shut until eight o'clock and then—Wow! That would have been the way to see it, first time. The full bedazzle. We can't film this crap—what did it take?"

"Twenty-five minutes."

"Ter-riffic. We got one hundred and twenty minutes and the goddamn sunrise here takes twenty-five."

She said a good cameraman would give the effect in ten seconds.

"Yeah, but people will *know*. My parents will know."

He wove his head discontentedly. As they went in from the balcony he paused to shake his fist at the sky. "Yahweh—you're an *alter kocker*. Hey, you know Yiddish, Danielle? I only enjoy swearing in Yiddish. Listen to this." While he made a speech in gibberish she thought, He makes me feel three hundred years old. And defeated. And timid. How many women in L.A. dream of earning "thirty big ones" at a hit? Women can't think like that—there is not one on the planet with a permit for such bold-ness. And yet . . .

His daring was like a spell; sometimes she thought, I'd give an arm and a leg to be able to think like you, Bennie. She won-dered if there was anything about her that he valued. Her pro-fessional skills seemed to her like parlor tricks.

In the dining room he said, "You're kinda mystical—this white cheese is terrific—aren't you?" Take more capsicum rings—the Israeli breakfast is the best in the world—he meant, well, he was a mystic, himself.

Now tell me you write poetry, she thought. Breakfast, the out-side world, was an antidote to infatuation.

"I used to write poetry when I was a little kid. I was real dreamy." Bennie remembered how he had driven his father crazy: he was working sixteen hours a day then, driving, to pay off the truck. He'd say, "Look at the boy! We've got a violinist on our hands. A rabbi!"

"When did you stop being dreamy?" she asked.

"When I got beaten up at school."—In the next village there were tough kids, blacks, who came over to the same school: illiterate parents. My mother used to drag me to school. As soon as she went they'd say, "Hello, Soap. Your grandmother was made into soap."

Aloud he said, "Hey! Did you see that? You know who the man in the sunglasses is? I'll be back."

The man returned with Bennie; he was pleased to meet Dan-ielle—he had not yet seen . . . what was it that had won the screen-writing award at Cannes last year? But, naturally, he had heard. And *Eleazar* was a . . . challenge. For a writer. And for the director, of course.

He had soft, pink hands and soft, greedy eyes; reputedly, one of the richest men in the movie industry. Bennie would hire his studios, his technicians, his secretarial staff, his carpenters, for *Eleazar*.

Were they going to the mineral baths? They should take the opportunity. He was here for his wife's arthritis—

"*Megabucks,*" Bennie said when he had left them. "*He* diversi-fied in the sixties." They watched his slow progress from the breakfast room. His wife's expression had the patience of a broken-winded horse being led out to graze, but her red fists on the walking apparatus belonged to a strangler. A lifetime of anger in those hands, Danielle thought; there she was—smiling at him still, apologizing for her inadequacy.

"I'll never get married," Bennie said.

Somehow, they simply forgot about Wili.

It was so quiet here, so perfectly still, so slow, hot, and deep. When they went outside at eight-thirty and looked up at the brown-pink mountains and the high bright sky, strolled across the desert highway, clambered up hillocks of mineral waste, followed crevices, and then sat down, distant enough from the resort complex to be out of range of the noise of its generators— when they rested there, with a view over the sea, they felt the air itself was sedative and healing. Yet this, Danielle was thinking, was the landscape that to the eyes of early pilgrims was a vision of hell. Here was its image, this deepest gutter in the earth. The snow of Mount Hermon flowed along the Jordan for rebirth, snowy-white, but in pillars of salt down here. Salt statues formed a submarine landscape that from a distance tricked vision, looking as if the surface of the sea had bucked into white waves. It was motionless. The eye argued with the mind, gave up, shifted, and rested on the hills all around. They were twisted into fantastic shapes, like cooled metal, like the residue from experiments—as if this valley were an abandoned laboratory and they should tiptoe, in case the alchemist was still on the premises, hiding.

They had stopped chattering.

The pulse seems to drop, she was thinking, the heart to beat more slowly; there is an invisible presence at work in this dense, lifeless place, something the body registers at a level too subtle for thought. A lid closes; you breathe differently in the deep.

Bennie wanted to shout. He wanted to yell and throw stones; his feet wanted to kick into the hump of minerals in front of the one on which he was sitting. He prodded it with his toe; tried again. None of it crumbled; it was seared hard.

"I still fast on Yom Kippur. Sometimes. Well, I never smoke. I didn't have a cigar last Yom Kippur.

"I wanted to go to yeshiva. I grew my hair long so I could twist the sides into *peot*. My father said I looked like a girl. In the photograph of my grandfather he wore *peot* to his shoulders.

"At the beginning of the day of Simchas Torah I danced all night with the older men; I took the crowned bride in my arms—

they allowed me to hold her! And I danced till I was giddy, singing, 'My joy is the Torah!' "

—I wish I *had* done that.

" 'How I love thy law; it is my meditation all the day. How
sweet are thy words—sweeter than honey to my mouth.' You see?
I can still remember—"

"Want a cigar?" Bennie added. "Here—I got some little ones,
panatellas. Girls usually like 'em."

"I don't smoke."

"So have an experience, Danielle. You're too conservative.
I'm going to have a joint later, on Masada. I'll see it better if I'm
stoned. You like hash?"

"About twenty years ago I did."

The cigar tasted disgusting. Bennie was watching her, eager—
no, she realized, anxious—that she should continue.

"You make me feel like a . . ."

A what? There was acute curiosity in his face.

—An old woman. And *hymen intacta.* I'm disintegrating, she
thought. You seem to know my weakest points. You've been
bullying me from the moment you arrived and I'm cooperating:
because until this film is finished I'm your prisoner. "A *nudnik.*"

"A *nudnik!* She speaks Yiddish already. You're holding it
wrong. Here, like this." He adjusted the smoldering turd between her fingers.

You have gentle hands, she was thinking. Even when you've
been in a temper, if you've touched me your hands have felt
tender, as if they remembered something that the rest of you has
forgotten . . . This place is as sterile as my life now that Katherine has left home. How is it possible, after eighteen years of
standing on my own, that I feel like a shattered vessel . . . ?

"You're doing real good," Bennie said. "I'll give you a Monte
Cristo tonight."

. . . now I'm one step away from the top? I feel dead. I was
in a fever when I first arrived, when I was sure he would welcome me. Now I feel as I used to when I was eight years old,
and could write, and he wouldn't answer my letters. I'd look
twenty times in the mailbox. It was like staring into an empty
tunnel. One day I thought: I'm never going to feel like this when
I'm grown up. That was how I got through Patrick's death:
howled for three days, then got on with life. You can survive, if
you're armored. Bonny was never armored enough—she just

sounded as if she was. I was her comforter, her protector, from when I was a child. Then I was Katherine's protector. I wish someone would be mine. Patrick was, for a while. But since then . . . James!

She laughed. "I was thinking," she said, "about my last boy-friend. He had me called out of a script conference one day so he could complain there was no toothpaste in the house."

"Yeah?"

"Yeah. I told him to make arrangements to live in a house where there was toothpaste. Before I got home from work that evening."

That figures, Bennie thought.

"Speaking of work . . ."

He helped her to her feet. "Let's ask Akram to take us to S'dom. We ought to have a look at the terrain from ground level before we go up." Siting the Roman camp, he said, was going to give him his first nervous breakdown. However, while they had been sitting there, he had figured out a way for driving the battering ram. "We'll have a tank engine inside the tower thing. I can buy one locally."

She returned his sardonic grin.

As they recrossed the desert road Danielle looked at her watch, saw it was nine-thirty, and frowned. "We've kept Akram waiting for half an hour."

Bennie deliberately slowed his pace. "Akram is getting one hundred and twenty a day, in green, and he can order anything he likes at the hotel on my account." At this moment he would be eating Black Forest cake and ogling the dames on the beach. "Akram's laughing," Bennie said.

Their emergency meeting that evening lasted almost to midnight. Jazzy was enraged. He and Saeed had gone to the room at seven-fifteen, before there were maids in the corridor. There was no DO NOT DISTURB sign on the door. The door was open but the lock had not been fixed by Wili in the way Jazzy had taught him—the door was just open, and the room was empty. No tools! Nothing. No sign of Kidron's clothes, no sign of Kidron except for cigar butts, a wine bottle, and an unmade bed. There were a woman's hairpins in the bathroom: did Wili suppose they could remove the paneling with hairpins?

What was Kidron playing at? Why had he suddenly changed rooms? Who was the woman he'd had there last night?

Do you know what it feels like, Wili, to be walking around with plastic strapped under your shirt? It feels like running across glass holding egg white in your hands.

What was making Kidron suspicious? He trusts the Green woman; he trusts you, Wili. *Doesn't he?*

As they were leaving, a waitress carrying a breakfast tray along the corridor had seen them. If the job had been done it would not have mattered: he and Saeed would be in Egypt when it was set to go *bang!* that night. What exactly had the woman from Los Angeles said? "Tell him I'll bust his balls?"!

How do you know she was telephoning from Los Angeles? Because she said so! Wili, the call came through the switchboard: she could have been ringing from inside Israel. Wili, they have taken your camera box. If they open it and see what's inside . . .

Jazzy said, "You came sobbing to me in London when you got out of jail because an Englishman had slapped your face five years before. Who fixed the brakes on his car? Who took the risk? Me and Saeed—you should kiss his feet. We risked our lives for your honor."

"I didn't ask you to kill him," Wili whispered. "I asked you to give him a fright."

"We did. For your honor we gave him a big fright. I'd like to give that Kidron a big fright for what he's done to us." Jazzy was thinking: the boys are becoming nervous. We've missed another opportunity. It was an error to believe Wili would be useful. I'll have to destroy the photographs he's taken. I'll have to rethink . . . "I'm going for a walk," Jazzy said. "All of you stay here."

He returned with a bag of the cakes called bird's nests; they frothed another *finyan* of coffee. Wili held Jazzy's hands. He did not dare to confess what the princess had said before they left the hotel that morning: that Kidron knew Saeed was a Palestinian. Because if Jazzy heard that, he would—

"You'll never know how grateful to you I am," Wili said. "For this . . . this . . ."

Weep now, Jazzy thought, for after tomorrow you will not weep again.

"I like a man who can cry," he said. "It's a sign of a good heart."

The landscape of sculptures soared against a sky of cyan-blue. The convulsed shapes changed from moment to moment, as did the colors: pink, like Bennie's kid jacket; white; every beige; lion-skin—the lion dozing in sunshine, lying in shade, or dull brown by moonlight. They gazed up at walls that contained them like ants fallen into a bowl.

"Mrs. Lot," Akram said.

The dirty white pillar, standing separate from and taller than others, was hundreds of feet high. Its peak tipped slightly forward—a head bent to utter a piece of advice.

As they walked to the car Danielle began to turn for a last look. Bennie seized her and clapped his hands over her eyes. "Just in case!"

They had been playing all morning, touching, feeding each other pieces of orange, laughing inordinately at one another's bad jokes. Without effort, some sort of camaraderie had been established. For a while, Danielle thought.

Sodom was a grassy knoll. What else? It must have been an oasis, like Jericho, once.

Bennie dashed up it ahead of her and ran about shouting, bending down, standing, waving. He had a fistful of wildflowers. When they drove back into the desert and again passed the outcrop named Lot's Wife the red poppies in their laps asked for silence in honor of a massacre.

They arrived at the base of Masada in the early afternoon. As the Mercedes' engine gave a final purr Bennie turned to Danielle and let his jaw drop.

"Know what?"

She nodded: Wili.

"Listen—if he's still here I'll say—um, quick, Danielle: you write the stories. You have to be a better liar than I am. What happened?"

"We changed the schedule."

"That's it? We changed the schedule?"

"And you fell on the camera bag, while holding a screwdriver."

"No! That's a lie! It attacked me. I fought it off with a screwdriver. Like that bloody hotel door in Rome. Did I tell you about that? My bathroom door in the Rome Hilton up and belts me across the eyebrow. You saw: I had three stitches."

"I saw sticking plaster."

"I needed stitches."

"I need lunch."

Wili was sitting in the cafeteria at the base of the mountain. Bennie saw him before he caught sight of them and whispered, "There's a saying in Hebrew . . . oh, oh, he's seen us." She watched his lazy stroll across the room, hands in the pockets of his loose raw-silk trousers. Then he was stroking Wili's back, calming him down. Wili's limbs jerked; he began to smile, then laugh, pleating the top of his nose.

Bennie was grinning when he returned to the cafeteria line. "All fixed. Juggy thought his other bunch of cameras had been stolen from the Plaza. He was so relieved when I explained they're stored in the porter's lodge that I told him the truth about busting his number-one bag. Happy ending."

They shuffled along the line holding their orange plastic trays. Bennie said, "You watch what Akram takes to eat, and take the same." She wanted to know why. "Do like I tell you: take the same salads as Akram."

When the four of them were seated at a Formica table Danielle asked Akram why she had to eat a yogurt salad with her humous. His tiny hippopotamus ears moved up and down in a fit of hilarity all their own.

"Farts!" he bellowed. "Stops farts."

Bennie almost tipped over his chair. "Akram—I'm going to put you in the movie. Listen, Danielle: you write a comedy scene for Akram. You want to be a Jew, or a Roman?"

"Who won?" Akram said.

"Who won! Danielle—don't write his lines. Just leave a blank page marked AKRAM."

They all felt slightly manic. Wili had eaten lunch and was raving about a new cure for carsickness, and the car he had hired—a tin Lizzy, but it had got him here all right, although he had to admit he had not arrived until ten A.M. and had hunted all over the mountaintop for them. He was fiddling with his traveling knife-fork-and-spoon set. Bennie said, "Give me! I've gotta have," and snatched it from Wili's hands to eat with himself. Wili insisted on getting the coffee: they must be exhausted if they had been working since before dawn. And he would just make a phone call—about his other camera bag.

He came rushing back to the table: *terribly* sorry—but the fact was the man he was talking to at the Plaza did not understand English very well and, since the bag was stored in Bennie's name . . . *Would* Bennie mind explaining that a young man would come to collect the bag from the porter's lodge?

When Bennie sauntered off, Wili leaned forward and said vehemently, "Princess, that Bennie Kidron is a real gentleman." She nodded gravely; Akram said, "Very gentleman." He was thinking about the lady he had driven home for Mr. Bennie two nights ago and of having noticed, this morning, that Mr. Bennie was feeding this other lady, his secretary, pieces of orange by hand, slipping them into her mouth. She had hit him across the face, in Jericho. Maher had seen her do it and they had all watched to see what would happen next. But Mr. Bennie had been most dignified and today he was courting the secretary in an ambiguous and playful fashion. He had picked red flowers for her, then thrown them into her lap as if he meant nothing.

Wili had to travel up in the funicular, because of the weight of his gear—"and the ticker, Princess. A few problems with my ticker." No—he wasn't going to keel over, and he didn't need the chauffeur (he said the word disdainfully, let it drop from his lips as fingers drop something soiled). He would carry everything himself—damn that Greek or whatever-he-was—but he could not risk the Serpent Path. She and Bennie ought to be careful, too: it was steeper than it looked from ground level and there had been some nasty accidents. One of the *Vogue* models had broken her ankle, needed plastic surgery on her face, and was useless for photographic work after that. They'd had to fly in another girl from London: she had no suntan and the makeup they put on her rubbed off on the clothes. And then it rained. An unbelievable downpour, worse than the tropics. Everything washed away. The camel bolted. Oh, yes—I know Masada, Princess. Did she have a walking stick? And gloves? Parts of that track had to be taken on all fours.

"For Christ's sake, Wili, there are handrails. I can see them from here."

All the same. Where had Bennie gone?

"He's smoking a joint."

I shouldn't have said that. Wili is more than a sycophant; he's almost spying on Bennie, she thought.

"I could get him some coke in Tel Aviv."

"Tell him."

Wili tipped a finger to the brim of the panama hat he was wearing today. "See you up there in an hour," he said.

The path was steep, a walk-and-scramble of forty minutes for somebody fit. Bennie was not. When he moaned for the third time, "We've been climbing for five hours. I'm dying," she began to note the minutes between each of his collapses: they averaged seven. She jerked him to his feet again, but when they reached the first really sharp incline he fell down and cringed with both arms over his head.

A group of young Israelis in khaki shorts and climbing boots was behind them. They halted and stared at Bennie, jabbering to each other and Danielle in Hebrew. They seemed to be offering to carry him, and could have, by the look of them: through rough shirts their bodies glowed. Bennie kept silent while Danielle repeated, "No. Please don't worry." One of the girls spoke a little English: "He is what?" she asked. "He's American," Danielle said. They had another conversation about that, then, unwillingly, moved off. When they were well away Bennie peeped from between his knees and giggled. She gave him a sharp prod in the rump with her sandshoe.

"Stand up! And behave yourself."

He stood up, raised his arms to the sky, arched his neck backward, and took a bite of the sun. Then he started off at a run, calling over his shoulder, "Beatcha!"

On the worst section, directly below the summit, Bennie jumped on the handrail and went sliding back down it yelling, "Wo-wo!" Alongside the rails there was a drop of about three hundred feet, but his arms held horizontal somehow balanced his slide and at the end of the rail he landed on his feet.

"You see me fly?" he yelled up at her. "It's fantastic! Danielle—try it."

She trudged on.

At the top of the path she entered the territory of birds, glossy black projectiles that threw loops of air around her ears then darted into crevices in the mountainside.

It was a pleasure to see Wili again when, emerging through what was left of the casemate wall, she met his black eyes, round as buttons from watching Bennie. "I think we should wait until he's safely through," Wili said, but Danielle was by now too angry and tired to care. In a tone that allowed no argument she replied, "You and I are working."

She wanted to see Herod's Palace first. Then the excavated granary. Third, the Roman camp on the western side of the mountain. Fourth, the synagogue. Fifth, the reservoir.

It was another hour before her temper had abated enough for her to be able to see anything properly. Then it seemed too late: ruined, the first razor-edge of delirium blunted. Her senses felt as sodden as cardboard and she thought, This is what Bennie did to me in Jerusalem.

Wili was starting to fuss about the light and the need to catch the last funicular ride down. But he had done well, and to work again with an old-fashioned professional had relieved some of her anxiety. Neither of them had seen Bennie for almost two hours. She told Wili to give up trying for more detailed shots of the synagogue and do what he could—given the lighting problems—with the casemate wall.

"I have to be alone for a while," she said. They agreed to meet in the upper palace in twenty minutes and go down together in the funicular. Bennie, no doubt, would want to walk down the Serpent Path in the dark: she had seen a notice stating that to do so was illegal.

Sunset was on its way and her shadow as she marched off toward the bow of the galleon-shaped mountaintop stretched out like a numerical progression, thin and limitless.

Herod had hired good architects: you have to admire the old brute, she was thinking.

The palace was sited to make the best of the climate and the view, which was staggering—like standing in the bow of a ship in a gale. Below was an ocean of seething rock; the cliff face beneath the palace's lower levels was unscalable. Someone had told her that men from the Israeli army had tried to climb it; she could not remember if they had succeeded or not, but that was irrelevant: they were not risking boiling oil poured from above while a tyrant laughed. Had he experimented with that test of his fortress on some of the more agile slaves? She could bet on it. The atmosphere was beginning to seep through to her now, Herod's fear of the beautiful, greedy Egyptian queen disturbing his sleep, in Jerusalem, and driving him to this crazy undertaking. At ground level in summer shade temperatures reached one hundred and thirty degrees. He must have killed thousands, making them climb with slabs of marble for his dining room walls.

She rotated her shoulder blades, loosening up now, sensing Eleazar's disgust when, exhausted from flight and the horror that lay behind him in the capital, he had scrambled on board this lifeboat and found it set up as a seraglio—gold paneling, marble baths . . . The nation was in ruins, irreparable; in Rome the Emperor was thirsty for the last trickle of its blood: "Take Masada, my dear Flavius, and the East will become calm." When that Emperor destroyed Jerusalem, he crucified so many hundreds of Jews he ran out of wood, and those not sold as slaves he had torn in the circus.

—And this is what Eleazar found: a mosaic-walled steambath.

And yet . . . They could survive here! Herod had planned well in his terror of Cleopatra. There was food for all—and weapons enough for a year or more. They had only to hold off the siege until summer when the tremendous impress of the sun would drive the Romans away. Yahweh must preserve them through another spring, into summer.

But He had not; He had forgotten to love them.

She remembered that armored units of the defense forces took their oath—"Masada shall not fall again!"—up here. Maybe where that figure . . .

A late-afternoon breeze buffeted his loose silk shirt. Bennie stood alone, close to the parapet of the upper palace, one arm extended. With the sun behind him his honey-colored skin looked darker. He was talking to something in the air—she couldn't make out what it might be—then she saw the way he held his hand steady, as if for a bird to alight on it. Maybe one of the blackbirds that nested beneath the casement. But Bennie was bracing himself for some larger creature—that was it! a falcon—he was seeing a hunting falcon return to him from the desert.

He turned slowly, smiling.

"Don't frighten him."

She waited.

Then, "Watch out, Danielle! He's getting bigger. Christ! It's turning into an eagle—he's going to rip my throat—!"

The parapet was only a couple of feet high but Bennie—thank God—was moving back from it. He rotated his hand so that now the palm faced upward, and he gazed at the invisible thing resting there.

"Look at it," he whispered. "It's pure white." He drew his eyes away from his hand and looked at her. "You turned it into a dove."

She did not dare touch him or speak again. How could he be hallucinating so wildly? Maybe the hash was particularly strong— or maybe he was pulling her leg. She felt mentally queasy.

"Would you like it?" he asked.

She nodded.

He walked toward her carefully, both hands cupped around the dove. "Promise you won't lose it," he said.

The evening breeze had vanished and there was silence. Around them drifted the seamless garment of the universe; the thread of it they knew, earth's sky, was transfiguring to gold.

Danielle walked backward, still holding her dove, then turned and ran.

Wili was thirty yards away, waving frantically.

When they reached the funicular landing the driver said, "You crazies! The last ride was fifteen minutes ago."

The kibbutznikim who ran the cafeteria grumbled and cursed but agreed to stay open long enough for them to drink coffee. The last tourist buses had gone and in the parking lot there were only the white Mercedes and Wili's red Alfa Sud. Danielle sat hunched over, inside herself. At length she said, "Bennie can't afford a drugs charge. He won't be able to make the movie here. If we tell them he's still up there . . ." Up there, alone, he could break his neck, or freeze. Once the sun went the temperature dropped abruptly. And there was no electric light.

Akram came in to the cafeteria, rolling his eyes. Danielle beckoned him away from the kibbutz people.

"Where is the hashish?" she whispered. "Is it in the car, or has Bennie got it with him?"

"*Hashish?*" Akram had no idea what she was talking about.

She said, "Akram, do you want to get paid?"

Akram took deep thought. "Very gentleman. I say, 'Please— sometimes soldiers come, make searches in motorcar.' Mr. Bennie very nice gentleman." There was a guard post on top of the mountain, he said; Bennie would not be alone.

They paid for their coffee and went outside to wait. The lights were switched off in the cafeteria, a jeep arrived to collect the staff. One of the kibbutznikim wandered over to the Mercedes.

"We're making a movie here," Danielle said. "We want to see how the place looks by night."

He stared at Wili, the inspection of a dog with its hackles rising, shrugged, and walked off.

By eight o'clock they were torpid with cold. The blazing desert sky had ceased to entrance them and its icy, spangled magnificence had begun to spin giddily, as if it would spiral them into itself and they would fall off the earth. Wili got out to take another look at the mountain.

"There's a light! He's coming down."

Danielle told Akram to switch on the Mercedes headlights and drive as close as he could to the base of the path. "You wait for him. He'll be here in fifteen minutes." She and Wili both sneezed; she was damned if she was going to catch pneumonia by hanging around any longer. Wili claimed he had a migraine coming on. She offered to drive, but he said he could manage.

As they got under way she closed her eyes and let out a sigh that felt as if she had been saving it for years. Wili patted her knee. He was driving carefully down the winding section of road, but when they reached the highway—hardly a highway by other standards, only one lane each way, unlit, without guardrails—he began to speed up.

"There's no rush now," she said.

"I've got to go to the lavatory."

She suggested he stop, but he did not want to; he wanted to get to the Moriah; he'd have an accident if he didn't.

"We'll have an accident if you don't—"

It was strange, watching the ground rear up, lit by the car's headlights, and to observe the jagged edges of stones galloping toward their faces in slow motion. Her body and Wili's sluiced from side to side, then there was the extraordinary flight, stars whirling beneath them, thunder, a terrific *crack!*—the sky turning slowly under their feet a second time. Another burst of thunder . . . Then nothing. They'd been killed.

TWENTY-FOUR

Death was ecstatic white-gold light.

She watched the overturned car, its wheels still spinning, and inhaled the pungent vapor of bubbling gasoline. Gallons of it spilt; were spilling.

"Wili!" she roared. "Wili—are you alive?"

She could not move very well, hanging upside down from a seatbelt. She seemed to be alone in the crushed cocoon. Wili had vanished.

She worked an arm loose and reached to where he had been; her hand met something hot and wet. She tried to grasp. "Wili!"

He screamed in reply.

"Are you alive?"

He did not seem to know.

"We've got to get out. The car is going to blow up. I smell the petrol."

"I can't," he murmured.

—We are going to be burned alive. He's unconscious again.

"Open your door, Wili!"

She jabbed her hand into the hot mess again—God knows what it is, his face? his guts?—and the pain brought him shuddering into consciousness. She held fast. Wili screamed and screamed. Then he faded once more. Danielle worked her other arm free and found a handle; it broke off as she wrenched. Maybe it was only the window handle. She felt again. This had to be the door handle. It had to open. Upside down, an astronaut, she used both hands to pry it slowly upward and pushed, pushed, gave her body to opening the door; the desert was holding it shut on the other side. One inch, two inches; a tigress energy empowered her. Six inches; ten. She could hear the metal breaking off the edges of the door as it grated over stones. She felt concerned about the petrol, but calm. She was calmly freeing her body.

Then she was free.

Tumbling out of the car head first, a rabbit breaking cover, she began stumbling and running, terrified. She squatted down at a distance of about fifteen yards and waited. Time went past so slowly it seemed to vanish. Then it did vanish. There was neither past nor future, but a permanent present. There was Is.

Akram was driving at seventy miles an hour when, rounding a bend, he saw the single headlight focused on the ground. The Mercedes overshot by a hundred yards; Danielle saw red eyes rushing back toward her. The silence squealed.

Time was back. She got up and ran forward, shouting at Bennie to stay away. Wili was dead and the car would explode any minute now. She tried to grab his clothes but he shoved her backward and, while Akram held her, crawled through the door she had opened. There was a lot of yelling. Akram let go of Danielle to help Bennie. She couldn't understand what they were saying so she wandered away again to escape the blast.

She felt sorry that Bennie was going to be killed.

—He gave me a dove, she thought.

She lay down, curved herself around its smooth elliptical form and went to sleep hearing them still shouting—people were always shouting here—in the distance.

TWENTY-FIVE

When they awoke the desert and blood were gone, washed away in the shower, and a sword of light split the room: they had not properly closed the blackout curtains; midday sun intruded.

Bennie and Danielle had gone to sleep around dawn. He woke first and turned on his side to watch her, a small-boned unconscious creature whose limbs, bruised navy and purple, lay limp on the other side of the bed. He had let go of everything—butted his head and shoulders through the door of the red car, untied Wili from the seatbelt, dragged him out, carried him to the Mercedes, steeled himself to the blood spreading over his trousers through their flight to the Be'er Sheva hospital, and then, in her room—

He'd helped her remove her shirt and jeans; blood crackled as the chrysalis of clothing broke open. The woman who stepped out came from temple rites; she'd smeared her belly and limbs with gore and her hair was wild from thrashing against the earth.

At the hospital they'd said: He won't die. A smashed arm, a shattered nose. He'll be okay.

You should see what a landmine does.

Or a hand grenade.

You should see shrapnel wounds. But—*nu*—more Israelis go this way; more are killed in car accidents than in all the wars—'48, '56, '67, '73 . . . Lebanon. If you work in a hospital you see what we really suffer from: enantiodromia.

From what?

We tear ourself apart.

But we'll fix your friend's face. Please—draw his nose, how it used to be. Like that! We make noses, not trunks. We'll make him a real nose . . . The arm will have to go. Good thing you knew to tourniquet it—but let me give you some advice: next time, loosen the tourniquet every twenty minutes. Don't feel bad about it—you saved his life with that tourniquet. He can get a prosthetic arm.

You believed the car was going to explode? It did! Seconds later?

You performed a mitzvah: the greatest.

Long life to you! Just put the woman to bed. Let her rest. Here's some cream for her bruises.

Long life!

They had arrived back at the Moriah at two in the morning: Danielle had said, "I want you to stay." An axe stood within her: in each eye he saw the glint from an edge of its double blades. I'm going to know you, and I'm going to change that expression on your face, Bennie had thought.

She was waking up, bruises blooming in tattoos on her thighs and hips and upper arm, a tiny cut on her chin from the desert flint she had fallen on. He picked up one of her hands and raised it to his lips: the smell of earth and blood was gone though there were still dark crescents under her fingernails.

She saw the sheen on his eyelids and came fully awake with one thought—not a thought: a state: she was in love. He was what she needed; he'd given her a dove, like the man in her dream.

"Yesterday, in the palace, you gave me a dove."

"I did?"

"Don't you remember?"

He did. Sometimes he could recall a trip. He'd practiced, back in the dawn of the seventies, when he and Raphael experimented with acid and mushrooms and everything else that you didn't have to put into your arm. Great movies: four great movies. They'd made *Running Hot* on nothing: none of them had any bread. Raphael had sold Marguerita's grandmother's diamonds and a rosewood chest, so they could hire the crane. The witch had nine lives—she'd been in the helicopter with Raphael but had escaped with a busted leg.

When I read the telegram from Brazil I felt like a husk, he remembered. I sat shiva for Raphael, and that bitch Marguerita had talked about money, about how much she'd get. On the praising day I smoked a joint for Raph, and we had a long conversation: he told me about Masada; he said I could go on alone but I had to make a *big* movie. He said, "Get rich, Bennie, get big. It's very small, inside a wooden box—but you won't mind it, if you've been big first." I've grossed twelve million in the past eighteen months.

He had done some research on Danielle before he'd hired her for *Eleazar*. She was fifth on his list, and the only woman, but it was the fact that she was a widow that had decided him. He'd thought, A widow on my side will be lucky, in case Marguerita . . .

—Maybe I've made a mistake.

He felt melancholy. If you were a hero, you were supposed to feel good.

—I'm not going to fall in love with her—she's terrible looking, well, she has beautiful hair and skin, and good legs: she ought to wear dresses, with those legs. She's got skin like Japanese women: like rose petals on the insides of the thighs. But she's a tough bitch. She haggled for a month over the percentage points. I was willing to give her three, but she screamed for five. I can't stand that woman Sarah she uses to do her contracts. Another JAP. They ganged up on me and Sam—Danielle sat at the back of the room looking like a girl frightened on her first date while that Sarah put on her glasses and said, "*Mister* Kidron . . ." And Danielle said, "Oh, Bennie, don't you see that I can't take less?" *Oh, Bennie.* What an act! Poor little girl. When they left Sam said, "We've been thugged. By a pair of dames."

—I ought to hire Sarah myself, to deal with Marguerita.

She's driving me crazy: I AM A THIEF, spray-painted on the Corniche, both sides. Ferdy couldn't sponge it off and we had to have the whole car repainted. So then she puts a rock through the windshield. She should be in jail. What did Marguerita do when we were starting out? She snorted coke and gave Raphael a hard time. She's a platinum nose.

"Bennie—?"

"Yes."

"Yesterday, when we were sitting looking at the sea—"

"I loved that. I loved being with you." And now I've saved a man's life. Not even a friend's. I can't stand that Wili: he's shifty and a crawler—but I saved his life. I was scared to death. Something said to me *do it. Just do it.* I thought, So I'm going to be burned to death, but I'll do it anyway. Danielle, you've been the instrument of my great mitzvah: if you hadn't tried to stop me, I wouldn't have had the guts. I would have stood back and waited for the car to blow.

"I'm in love with you."

"Do you fall in love with every guy you screw?"

"No."

—She's got crow's-feet around her eyes; but the skin on her body . . . I've never seen such—what was it? cruelty?—in a woman's face as last night. There's a mystery in what that made me feel, in seeing the real thing in someone else. Cruelty is not the word. It's the concentration of a subtle energy. Funny about her name: Daniela. "God is my judge." She probably doesn't know what it means in Hebrew. I'm definitely not going to fall in love with her. I spend too much money on dames already.

"I haven't fallen in love for years," she said.

"Neither have I. Falling in love is a mess."

—I fall in love at least every six months. Sam says if I'd get married I'd save ten grand a year. I spent forty-five thousand last year, at the Wilshire: he showed me the figures. That included what I bought in the flower shop. Sam says I must quit walking past the florist with them—get a headache; get a toothache. He says I'm pathological about buying them presents. He does what he can with offsets on the gift allowance. I won't tell him about the jacket I've ordered for Daniela. I won't tell her, either. It'll be a surprise, when we get back to Jerusalem.

"You're all bruised." He stroked her shoulder.

—Sam says I have an urge to adore women, but I resist it, so the whole thing becomes a game of winners and losers. What would he know? If you take a dame to the Wilshire she knows it's a contract: she won't give you herpes. She understands: the room, the Dom Perignon, mean it's a *deal*. A clean deal. What

would Sam know, married to Debbie for thirty-five years and
never looked sideways? First and only, for both of them. Grandchildren!—do I want children and grandchildren? Jesus—Sam and
his grandson go painting together. A great kid, a genius . . .
Danielle could be a grandmother herself: she's got an eighteen-
year-old daughter. I could screw both of them—like I did with
that crazy actress and her mother. They're all crazy. And JAPs
are the worst. Danielle's half-JAP. Even Wili picked that up—
called her "Princess." That's her—Jewish Australian Princess. I've
got to get out of bed—oh, oh, here we go.

"No. I don't want to," Danielle said.

"You're in love with me and you don't want to?"

"That's right."

"Why not?"

"Because you don't want to."

"*Motek*, take a look."

"It's what you're thinking that counts."

—Now she fancies she's reading my mind. I'm not going to
have a JAP mind reader rejecting me. And I do want to know
her again.

Bennie said, "Hey, let's have some sunshine. It's full of vitamins."

When he tore open the blackout curtains there was the dazzle
that they should have experienced yesterday. Light bouncing off
the sea below came roaring in, wrecking the room—flinging their
bloodied clothes on the floor, tossing wet towels over chairs,
mauling the bed. For an instant their eyes ached; the night lay
revealed. Then it was just sunshine. And time for room service.
It was five past noon.

While Bennie was ordering brunch Danielle went to the bathroom and examined her bruises. The wince of neon light made
them more livid: most of her right side was charcoal-colored, in
cabbage-rose whorls. She looked, she thought, like an eighteenth-
century image of the child of miscegeny. She felt ashamed of
herself. The joy of waking up, in love, seeing Bennie kissing her
hand, had been draining away while they spoke, and now it was
gone. Her body ached, she looked ridiculous, and she'd done
something unprofessional. She had promised herself again, after
smacking Bennie's face, that she would not have an affair with
him. He had not wanted to complicate the relationship either;
he'd made that clear the evening he arrived in Tel Aviv. But

there were so many levels of intention; suddenly the deep ones could arise and sweep those on the surface aside.

Going to bed together has given us extra reasons for hostility to each other, she thought. It's his fault I'm in this state. If he hadn't got stoned I would not have been in Wili's car . . .

She turned her back to the mirror and twisted her head over her shoulder to see how badly her backside was battered: it was hideous, as if she had gangrene. Then she turned and met a steady, cold gaze: a woman's eye was appraising her. Her demeanor was cool; it said, "Don't twist the truth. Of course it was not Bennie's fault you were in Wili's car. It was your choice. You may fool yourself, but you can't fool me."

They smiled at each other ruefully, sharing another recognition: she would be tormented in the days to come by memories of making love. It was something to do with female physiology, or perhaps with the act itself, that the man left part of his body within you.

"Hey, you look terrific," Bennie said when she came out. "The rainbow lady. Three days from now you'll be all green—how 'bout that? Green Danielle Green?"

The wit of a nine-year-old, she thought. "What did they call you at school?"

"Aw—something in Hebrew. I can't translate it."

"I hated primary school. I was the only girl there without a father, and the only kid whose mother worked."

"What at?"

Bonny had been styled a *vendeuse* in a shop in which all the clothes came from France. "It's in a part of Sydney that's like Rodeo Drive—Double Bay. Known as Double Pay. She earned— oh, ten pounds a week, plus clothes at eighty-percent discount. But she still wanted to live as if she had Arab servants." Danielle added, "She was very good-looking."

Bennie smiled: he got the picture—Mama laid it out, for old boys. They probably called by to give Danielle a grope in the afternoons, too, when Mama was in the dress shop and the kid was on her own, home from school. So she gets married at eighteen, to escape; widow at twenty . . . The legs came from the mother—he could practically see her: one of those blonds as haughty as a camel, Vaseline on her eyebrows. They lift your wallet if you blink. "I'll tell you what your mother used to look like, at your age."

When Danielle laughed her face was as delighted as a little kid's—that amazing gap! Mama should have had her teeth fixed. But she was a selfish bitch: wouldn't send the kid to an orthodontist, spent the money on cocktail dresses.

"I get it right?" he asked.

"Exactly."

—But only her nasty, beautiful side. Bonny came to fear her looks. She said to me, "No man will ever love *you* if you're beautiful. They'll only love the outside." She'd say, "Don't make my mistake." There was no chance of that. Unfortunately.

"C'mon, don't look sad. Come and sit on my knee. I promise—well, we couldn't anyway. The waiter will be here in five minutes."

They had dressed in bath towels. She perched, then relaxed against him.

"You know what we are?" Bennie said. "We're war orphans. And we know it. That's the difference between you and me, and everyone else. You know why I hate Israel? I tell you, I hate the place. It's a whole country full of losers who are kidding themselves, trying to believe it's all going to work out in the end. They go on believing in a personal God who looks after the Jews. If I weren't an optimist . . ."

His physical presence, his eyes so close they blurred into one, the rasp of his beard on her cheek, overwhelmed her and instead of trying to think, she nuzzled at him like a calf to its mother.

"Why are we making *Eleazar?*" she murmured.

"I dunno. Because I want to be rich. Because I think Ariel Sharon is going to take over the country . . ."

"Bennie!"

"No—listen—don't give me that left-wing crap. If there's a de Gaulle in Israel, if there's somebody who can stitch it together again, it's Sharon."

"They'll never forgive him for starting the Lebanese war."

"Rubbish. He was fired, remember? Israel will have to get back self-respect after messing up in Lebanon. And Sharon's got the hero-stuff Israelis need."

"All the good people will leave."

"The good people? This is the Middle East, girl. This is a country of *schwartzes* now. Sixty percent Sephardi." He removed her hand from his crotch. "The waiter is coming. Listen—we're going to eat on the balcony. Then you're going to stay here and rest, and I'm going to leave you alone. I've got the plane hired for tomorrow—"

"I can't. I can't face a small plane yet."

"I'll do the aerial stuff. I'll be gone a few days. You're to sit in the sun. Sit in the Salt Sea and read the newspaper. Sleep. They told me at the hospital, The woman has delayed shock. Let her sleep. They said, She'll cry a lot; she'll think she's dying. But you'll be getting better, okay? Here's breakfast!"

She hid in the bathroom until the waiter had gone.

Bennie had ordered lavishly. They were both hungry at first, but Danielle soon realized that her appetite had gone; she picked at the cucumber and chewed an olive. Bennie said, "I can eat for two. Do you think I'm pregnant? You hire me a photographer who cuts his arm off, and a Palestinian pretending to be Greek. You haven't got me pregnant, too, have you?"

She tried to be amused. It was blindingly bright on the balcony but her mind felt misty. It drifted. With effort she could bring ideas into focus, but they slipped away again, returning her to the desert by night, waiting for the car to explode. It was no use; she felt somber and said somberly, "What about being war orphans . . . ?"

"You make money. You eat while you can." He held back his head to lower a crescent of honeydew melon into his mouth. "You don't get attached. That way you don't lose anything."

"But you're attached to me. I know it intuitively."

That was typical, he thought. As soon as a woman was old enough to have crow's feet, she believed she was psychic. It was vanity. She looked in the mirror, saw the face was on the way out and said to herself, "But I've got psychic powers."

"Sure I am. We've got a contract."

—My mother *is* psychic. She never goes to Diezengoff, but the one day in almost twenty years when Bennie is sitting on the sidewalk in Diezengoff, something tells her to go there. She wasn't going anywhere; she was just wandering around looking at the shops. She thought I was in Hong Kong. —She knew there was going to be a war, in '67. I'd been four months in the army. She said, "Bennie, you've got three days' leave. You're pale. They're not feeding you properly. I'm taking you to Cyprus for the weekend." And when we got there she said, "Now we're staying here, until the war is over. I want you alive." She said, "Your father will never speak to you again." She said, "You'll never be able to go back." She said, "Your *bubeh* in New York can get you American citizenship. She knows a senator. I can't give you much money. But you've got your health. You'll sur-

vive." She said, "Israel isn't for you. You should have studied
Talmud, like my father. I don't want you driving trucks, and
tanks. I don't want a dead hero." Now I'm a hero and I should
be feeling great. When you haven't done it, you think it's everything; when you have—you know it's nothing.

He said, "Either you want to have a serious conversation, or you
want to talk about intuition. Make up your mind."

She was aghast at herself: I've done it again! I've behaved
like a little girl. "Serious."

"Serious is making megabucks. We're going to win an Oscar,
remember? Two. Best Screenplay. Best Director. Now, eat!"

"Maybe we'll win Best Movie."

"Why not?"

At the door to her room he said, "I'm ashamed to be seen like
this." The silk trousers wore a brown apron of stain. He had
averted his face, grimacing, while he dragged up his fly, shed-
ding grains of dried blood.

"Do you love me?" she asked.

"Of course. Hey! I can't stand women crying. It's just shock.
Listen, I've got a car waiting." He felt that horrible, delicious
clutch in his loins, like a shudder of electricity from within.
"I'll be back in two, three days." He kissed the limp hand.
"Shalom."

He was gone.

TWENTY-SIX

When the hotel door shut behind him at two o'clock in the afternoon a door of night closed upon her.

At first she tried to sleep. She drew the blackout curtains again and lay down on the bed. She had barely been aware of physical pain in his presence; now every joint flamed and her flesh throbbed. She felt like a lump of wood caught by the lick of fire. Lying still was impossible, but movement only sharpened her awareness of being damaged. She thought: my neck is broken! They've made a mistake—I'm going to be paralyzed.

She tried to remember what she had read of quadriplegia: it was difficult to diagnose, the nerves of a broken spine could remain connected for weeks, like a spider web, then a trivial movement would snap them. The wail of a siren fled around the room, and another, and again. She lay rigid.

Danielle knew her neck was not broken.

Israel has the best physicians in the world, she told herself. I have to trust them. They said I would be in pain—but nobody tells you what pain is, as nobody can tell you what a painting or music is, they can only describe it by reference to another sight or sound: it's like this, it's like that. Words are ghosts. When

have I known such bodily anguish . . . ? Giving birth to Katherine—that was different because the terror in my bowels was
lightened by joy and all those hours of darkness were touched by
an inward voice that murmured, It's hard, it's hard—but your
reward is coming. Push, you must push—you won't be torn apart,
I promise. Yes, you can scream. This pain will vanish and be
forgotten.

She lay panting on the bed. This was different. There was no
reward, no nurses around her murmuring, "Darling, darling—it's
opening. Three fingers now . . . we can feel the head." There
was only pain—not so sharp, much less. Compared to childbirth.

This is like a cut finger, Danielle said. I'm just sore.

A couple of yards away, on a table, she remembered there
was a packet of analgesic tablets they had given her at the Be'er
Sheva hospital. She could not see them in the dark; the idea
came that she should switch on her bedside lamp, stand up, go
to the table, and take a tablet. But willpower had deserted her;
her arm could not be bothered to reach out for the lamp; thought
and action had been disconnected by a different, subtle quadriplegia. Something other than her spine was broken and she
gave up hope of ever moving again. Of ever doing anything.
She turned her face to the wall and waited to die.

For the rest of that day and those that followed she mourned,
slept and mourned her own death and the deaths of others. Sometimes her dark companion of the road returned and made her
howl with anguish. "Let yourself die," he'd say. "I can't help
you unless you do. You have to change—the time has come. But
this comes first. Accept it," and he killed her in many different
ways, sometimes with clubbing, sometimes with nails through
her wrists. At night she sat on the balcony and looked at the sky;
the moon grew fatter and floated unruffled on the glistening sea;
stars in sprays hung before her close enough to pick, but she
could not be bothered to reach for them because they were so
familiar they seemed as worthless as everything else. When the
sun shone she hid from it in the blackened room. She arose when
the muscle of night contracted and in the cool, arid air she contemplated the dryness of her life, the fact that she was ugly,
talentless, and alone.

She dug up memories—of thirty-four years' longing: longing
that it should not have happened, that Geoffrey should not have

been killed, that her father should not have turned into a monster. Her pilgrimage seemed contemptible, another bead on a chain of follies that stretched back to childhood and forward toward the end of her days. She had been deluded at every moment; she loved no one, and no one loved her—not even Katherine.

Katherine is sick of me, Danielle thought; she said as much on the telephone. As for my clever career: what a joke! I've been a gun-for-hire, writing manipulative junk for advertising agencies, then sentimental junk for television, and now rubbish for the movies. My ugliness goes beyond looking like a gap-toothed witch. I have an ugliness of mind that no orthodontists or hairdressers or cosmeticians can alter: I'm stuck with it. I'm a whorish woman, as my father predicted about Bonny and me. Who was I to hit Bennie in the face for stealing Wili's films? He's honest about being a crook. He's not self-righteous, like me.

Every thought of others was a rebuke; each quality of theirs marked a lack in her.

I'm not intelligent, just sharply skilled in deceit, she thought. I learned in high school how to trick the teachers and the kids into believing I had better wits. I was as dumb as the girls who sat at the back of the room and never spoke. I had the nerve, simply, to interject with questions and arguments . . . Maybe they saw through me. Alice did. She knew I was more cheek than intellect but she played along with the game. When I first dyed my hair she said, "Ah-ha! You are taking a road . . ." I can't remember the rest, but she had been amused. She had dyed her own hair, she said, until she was fifty, when she asked herself: Whom am I trying to deceive? . . . I no longer know what color mine is: brown, I suppose. But which brown? Chocolate? Honey? Mouse? Not even to know the color of one's hair . . . I've been drawn to the fake all my life.

The foreshore below was lit with orange electric light. She hated it because its brilliance diminished around the edges of the lake the chill purity of the moon. She thought, How like the Israelis to violate moonlight: stoic virtues without the graces. Warm hearts, giant national passions, but no courtesy, no sense of harmony . . .

She watched her mind tricking her again, leading her off into criticism of the wrong in others, when its proper course was to examine her own faults. For a while she wondered what would happen if she let herself drop from the balcony to the concrete below. But she was too small even for that. It was only four floors. Some staff member would be awake, would hear the thud as she landed. He and others would gather together her unstrung puppet limbs and take her to the hospital, where they would patch her up. As they were patching up Wili. As they could not do to Geoffrey, or Patrick.

I wept for neither, she thought. My tears were for myself, robbed of my brother and my husband. I didn't cry for them to return for their own sakes, but for mine.

This truth was so painful it pierced her heart and opened the way to a well of tears that did not gush but somehow seeped upward into her eyes drop by drop. It was as different from the crying of self-pity or excitement as cheerfulness is different from joy. She felt as if she were not weeping for them but that brother and husband were inside her chest mourning themselves. They used her tenderly, clearing channels to allow a flow of emotion that gradually changed from sorrow to love. It was a feeling without desire or yearning, complete in itself.

For a while she felt happy and believed she had nothing more to learn. But that passed, too, and the dark returned. Sometimes she telephoned room service and had food brought up. Staying awake until dawn she would sleep until midday, then heave herself off the bed when the maid arrived. She lay in a chair while the woman dusted and vacuumed around her. The maid was an Arab or a Sephardi and each time she had finished the cleaning she would waddle up to Danielle, lay her leather palm on Danielle's forehead, and nod. She seemed to know something. Her fat cheeks were as unlined as a baby's, but up close her strong brown eyes had a penetrating and chastened wisdom, as if they had seen the secrets of many beds, many bathrooms, in their time, and knew what misery was. When she left, her sweat smell hung in the air for minutes afterward.

Danielle began to crave the calloused hand pressing its heel on her forehead. She had long ago decided to give up writing *Eleazar*—what was the point of burdening the world with further distractions?—but one afternoon, lying underneath the maid's hand, she felt energy passing from it into her wilted mind and limbs, a faint stirring of interest in . . . in the mysterious order hiding inside life. It felt no bigger than a drop of rain to the desert without and within. However as the hours dragged toward night, she became aware of this drop's deep penetration.

The woman returned each evening at six o'clock to remove the bedspread. They had not spoken to each other; they had no common language. At five o'clock that evening Danielle began to draw pictures of what had happened: she wanted to show them to the maid to explain her state. At first she drew the car overturned, herself and Wili trapped inside (like Patrick and his Thames TV girl), then her figure crouching in the desert clasping the dove, then Bennie and Akram dragging Wili from the wreckage. She sketched carefully at first but the drawings began to have an urgency of their own and turned into cartoons, then abstracts. She had only a pencil and a few different-colored ballpoint pens; the need for proper colors became a frenzy. She had cosmetics: eyeshadow pallets, lipsticks, kohl pencils.

When the maid entered she found the sick girl sitting on the floor in an ocean of paper that she had covered with scrawls. She had drawn on everything: on her own notebooks, on all the hotel stationery in the room, all over the newspaper, on the room-service menu; the bedroom mirror was an explosion of lipstick; in the bathroom she had scribbled in gold eyepaint and black on the glass and these colors and the same design were what she was repeating, now, on the pages of the telephone book. But she was smiling. The maid had not seen this crazy one smile before. She cleaned the mirrors and helped Danielle gather together her drawings.

Later that evening Danielle answered a knock and met someone from the hotel management.

"You've been in a car accident?" he said.

She nodded. He asked if he might come in, then walked up and down the room, glancing in corners. After a while he said, "You're an artist?"

She shook her head. She had no idea what he was talking about, but he seemed benevolent; he made small talk, asking about her work. She told him about *Eleazar*. He sat on her bed and smoked five cigarettes while they chatted about movies. When he stood to leave he said, "We've got an excellent masseuse in the hotel. Do yourself a favor." He said he would book her for a massage at eight A.M.

She was awake at seven-thirty when he telephoned her to say, "Get up. Get dressed and go to the lower ground floor." She felt different this morning; yesterday was a bit of a blank, as were

the days—she did not know how many—before. But this morning
she felt almost alert. It seemed the resort was for invalids, as
well as vacationers, and according to a brochure the hotel's
lower floors were set up with exercise equipment, spritz baths,
and a mineral pool. A couple in the elevator said that some
Scandinavian country allowed trips to the Dead Sea as a claim
on the national health scheme. Was she here for a cure? By accident, she replied. And from what country? She was confused by
the question. But before they had bumped stage by stage to the
lower ground floor she had said, "I'm not sure. Maybe I live
here." The husband cocked his head, puzzled. "You're a guest
worker on a kibbutz?" Danielle nodded. He held out his hand
and she shook it limply. "Good for you," he said.

The masseuse was a Georgian—"No, darling, *not* a Russian,"
she said. Her thick body strained the seams of her uniform,
while her hands, strong enough to heave coal, felt like butter-
flies. She put a stethoscope on Danielle's belly and linked it to
a machine: battle noises ricocheted. "World War Three," she
said. "Inside you." An hour and a half later Danielle woke up;
the masseuse was offering her a glass of mineral water. From her
disjointed explanation Danielle gathered that the flow of energy
in her body had been disturbed, but the masseuse was putting it
right. She was to return the next morning, for work on the
bruises.

Waiting for the elevator she saw the wife of the movie chief.

"Look at my hand." The woman extracted it from her walking
apparatus and very slowly, like a lobster claw, opened it with
an act of will rather than muscle and nerve. "I couldn't do that
three days ago. They say that in another week . . ." She gossiped
on about her joints, not noticing—not caring? thinking it normal?—that she was addressing a person who was lime-green and
indigo from shoulder to ankle. The intense selfishness of the sick
was soothing, Danielle realized. Maybe they drove the staff mad,
but they made few claims on each other, oddly detached by
their personal obsessions from much prying or attempts at contact. They spoke softly, they moved slowly. They were fully
united only in an unvoiced dislike for the vacationers, who ran
about, made noise, and did not have the time to listen to them
describe the course of their aches and pains. We are like shades,
she thought, asking each other briefly how each has landed in
this hell. When the crippled woman had made her own report she

waited for Danielle's and nodded as she stared at the bruises; she too had been massaged by Bella the Georgian. "A genius," she said. "You know how she developed her technique? She worked in a lunatic asylum in Moscow. She cured hundreds of mad people." For a moment they looked directly into each other, bright-eyed, sharing with affection a mutual burden that did not need a name. "Come and see me," the woman added. "I have a house in Jerusalem." She had others in Rome, London, New York, and Los Angeles, according to her card.

Bella had told Danielle to take twenty minutes of sunshine on the balcony and she saw the emperor's wife again that day, seated in a deck chair among a row of others, gazing in reverie at the water. A young boy ran from his parents and dived head first into the Dead Sea, to surface screaming. The parents and other tourists carried him to a fresh-water shower on the beach, all talking at once and rebuking each other. The row of heads of the invalids swayed back and forth like a stand of wheat struck by a wind, then fell still again, uninterested.

Danielle returned to the darkness inside, and Patrick's death.

She had not asked if his car had rolled. Now she wondered if he too had experienced that ecstatic flight on a whirlwind and had been swept so high that the stars were a carpet for his feet. She tried to concentrate on Patrick but found instead she was thinking about Geoffrey or Wili—poor, hopeless, horrible Wili— and Bennie, or at other times, about the man Amos. He had been severely wounded in the Six-Day War, Alice said. There was no sign: he did not limp, his arms were his own. Her mind rambled without discipline; repeatedly she called it back to Patrick, putting the scraps together.

They had lived with each other fewer than four years, she recalled. Their first house was a basement apartment in King's Cross.

—We were a pair of young dragons intertwined. Below ground level, an inferno of lovemaking.

On weekends they would surface to buy fuel from a hamburger joint that stayed open until three in the morning. Once a troupe of performing dwarfs was there. They had capered around her and Patrick and told jokes in a ribald patois that was neither English nor not-English. One had cried, "Take me up! Take me up!" He had put his hand up Danielle's skirt and pressed her thigh. Something in the indecency had robbed it of offense, as if his were the touch of a wise one. She remembered, but still did not understand what the little monsters had meant; she had felt like a queen to them.

It was three o'clock in the morning. Hours ago the moon had sailed over the roof, off toward the Judean Hills, and by now would be diving into the Mediterranean. She told herself, I must try to sleep.

She felt she had not been asleep at all when a shout in the room woke her. A voice cried, "Hooray! Hooray!"—it was the peasant girl cheering forward her wonderful bull as they galloped through a meadow to freedom. Clasping his giant neck she looked the size of a dwarf.

—To be alive!

—I forgot. I thought I was remembering—but I was forgetting what an adventure it is to be alive.

She wanted to get back to work on *Eleazar* immediately.

As she and Bennie had told each other often, the timing of the suicide scene would determine the whole movie. In Los Angeles they had watched the TV videos made after the Jonestown mass suicide and the massacres in the Sabra and Shatila camps in Lebanon. Danielle had timed at thirty seconds the onset of an unbearableness that transformed into boredom; Bennie at a minute and a half. "That's the time people spend on a roller coaster," he said. "You think amusement parks all over the world haven't got the timing right? I tell you—the public wants ninety seconds of horror. *Then* the brain goes blank." I've had a blank in time, too, she thought.

She sat up in bed and snatched her watch from the shelf beside her. It had been broken during the accident and its hands stood permanently at a quarter past eight. That was the question that had been niggling at the back of her mind for—what was it? three days. There had been something wrong about the gap in time from when the car ran off the road and turned over twice and when it had blown up. Even though the engine was still running, in gear, the wheels spinning madly like the legs of a beetle on its back—even though with each second petrol vapor was spreading . . . there had been an eon before fire had engulfed it. Bennie had been at least ten minutes behind them; another three—maybe five—pulling Wili out. And only then, a quarter of an hour later, had the blast made all three of them dive for cover.

For all that time she had somehow known the car would explode. Wili had *said* something. So many things had happened at once as they began to run off the road; she had been hypnotized by the sight of the desert rushing toward them and the feeling of hallucination. But she and Wili had kept on talking to each other, and he'd said . . .

—He said, "We've got no brakes!" Then, when we were airborne, he said, "They've killed us. Get out if you can."

That still did not make sense.

There was no clock in the room. After a long while someone bad tempered answered at the reception desk. It was four in the morning, he said: was there anything else she wanted? Maybe a string quartet? No? She only wanted to know the time? Would she be ringing again, to ask when it was five o'clock?

"Don't be rude, or I'll complain to the manager," she said.

"Lady, you complain to the manager, you'll get nothing to eat." He hung up.

I'm back in Israel, she thought.

She waited a few seconds and rang again.

He answered with, "What do you want now?"

"I want you to tell me where Mr. Kidron is. Benjamin Kidron—he's left a message at the desk, saying where he is. Please find it."

" 'Find it. Find it,' she says." He went on in murderous-sounding Hebrew. Then, "The date today is . . . one moment, he has written in Roman letters. Lady, I speak, I don't read, English. You want I wake up someone else?"

She asked to be called at six A.M., when an English-reader would be on duty.

Bennie was in the Tel Aviv Hilton: she had to follow all the instructions he had left before the receptionist there would connect her to his room.

He said, "You ring me at six-fifteen to tell me Wili's car was going to explode? It did explode. I saw it. You saw it. Akram saw it. Listen—I had to go to a nightclub in Jaffa, great Yemenite singer there—I've been asleep for just half an hour. Can we—?"

"Oh, damn you."

Bennie said, "Tsk, tsk."

The Yemenite opened her huge black-coffee eyes. "I'll call you back," he said to Danielle.

"Who was that woman?" the Yemenite asked.

"Nobody. Go to sleep. You're going to be a movie star, okay?"

For his taste she had too much body hair, and she was too

young for the part he had offered her—as leader of the Zealot
women who had disobeyed—but she would be fine as someone
else, a singer. He'd get the casting director to tell her that her
acting was lousy so the role was being given to another, and
that Mr. Kidron was disappointed. He had not wanted to go to
bed with her; she had persisted. And then she had given a running commentary: You're wonderful—you make me feel wonderful—you're the best—you're such a man—you make me feel . . .
As if it were a social event, a civic reception, and he was there
to be given a prize.

"Hush, *motek*" (he could not remember her name). Hush?
Why hush? she'd asked. Don't you want to know . . . ? Oh,
you're tearing me apart. It's wonderful.

He'd thought: Some know; some cotton on. Most ruin it.

Elohim speaks to me in silence. "Because I'm concentrating,"
Bennie had replied.

Over the years he had trained himself to yearn toward release,
then hold back, and this delicious agony of willpower had become a life habit.

At least it's exercise, he thought.

He had a routine for discovering their names: when they woke
up he'd say, "Hello. I think my name is Bennie Kidron. What's
yours?"—as if they had both lost their inner selves during the
night.

She told him her name; he gave her his card, asked her to
write *in English* to L.A.—no, no, not to him, to this man, Hal
Mathews, the casting director. The car was waiting; he had to
rush. Yeah, next year in Jerusalem . . . Do you mind eating
downstairs? I have to lock the room . . . documents.

"Come on, donkey, give me breakfast," he said to Akram, who
had another giggling seizure, but handed over his bread roll
filled with a hard-boiled egg and sprinkled with olive oil and
marjoram.

"It's going to rain," Akram said.

"Don't be anti-Israel." More laughter.

Bennie could see that Akram (who had accompanied him to
the club last night) was busting to ask about the singer, so he
told him—"like a gorilla, horrible—a man's better off with a wife."
Akram had seven kids.

They had stopped again at Jericho on the way back from the
Dead Sea to buy fruit for the children and Akram had taken

Bennie through the ghost towns on the fringes of the city. Mud walls, reed roofs, the refugee houses were as quiet as graves.

Bennie said, "My parents didn't come to Israel for this." He thought: my mother did not—but maybe my father did. Akram had not giggled.

—My mother told me: "When your younger brother was born he came out yelling. But when I had you, I screamed and you did not. They put you in my arms while you were still bloodied from being born and you just lay there, and looked at me. I'm sorry, Bennie. I wasn't used to Israel when I was pregnant with you. I'd only been in the country a few months. I fell pregnant here, on Cyprus, in the displaced persons' camp . . . You're a Jew, not an Israeli."

—She married the first able-bodied man she met; they had not even shared a mother-tongue, because hers was Czech and his Hungarian. "I was a scarecrow." But she conceived me, the first night. It was like that: a rage to rebuild the race. They had no idea then that the gap was six million. When you see them planted out as trees—that memorial forest we went to yesterday, or whenever—it's difficult to believe.

—"Your father will never speak to you again."

—"Your *bubeh* knows an American senator—knows him well: you take my meaning?"

—I said, "But she's over sixty!"

—"Bennie, Bennie: when you're older you'll understand. Desire does not stop."

Sometimes he had heard his father grunting over his mother in the night. Next morning she would wash her hair.

Daniela had washed her hair.

I don't want to think about Daniela, he thought. I had no time to call her back; as it is I'm late for the helicopter. The question is, will I spend tomorrow in Israel and see her again? Or should I send Akram to collect her, deliver her to Jerusalem, while I catch a morning flight to Athens? The lilac jacket has arrived. I could leave it with a note saying . . . I'll think of something today, on the chopper. The pilot is going to let me fly it this afternoon. I must be practical about Danielle: she and I need an extra script conference, so I should stay another day. On the phone she sounded crazy. She asked me to find out something from Akram . . . God, what was it? I didn't take a note. Sam drilled it into me: Bennie, you are disorganized, so every phone conversation, every business lunch, you take notes. People who take notes don't go bankrupt. You want to lose two million dollars, like you did in 1976? You want to drive taxis again? Bennie—you haven't got the financial fat; when you've got it, you can quit taking notes. God, I'm tired; Danielle's right: this place erodes you—

"Akram, you got any more chocolate? I'm still hungry."

"Too much ploughing last night."

"And I'm getting too old for it. I'm thirty-four and falling apart."—Akram laughs at anything; I tell him the truth and he pisses himself.

"Long life to Mr. Bennie! They said at the hospital you will live to great age."

"Yeah. I could save myself years of trouble."—That one went over his head. Hell, he's an Arab; only Jews understand jokes like that.

—Sam said to me: The money you spend on dames—Bennie, you transform every one of them into a prostitute. Is that what you want? I couldn't tell him the truth: I do. Prostitutes are unowned, they're kind of virgins. They used to be in the temples so men could taste *Elohim.* The Hasid tried to tell me that when I saw him in the cathouse in Tel Aviv. I thought he was just another hypocrite.

—My father says they're all hypocrites, taking advantage of having a Jewish state, somewhere they could not be persecuted, but refusing to serve in the army, to work the land . . . Superstition! he'd say. "What's Judaism? It's a four-thousand-year-old superstition—and what's it done for us? Given us Auschwitz! It makes me sick to hear Jews boasting about 'the great Jewish contribution to civilization—Einstein, Marx, Freud.' I remember the contribution we made at Auschwitz. You know what they do in Mea Sha'arim? They pray for rain! We have witch doctors in this country who pray for rain and burn the national flag on Independence Day because they think the State of Israel is unholy, that it's been made by men, and only Yahweh can make it when he sends the Messiah. Bennie, there is no God looking after us: only Jews look after Jews." He made a point of eating too much, and smoking, on Yom Kippur. My mother refused to cook him pork: "You want pig on Yom Kippur—you cook it," she said. She taught me how to fast. I should call her. I will, from Athens.

—I told Sam, "They don't think they're prostitutes. They think I'm a nice guy." He said, "You're a sucker, kid. You break my heart."

When Danielle put down the telephone, she was shaking. His sleepy voice, the intimacy of his breath in her ear . . . if he had stood before her she could have opened her mouth and swallowed him. She craved to know him all over—what he was thinking; what he was doing; his dreams. She wanted a total possession.

Friendly sunshine flowed over the carpet, onto the bed, hauling her from the deep like a fish. She got up and searched the room, looking for some part of Bennie: a belt, a sock, a piece of paper with his writing on it. There was nothing. She felt as flat as a shoelace.

Then love erupted again. She was in love! She didn't care what he felt about it.

He must feel the same! she thought.

—But maybe he doesn't. Maybe I'm just another of his one-night stands.

What was he doing? Who was he with? He'd be with some tart he picked up in the nightclub. She'd strangle her first, making Bennie watch . . . She thought, I'll ring back and say, "Get that girl out. Throw her out, or I'll be there in five minutes to tear her up."

Danielle looked at the telephone. Then she began listing his faults: Bennie is a crook; he's a womanizer; he's ruthless. His charm is seditious, all of it employed to the one purpose of making a mountain of money for which he has no use . . . But his vices had a high polish to which she—

I can't help it, just yet, she thought. His perversity enthralls me.

She tried a duller path: My financial security hangs on this film. I will lose my house if the contract is broken. If I have a fight with Bennie—and I will, if I can't recover from this madness—I'll be sending twenty years' work down the drain. And Katherine's education. I *must* give her a better chance than Bonny could give me: my life would be a disgrace if I couldn't believe Katherine is a finer being than I, with a brighter future. She's like a growing shoot; I'm her tree.

She pictured her view through the gum trees, the little bay

with white boats in it, the thousands of suns dancing over the Pittwater, from the boat moorings all the way to Lion Island.

She thought, I shall not jeopardize that for . . . a fuck.

She realized they needed one more script conference, but after that they could communicate by telephone—and if they *had* to discuss the final draft face-to-face, she could take Sarah with her.

Danielle began to smile, then laugh.

Sarah wore a tracksuit to the office and smoked eighty cigarettes a day. The morning they had squeezed five profit points out of Bennie and Sam she had said, "Daniela—you forget what your momma told you about being polite. I know this boy. And I know Sam." The first fifteen minutes were quiet; for the next hour and a half Sarah and Bennie had screamed at each other. It was so exciting they all began to believe what they were saying. At one point Danielle had been inspired to shout, "I refuse to be your piece of cheap territory!" At the end of the conference the two sides had kissed each other and they had gone out to lunch. Sam was so agitated he couldn't eat; Bennie, who half an hour earlier had been saying, "You're crucifying me! You're killing me!", turned to him several times to whisper, "It's only money, Sam. Listen, this soup is good. Eat."

Danielle was laughing so much her nose ran and she needed a Kleenex. In the bathroom she saw the cold woman-of-glass watching; the woman had a faint, ironic smile.

I need ice in my heart, she thought. I want to burn my eyes against Jerusalem one last time; I want to see the Judas trees blooming in the Kidron Valley . . .

—My father holds me in a rock of ice; I've come to accept that in these past days: he's not going to melt.

The glass woman nodded slowly. Danielle said to her, "But what now? Who am I now?"

Her companion looked thoughtful. Then she mimed a curse.

"Damn it!" Danielle said. For more than an hour she had forgotten the practical reason she'd had for contacting Bennie: the timing of the car's explosion. She hoped that Akram would have noted the time they left Masada.

She had another massage and spent the day dozing on the beach and walking again through the foothills; sitting among the deformed, petrified minerals with a clipboard and pad on her knee she wrote up her notes of Masada as if there had been no five-day gap between being there and being now.

Her bruises had gone, their greenish traces hidden by skin turning biscuit-colored. Bella's peristaltic machine that morning had made soft gurgling noises. "You flowing goot again," she'd said.

Bella could see auras and spirits, but she rarely told her clients; each time Danielle entered the massage room a young man accompanied her, an insolent fellow, but he was fond of her. "You got husband? You got brother?" she asked, shrugged, and went on with her work. People wanted to think they were free; they didn't like to be told what was in their auras.

At four o'clock in the afternoon Danielle returned to the hotel, where the desk girl handed her a message: Akram will collect you at seven P.M. Script conference tomorrow morning in Jerusalem. Love. Bennie.

She felt faint, and in a panic. She had to get ready, pack her clothes, organize her ideas for the morning, arrange everything under headings. There must be no spaces during the conference—she would write out an agenda, give it to Akram to deliver tonight to Bennie, so that when they sat facing each other in the morning they could go straight to business. Bennie must have decided to leave on an evening flight, tomorrow. Danielle turned and dashed back to the desk. A man—maybe he who had offered her a string quartet—was glowering behind the cash register.

"What day is it?"

He sighed and gave that flap of the hand from his wrist.

"Thursday," he said. "From last night it's been Thursday."

"Are there flights to Athens—or Rome—tomorrow night?"

"You have an airline in mind? Not El Al, I hope. El Al does not fly on Shabbat—it doesn't even fly, the pilots go on strike for four months. Now the doctors want to go on strike. Lady, this is a democracy. What can I do about it?"

"Do you have an airline schedule?"

"Am I a travel agent? Do I look like a travel agent?"

She could hear him shouting after her as she strode back to the elevators. Unless tomorrow went like clockwork, Bennie would be unlikely to get a seat on any of the crowded flights out on Friday afternoon at this time of year. Or so she imagined. It could mean a whole day followed by a jagged night under the same purple sky.

Packing, which she thought would take an hour, needed ten minutes; the unendurable wait began. She tried to write an agenda, but it seemed both muddled and stilted. She threw that out and began again: the result was only marginally better. Or maybe it was worse. She tore it up. She walked up and down, she ordered coffee and sandwiches and when they arrived did not like the look of them.

The earth rolled and a gentle sunset flowed up from the Mountains of Moab, turning them from violet to gray; the swelling moon, which would be full on the first day of Passover, soared away, chased by Polaris. The sea held its color, the astonishing chemical shade of blue like a public swimming pool, then in a moment became an ink lake.

"Good-bye," Danielle whispered. The telephone began ringing: Akram would be in the lobby.

She took a final look—for Eleazar. He had not stood so close, but had been able to watch the sea well enough, from up there. It was this time of year: around Passover, a time when the moon was always full. When Eleazar had looked into that pit of ink . . . It was so frustrating: the historical record was as frail as a remnant of silk found in a grave. The Romans hadn't bothered to record the Masada suicide, as they had forgotten to make a note about the execution of a troublemaking rabbi from Nazareth.

If the Masada women had not disobeyed the Zealot council, then gossiped about it, the story would not be known at all. And now archeologists had turned the event into the hack of contemporary politics; the official view was that Eleazar was an Orthodox Jew dying for Israel: Death before Slavery! How plausible, she thought. How convenient to have Eleazar as the hero for young soldiers. At Mira's place someone had said, "Listen to our propaganda: it's not accurate, but it's plausible. 'Never Again.' 'No Alternative.' 'Created Facts.' 'We don't forget 1492.' Our slogans are so good we don't need to think: they explain everything."

"Okay, I'm coming," she called.

String Quartet was at her door. "This is all? What do you need me for?"

"I don't. I could carry it myself—but I thought you'd like the tip."

He cocked his head, eyeing her one bag, wondering if he should stoop to an act beneath his strength's dignity.

In the elevator she asked, "Where were you born?"

"Al-Khalil. You call it Hebron."

"That's an A." She looked at him again and began to smile. She had a dollar bill ready, replaced it, and pulled out a five.

"The dollar was okay," he said.

"Take the five." She was still smiling at him, and herself. "I don't often meet Arabs like you."

He shrugged and pocketed the note. He was used to being patronized.

When she saw Akram's piano-key smile stretched to his ears she kissed him on each bunched cheek before thinking of what she was doing. There were grayish circles around his eyes.

"Have you and Bennie been enjoying yourselves?"

She got the whole story between foyer and Mercedes: Akram had been in a helicopter that day—Mr. Bennie had flown it himself—Akram had made vomit, from frightened—right there, over Masada, taking photographs, Mr. Bennie falling out door of helicopter . . .

"What!"

"Almost. Almost falling out door. Mr. Bennie says come to Los Angeles, drive Rolls-Royce car."

Danielle pulled him up. "Don't be crazy, Akram." How to explain that Bennie's life was half fantasy?

Akram seemed unconvinced. She, however, felt strengthened by the exchange, and ready now to enter the space lilting from Bennie's presence in it. The car smelled of Monte Cristo cigars, there were his orange peels on the floor and a pair of his sunglasses tossed on the backseat. She became sleepy as soon as she sat down.

"Akram, what time did you leave Masada on the night of the accident?"

He could not remember the order of the days anymore; she asked him to try and announced she was going to sleep.

When the car reached sea level and the temperature began to drop Akram switched on the heating system to keep her warm. He had been puzzling over the question he had been asked twice that day: Bennie had wanted to know this morning at what time they had driven away from Masada. Akram had thought he was hinting about an overpayment for that day, although Bennie never argued about money—just peeled off the notes. A few days earlier Akram had felt it on his honor to tell Bennie that he had, last week, made an error. Of three hours. Actually it was five and a quarter hours, but that was an undignified number. "Aw—keep it. Buy something for the kids," Bennie had said.

Akram had to concentrate on driving up the Judean Hills, but when he caught the first glimpse of Jerusalem—the Hilton tower—he remembered: Bennie and the soldier who had brought him down from the mountain had talked for a while, beside the car. The soldier didn't want money, so Bennie had given him a cigar and had lit it for him. Then Bennie had given him the hashish.

"Makes you fly," Bennie said. "C'mon, Akram. We've gotta fly. What time is it?"

It had been 8:45, Akram now remembered.

He told her this when he carried her bag to the door on King George Street. She was still half asleep.

"As late as that?" She looked reluctant. "What about Wili? Has Bennie had any news?" Danielle had sent Wili flowers and a message—Get Well, Love to you from the princess—feeling ashamed while spelling it out to the woman at the Moriah reception desk.

"Sat-*is*-factory," Akram said. "Four days more, he returns to England. Mr. Bennie says, more handsome."

"Isn't that good?" He could see she was so tired that she might be about to cry. Foreign ladies, in Akram's experience, did not know how to live: they worked too hard; they were rich but they never enjoyed it.

"You sleep," he said.

Jazzy had long since satisfied himself that the timing device Saeed had invented in fact worked. While Danielle and Bennie were asleep together, he had driven down to the Dead Sea for a beach picnic with Saeed and a couple of the other boys.

"Their driving," he said when they passed the black remnants of a car by the side of the road. He had the bored, dry expression of someone used to all sorts of uncivilized behavior. A tire in perfect condition was twenty yards away, available to any collector.

"We could use that," one of the boys said.

"I would not soil my hands," Jazzy replied.

Saeed looked at his knees. While the others were in the water Jazzy told him: "That's what has to happen to traitors." The other boys believed that Wili had returned to London on a special mission.

"But *why* did he tip off Kidron?" Saeed asked.

"It's my opinion he worked for MI6. I think they recruited him while he was in jail, and when he came out and I met him: 'Oh, Jazzy—save my honor! Give me revenge.' It was a trick from the start."

"Then they know about us."

Saeed had genius only in his hands.

"Of course they do. But do the English love the Israelis, who sold weapons to Argentina for its war against Britain? And because we are independents . . ."

Jazzy knew what could happen to Palestinians who joined political groups; for Saeed he recounted again the story of a perfumed scorpion.

"It happened in 1969, I was thirteen years old," he began. His only brother had joined Fatah and made an ambush that destroyed an Israeli armored car. He was betrayed one night, and shot dead. It was the time of year when almonds ripen. For two days Jazzy had been picking almonds, loading them on the donkey and returning home only in the evening. Then he and his mother would shell the nuts. They were doing so, sitting on the doorstep in the sunshine next morning when an Israeli officer and soldiers arrived. Jazzy's mother knew, then, that she had lost her elder son. The officer was very precise, very correct; he said: "It is my duty to inform you that this, being the dwelling of a terrorist, shall be demolished." He quoted the military regulation. "In exactly," he looked at his watch, "twenty-seven minutes. Please collect your belongings and leave the premises."

Jazzy's mother shelled another nut. Then she said, "My husband is dead, my daughters are married and have gone away. My strong son has disappeared and I have only this child. It's a nice day. These are beautiful almonds. Allow me to offer you some coffee and some almonds? Let us sit in the sunshine a little longer." The officer turned to the two soldiers with him and said, "Come back in one hour." He sat down and enjoyed his coffee and almonds; he talked about the weather and the crops with Jazzy's mother. The soldiers returned with the bulldozer; the officer said, "Thank you for your hospitality," then directed the demolition of their house.

"What did he do then, Saeed?"

"He returned to his office and resigned."

"And why?"

"Because he was a scorpion."

"Because he was the very man who, a few hours earlier, had killed my brother! . . . And then?"

"His resignation was rejected. He was promoted to major and moved to army psychology."

"Yes, yes. A perfumed scorpion. Our land is full of them." Jazzy and his mother had gone to live with relations and it was through them they learned what the officer who had eaten almonds had done the night before.

When he was fifteen Jazzy met an Englishman. The man took him to London, but Jazzy got bored and, when he had finished high school, left him. Soon afterward he met Saeed, who was already famous for his hands. They worked around Chelsea and Hampstead, robbing the parts of London Jazzy already knew, and met Wili a few days after he'd left jail. They had dreamed up the idea of fixing Wili's enemy's car for no special purpose—just to see if they could do it. Since then, whenever they needed money they'd asked Wili—not that he had much, "but it's good for his memory," Jazzy would say. When the man had been killed Wili had shat himself, like a baby. "Your girlfriend's brother had an accident. Look, the newspapers say so," Jazzy had reassured him.

He was not concerned that there had been no newspaper stories of the death of a foreign photographer on the Dead Sea road: tourism was suffering this year because of the Lebanese war and it was undesirable for the Israelis to make things worse with negative reports.

They lay and dreamed in the sunshine and when some foreign girls in bikinis walked past they called, "Hey, darling!" One day it would be all theirs: "every centimeter, every almond tree," Jazzy said. The girls turned and waved back at the boys whose creamy winter skins gleamed like the fur of cubs as they played on the beach.

TWENTY-SEVEN

The Plaza had a downstairs area that in the evenings served as a reception room or could be used as a theaterette. It was furnished with comfortable chairs and low tables and at this time of day it was quiet. When Danielle telephoned Bennie from the lobby at five to nine she said, "I can't stand bedroom walls for another day. Meet you downstairs."

Bennie had an insolent walk. Danielle watched his pale blue jeans descending, each leg allowed to relax, almost collapse onto the step below, in a lazy movement that no sensible person would use on a staircase. He was wearing an electric blue leather jacket and had not shaved for a couple of days. A box of Monte Cristos was tucked in his armpit. As he sauntered down the steps, he tossed into his mouth and munched some green things he held in a plastic bag. The Bored Hoodlum, she thought.

"Have some," he said, holding out the bag of small egg-shaped fruit with softly prickling skin. He did not know their name, in English. "We used to call them Martian's nuts." He added, watching Danielle grimace, "Chockful o' vitamins."

She was thinking, Our defense systems are working efficiently.

She had dressed up—the Rodeo Drive boots, a cream silk shirt, her best cream trousers, and a black angora pullover knotted by its sleeves over her shoulders. Although she saw better with contact lenses, she had decided not to wear them but instead her Dior spectacles with the thin black frames. Bennie had not seen her in glasses before; he made no comment.

"You had breakfast? I haven't. Have some Black Forest cake and coffee." He strolled away again.

When he returned he said, "Right. Now we work. How are you, *motek?*" The endearment, offhand, small change, clinked into place as the cue for their act. She was just "Sweetheart" or "Sweetie-pie" or "Darling"—showbusiness Darling—one of the herd.

Life's safe again, she told herself. We've been there, done that. Bennie's tired of that and now he wants to play a new game. Things move fast, when he's driving.

—He said all that to me in one word.

Well, that's that, she thought.

—Grasshopper brains.

When he worked, however, he got himself "into gear" as he called it. His appetite, which was like a constant inner erosion, vanished. He drank cold coffee; he did not notice the cigar he was sucking was unlit. His eyes did not wander over women who passed. She thought, He's almost articulate.

By two o'clock she felt her concentration flickering. They had worked through the major plot (the Zealots) and the minor plot (the Romans), the characterization, the locations, the themes, and had reached once more the sticking point: the motivation for suicide and the motivation for the women who had refused to die. Bennie said:

"It was inspiration! Eleazar was inspired—and the women were inspired. Simple."

"We're not dealing with simpletons." She heard the razor in her voice; a black sulk played over Bennie's lips.

—Thick, deft lips.

"I need to take a walk," she said.

For a moment he hesitated: she had not meant it to sound like an invitation, but it had, all the same.

"I'll make some phone calls," he said. The day was too far gone for him to catch his flight that evening; he would rebook on another. "How long do you need?"

"An hour. Or so."

"Take three."

Typical: make it excessive, she thought. I could be back at three-thirty.

"See you at five," Bennie said. His arms were resting horizontally on the back of the settee; he flapped a hand in dismissal. Danielle did not look back, and he watched her leave with a feeling of relief.

He had thought about her a lot since that night whenever it was—a week ago—and had worked out what it was about Daniela that unnerved him (apart from the fact that she was too damned smart). It was this: she had too many personalities—like some good actresses, who were bitches to deal with off-stage because they played to you, and you never knew where you stood.

He and Raphael had a motto: never screw a good actress. Bad actress—that was a different story; you were in control with them. But that Danielle. There was a part of her that held him in contempt, even though she was still infatuated with him, too scared to come up to the room, wearing glasses that kept slipping down her nose. When it suited her, she allowed the contempt to show. Of course, she was an egomaniac who thought she was right about everything. For example, the motivation: when she came back from her walk she would announce the solution. She would get that oracular, fixed expression in her eyes and say, "Bennie, I *know* . . ." It would be some crazy piece of intuition. He would humor her. Come third-draft time Danielle would discover who made script decisions on *Eleazar*. He had said to her again this morning—very gently—"We must not lose sight of the dramatic impact," and she had replied, "That's the editing job," as if it were something for the servants. She talked about the movie in terms of a search for Meaning and Truth.

Well, he'd warned her. He'd told her: megabucks.

He watched the heels of her boots disappear up the stairs and smiled to himself: there was a distinct possibility for tonight. Now that he had worked out that he did dislike Danielle, and why, he felt calm about going to bed with her again. She didn't talk.

I'll give her the lilac jacket this evening, he thought. I'll also negotiate on the suicide motives. The reality is that if I thug her too soon, she can refuse to write the third draft—Sarah knows how to draw up a contract—and then I could be in trouble.

—I'm a real nice guy and I'll be real nice to her this evening.

*   *   *

Danielle crossed King George Street, changed into jeans and
and sneakers, then realized she did not know where she wanted
to go or what she wanted to do. She could buy a new watch—
that would be a useful activity—but the West Jerusalem shops
were already shut for the coming Sabbath. In East Jerusalem
many would not reopen until five; if she wandered along Salah
el-Din Street looking for a watch shop some helpful young or
not-so-young man would trail behind, until he had worked up
the courage to grab at her bum.

She had a sense of being out of rhythm with herself, and
jittery. Of course, she and Bennie were getting ready for the
argument they would have this evening—but it was more than
that.

She wrung her hands—sometimes she did that, unconsciously,
when she was in a quandary—then noticed what she was doing,
and noticed that her hands enjoyed each other. They were silky
and her nails were long. Of course! They had done no housework for almost two months. Since leaving Sydney she had not
cooked a meal, used a washing machine, watered the garden,
fed the dog, picked and arranged flowers, ironed a blouse (there
was no iron in the painter's apartment; she had searched), staggered outside with a garbage can . . . She had been out of
touch with all the small activities that, back in the seventies,
she, they, feminists, everyone with a sense of justice, had condemned as "shitwork"—but that, in recent years, she had found
fundamental for well-being.

For a sense of groundedness, she thought. We should have demanded that men share housework not because it's nasty, but
because it's soothing.

"I'm going to cook," she said aloud. In the Old City the Christians would have their shops open.

The painter had an African string bag on a nail beneath the
spirit mask.

She now knew the fastest route, through the Independence
Gardens, along Mamilla, straight up the hill to the Jaffa Gate.
Spring was beginning to blossom, there were flashes of flowers
and light perfume in the Gardens, but she was in too much of a
hurry to enjoy them now that she was craving contact with the
deep odors of fruit and vegetables, nuts and raisins . . . and
those glass bins of spices that give out scents to lift your head from

your shoulders. She could buy cardamom to froth with the coffee, and dried oregano, and salty white cheese.

In fifteen minutes she was at the top of King David Street—or Suq el-Bazaar, depending on politics, language group, and all the rest of it. There were sandbags outside the Jaffa Gate and there seemed to be more police and soldiers around than usual. She reached the entrance to the souk and saw why: the place was packed solid with Passover and Easter pilgrims. Merchants who on other Fridays would have boarded up their premises were leering beside their mounds of dried apricots and jute sacks spilling coffee beans, shouting, "Yes, please? What is it you are wanting? We have it—" and dispatching nephews and cousins of nephews to run to other shops for whatever it was—halvah coated with chocolate?—that some potential customer had fancied he might have an interest in buying. A boy tried to sell her dried Holy Land flowers, a crucifix, and a transistor radio; a donkey was being unburdened of a Christ; a couple of tourist hippie girls were poised to steal a scarf with silver thread through it, and someone in the vicinity was smoking hashish. What about a genuine Roman glass? Or a Hebron plate—here, beautiful painting of Jesus on it, His face . . . ? Or the Virgin? His brother from Bethlehem who carved this wonderful, exact Virgin in tears also sells exciting pictures of ladies and gentlemen. Together. Or would she like ladies together with ladies? More nice for her? She was Californian, yes? There was also a Buddha . . .

She took a stranglehold of the string bag with her wallet in it and elbowed ahead. The fresh produce was further down through an alleyway to the left, as she recalled.

Abruptly she had to throw herself against the stone wall. She either had missed her turn or had confused the point at which the labyrinth did a sudden switch of personality and became the Via Dolorosa, a street that broke in half and ran in two disconnected parts through the Old City. Toiling toward her were a group of people carrying wooden crosses on their backs, led by nuns. They had reached a Station of the Cross and all paused, blocking the way. Danielle ducked her head to avoid a blow from a passing cross. Then she saw that this melodrama was not all, that following those on foot were nuns on their knees, three of them, aged at least sixty. A snail's thread of blood traced itself out behind each of them and she could see darker patches seeping upwards into their black skirts. She felt her skin goose-step. A nun was right beneath her now, and as the crone gazed up to the Roman letters carved above a doorway she muttered, "De fiends. De filty, rotten, stinking murderers." She banged her head on the ground and crawled on. There was a hissing and clicking noise: a Japanese was taking photographs.

Danielle was still pressed against the rock when Alice appeared.

"Dearest! What joy."

She saw the desert suntan and that Danielle was pale underneath it. The Friday procession tended to get out of control, around Easter, and however Israelis laughed at its naive barbarity, it sickened them. "It sickens me, for that matter," Alice said.

She, too, was food shopping. They went along in silence, Alice guiding the way to the fresh food market while Danielle held her elbow to steady her over the uneven alleyways. Alice couldn't hear in crowds, she could only talk. She said after a while, "Some of those nuns have saved their whole lives to make a pilgrimage, and when they arrive in Jerusalem they're rutting to touch the holy places. I've seen them fight each other to crawl through a doorway in the Church of the Holy Sepulcher to get at the crypt. The disgusting Armenian priest on duty would kick their behinds to make them hurry so he could demand sixpence a head from the next lot who wanted to kiss the ground. One Easter he asked two bob. A big brute, prowling his small domain. He flattened a Greek Orthodox brother . . . was that in the thirties? I can't remember."

She was wondering when Danielle would try to tell her about the car accident—her normal way in the old days was to announce good or bad fortune instantly, and expect you to join in rejoicing or disappointment. It was a pleasant surprise to find her less of an egotist.

She continued, "You've never seen Christendom in spasm, have you? You've never seen the tide that swells up from Passion Sunday, through the vernal equinox, Lady Day and Palm Sunday—when the pilgrims trot down from the Mount of Olives on donkeys, waving palm fronds and singing. Then Maundy Thursday, Good Friday, when they fast—and then Easter Day, when all the bell towers roar and ring and the walls themselves chant, 'He Is Risen!' . . . The older ones easily forget that the Pope was kind enough to pardon us in 1962." She whinnied.

Danielle was grasping her arm so tight she was hurting. Alice patted her hand and it loosened a little.

"You should experience Bethlehem on Christmas Eve. It was wonderful until recently, but now the terrorists say they are going to bomb Manger Square, so it's all sandbags and body searches—soldiers kneeling beside machine guns as you drive into the town. Funny, what we kneel to . . . I took Gideon to the Church of the Nativity a few years ago. When he saw the rubber doll in its white nylon dress and the red velvet manger he had an attack of *fou rire*. It's a nervous reaction he gets from his father. I told him, 'You mustn't laugh,' but he couldn't help it. He kept saying, 'A plastic baby' and we had to go outside. I tried to explain to Giddy what an enormity it's been that in Judaism, Christianity, and Islam the masses have been served up concrete in place of the metaphors of religious language. He listened, too—until I said, 'And that includes the story of the Promised Land. Read your Kabbalah. It was never a *territory*. It's the land *within*.' When I told him that, his face turned into a barricade." Danielle has something of that look about her at this moment, Alice noted and thought, I'd like to introduce her to Father Gilot. When I brought him to Giddy it was already too late: Amos had taught Giddy to distrust religion, and Giddy lacks his father's discrimination. He must, poor child, being in the army. "It's all been vulgarized, you see," Alice said aloud. "You can make passion popular, but not truth." She added, "Amos has read the Kabbalah. He has no illusions about territory. But I've seen the battle-hunger in his eyes, when he was younger. When I asked him, 'What would happen, Amos, if we all got revenge for everything?' he replied, 'We'd all be happy, my dear.' He had the wit to laugh."

They had reached the entrance to the fruit and vegetable souk, a cavern fragrant with fresh food and stinking from dead. Alice averted her eyes from the butcher shop where the head of a baby camel swung from a hook through its nose. Danielle said, "Erk!" Then: "I feel like buying that thing—for Bennie."

"You're angry with him. Why?"

"Oh, the script—"

Alice noted the alert, nervous glances Danielle was casting everywhere. She knew it could be hours or months before the effect of the performance on the Via Dolorosa had worked its way through her. That's the trouble with these quick-witted, hard-driving types, Alice was thinking: they're unkind to themselves. When they have an emotional shock, they hit it like a brick wall. But she'd been a joy to teach as a child . . .

She said, "We have to bargain. I do it by turning stone deaf. Good-bye. Follow me."

They wanted much the same stuff: cucumbers, carrots, a melon, herbs. After a while Danielle became aware of peace spreading to her from the small beauties of the food she handled.

"That nun," she said.

Alice switched on again.

"That Irish nun—" Her voice snagged.

Come on, come on, Alice thought. You want to be Jewish, you face up to anti-Semitism.

"—perhaps she was cursing the Romans. But if she wasn't—" Danielle was sniffing melons to check if they were ripe. "If I'd been born in Europe a few years earlier . . ." She nodded to the grocer that the melons would do, he could weigh them. "I mean, how odd that I should have got to this age, without any sense of . . ." Her face, turned to Alice, was puzzled. "You know, I thought it was glamorous. To be a Jew."

"Did you indeed? Of course, your generation has had that luxury. But I don't remember it like that. I remember that you wanted to be like everyone else, but one day when you were about twelve, you and Bonny came to the school concert, both of you dressed up like courtesans. You were wearing an Omega watch that you'd got for your birthday from Bonny's current gentleman friend. That was a Saturday. On Monday that little swine Helen Kelso said as you were going in to chapel, 'My mother says your mother is a loose woman. And you're just a Jew.' Have you forgotten you were expelled for a month, for blackening the Kelso child's eye? Have you forgotten I put my job on the line, so they wouldn't chuck you out for good, and came and coached you on the weekends?"

Danielle was looking abashed. Alice shook her head. In Hebrew she said, "I'm deaf, not blind. You reweigh them with your hand off the scale." To Danielle she added, "You were more honest about it then than you are now. You didn't think it was 'glamorous'—you saw it was inescapable. And you were furious. You demanded to be excused from attending chapel from then on."

Danielle allowed Alice to bargain for two lemons. The man wanted to sell no fewer than five. He worked himself into a rage over four carrots: four *kilos*, she meant. No: four carrots.

"Can't hear a word you're saying," Alice piped at him. "And she can't understand you, so it's no use abusing her." To Danielle she said, "I've known him for years. We have the same fight every week. Ah—you see, he's saved me a ripe avocado."

The man waddled around to their side of the stall and re-arranged both their shopping bags so that the more delicate items were on top. Then he gave a satisfied upward jerk of his chin. Danielle thought: *Arab.*

"They're feeling the economic crisis that's coming," Alice said. "But they've no conception of how bad it will be. Even Amos refuses to think of what's around the corner. I told him, infla-tion will reach a thousand percent next year, and he scoffed. He's distracted by the war, like everyone else." She could see that Danielle was not listening to her; however, she was delighted by the changes she could sense in the girl already. Nobody was un-affected by Israel, but the effect was negative for many. It was especially confusing for Jews, whatever their temperaments—cold fish or firebrands. Oooh, firebrands! Her mind was wandering a bit, Alice realized; she got tired in the souk—there was too much stimulation.

"You know, there was not a cause—female suffrage, the war in Spain, vivisection—that didn't involve my heart and mind. I *loved* being a firebrand. It's so much easier to reform the world than to reform yourself. You need not surrender anything if you're forc-ing others to give up their wicked ways. Reform is so democratic. And don't we all worship democracy?" She and Bernard Gilot discussed their dreams for an anarchy: "It will come, it will come—when man is complete," Alice said.

Danielle said, "I now remember that scene at school about anti-Semitism. You said, 'The Holocaust is within the power of each of us. And we must each overcome it.' I thought I knew what you meant. But I've forgotten." She tapped a finger against her ear, miming for Alice to tune in.

Alice had heard her but decided to stay in her own world a while longer. "I think democracy is a system of bribery, and it's working worse and worse in every country you look at. Well, that's the way of things—everyone needing to protect his own tiny pile of goods and flesh. So he thinks." She gave Danielle a nudge to let her know she was now ready to answer her: "It takes years to learn to love," she said.

To avoid the crowds they decided to leave via the Lion's Gate but it too was clogged with tourists. A guide with one group was explaining how, in 1967, Jerusalem was captured through this gate and that a military decision was made not to shell the Old City—although the Jordanians had used shells in '48 and had destroyed the Jewish Quarter. The tourists listened to the self-righteous rigmarole spinning on and on. "We took Jerusalem on foot. Here, look, the bullet holes." They peppered the iron cladding of the Lion's Gate doors. Who wanted to take photographs? He rammed his index finger through a hole. A member of the tour group asked him to adjust the angle of his head—there was a shadow on his face, spoiling the shot. Smile for us. The cameras seized him.

In Danielle, a rift opened. Real photographers—like Wili—used the light as it was; he posed nothing. He grabbed the instant. He'd been quick. Wili had had two arms.

"I'll get a taxi," she said.

When they were settled in the backseat Danielle started to weep. Alice patted her knee, but Danielle said jaggedly, "Don't comfort me. I've got to go back to a script conference with Bennie, and—"

Alice closed her eyes and waited.

You need patience with the turmoil of the young, she thought. Bennie had been in a fearful state about the accident when he had telephoned her from the Dead Sea and asked her to contact Professor Garin.

The old brute was unmoved. Marilyn had shown more concern, Alice recalled, although she could not resist remarking that "the Lord has taught Danielle a lesson"—and when I inquired what the lesson might be, she had the gall to reply, "If you came to church, Miss Sadler, you'd find out."

"Bennie can be very trying," Alice said.

Danielle blew her nose. Abruptly she was able to get a grip on herself. "You know what? We had a car accident near Masada. And Wili's arm has been amputated. It's Bennie's fault. And mine. We were getting on each other's nerves." She realized she was botching the explanation. She turned to face Alice and stared into magnified, steady eyes. Alice was thinking, The same reaction as Bennie's: guilt, exaggeration, oversimplification, self-punishment. You and he are a fine pair.

"Who was driving the car?"

"Wili."

"Just so. It could have been your arm, instead of his."

Danielle had not thought of that. There, see her swoop on the crumbs of comfort. But guilt's twin is irresponsibility, Alice was thinking. When Bennie came swaggering into my apartment last night it was like allowing an orchestra through the door, all out of tune. I thought my head would split, from his boasting and his cigars. Then he burst into tears and wanted to know what he should do about Wili: put him on the payroll for life? It was something to do with workers' compensation, for which he had no legal responsibility, but his lawyer had told him he was probably morally responsible. When I pointed out that it was up to the driver to drive properly he said, "You're damned right. Little schmuck." And that was the end of it. He ate a whole box of matzoh and smacked my backside when he left. She hoped Danielle would be less callous.

Danielle saw that Alice had gone to sleep.

The shopping had taken longer than she expected and there was no time to change. She thought, I'll go like this, and ran across King George Street in her sneakers and jeans. It was already five past five. Bennie was not downstairs and the hotel staff was rearranging the furniture. When she rang his room, he said, "They threw me out for smoking. Bloody *Shabbas*." The Sabbath elevator stopped at every floor and of course his suite was at the top of the building. When he swept the door open she saw he had shaved and that he was in a good temper.

"I called New York. You know what? My shares are up. I've made a few grand." Thirty or forty—he wasn't sure.

Danielle felt as if he were an acrobat who had back-somersaulted and landed with his feet on the highwire. Again.

"Capitalist pig," she said. "I'm only working until seven-thirty." She explained she was going to make her own dinner tonight, and noticed he was at once on the alert. "I haven't enough for you."

Bennie shrugged.

They were finished before seven o'clock. Bennie had taken a couple of notes, chewed a piece of paper, and listened. His only suggestion was about a singer—"to relieve the tension, you know?" Danielle said: of course there would be singing.

"Yeah. But give one of the female singers a little role. Give her a couple of kids. Let her decide that—aw, she'll kill them herself. Real pathetic."

"So who's the singer?"

He was annoyed with himself for being unprepared with a good story, so he just talked. "She's got a terrific voice. Terrific looking. Listen—" He couldn't help it: she was all over him. "You know what dames are like when they want to get into a movie, they'll—" he stopped himself at the coarseness that had sprung to mind, "hassle you."

I'm really screwing up my chances for this evening, he thought. Danielle knows I've laid What'shername.

Then it came to him. "I met her in the lobby, just after you left this afternoon. She has a cousin on the staff who told her who I was, and . . ."

Danielle was looking skeptical, but she half-believed him. He jumped up. "Hey! I won't be seeing you again—"

She watched him saunter into the bedroom. She was already thinking about preparing dinner: half the avocado, with lemon juice; then a Greek salad of white cheese dribbled with olive oil, long brown olives, the small, firm tomatoes; halvah; coffee; oranges. And for breakfast, a honeydew and the granola Alice had given her.

"What's this?" she asked without curiosity. Bennie had laid on her knees a large gray cardboard box.

He helped her open it; tissue paper crackled inside. She began to scrabble it away, excited, then—

"Bennie!"

It was a garment sold by the kind of shop with only a vase of flowers in the window; you made appointments for fittings.

"But," she said. She had nothing in her wardrobe to wear with it.

He was gaping with pleasure. "C'mon. Does it fit?" Perfectly. "Now you can throw out that monkey suit." Yes—she could: the fox jacket was too hot for the Sydney and Los Angeles winters. She'd kept it for Patrick, a memento of their only winter in London, two freezing Australians who'd come from a summer of one hundred degrees into snow, with no jobs and nowhere to live, and £40 between them. Patrick had scoured the pubs until he'd found where hot goods were sold. It's a scar I can throw away, she thought. And not because of this fragrant, silk-lined replacement but because at last I've let go of Patrick. He can rest in peace.

Bennie was saying, "Hey, hey." His arms were around her. "Aren't you pleased?"

❖　　❖　　❖

There was, after all, enough for two. He watched while she put it together. For dessert they ate the honeydew, then had coffee and halvah. Bennie said, "Let's go for a walk." The night air was cool and had a Sabbath freshness now that workday traffic had vanished from the city. They walked aimlessly, like tramps, people going nowhere in particular. Bennie slung his arm over her shoulder and they talked by following ripples of thought that led into memories and secrets. She told him about the nuns and how horrified she'd been; he told her of his terror on the night of the accident, when he'd crawled into the car. "You said there was a time bomb in it."

"I said that?"

"Sure. You were crazy."

The collected memory was suddenly unendurable, for it contained so much guilt for each of them. The event seemed fated by their own weaknesses—her high-handedness the night she dined with Wili, which she had offset by offering him a job; Bennie's fear about returning to Israel, which he had diminished by verbally assaulting her, and by getting stoned. They began to detach.

"Well, it did explode."

"Yeah! You think there was a bomb? Hey, maybe Wili was a terrorist . . ."

They started constructing a plot—remember the assistant? the "Greek"? Wili was on a suicide mission—but everything goes wrong—because you got stoned. And Wili, while he's a real hot photographer, is a dud terrorist, so he doesn't set the bomb right—it was meant to blow up the Moriah Hotel and all those people with arthritis and skin sores—but he blows away his nose. It's a circus act that's not coming off: the lion won't jump through the flaming hoop, the trapeze artist misses and falls in the net. And then—

"Look, look," Bennie said. "This is what he does." He had his arms upstretched in a V for victory. "He takes a bow, very dignified."

"As if that were the whole point—to fall arse over tit—"

"—in front of three thousand kids."

They were shrieking with crude hilarity. Families gathered in the glow of Sabbath candles heard laughter outside.

"You know—I haven't produced a comedy since *Running Hot.* How about, after *Eleazar,* we do a comedy?"

"With terrorists and vitamins!"

"We'll set it in Peru. They got flying saucers there—common as dogs' balls. Raphael told me. Okay, so the terrorists, disguised as Rolfing masseurs . . ."

There has got to be an alternative to evasion, Danielle thought.

Raphael and I used to rap like this, Bennie remembered. I had so many good ideas when Raph was alive.

"Raphael was mad, by the way," he said. "He didn't own a pair of shoes. He owned one set of clothes. When they were in the wash, he wore a sarong. As soon as he married Marguerita she bought him Bloomingdale's—and he gave it all away to a black kid he saw clipping a hedge."

We hedge, Danielle thought. "So she did it again?"

"And he did it again."

"That's marriage."

Their shouts of laughter rang through the night. And what's funny, Danielle wondered, about a man and his wife hurting each other's feelings? What's funny for Wili, now?

They had wandered to the entrance of a public garden, a small inky area scented by spring flowers. A pearl shone in the Passover sky. Bennie looked down at her and the moonlight mirrored itself along his eyelids. She was filled with longing and fright.

I can't go to bed with you tonight, as you are planning, she thought, because sex makes me childish. And when I'm childish, I get hurt.

Bennie said, "There'll be a seat inside."

Out of the orange glare of a streetlamp they had to stand still for a while to allow their eyes to adjust to the unlit garden. After a few minutes they found themselves in a shimmering, vaporous light, enough to see their way to a bench under a trellis. Across the valley the lights of a West Bank settlement town signaled. At night one saw parts of the fiery ring of fortress towns built to defend Jerusalem.

"That must be Giloh." Her tone was dull.

—And Absalom sent for Ahithopel, the Gilonite, David's counselor, from his city, even from Giloh. The books of Samuel had been Bennie's favorites, David his favorite ancestor. He began to sing.

She recognized the tune and that it was different from his childhood Israeli songs, which sounded Russian. The words were unfamiliar; she picked out Lord, and in the last line, Israel.

"What is it?"

"A psalm of David."

"Which one?"

"I dunno. It says in the last line, Redeem Israel. From its troubles." He took a cigar from his breast pocket and a gold lighter with a clipper attachment. The gadget, which she had seen before, reminded her of Wili's folding knife-fork-and-spoon set. A thought that was feathery around its edges began to assemble itself: that Wili had played an extraordinary role in their lives, that they were seated together in a cocoon of anguish and tenderness because of that . . . creep. He had given them something to share that had uncovered them to the bone.

After a while she said, "I'm frightened of you, because you make me come to terms with—or see—weaknesses in myself that I don't like thinking about . . . that I'm not good-looking enough, that I'll be rejected and abandoned. I feel I have to defend myself against you. It's the *worst* thing, to be permanently scared of being hurt."

Bennie felt his heart swell. "I'll never abandon you," he said.

They did not talk much on the walk back to the Plaza. Between every stop of the Sabbath elevator ascending to the top floor Bennie kissed her face.

In the morning they stood on the balcony and admired the Old City and the dark green patches of garden that could be seen from this height but, from street level, were hidden behind walls.

"I got Alice to contact your father," he said. He was winding her wet curls around his fingers. Neither could stop touching the other and their fingertips had an extra sense, like that in the hands of the blind.

She told him she had given up. "I was sure he'd come around. But now—" Nothing is resolved, except that now what I thought was a homing call turns out to be a noose of unfinished business. He spoiled me so much when I was little. He used to hide chocolates in his pockets for me to find.

She had been speaking aloud.

"Still looking for 'em?" Bennie said.

They let the topic drift away into the pale blue of day.

The next afternoon they sat holding hands in the back of Akram's Mercedes, lurching against each other as the car sped down from Jerusalem, past the iron memories of the '48 war,

through Bab el-Wad, across the Valley of Ayalon, toward Lod.
Bennie was running late for his flight. When they arrived at the
airport they were allowed to stay together for only a few minutes
before Security separated them. She had to watch from a distance while he opened his siutcase and answered the set questions: yes, this was his case; yes, he had packed it himself; no,
he was not carrying anything for anybody else; yes, it had been
in his care since he packed it; yes, he had relatives in Israel. And
being searched. He was speaking Hebrew, his accent was native,
his bag was searched all the same. Men with walkie-talkies pa-
trolled the linoleum. She watched a man without a walkie-talkie
cover a territory around the cafeteria where the tables were tall
mushrooms.

There were no chairs: people left bombs under chairs. The
man suddenly picked up a shopping bag that a woman had
abandoned to run after her toddler. He disappeared with it.
When the woman returned with her child and found her bag
missing, she began looking around frantically; the man observed
her from a distance. After a while she got the idea of accosting
one of the walkie-talkie officers and the plainclothesman resumed strolling about.

One tended to forget
The hatred.

One tended to forget that a few years ago hooded figures had
leapt out of walls here, in this airport, to machine-gun fifty people to death, Jews and Gentiles—they weren't fussy, it was the
daring of the stunt that counted, for daring got publicity. Terrorism lusted for headlines. She thought, If their attacks were
reported by theater critics—"another vulgar cliché of the weapons cult" and run on the crossword page . . .

She watched Bennie's head being carried away on the tide of
travelers. He turned, his eyes straining across the crowd. She
shouted and the direction of his gaze swerved toward her. A
gate opened; the flood toward it swept him through.

Akram drove her back to Jerusalem and took her that night
to dine with his family in the eastern sector, down a lane, up a
flight of iron stairs. He had a plastic chandelier and Swiss Alp
wallpaper in the dining room. A VCR stood beside the TV set
on a carved wooden chest. Akram blew dust from the vase of
plastic roses with proprietorial dignity and they sat down and
waited for his wife to serve them. She was shy—because she
spoke no English, he explained—and at first did not want to join

them, but Danielle kept smiling and nodding, and at last Mrs. Akram subsided onto a dining chair. The younger children were made to shush and ordered from the room. They peered around the doorway giggling, and for seconds at a stretch became brave enough to take a steady look at Danielle, who jumped up, chased, caught, and tickled one, sending him into convulsions. She did it to prove she was human, underneath. "Western Lady," Akram said, and his wife nodded agreement; they made it sound as if she were neither one sex nor the other, but a hybrid species. Maybe they're right, Danielle thought.

The domesticity—the plastic potty in the hallway, the smell of children and cooking—made her want to be home.

Next day the first of the farewells had to be made. She called again on Professor Garin, who was out, Marilyn said. Marilyn had washed her hair and was wearing a new Indian cotton dress; she invited Danielle to the kitchen for mint tea, asking after a while, "And how is Bennie?"

"Fine. He left yesterday."

Marilyn looked down then up with the uncertain expression one sees in the eyes of small, purebred dogs when they meet strangers.

You're as hopeless as I am, Danielle thought. "He's gone to New York for Passover with his grandmother. Then he's returning to L.A."

They bumped cheekbones at the front door. Marilyn clutched the bottle of Passover wine Danielle had brought, saying, "He'll be thrilled." They called, Peace, Peace, up and down the stairwell.

When the door was shut, Professor Garin came out of his study. He felt frail and dispirited, as if Danielle had got the better of him. And what was worse, ever since he'd come home from hospital Marilyn had taken to scolding him. Just now she'd kept him locked up in the study for forty minutes while she and Danielle chattered in the kitchen.

Marilyn had her hands on her hips. "Some people would say you were very selfish not to see her," she said.

"Dr. Wilensky told me: my heart can't stand it," he replied.

"Your heart. Your *pride*." Marilyn snorted. "And *I've* told you, Professor Garin, not to wear that pullover indoors. That's your best pullover, which I hand washed . . ."

After a while he asked shyly, "Did she bring me a present?"

* * *

Danielle spent an unorthodox Passover dinner at Amos's house, with Alice, Phil, the silent Tikva, and a crowd of academics who argued all night. There was no ceremony except for a moment at the beginning of the meal when Amos lifted his glass and said, "Lord, lead us out of Egypt!"

Danielle and Phil were the only ones who spoke no Hebrew; the others would remember every so often and make some remark in English, but mostly he and she were left to themselves. Phil was alarmed and depressed: he did not know how he could write his *Washington Post* articles without sounding as if he were delivering a stab in the back. What was published in the Hebrew press (Amos had got him translations) would make your hair curl, but . . . That was in the family. "Israel was the most optimistic undertaking of the twentieth century," he said gloomily. Danielle tried to cheer him up, without success; Tikva brought them cups of coffee and he brightened momentarily, asking her about Gideon, but she shook her head with a remote, smiling look and passed on.

"So many of the young women here—" Phil began. His amiable face wrestled with something he did not want to say. "—are hard. And disappointed." He checked himself—"I don't mean to sound sexist"—if he were giving Danielle offense. "I think it's the army. The cult of militarism."

She nodded and sighed. Bennie had put it brusquely: "Most of them look like sluts." She'd hoped that he'd really meant they felt imprisoned by the military system—the No Alternative— against which they were instinctively in revolt. She had the cheap idea that she was pleased Bennie had not met Tikva. Chatting with Phil, her thoughts were on Bennie and she barely noticed Amos's hostly gestures, that it was mainly he who threw sentences in English for her to catch and turned the conversation to her research, and the accident.

At the door Amos said, "I'll see you in Sydney." He was taking his sabbatical leave in Australia. "Orstralia." He rolled the word around his mouth, testing it like an odd flavor.

"Will Mira be coming with you?"

Amos shook his head. Mira was going to spend six months at Oxford. "If I run into your father—"

"Yes. I'd be grateful."

"You're so *English*," Amos said, and his head reared away in amusement. "Are all Orstralians so polite? Will I need a tuxedo?"

—Smartarse. Wisenheimer. "Sure. We dress for dinner."

"See you in a white tuxedo," he said, rolling his yellow eyes.

Downstairs Alice said, "Amos has taken a fancy to you."

Danielle felt trespassed upon. She longed for her own house, for Emma prancing with excitement, for cooking special lunches for Katherine on the weekends, for the boats turning slow circles in the bay beneath her windows while she wrote letters to Bennie in her head.

It will be autumn and there'll be Queensland mangoes as big as soccer balls in the greengrocer's shop, she thought. And porpoises will be torpedoing through the dark blue water. And we're not at war. And we don't have nuclear weapons. And nobody wants to wipe us out of history, as an experiment that failed.

A string of negatives, she thought.

"He's wasting his time," she said to Alice.

Early next morning she braced herself for the Old City. You could walk part of the way along the parapet of the walls, something she had done once already, weeks ago, but it had been late in the day and groups of other sightseers had forced her pace. The Old City was a Chinese box. No sooner had one set of buildings been revealed than another was discovered within. To walk around the Old City's circumference took a couple of hours and yet there were people who had spent thirty years exploring inside the circle and not seen it all.

She arrived before the day's onslaught of pilgrims and as she passed through the pedestrian doorway on the left of the Jaffa Gate she put on the purposeful expression necessary in this part of town.

Saeed, who was hanging around waiting for tourists, saw her and decided to get Jazzy. She was making for the parapet; Jazzy could catch up to her there.

Danielle had not been long on the bowmen's path when from one of the houses in a section behind the Street of the Greek Patriarch a man emerged thirty feet below her, glanced up to right and left, saw she was alone, and exposed himself. He began to masturbate. Her instinct was to hurry away. Then she thought, Damn it! and laughed. The man shot up a furious look and pumped harder.

She yelled down, "Monkey! You should be in a zoo!" She capered back and forth, miming his flailing hand, until, after less than a minute, he stamped inside his backdoor. She was jubilant.

But ten yards on, when the house and the man were safely out of sight, she felt dizzy and glum. You forget the hatred, she was thinking. You forget men want to punish women. And vice versa.

She decided she would walk only as far as the Damascus Gate then return to the apartment, pack, and have a rest. Her legs felt unreliable and something worse had happened: she was intensely sexually aroused. Her crotch was jumping with electricity, and wet. She felt frightened of herself and for herself: everything seemed tenuous and reversible; anything could capsize.

She realized someone was trying to catch her attention and turned, scowling. A young man was jingling his gold bracelet as he waved at her. He repeated his greeting: "I say, aren't you the lady photographer?" He had a Pommy accent.

She shook her head, frowning harder. She didn't like the way he had snuck up behind her. He didn't look English, but there were plenty of Jews and Arabs around who had been brought up in England. He was vaguely familiar.

"I say," he repeated. "Didn't I see you taking some marvelous shots of St. Anne's the other day?"

"Not me. Sorry."

He seemed crestfallen. "Well, I don't know if they were marvelous or not—rude of me to assume. Look, I've been given this *unbelievable* machine—" He had a Nikon. "And I can't work the ruddy thing. Do you know about cameras?" He prattled on about his vacation and his mother (for whom he was taking the photographs) while she had a look at the camera for him. The problem was simple: the cover was on the lens.

"Gosh, aren't I an idiot! And don't you know *everything!*"

He was as effete as Wili. She smiled. He had fallen into step beside her. Mother would scream when he told her he had spent six weeks searching for people to rescue him from La Nikon—there'd been a simply *marvelous* man, a professional photographer, who'd explained all its working parts a week or so ago—they'd met in a camera shop—and you know, he had, I promise you, the biggest nose . . .

"Really? What was his name?"

Gosh. He had such a bad memory. William? Wilfred? Winston?

"Wili," Danielle said. "That was Wili Djugash. He's one of the best photographers in the world."

Go on! She didn't say. Mother would—! "And you know Win— Wif—?" Gosh, he must write down the name. And address, if she knew it. For a lark he would love to send one of his snaps to . . . Win?

"That might cheer him up," Danielle said. "He's in pretty bad shape. He had a car accident."

"No!" He stopped walking; his hand with the gold bracelet flew to his forehead. "What happened?"

"His car crashed. And he's had an arm amputated."

Oh, God. But he was alive? He wasn't going to . . . die? Or anything? No . . . *brain damage?*

She felt nauseated, as if she'd had a blow in the stomach. In the cosmetic-perfumed muddle inside her shoulder bag she found one of Wili's cards.

"Here. Bye. I'm in a hurry." She reached the Damascus Gate with his "Thanks ever so!" trailing after her.

Two days later, after hours in airports and airplanes, she arrived in Sydney.

Emma's welcome festival continued for a week. Every movement of Danielle's was an invitation to skip, leap on and off the chairs, and perform her specialty, the flying kiss, which began at a distance of five feet. Emma's nature was love; she delighted in the force of love and in impetuous contacts.

When Danielle struggled through her high wooden front gate carrying what she could, with the cab driver acting as porter for her heavy suitcase, Emma rocketed from the kitchen door and knocked her over. A bronchial wail arose from Mrs. Wellsmore, who, with the cabbie, tried to pull Emma back. Their yells and tugs at her collar were futile.

"Leave her, leave her," Danielle said.

She lay flat on the concrete of the driveway, panting as paws smashed into her chest and belly. Sometimes the dog's physical power appalled her; sometimes on the beach Emma would grab something in her jaws and begin shaking her head in a frenzy, a switch would tip in both of them, and Danielle would see Emma in the pack of dogs in a Staffordshire bullring, tearing the beast to death, as she had been bred to do.

Emma was saying, "I love beyond endurance. My being overflows!"

The taxi driver went away wagging his head and Mrs. Wellsmore, the drawstring of her lips jerked tight, returned to the house to make a pot of tea.

That night Emma slept under the blankets instead of at the foot of the bed. Every couple of hours she crawled up to the pillows to cover Danielle's face with caresses and to explore her armpits, the flavor of her palms, the webs between her fingers.

Like Bennie and me, Danielle thought. "But you're better than Bennie."

Early morning and after dark when they drove to the surf and went running along the beach Emma pleaded with Danielle to try harder to keep up. "Beloved, Beloved," she cried. "Like this— like this!" She never tired of trying to teach Danielle how to run.

It took Danielle some days to discover the source of the smell in the house.

At first she thought Mrs. Wellsmore had neglected to air the clothes. Then she discovered the huge burned spot on the underside of her mattress. Emma came in to stare at it, too, then looked up at Danielle, smiling to her back teeth: it was she who had dragged Mrs. Wellsmore, drunk, and having a last cigarette for the night, from Danielle's bed.

"Yairs. I did spill a spot of tea on it," Mrs. Wellsmore said.

DIARY
1 9 8 4

I found home-people half-asleep after Israel and I didn't feel like talking to them about what had happened to me there. I knew nobody who I thought would understand even as much of it as I did. I felt lost.

When I first returned home I spent hours in an armchair, pretending I was recovering from jet lag, but in fact admiring what I owned—perhaps like the Jews who first settled and farmed in Palestine and rejoiced in the feel of their earth on their hands, their cows giving Jewish milk, their cotton fields growing Jewish cotton, their hens laying Jewish eggs. I was in *my* house; its solidity reassured me. I thought of it as the sturdy vessel containing my life again, safely, after all that shaking around. *My* house. I'd worked for it; I'd built it up. I knew Mrs. Wellsmore felt as kindly toward me as the Palestinians did towards the Israelis— but what could I do about that? She'd sold the husk of it to me.

I was wearied by the excitement I had left behind and by the heaviness of love. I thought constantly of Bennie Kidron as I sat by my wide front windows.

I'd been extravagant when I rebuilt Mrs. Wellsmore's cottage and had knocked out the north wall to replace it with glass. In front of me was the wooden-decked balcony with balsam and

geraniums in pots. Beyond were the tops of the trees in my garden, a steep slope that, at an invisible equator, changes to native
forest, virgin except for the track that leads through it to the
front door of Mrs. Wellsmore's own fibro-cement shack. It was
once a dinghy shed; high tides bring shoals of transparent fish
to her back-door mat. I, in her former house, look clear over her
roof and the canopies of eucalyptus to the bay. I have a T-shirt
printed with a drawing that could have been made from my balcony. Under the picture it says: FROM MY FRONT WINDOW I CAN
SEE LION ISLAND. It's the sort of thing the Avalon boutiques sell
mainly to the inner-city people who rent houses here for the summer. One feels cut off from Sydney; the city is almost as far away
as Jerusalem is from Tel Aviv.

Thoughts of distance distressed me.

Bennie was a planet away.

He telephoned me from New York the morning after I arrived
home. I was about to leave for Emma's early run, but it was evening for him and he was going to dinner with his grandmother—
that outrageous old woman who enjoys piano bars and the atten-
tions of an elderly senator. Then they were going to a new
Coppola movie. He said he wished I was there.

We pretended. At least, I did. My own nature was largely a
mystery to me then: many of my actions seemed alien events
over which I had no control; I would think out the explanations
afterward. If you are a mystery to yourself you cannot change. I
was half-blind, in those days, not only to my own faults but also
to Bennie's. It had not occurred to me that there are people, of
whom he is one, who arrange their affairs in a way that invites
disaster—and that I was another.

We pretended for a few weeks that distance did not separate.
He telephoned me every couple of days. In between I suffered
frantic bouts of jealousy. At first we talked for an hour at a time,
but we found less to say, and the interlocked threads snapped
one by one. I was embarrassed by the irrelevance to him of the
things I had to report—that I'd discovered Mrs. Wellsmore had
almost burnt the house down, that Emma had a tick (he didn't
know what a tick was)—yet I felt resentful that they didn't interest him. He returned to his seesaw of complaints about Marguerita Schultz and his boasts of how he was outwitting her, the
Internal Revenue, his bankers, the whole financial world. Once
he was drunk: it was four in the morning in Los Angeles, he

said, and in a few hours he was going to have to appear in court. He'd been up all night with Sam "and the boys I hired in New York—best attorneys in the world." The witch was closing in; he and Sam believed Raphael died leaving only one will and that the alleged second one produced by Marguerita was a fake. But the courts had accepted it as genuine, invalidating the first, which had left Raphael's share of the company to Bennie.

It was ten o'clock in the evening in Sydney; I was working on the screenplay and my mind was sharp. But the interruption had shattered an image that was taking shape. Bennie said, "What am I going to do? The bitch wants to tear me in half."

He had not told me before about the second will. He had not told me that there was a real danger he could lose control of the company, that Marguerita Schultz might be able to stop production of *Eleazar*, that the whole project could be washed away like a sandcastle. My contract was with him; I could be out of a job. I suggested he volunteer for military service in Lebanon.

"Thanks," he said, and hung up.

I had set a tough routine: from six to nine playing with Emma and so forth; nine o'clock to one-thirty writing; lunch and a sleep until three-thirty; writing until seven; another run with the dog, then dinner; nine till midnight, work. I took Saturday mornings off to do the shopping while Mrs. Wellsmore cleaned the house. By midday she was sometimes drunk. "Touch of the flu, dear," she'd say when she lurched against the furniture. She found excuses for hanging around me on her cleaning day, suggesting extra work. (This was to earn another five dollars, which went, that evening, for gin.) One day she said she had to clean the silver—I didn't have much, only what Bonny had salvaged when we fled Jerusalem—and I saw her fling a tablespoon out the kitchen window. I found it in the azalea bed and brought it back to her.

"Oh," she said. "I thought it was a lizard."

I never knew what strange bestiary was in her head. The day, a few weeks after my return to Sydney, when I arrived at the house with bands on my teeth and a black knot of surgical string in the center of my gums—the orthodontist had had to cut a little ridge of bone between my incisors—Mrs. Wellsmore screamed. I was groggy from the anesthetic, but I rushed to her, thinking she was going to faint. She staggered away from me, saying, "Come no closer!" When she calmed down, she explained that she thought I had a spider in my mouth and that I'd been out in the garden eating their webs.

"I'll do your shopping, dear," she said. "You can't go down to the village looking like that, like the grille on a 1955 Holden."

The moment when I had decided to get my smile fixed, my looks had ceased to worry me. It was extraordinary to realize that I had been trapped into one misery by attempting to evade another—Bonny's warning to me (when I was about eight years old) that I would never be loved if I were too handsome. I had been planning to tell Bennie about my teeth next time he called, but he did not telephone again for a month and by then I had realized that it was not his business, but my own.

I had returned outwardly and, in time, inwardly to a celibate life. Katherine was secretly delighted although she pretended to be permissive about me. She whined a bit: "Aw, Mum—you should have a boy friend." These days she put gel in her hair, making it look like a lavatory brush, and arrived home for weekends of windsurfing in mauve or purple faille dresses with silver beads around the necklines. They cost two dollars each from St. Vincent de Paul and apparently she wears them to lectures with fishnet stockings and canvas shoes made in China. They are her disguise: she's as steady as a bank clerk.

She discovered my new kid jacket on her first visit. I made her promise to lend it back to me on short notice: perhaps even then I had an intuition that Bennie would turn up without warning.

When he telephoned after the month's silence he was more like his pre-Israel self. I had almost finished the first draft. We were businesslike and kept to technicalities. He was obviously talking from a list of headings, and taking notes of my remarks. He'd signed contracts with an art director and a composer. Toward the end I asked, "What's happening with the evil Mrs. Schultz?"

"We'll settle outta court," he said. "Jesus, have I had a hard time." He asked me to hold. I could hear another phone ringing and heard him say, "Great. Terrific. Can you hold? I'm talking to Australia—" and I thought how accurate that phrase was: he was no longer talking to me.

I can say now that I love Bennie. I know he does not love me: his deep feelings end when he senses he has the upper hand.

He telephoned me again to say the first draft was brilliant, but I knew he was dissatisfied with the ending. I was, too. I refused to fly to Los Angeles for a discussion, although he offered to pay the fare. I'm not sure now why I was so stubborn—I think it was panic at the thought of having to meet him face-to-face, although the excuse I gave was "family commitments." It was my first mistake, for in fact I had done what he wanted me to do: create a problem. He needs crises to reassure himself that he is alive, and where there are none he will invent them. He craves excitment, not fulfillment, from life.

I set to work on the second draft, trusting something would turn up, a phoenix rising at the end of the story.

What turned up, however, was the first of the dolls. It was a dreary day, rain coming down in long needles. The Pittwater was as gray as anesthetic and treetops were lashing about; people in yellow or orange oilskins clambered around their boats, pumping them out and refastening tarpaulins that had blown loose in the gale. The mother possum and her overgrown baby had tucked themselves in a niche under the roof of the sundeck and Emma had spent all morning barking at them, until I shut her in the bedroom. It had a sliding door which, if she was determined, she could open by hooking a claw under it, but usually after a scolding she went to sleep. The postman must have rung the bell on the front gate, but I did not hear him. I heard Emma, at large again: her shoulders and back became a wild boar's quills when there was some serious intrusion. The postman, a waterfall, was wedged between the wooden door and the screen inside it, saying hopefully, "Good dog."

The wrapping of the parcel was so sodden that I put it in the garbage without looking at the postmark. Inside a shoebox there was a nude rubber doll of a dumpling-nosed girl with Jean Harlow hair and an open-lipped smile. It was the type that came into vogue in the early 1970s, with the "sexual revolution"—that is, it had a plump little Mount of Venus, grooved, and a hole between its legs. But no anus. I'd been to a raffish, ritzy dinner party in Woollahra when these dolls first came on the market. The hostess had run to the children's bedroom and brought out boy and girl dolls, holding them up as proof of her broadmindedness. Then the guests made them copulate on the dining-table in between the candelabra and the crumbs of baguettes. I asked why, since the dolls had everything else, they had no arseholes. The hostess said, "You *would* notice that." On impulse she added,

"Vere are ze anuses, I ask you?" She rubbed together her index finger and thumb.

I thought somebody had sent me the doll as a joke. A number of my friends knew that I was back on what they called "the chastity kick"; some of them were compiling lists of eligible men—no easy matter in Sydney. The bands were due to be removed from my mouth; soon I would have teeth like anybody else's, lined up straight as milk bottles, a kind of portcullis. My best friend, Nell, was threatening to have a "fangs frolic" to celebrate; there would be five guaranteed heterosexuals at it, she said. I thought the rubber sexpot was probably from her. I gave it to Emma.

A couple of weeks later when its partner, a boy doll, arrived, I gave her that, too. Nell and Katherine, the only people I could think of who might have the inclination for such nonsense, denied knowing anything. Both dolls floated and for as long as they lasted made good beach toys for the dog, so by the time the third lot arrived, their two predecessors had been chewed to pieces.

Amos called me in late winter. He had been in Australia for some weeks, at Melbourne University, and was to come to Sydney for a weekend. Of course, he did not start off by saying that; he began by saying that he was calling from the swimming pool of the Singapore Hilton, where Malay beauties were massaging his feet. I was unexpectedly thrilled to hear from him—Amos brought back for me the poignancy of trying to stay civilized, in Israel, in 1983.

He said, "I wrote you a fifteen-page letter. You mean to say you didn't get it?" It took me a while to realize that Amos was shy; much longer to know that he was a man who, yearning for comfort, rejected it.

I told him I would love to see him but added that Sydney was vast and I lived a long way out of town.

He said, "I understand the geography. Seven hours. We crossed the northern coastline, saw something called Dar-win, and I fastened my seatbelt, ready for Melbourne. Seven hours later we got there. How are you going to defend this country?" I told him we couldn't, but we kept an army, navy, and so forth, to be polite.

Of all the things to do and see in my barbarically glorious city, which on hot fine days looks to me like a shipwreck of bright-skinned mermaids and sailors washed ashore, Amos wanted to visit the zoo.

I told him to take a taxi from the airport, then a ferry, so that he could see something of the harbor, the famous and ugly Opera House (an albino tropical plant rootbound from too small a pot), and the famous and ugly Harbour Bridge (shaped like a costive tortoise suspended between stakes). We Sydneysiders are proud of these monuments; their cost was awesome. I was to meet him at eleven next morning.

As I drove toward the smog, I had a bet with myself that he would not notice my new smile. I won, but Amos did realize something was different: "You've had your hair cut?" he said.

We lived in different worlds.

As we were shaking hands I noticed his kippered skin had been smoothed from a few weeks in mild, damp Melbourne and that the navy pullover he was wearing was cheap lambswool, probably from Myers. His tough-guy bearing—big chest, slim hips, and legs held rigid at the knees, jutting chin, small, pouted lips—could have won him a role, I thought, as a detective in a French movie: a plainclothesman from Marseilles who'd seen it all, but still had a heart. His look was of military *service;* I mentally placed Bennie beside him and saw a rebellious thug.

"I *had* to get away from Israel," Amos said. "Everything is degenerating there." He had been enchanted by his ferry trip from Circular Quay to the zoo, but when I asked him what it was that had particularly attracted him he could not say; it was just Sydney Harbour, the yachts, the ocean liners, the great cargo tankers. Nothing specific.

I had not been to Taronga Park for years; it was agreeably changed. As cruel institutions go, it seemed kinder—at least to some of the birds. Ibis and peacocks roamed through luxuriant gardens which, when Katherine was a child, had been acres of concrete. We saw the snake house, the languid kangaroos and wallabies, the horrible tiger cage, and the seals who mewed to each other underwater in voices that we could feel vibrating through the walls of their pool. Amos loved the giraffes in a paddock with a view across the harbor. A foal galloped on bamboo legs, teetered, then folded itself down like a telescope.

We took our sandwiches to a bench by one of the artificial lakes where the iridescent ducks begged brazenly. A sign said PLEASE DO NOT FEED . . . Amos threw them crusts. "It's okay. They can't read," he said. Liquid silver spouted as the ducks fought each other. Then around a curve of the lake a black swan came swimming fast. Its gaze focused down on the water made it seem bashful. Amos threw more bread, the swan snaked out its neck, swallowed, then turned to face us. It was a fine, full-grown bird, as composed, as it stared at us, as a king.

Amos had never seen a black swan. "Okay—who's painted it?" he said. "Swans are white. What's going on?"

The bird came ashore on its red frogman feet. Amos had walked forward to the lake's fence to feed it by hand.

"They can be savage," I said. "Don't tease it." He was trying to make the swan come closer. Suddenly the curved serpent straightened into a rod; Amos leaped back shaking his hand.

"You bastard!" he said. The swan was eating the food he had dropped. Just before it slid back into the water it gave a kind of salute, raising one wing. There, hidden by the black plumage, was a sheaf of long white feathers like the pages of a manuscript fanning open.

"Look!" I said—but Amos could not see that the swan was hiding a film script beneath its wing.

"You're really funny," he said. He was smiling in amazement at me. "Tell me—is all your family odd?" Later that afternoon, because he seemed at loose ends, I asked him to stay for the rest of the weekend. We were both embarrassed.

When we arrived at Avalon, after dark, Emma behaved shamelessly. Amos was good with dogs, as people who feel unloved often are. She flung herself on the floor at his feet, belly up, and he smooched with her while I breaded and fried some veal and threw together a salad. The meal was skimpy, but he was ready to be charmed by everything: the house, the dog, the possums that arrived during dinner for bread and sugar. He came with me on Emma's evening run at the surf beach. It was high tide, so we had no trouble with the swags of brown kelp that can be booby-trapped with bluebottles. There was phosphorus in the water. He'd never before seen the cold fire that sparkles around your feet in the dark. When I finished throwing a ball for Emma and returned to him, I found him playing with the phosphorus— but as a scientist might, scooping up handfuls of water, trying to determine its various qualities. I guessed he had never had a chance to play in childhood; at that stage he had not told me what had happened to him during the war in Europe. I began, at that moment, to try to adjust my vision to his. It was a flaw in my nature, and, I suppose, in that of many women, to accept, out of some inchoate sense of pity, burdens that were not my own.

Sharing, I discovered, does not halve the weight; it doubles the quantity of unhappiness.

Amos made fewer wisecracks that evening. But he was barricaded with them again next morning, and tense with politeness about keeping out of sight until I had showered and dressed, when he scuttled into the bathroom in a shoddy new checked dressing gown.

The day was overcast and drizzly; Lion Island was hidden in mist. I was piqued that the view was so poor and the weather too miserable for fishing from the jetty, but he said, "This is paradise. I tell you—you've got yourself into paradise." He seemed happy to do nothing more than sit around and talk, but I became restless and in the afternoon I coaxed him out for a walk. The neighborhood is hilly and we had to go slowly because he was short of breath. "What are you? An Orstralian paratrooper?" he asked. "I tell you—you've got a military profile of ninety." We'd got back to the war: Gideon was out of danger because the government was frightened of stimulating the Yesh Ge'vul mutiny by dealing too harshly with the situation, he said. When Gideon had been released from jail he was told—unofficially—that he would not be sent back to Lebanon.

"What's he doing?" I asked.

"My dear, I don't talk about those things."

I felt foolish; I'd forgotten that Amos was in the army reserve, and there were oaths of secrecy. I said irritably, "I could never live in Israel. It gave me the creeps, knowing every male between eighteen and fifty is armed."

"There's a reason for that. Oh, fuck it—I don't want to argue with you, okay?"

I realized he meant he did not want to argue because he was certain of winning.

We moved to the steadier ground of politics: when the government might fall, if Mapam would split from Mapai, the future for General Sharon, the Labor Alignment leadership issue. In Jerusalem Amos was part of a group working to unseat the Alignment leader ("a piece of shit"), who, "with a disastrous war, the economy falling to pieces, the Americans turning against us—in *those* circumstances probably can't win an election." He lived politics; he had that obsession with power and powerlessness that in centuries to come may seem as quaint as schoolmen's debates about angels on the head of a pin. I had begun listening not to what he said about policy issues, but what he was saying about himself.

It was then I remembered Shula's remark about his cynicism; I knew from my own experience how we cling to what we have made of ourselves—how we see the world—and that surrendering it is terrible. I'd felt as if I was being battered to death—and I was, in a way. The old was being murdered. It occurred to me that Amos, having developed his mind so highly, would have a worse time of it than someone less formed. He could even be violent; the thought of it made me uneasy; I'd been told he was an eloquent, even suave public speaker. He must have known his language in private conversation was harsh; I suppose he believed he burned out his anger with words. However, everything he said about politics was so well argued, sensible, and concerned with the national good that I felt cheap for criticizing him to myself. He was saying:

"Israelis now want three things—Greater Israel, a Jewish state, and a democracy. They can have any combination of two, but not the three. A democratic Greater Israel means the Arabs will take over Parliament, and that will end the Jewish state. A democratic Jewish state requires us to give up the West Bank and Gaza, so we lose Greater Israel. What we've got now is a Jewish Greater Israel, with the result that we're degrading morally, spiritually, and intellectually. A few years back I was talking to Koestler . . ."

"*Arthur?*"

His eyebrows asked: How many Koestlers are there?

". . . who wrote in 1948 that our system of election to Parliament was so obviously ill designed and counterproductive that, within a year or so that fact would be clear to everyone, and it would be changed. It wasn't." He kicked an invisible stone. "I tell you, the reform of our system of election . . . We need a Messiah. Better still, his Old Man."

I remembered the Sephardi hairdresser. "Do you believe in God?" I asked. I'd made the common mistake of assuming that the antireligious are atheists.

For the first time he looked at me as if I were, after all, a student not really sound enough for an honors class.

"Of course. I think He's a cunt—excuse me—but, of course. My dear, what is our life but chipping away at that huge mind?" He reverted to a comedy routine: "Einstein said life is relative; Marx said . . ." And so on.

Next morning he gave me a peck on the cheek with his lips. A few hours after he had left a messenger arrived with a plastic tube wrapped in lime-green tissue paper and with a red bow on top. Inside the tube was a red rose on an eighteen-inch stem and a great deal more ribbon arranged in a spiral pattern.

I had to call Nell and tell her. Nell inherited a lot of money which she has managed to squander with unflagging cheerfulness. She's had two husbands, left one, and the other, she says, died of bad temper because she was so extravagant. Her dinner parties of more than a decade ago, in the days when she could afford them, were known for the drama of their cuisine: raw duck with beetroot; radish sorbets; tuna ice cream. "It really is delicious," she would coax well-bred, terrified guests, looking from one to the other with her big, open, untidy face, trying to guess what it was that was holding them back.

"For pity's sake!" she shrieked. "Is it worth it, I ask you? Is it worth cooking for them and listening to them and . . ."

"No," I said.

"Give the thing to Mrs. Wellsmore *immediately*. Before it bites."

I cut the stem and put the rose in a vase. It died that evening.

In any event, I forgot to thank Amos for the flower when I telephoned him. I called him because that afternoon the detective had asked me if there was anything to do with my work or with Israel that could have provoked someone to send me the third lot of dolls.

They had been delivered soon after the rose. When I opened the shoebox and saw the mangled contents I managed to get to the bathroom to vomit. I now know who sent the dolls and can see that the action made sense in its own terms: when we constrict our sympathies tightly enough anything becomes reasonable. At the time the dolls were a mystery to me and the detective, who had the smooth reddish skin and bright smile of a chronically short temper. "There are a lot of angry people in the world," he said.

Amos said, "Jesus, you're alone up there." He offered to come back to Sydney the following weekend and arrived in time for dinner on Friday. Emma was so alert with tension that at first she would not let him through the front gate. We talked until three in the morning, listing all the people I could remember meeting in Israel. Finally he asked, "Could it be your father?"

I had never fainted before. It makes blackness, like an anesthetic. When you come to, your hands tingle. Amos had lifted me onto the sofa and was kneading the nape of my neck, saying, "I'm sorry. I'm sorry I said that." When I sat up he pulled me to his chest and held me lightly there, rocking a little now and then. He told me what had happened at another interview Phil had had with Professor Garin: Phil had said something about me and my father had replied, "My dear man, you puzzle me. I have a young housekeeper, an American gel. I do not have a daughter." Amos added, "I hate crazies. Especially crazies in politics."

I said, "I'm going to bed. Do you want to come with me?"

He said he would put on his pajamas. I put on mine, and turned out the lights. We did not make love, but lay still alongside each other, each, I know, wishing we were elsewhere— anywhere—yet not knowing how to escape. At last he said, "I'm going to sleep," and did so, instantly. It's said they learn to do that in the army. I stayed awake for the rest of the night, in the guest bedroom.

At breakfast he said, "Things between me and Mira have not been good, but all the same . . ."

But all the same there are certain things we are all incapable of resisting: fantasies.

And so, with the unreason and inevitability of a dream, I obliged Amos to become my lover. A month later he moved to Sydney, and spent every weekend at my place.

At first I thought I knew what I was doing: I wanted the sense of security that can come to a woman through bonding a man to herself. No accident, I think, that at this time I chose a partner with an underside of violence. You fight fire with fire. But what *is* the original fire? I believe it's the many forms that vulnerability takes in the minds of women if they are imprinted, often at an age too young to remember properly, with a violent example of male rule. It's a female—and a Jewish—fear of The Other Side. Over decades I'd built a shell—certainly it was imperfect—but for day-to-day, twilight living it was good enough. It had splintered under the impact of the third doll. I saw myself naked, now, as I had been then, four years old and witnessing my father try to kill my mother. I'd thought, "I'm next!" The image of her broken, on the floor, lived in the basement of my memory. When I opened that third parcel of dolls I was a house that screamed from cellar to attic.

And so, Amos: my protector.

He was grateful, at first. He was nine years older than I, but sexually we were not only separated by age, gender, and an experience of holocaust, we were also of a different species. I had been harem-raised. I knew at twelve that you put scent on the pillows as automatically as you put potatoes in water when you peel them. I had a whole aesthetic of sexual ritual and gesture. Amos seemed enthralled and horrified—like a European explorer coming across Hindu rites. There were only a few ways in which he could enjoy himself with me without feeling threatened. He liked taking me to concerts; he liked holding hands; he was grateful to me for stroking his dark steel-wool hair; he was grateful to Emma. "You're both so lovely," he'd say. But he was more comfortable with her trollop behavior than with mine. He began to call me Jezebel, and I wondered if he remembered that Jezebel had been thrown to the dogs to be eaten. He would say, "Not tonight, Josephine." I was struck with compassion, with wanting to unlock his frigidity. I felt that if I stretched myself out as a bridge for him to cross he might reclaim that part of himself he had rejected. And that was foolish of me, too: later I realized I had been trying to force on him something he did not want—and that what I had really been doing was assuage my own desperate need for security.

He told me how he had, as he believed it, lost his wife's love. In 1967 his unit had fought on the Golan Heights against one of the Syrian foxholes that had tormented their kibbutz. "We were sent in like Russians—we'd never fought like that before, flinging men at the enemy." The Syrians had a last resort: flamethrowers. Amos was lucky his face and neck escaped. When he came home from the hospital, his wife had turned her head away from him. I did not like the look of that burned flesh, either, but I felt tender toward it; with my head laid against his heart, I could hear the crepitations of his cigarette-ruined lungs. When Miki would not touch him he had wanted to die, he said. "But not for long, Jezebel. I tell you—alive beats dead. Rule One of the Israeli Army." He added, "Used to be."

Sometimes I lay awake beside his tightly curled sleeping body that feared to be aroused. Drifting into sleep I would imagine that against my thigh lay the dense, soft barrel of a penis, and that it was mine. I have asked other women about this phantom. Those whose lives seesaw between infatuation and loathing the partners they collect one after another have laughed. But others, more alone by temperament, have admitted that yes, they have had such imaginings, and usually at moments of crisis: when they decided to leave their husbands, at the time they realized they disliked their jobs, or the way they were running their lives.

I will always be grateful to Amos for creating that cold boundary in my bed.

I had been so upset by the third batch of dolls that I gave up work on the screenplay.

Emma considered any time I was not typing was hers, so we went walking day after day, finding tracks through the bush, paths to unfamiliar beaches and over and between seamed boulders that divided one bay from the next. Sometimes we fell in the water; sometimes we were trapped by a tide gnashing at the rocks and would have to swim for it, arriving home freezing, scratched, and mapped with salt crust. I had vivid catalog dreams of the sights of the day. One was of a cormorant, a bird committee-designed: greasy-looking dark feathers, question-mark neck, and so insatiable it seems to have time only for fishing, drying out, and fishing again. Cormorants are hunger-on-wings. Their wings are odd, too: when they alight they hold them up, like heraldic birds. I dreamed a cormorant. The next night I dreamed it again, but when the bird stood on a buoy to dry itself it wonderfully changed to a black swan. *The* black swan—a white fan unfolding beneath dark pinions. I was so astonished, I woke and sat up. I waited with my eyes closed; maybe I dozed.

Suddenly the swan returned: a cube of brilliant light became the image of a huge white bird. Its immense wings vibrated close to its sides, ready to soar open. I was gripped with awe and a yearning to be near it. A loud voice said: I have shown you.

What?

I knew when I woke up again. I went to the typewriter and urgently rewrote the final scenes at Masada: white specks in the distance growing larger, then the air wild with beating wings as the angels swooped down to the rock, gathered the hundreds of Zealots and lifted them off to a smiling sky. Strewn on the earth was a spatter of husks, the corpses left behind for Romans to gape at.

✿   ✿   ✿

On the telephone Bennie said, "I love it! It's the best final scene in any movie ever made." He added, "But I think we've got a few problems . . ."

He asked me to Telefax the entire second draft and I did so, from an office in central Sydney that afternoon.

A day later he telephoned and said, "It's a bit arty." His voice wheedled. "We've got a miracle problem, Daniela. The fire turned back on the Zealots by Yahweh is one miracle. One for the Romans. Now I think it gets tricky if Yahweh sends angels . . ."

I wheedled back for a while. I asked him to show the scene to the composer. I said, "It's a marvelous opportunity for a musician. Bennie, you could win Best Original Theme Music."

He is too skilled a negotiator ever to say no until the minute before midnight. He has a way of listening to an argument that defeats your confidence in it because although he is apparently paying attention to every detail, something in his manner tells you that his mind is elsewhere and he is bored. He was saying, "Yeah . . . yeah . . . yeah," drawing me into thickets of justification. I was not persuading him. I was ambushed.

I said, "Stop conning me. You know it's the right ending. It's redemption. What you dislike is the politics. You want a movie that says: Look at what a *momzer* Yahweh is, but we Jews won't be beaten by Him. Israel has struggled from eternity and will struggle to eternity with God. That's what you want—isn't it?" It seemed clear to me why Christianity had been a heresy of Judaism: it forgave God—all those forgiven sins were His, not ours. The wrestling match was declared a draw.

Not so with Judaism.

Bennie said, "Girl—you're overexcited. How 'bout you come to L.A.?"

In those days if anyone called me a child, I became one. I replied, "How 'bout you bite your bum?" and hung up.

Ten days later Bennie arrived. He telephoned first from the Sydney Hilton to check that I would be at home. I offered to meet him in town but he said, "My coproducer is with me and we want to go for a drive." He said they had flown in via Tahiti. I could picture him drinking the pale rum of the tropics and feasting himself on whatever it is they feast on in Polynesia.

"Who's this coproducer?" I asked.

"Someone fantastic."

I told him about Amos.

"Doncha love me anymore?" Bennie said.

By now it was December; summer heat was adding its first increase to the weight of gravity, which by February in Sydney is so heavy people cannot easily rise from their chairs. But the weather of this weekend was exquisite. The air felt refined and eventful, brimming with summer life—the high-pitched whirr of cicadas and the sugary smell of pollen. In my garden hummingbirds stabbed their curved beaks into flowerheads, held aloft by wings moving so fast they were invisible. The gum trees all around breathed out the clean, medicinal aroma that in a few more weeks, when heat began to strain them, would change to a shimmering bluish halo and a reek of fire within. It's a smell that arouses national unease: bushfires are fated to Australia by the inflammable sap of her native trees. My garden had a fire-colored bougainvillea, planted years before my time and now growing in a neon blaze over the shed beneath the sun deck. Visitors admired it but I didn't like it much: its flowers were bits of paper, without scent. I kept it going for its blaring contrast with the silery grays and pastels inside the house.

When I went to the front porch to welcome Bennie I was forgetting my appearance had changed. I suppose he might not have recognized me, with a Colgate smile. I might not have recognized him, behind black sunglasses, with his gut breaking open his shirt buttons, and his double chin.

"You're looking two hundred percent!" he said. He had noticed immediately, and made me aware again, of what it was that had changed. I saw then the wince of embarrassment run through him, as if I were a mirror in which he was suddenly seeing his own degeneration. Bennie did not look older; he had the appearance of infantile debauch.

He was well tanned and when he took off his sunglasses the whites of his eyes were stark.

"You too," I said.

And this was Amos.

And this was Naomi, my coproducer.

She limped forward, leaning on a walking stick, the hand on the silver knob wearing a platinum wedding band on the ring finger and a huge pale sapphire in the shape of a heart, the same color as her loose silk dress and the worm of a vein at her temple. She had fair hair and a weasel face like that of the waitress Ben-

nie had eyed on Diezengoff. I left Amos to entertain them on the
balcony while I hid myself away preparing drinks and food. I
used the wrong knife, a Sabatier with a ten-inch blade, to slice a
lemon, and cut my finger. The sharp pain released a shiver of
tears and as I stood in the kitchen sucking the thin wound I realized that Bennie and Naomi were married. They were probably
on their honeymoon.

Betrayal, humiliation, dignity. The sequence worked itself out
and I was able to join the others feeling detached, and wondering what trick Bennie would try next. Naomi was lying in a deck
chair, one arm trailing over the side as if she had drowned there.
She had little to say—she thanked me for a glass of mineral water—but sat gazing into the crystal heart on her finger as if trying
to read something in it. She too had a suntan but the skin around
her eyes, which had been protected by sunglasses, was tinged
pale blue; she seemed a creature who had lost her will. Amos
asked her stiff, trivial questions which she answered in a small
Californian voice.

Half an hour later Bennie blundered and said, "Hey, Marguerita, what's . . . ?" Of course! "Naomi" was the widow Schultz.
Bennie had settled out of court, all right.

He was leaning on the balcony rail beside Amos; we three
were talking about Israel but Bennie, as usual, had half his mind
on other things.

"So this is what it's like to live in Sydney," he said. "Dolphins
in your back garden."

A school had come somersaulting into the bay. "Naomi" stirred
to life and stood up. Oh!—she loved dolphins; they'd seen none
in Tahiti . . . Amos offered to take her down the track to the
beach.

When they had gone, I said to Bennie, "Neat."

He grinned and the fat under his chin flattened as it pulled up
toward his ears.

"We had the full Orthodox thing. She converted to marry Raphael. They both thought it was a joke, but it satisfied his parents, and the rabbinate."

"Do you now own the whole company?"

He weaved his head: it was not as simple as that; she had
good lawyers. *They* had drawn up the marriage contract.

I asked why she had changed her name. Bennie shrugged.

"New life. You know?" He added, "It was the only way out. For me."

The old defiance shot through his eyes: "Listen—I'm a real good husband," but he could not maintain it, his body was laughing inside, shaking him, and he started to giggle—until a whoop of energy escaped. I was laughing, too; we hugged each other, shuddering with laughter, pressed so close the boundaries of our skins got lost and we were clasping not one another, but ourselves, in silence.

After what was an eternity, very short and very long at the same time, Bennie said, "Look out—they'll see us." We could see them: Naomi had tucked up her dress and was standing crookedly in the water, one hand outstretched to the dolphins as if calling them, but they were already diving out of the bay. Amos stood on the beach behind her, watching with his hands on the hips. His head was cocked to one side.

By the time they returned, Bennie had told me: I was fired.

The contractual situation, he said, was straightforward: I had twice refused to come to L.A. to discuss the drafts (although he had offered to pay my airfare), and I was insisting on an ending to *Eleazar* that was "impossible. Technically impossible, religiously impossible." Didn't I understand the political clout of the rabbinate in Israel? Not to mention that the Hasidim when aroused were capable of taking the law into their own hands: did I want, maybe, that filming would be forced to stop? Or that he would have stones thrown at him? . . . I let his monologue flow on until abruptly I was furious. He was offering me elaborate excuses for stealing my copyright. As he had shoplifted to pay for his adventures in the Tel Aviv brothel, as he had stolen Wili's film negatives, as he had stolen (with some legal complications) Marguerita's share of the company, Bennie was now stealing my work.

"Whose name will be on the credits as writer?"

Bennie drew himself up. "Mine. I'm writing it, now. It's almost fixed—I can go to shooting-script stage in another few weeks."

I grabbed a handful of ice cubes from their bucket and flung them into the bougainvillea. Then I sat down peacefully.

Bennie was grinning. He had worn his thug's sunglasses to sack me; he twitched them off his face and said, "I'm going to do something that's not to my advantage." His eyes were shining

with pride. "Here." The slip of paper he handed me was a check
for a quarter of a million dollars. It was what I would have
earned if the contract had run its normal course. Minus the
profit points. Bennie said, "Be nice, don't make hassles. Don't get
that Sarah involved. I warn you: I've got better lawyers than
Sarah. If you try to sue me, you'll waste yourself."

"What about the profit points?" I asked.

Bennie's expression was scandalized. "Danielle! I'll never let
you down—I told you that in Jerusalem. When the movie is made
and the receipts are in . . . Listen: I'll pay you. Maybe not five,
but two, three—"

"Five!" I said.

He sighed. "For you, five. I give you my word."

The appearance of Amos and Naomi in the doorway cut the current that flowed between Bennie and me.

Bennie said, "I think, Naomi, it is time for us to leave." He
stroked Amos's back as he said "Shalom." Amos still looked
puzzled, watching Naomi limp toward the white Daimler, the
chauffeur helping her into the back.

"What sort of guy marries a cripple? She was in a helicopter crash . . . I mean, it's kind of him to have married her,
but . . . ?"

Amos, when I had explained to him as much as was explicable,
spent an hour walking up and down the living room, swearing
and kicking at objects that weren't there. He lapsed into Polish
and Hebrew and would turn to me with incomprehensible questions. In English again, he asked: was it *true* I had breached the
contract? Didn't I know—for Christ's sake!—its terms? And there
remained the question of copyright: I could *prove* I owned it . . .
And what about the profit points? If the film were a success I
stood to earn up to an extra million dollars. Did I imagine that
bastard would hand over . . . ? He was getting away with mur-
der. And I trusted him! That was beyond all logic.

Love is.

"He's ruined your career!" Amos said.

I had started making lunch.

"You're chopping up celery as if nothing has happened. Women!
God Almighty . . ."

Amos insisted on knowing Sarah's home number and spent an

hour on the telephone to her. He came out of my study fierce with triumph because he now understood the contract. Sarah was as furious with Kidron as he was, he said—but it was sticky: if I tore up the check, Sarah could get an injunction.

They had both missed the point: I had had the pleasure of creation. In the meantime, I had enough money for a three-year holiday.

"If you rip up the check, Sarah will fight for you. She'll be able to delay production so long that Kidron will lose his financial backing. You can ruin him, she says. He's been bankrupt before. If he goes to the wall on this one, he's finished."

I knew that already.

"Money is all that Bennie has got to live for," I said.

Amos sat down heavily. When his face was in repose its underlying worldweariness and distress showed in every line and angle. The phrase he had not used for weeks returned: "You're a lovely woman." I felt ashamed of what I was keeping from him— that if I had not loved Bennie, I would have gone ahead and ruined him. But I did love him. Through desire, possessive love, anger, hatred, despair, and humiliation, I had arrived at equanimity about him, which is wrongly thought to be evenness of mind but is a state of balance in the soul. It's a state that admits only love.

"I'm being practical," I said. "What, having ripped up a fortune, do you and Sarah propose that I live on?"

Now that he felt himself in charge of my life, now that I was not Jezebel but just a woman, one of that species condemned at birth to passivity, Amos was transformed. He came over and ran his hands through my hair. In five days he had to leave Australia.

"I've been thinking," he said. "Perhaps if you rented out this house and came back to Israel for . . . ?"

A while. He could get Katherine into the Hebrew University in Jerusalem; there would be no difficulty importing Emma . . . I could picture it, too: a ready-made family of females around him, replacing those he had lost.

That night Amos made love to me, tentatively and without expertise; he was baffled when I cried.

As it turned out, because of other events I would have returned to Israel anyway.

My father died. Alice telephoned me with the news and my

first reaction was triumph. This changed to anger, then sullenness against the enemy who, by slipping away, defeats one's great purpose. I wanted to return to Jerusalem to see for myself that his house was empty.

He had willed his apartment and everything else to Marilyn, except for the money to cover my plane fare from Australia to Israel. Whether he intended me to sit shiva for him or that I should return "home" I don't know. I could not attend the funeral and the initial mourning period because on New Year's Eve, Tuesday December 31, 1983, while I was buying food in Avalon village to tide me over the holiday, Mrs. Wellsmore set my house on fire.

I saw the two firetrucks hee-hawing past as I came out of the supermarket and did not relate them to myself. By the time I got home there was a crowd in the street outside, an ambulance, ambulance men pressing an oxygen mask over Mrs. Wellsmore's face where she lay on the pavement, and some kind soul was nursing Emma, who screamed and groaned. When she saw me she stopped, and I stumbled up to her and stroked her head for a few seconds. There was a barbecue stench and her hind legs seemed to have melted into reddish-black molasses. Then one of the policemen asked me to come with him. He was a big man, more than six feet tall, and he held my head against the blue cotton of his shirt. Through his hands covering my ears I felt the reverberation of the pistol shot his companion fired.

Mrs. Wellsmore, who otherwise would be in jail for arson, is in an asylum for the insane. She had sent me the dolls as a warning that "everything must be destroyed." I had to be punished for living in *her* house, she explained to the police. While I was out shopping the bougainvillea had told her to set the curtains on fire.

I spoke often by telephone to Amos and Alice, whose David had died. Both warned me that the situation in Israel was worse than ever: the economy was moving toward hyperinflation, the government was rudderless, and the war dragged on, costing Israel a million dollars a day and another life every week; the Shi'ite revolt was growing. Not only was it 1984; the Jewish calendar year also spelt out the word Destruction, Amos said, and there was an atmosphere of doom and superstition. Rabbi Kahane was becoming more popular. General Sharon, the architect of Operation Peace in Galilee, was not finished politically as everyone—he meant, the Left—had believed six months earlier. There had been bombings in Jerusalem: buying a pair of shoes in Zion Square on Thursday night, Amos had to run outside in his socks while the bomb squad investigated a suspicious brief-case. After his months of chewing nicotine gum, in Australia, I could hear that he was smoking again.

I left Sydney at the end of January, on a tourist visa. When Amos met me at the airport his face had resumed its crumpled brown-paper look. I went to bed in his spare room and slept twelve hours on the lumpy iron-framed bed. Next day I visited Alice—and later in the week went to my father's place.

This winter in Jerusalem was not as cold as last year's, but times were harder. Walking from Rahavia to Jabotinsky Street I could see small signs of decay: cars were dilapidated—dents in the paneling had not been beaten out, broken taillights gaped—and people's clothes had a scruffy look, as if dry cleaning were now a luxury. The local matrons were not going as often to the hairdresser to be set and sprayed—but Marilyn:

Marilyn had discovered shampoo, and a pure wool well-cut gray dress with a white Peter Pan collar. A sticker on her front door said in English LET MY PEOPLE GO.

In the hallway she introduced me to someone called Clovis, aged about twenty and with a forehead no lower than a chimpanzee's. "My tenant," she said. He seemed an obliging one, particularly in the matter of tattooing her white neck with love bites.

"Clovis is full of the Spirit," Marilyn said. He grunted appreciation, and went on gnawing at his thumbnail.

We all went to the kitchen where there was a photograph of Jesus on the refrigerator. Clovis was ordered to open a bottle of wine and then sent out to do the shopping while Marilyn and I settled down to get mildly drunk, although it was before noon.

My father had died *so happy,* she said, because he had known that soon Israel's population would be augmented by three million Russian Jews. It seemed there had been a hitch to the Temple Mount project, so in his last months Garin had turned his attention to the refuseniks. Apparently the Lord—I was never sure who Marilyn meant by this—was about to release a plague on the Pharaoh of the North (she explained: Uri Andropov) in punishment for denying exit permits to Soviet Jews. Throughout northern Europe people were ready to welcome the Prisoners of Zion who would be freed when Pharaoh fell to his knees. They were storing food, bedding, and medical equipment; someone had bought a castle in Sweden and converted it to a hospital. She did not mention the oil well of Deuteronomy 33:24 that would turn the shekel into gold; the newest large-denomination shekel notes, as Amos had pointed out to me, had a printing error on them that showed precisely what the currency had turned into.

He had been appalled that I was going to spend the morning with Marilyn. But I had changed enough in a year to find her somehow beguiling. Her monologue seemed to me now a kaleidoscope that constantly formed new patterns within itself, and if I just listened—as you just look through a kaleidoscope, without growing angry that it does not make something "true"—I could sense an interplay of images in her mind (and my father's) that was enchantingly full of surprises. Surprises and paradoxes abound in real life: Amos had said to me the day before, driving back from Lod, "You know who's won this war? The thing we crushed: Terrorism."

Toward the end of the bottle, Marilyn fetched from the study an envelope marked "For Miss Danielle Green, by hand." Inside were my baby photographs and some snapshots of the whole family, Geoffrey standing, my parents seated, me aged about three sitting on my father's knee waving a chocolate at the camera.

I put the envelope in my handbag and walked out into the cold, smiling uncontrollably on the outside and the inside. The photographs had put back together things that time had pulled apart. He had loved me. And I him. I'd been his "baby doll," his "angel," his "little mouse"; he'd carried me on his shoulders along the Street of the Prophets and I'd waved to the Ethiopian priests and all the people below, while I rode in a chariot. I felt the exaltation of that again.

He'd told Marilyn, "I can't see her. She'll tell Bonny I've gone bald."

I was to have lunch with Alice and thought I should try to sober up first. I walked from Jabotinsky Street and found a seat in Einstein Square, near the Van Leer Foundation building. It's a quiet part of town and at this time of day was almost deserted. I sat there oblivious of the cold as I thought about the challenges that still faced me in Israel. One was Amos: I had discovered he had begun drinking quite heavily in the evenings and, I felt, now that he was home again, didn't really want to live with me.

The other challenge came from Alice.

David's death had not diminished her, as I had expected it would. In fact, she seemed brisker and younger, moving with a sprightliness that was almost uncanny. Some of the sharpness I remembered from school was back in her eyes—and her tongue. When I told her about my relationship with Amos, that it had begun in Sydney after the doll affair, she stared at me for a while, then remarked, "So he wasn't wasting his time." I tried to explain that I did not think he and I would stay together, that it was understood I was only a visitor, that I had a life of my own. Alice replied, "A life of your own?" and her eyes locked on mine, demanding, *When* will you ever have a life of your own? What you've had, so far, is a succession of men to hang on to—father, husband, lovers, now Amos, your father-substitute lover . . . She said aloud, "I don't think that phrase 'a life of one's own' means much for a woman, you know, unless she is the equal *in spirit* to the men she associates with. If she merely has *a job* of her own . . . I see so many who are just hard-working parasites attached to male hosts."

I'd blushed, and after a moment whined, "But I want to be *special* to someone."

Alice sighed out her disappointment while I sat looking at the rug in her parlor, thinking, You handed me a torch in childhood, and I've dropped it. Every few yards.

The muzziness from the wine was beginning to clear from my head. I thought, She thinks she's teaching me something I don't already know. I mightn't have always known it, but I do now. And what next? What happens to the parasite when it drops off the host? It becomes a bigger, better, more successful parasite?

I looked at my watch; unless I caught a bus now, instead of walking, I would be late.

The young man I'd met on the ramparts, the queen who couldn't work his Nikon, was seated next to a window. The hourly radio news that is relayed on all buses—in case the country is attacked—was being broadcast. I yelled above it, "Hello. Did you get in touch with Wili Djugash?"

He looked astonished. "Oh, yes," he replied. He put his hand on the seat beside him to prevent my sitting there. "Do you mind awfully? I've got to get off now." He had some sort of bag beneath the seat which he heaved to his shoulder and with a girlish toss of the head made his way past me. I went one more stop, to the little group of shops on the Gaza Road, where I bought four slices of Sacher torte and a bottle of wine. It was no use being mildly drunk; I wanted to be Purim drunk—then sleep until it was time to go out to dinner with Amos and Gideon, whom I had not yet met.

I recognized him as soon as I saw his army boots thumping down Alice's peeling stairwell. When his head with its punitively short haircut bobbed to avoid hitting the ceiling above the final few stairs and he caught sight of me he said, "Danielle!" and swung me up to him with no more effort than if he were lifting a child. The cakebox fell open. He had the high color of momentary exertion, excitement, and good health. His eyes fixed on the cake. We sat on a step side by side and ate a slice each. He was as taciturn as Amos was garrulous; he ate with one hand on my knee. Then he wiped his mouth with the back of his hand, said, "I'm late for duty. Till tonight," hugged me, and ran out of the foyer.

Even Alice heard the explosion ten minutes later. The newspapers next day reported that the bus tore apart like a rag, releasing a fireball that went rolling across the road, where it engulfed a car and its passengers. Eight were killed instantly, two died in hospital, and another sixteen were wounded.

All that afternoon, at first from Alice's and later from Amos's place, I listened to the rising *wah-wah-wah* of ambulance and police sirens coming from the Gaza Road, wondering if I could tolerate even a week longer in Jerusalem. Amos got home at six o'clock and asked, "What's happened?" His car radio was on the blink. I told him as much as I knew: a bus had been blown up on the Gaza Road and the area was cordoned off.

Minutes later some Israelis came to the door. I could hear them speaking softly to Amos, who, when he sauntered back to the cluttered living room, lit a cigarette and examined its glowing tip as if seeing one for the first time.

"That was the military police," he said at length. "Gideon's dead."

I jumped toward him. His jaws gritted.

"Don't touch me. Don't come near me. And *don't cry!*" Desperation settled on his face as the sudden marks of a fatal disease, smallpox, a cancer, diagnosed too late and now raging.

In the guest bedroom I pressed my hands over my ears to dull the noises Amos was making as he smashed things. After a few seconds I pulled the chest of drawers across the doorway. I was too frightened to weep, and too horrified. I had lived this scene before: my father had smashed lifeless things, at first.

When there had been no sounds for half an hour I removed the barricade and went out, stepping carefully through the broken glass and china and trying to move silently in case he was still there. Then I began cleaning up.

Amos returned around dawn. I had replaced the chest of drawers against my bedroom door but he walked straight past. At eight o'clock I took him a cup of coffee and he said, "Thanks." He seemed tired but normal.

The funeral was that afternoon. Then there was a week of shiva, with no formalities, just scores of visitors, arriving at all hours. Dvora (Amos's sister), Mira, and I were constantly cooking for them or trying to find space for the food and flowers they brought. Alice did not come. When she heard of Gideon's death her right arm became paralyzed. She could only just creep about at home and was almost totally dependent on the girls from the home-help agency. When I went to see her she looked at me as if she were blind and after a few minutes asked me to leave her to her grief. But she did lift her face to me to be kissed. Back at Amos's house Tikva sometimes asked if she could help us and would stand in a stupor dropping tears into a bowl of cake batter before wandering off again to my bedroom. I had restocked the kitchen with china and glasses, a coffee-making machine, a juicer, a food processor, and good chopping knives. We needed all of it. Politicians of every party came and even two frock-coated Hasidim who turned their eyes away from us women and spoke to Amos in Yiddish, then recited prayers. From Tikva they accepted glasses of water, all they were allowed in a non-kosher house. We women blended easily together, as we always can when we sink ourselves in the pool of female memory that surrounds the maintenance of life.

We—or at least, I—lived in an automatic state of doing each task as it came to hand, so I cannot remember which day of shiva it was that the world turned upside down and dragged me back to my first afternoon in the Old City. Certainly it was the same day that photographs of the young man with the Nikon and of Wili's assistant, the "Greek" whom Bennie had disliked, were published. They had been arrested on suspicion of bombing the bus on which Gideon had ridden.

Antiterrorists interviewed me in the apartment. They wanted to know everything about Wili and Bennie and the car accident near Masada. They were Sephardim; the man was a flirt. Before his woman colleague could stop him he winked at me and said, "You're very good friends with Kidron?" Amos walked out of the room. Within twenty-four hours Wili had been arrested in London, traced through the national health system to the kindergarten where he was working as a teacher's assistant under the name of William Ash.

He may escape prosecution by becoming a witness because, it seems, the Israelis have been unable to get a confession out of the other two.

When shiva ended, Amos went back to work at Mount Scopus. I continued to sleep in the guest room; I kept the household running. Amos had become silent; he never showed any sign of being drunk but he was drinking a good deal. Sometimes when I stood close to him, as when I brought him food, I saw something pacing behind the cage to which he had withdrawn. I decided I had to get away from him for a while, to rent a car and go touring. "Good," he said. "You came here for a holiday." He made it sound like an insult.

I invited Marilyn to come with me. Of course I would have loved to take Alice, but although she had recovered and was able to do most things for herself again, she was not well enough for traveling, so Marilyn would have to do as a companion. She was unemployed until the end of the month, when she would take up a job as a social worker for aged Jews. "That was *why* I studied sociology in the States," she explained. She had not understood at the time why she chose that course, but now she did: it said in the Bible "Comfort ye my people." Fortunately Clovis was unable to get leave from his work in a laundry, so for two weeks she and I ranged the Galilee, free. Visiting every church where He had said or done something was a small price to pay for the mountainsides rainbowed in wildflowers, for the flocks of brown sheep wallowing in clover, and the pastel, shimmering Sea of Galilee. Here was the easy land, the milk and honey. We lolled on the foreshores of the lake at sunset watching it dissolve into pink sky; we drank arak and Carmel wine and ate St. Peter's fish.

Marilyn had forgotten none of her hippie skills. When men pestered us she lied to them quietly, "I've got a pistol in my handbag"; when she complained about the bones in her fish fillets and the waiter clamped hands on his hips, demanding, "What do you want? Feathers?" Marilyn smiled and replied, "I am just a stranger within your gates. Please take it back." The Lord provided her with these responses, she explained, via the Bible; she would quote the verse. Each night she spent an hour learning one and writing out its uses in daily life.

I came down with church fatigue: too many hymns, too many candles, too many icons. One day it all blurred into a *son et lumière,* a sort of low-tech movie. I was sick of Christian entertainment and of Marilyn, who spoke so often about "Jesus, who brought me to a place of loving surrender," that I replied one evening, "You apparently enjoy surrendering to Clovis, in particular." She'd been eager for a girls' talk. I got the whole story about her life of drugs and sex and rock and roll.

"I was so innocent!" Marilyn said.

Next morning from our hotel in Tiberias I telephoned Bennie. He ran through his usual preface of telling lies (he had telephoned Jerusalem to speak to me; he had broken his leg) more quickly than usual, to silence. Then he said: "You wooden believe it—that bitch of a Naomi . . ."

What had happened was immensely complicated, something to do with the marriage contract, the coproduction contract, and her shyster lawyers. The upshot was that Marguerita had left him and they were countersuing each other. He was as thin as a pencil, with worry. He expected to spend "the rest of my life in litigation." Listen: did I want a screenwriting job? *Eleazar* was on the back burner; meanwhile he was going ahead with "a great little movie, tight, low-budget . . ."

His interminable battles, material increases and decreases, his frustrated creativity, sounded like an allegory for the history of Israel. I remarked as much and he shouted, "Terrific idea. How about you write me an outline about a patriot who . . ." Then he had a moment of dread, on his own account and on Israel's— because maybe Marguerita would win, maybe the Moslems by force of numbers would overwhelm the Jews, and then the fine, hell-like balance to which the inhabitants were so accustomed that it seemed normal and desirable would be ended.

"But set it in South America, okay?"

I said, "Bennie—eat! Enjoy!" and he laughed.

An hour later Marilyn and I were driving north on a new road, not marked on our map, and were more or less lost when, over the crest of a hill a dinosaur appeared. I don't know what sort—Merkavah? Tyrannosaurus Rex? Its great neck was out-stretched and its flanks caked in gray muck from the swamp. It had eaten and was lumbering home. I pulled to the side of the road to let it pass and as I looked up at the mud-covered belly a man riding above on its back waved. I knew then that whatever became of my relationship with Amos I was unwilling to live in his country. It was too noisy; the dinosaurs had woken up.

I have, however, been detained here.

After the northern warmth Jerusalem was unpleasantly cold. I returned to it the day before we were due to visit Gideon's grave to mark the first month after his death.

Amos seemed easier.

After so many restaurant meals I was looking forward to cook-ing, but he said, "You spend enough time in the kitchen," and we went to a Hungarian restaurant for dinner. He talked about his work. I had been careful not to touch him but walking home, af-fected by food and three glasses of wine, I linked my arm through his and when we closed the front door, we started kissing. His penis erected in a spasm, then subsided again. I made a half-witted remark. "Want to go to heaven?" I asked. He nodded, but when I got into bed beside him his face was rigid and his body felt cool, as if the blood supply to its surface tissues had been cut.

I said, "It's not meant to be an ordeal, you know."

He asked, "But what *is* meant?" and I felt so sad for him I gasped.

Amos said, "You've been wonderful. Please don't ruin it. Don't start crying." After a while he added, "You're a grown-up woman. You know what I mean?" I stroked his hair for a while, then went to my room; I awoke feeling unwell.

But because I was the last and least member of the family, so to speak, who had seen Gideon alive there was special signifi-cance in my making the trip to the cemetery. At least that was so in my view, if not in Amos's and all the others who came that day to stand on the hillside beneath pine trees. Fresh graves of other dead youths were around us: in twenty-one months Opera-tion Peace for the Galilee had cost in lives twenty years of ter-rorist attacks on northern settlements, and here was Gideon laid beside soldiers in the war he had refused to fight.

Amos and I drove home in silence. As we turned into his street

he swore: his parking spot on the pavement had been taken by
a large white Mercedes.

"That's Akram," I said. "I sent him a postcard from Tiberias
and told him I was here."

"Did you ask him to take my parking spot, too?" Amos muttered. Just then Akram came out of the apartment block; with
him was a man I didn't know, a big handsome fellow.

I said, "I'll get out and say hello to them."

Akram flung his arms around me and kissed my cheeks; he'd
come to invite me to a traditional wedding ceremony in his cousin's village, Abu Gosh. I shook hands with the cousin; we chatted
on the sidewalk for a few minutes until Amos, having found another place to park, walked up. He nodded to them and went
straight on into the building, with his head down. I said, "I'd
better go."

"Who's the big dude?" Amos asked when I caught up to him
on the stairwell. I told him about the invitation to Abu Gosh.

"They're brigands in that village," he said. "It suited them to
side with us in the War of Independence and since then they've
been anathema to the rest of the Arabs." He added, "They're a
bunch of jerks. Abu Gosh used to make its living by robbing
travelers on the Tel Aviv–Jerusalem road. Nobody can trust those
bastards."

I felt abashed, and irritable with him, as I had been when we
first met.

"Stop trying to fight the world," I said.

He replied, "Spare me the banalities."

He had done no housework in the time I was away and the
apartment was dirty and dusty. He paced about saying, "This
place is a pigsty," but made no effort to clean up. I said I would
fix the place after I'd made lunch. The kitchen table was littered
with newspapers but I coaxed him to sit at it, to talk to me while
I prepared the food. I took out the big meat knife and when I
began sharpening it he winced at the fingernail-on-blackboard
noise.

"Women!" he said. "Why do they make everything complicated? Why . . . ?" He was trying to get a grip on his bitter-
ness, but as I made a final scrape of the blade across the stone
the sound seemed to twang a nerve inside him, and he jumped up.

"You knew the bastard who killed Gideon," he said. "If you
hadn't got on that bus . . ." He moved toward me. I could feel

my scalp bristling. Amos had picked up a rolled newspaper and began tapping it on the kitchen table. I was so tense a little noise came out of my throat, like a whinny. "It's funny, eh?" he asked. "It's bloody funny!" Suddenly he gave the table a terrible blow with the newspaper. "You knew!" he repeated, and he hit the table again.

I said, "Amos, if you hit me—"

He said, "I'm not going to hit you. Look at you—threatening me with a knife. D'you imagine"—he was still struggling to come out with a joke about it—"that armed with *Haaretz* . . . ?" He gave the table another blow, not as hard as the last one, then swung his head toward me. I saw that the demon had subsided. There was a moment of stillness, then into Amos's eyes came the panic of a creature on which a trap has snapped shut. I felt a thump of energy strike the room, like the *whoof!* of an explosion.

His aorta had burst.

Today is the last of sitting shiva for Amos. There weren't as many visitors as for Gideon.

Amos haunts me. He was a tiger who has seen the bars ten thousand times, until he saw nothing but bars.

While I, it seems, am free. I will not try to make Alice believe me. I will say nothing to her of those last minutes between us. But I know that if Amos had struck me, or even if our fight had lasted a few seconds longer, I would have gone for him with that knife. But he controlled himself; in the end he stayed civilized.

Amos!

Tomorrow shiva ends; Tikva will drive me to the airport.

EPILOGUE

One Saturday in the winter of 1986 Marilyn visited Alice Sadler, bringing a copy of *Time* magazine. The People page carried a photograph of Tikva Kahalon and a caption: "Kahalon: New star?" The story said:

SCREENWRITER-TURNED-DIRECTOR *Danielle Green* CHOSE AN ISRAELI GIRL SOLDIER, *Tikva Kahalon,* TO PLAY THE LEAD IN HER FIRST FILM, *Moses Cafe,* THE DROLL COMEDY ABOUT TERRORISTS THAT OPENED LAST WEEK TO ENTHUSIASTIC REVIEWS, NOT LEAST OF THEM FOR THE MILITARY BEAUTY'S ROLE AS AN *agente provocateuse.* KAHALON WILL TOP THE CAST IN GREEN'S NEXT MOVIE, *The Gaza Road,* A LOVE STORY SET AGAINST THE ISRAELI-LEBANESE WAR, IN WHICH THE ACTRESS WAS A PARTICIPANT. ASKED IF THIS GRIM SUBJECT WOULD BE GETTING COMIC TREATMENT, TOO, GREEN QUIPPED, "THE JOKE MAY YET BE ON ME." FINANCE HAS FALLEN THROUGH ONCE ALREADY, BUT GREEN ADDED SHE WAS NOW CONFIDENT THE PROJECT WOULD GO AHEAD.

Alice was growing frail. She sighed once or twice as Marilyn read to her. She'd heard little from Danielle for a year and had seen her only briefly while she was in Jerusalem directing the location scenes for *Moses Cafe*. Danielle had invited Alice to lunch at the Plaza, where she had taken over a whole floor for eight weeks, had arrived an hour late, then had to leave after twenty minutes. Alice had not been surprised: Danielle was a selfish, ardent creature.

"Well, just look at our Tikva," she said. "See what Danielle's new confidence is doing for them both. New confidence or new desperation; one wonders sometimes which is the stronger goad . . ."

"It must be God's work," Marilyn replied. "Confidence means 'with faith,' Miss Sadler."

Outside, the city was quiet because it was the Sabbath. A daylight moon had floated up from behind the Mountains of Moab. It was almost round, a white face lopped by a blue beret worn at a jaunty angle.

"Indeed? And I have not yet forgotten my Latin derivations, dear girl. Now, if you'll just take my arm, we'll be off for our walk in the Old City."

ABOUT THE AUTHOR

Blanche d'Alpuget was born in Sydney and lives in Canberra. *Winter in Jerusalem* is her third novel; she has also written two biographies, one of them on the prime minister of Australia, Bob Hawke.